The Lavender House

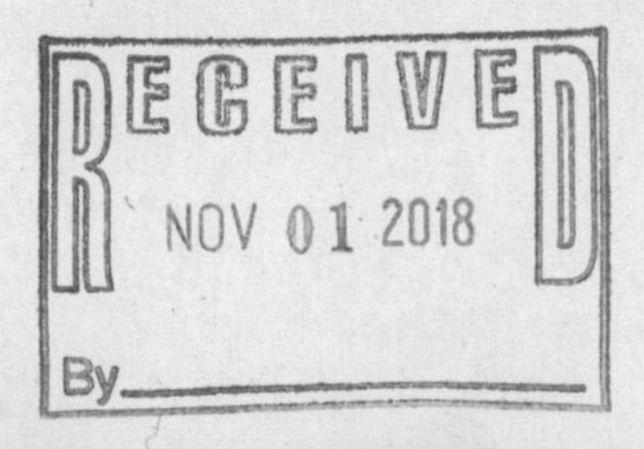

Also by Hilary Boyd

Thursdays in the Park
Tangled Lives
When You Walked Back Into My Life
A Most Desirable Marriage
Meet Me on the Beach

Hilary Boyd

Quercus

First published in Great Britain in 2016 by Quercus
This paperback edition published in 2017 by

Quercus Editions Ltd
Carmelite House
50 Victoria Embankment
London EC4Y 0DZ

An Hachette UK company

A CIP catalogue record for this book is available
from the British Library

PB ISBN 978 1 78429 414 4

10 9 8 7 6 5 4 3

Typeset by Jouve (UK), Milton Keynes

Printed and bound in Great Britain by Clays Ltd, St Ives plc

'A woman is like a tea bag – you can't tell how strong she is until you put her in hot water'

Eleanor Roosevelt

PROLOGUE

Nancy was in the kitchen preparing supper, listening to *The Archers* on the radio, drizzling olive oil over some summer vegetables for roasting, when her husband, Christopher, walked in and told her he was leaving. The July evening was breezy and cool, but the doors to the garden were open, the tortoiseshell cat from next door prowling around the tubs on the flagstone patio, rubbing his body luxuriously along the smooth earthenware sides of a pot of lavender.

Christopher stood across the room, the island worktop between them. He was dressed in jeans and his navy sweater, the high zip-neck brushing his chin, although the zip was partially undone. Thin, small and tidy, tanned from his endless walks in the Suffolk wetlands, his grey hair short, almost monk-like, he seemed determined, almost fierce, as he clutched his brown leather holdall in his left hand.

'Where are you going?' Nancy asked, holding up her oily hands, like a surgeon ready to operate, as she paused in her task of tossing the onions, courgettes, peppers and baby tomatoes. 'It's nearly supper time.' She reached across to turn the radio off, using her elbow to press the green knob: Christopher hated *The Archers*.

'I'm going to see Tatjana.'

'Now? Why?'

Tatjana was the newest member of the Downland Singers, a small madrigal group Christopher had set up nearly thirty years ago. From Latvia, she had auditioned when Gillian Perry – Christopher's protégée – had left because of her husband's cancer. Christopher had been very enthusiastic about her, said she had an extraordinarily pure soprano voice. Which obviously – as Nancy was about to discover – was not her only asset.

Not answering her question, her husband said, 'I won't be back tonight.'

Nancy frowned, not getting it.

'I won't be back,' he repeated.

'Won't be back? Why not?'

'I'm staying with Tatjana, Nancy.'

And when Nancy, still baffled, continued to look blank, he added, by way of explanation, 'We're in love.'

She stared at him. From a man of sixty-nine, the words sounded made up, fatuous. Genuinely unable to take them in, she lowered her hands and reached for the kitchen roll, wiping the oil from each of her fingers one by one. 'Well,' she said, 'if that's the case, you'd better get off, then.' Her gaze was fixed on his face and she saw his shock, almost bewilderment, at her reply; shock that must mirror her own.

'I'm sorry,' he said, looking away.

And she thought that he probably was, in his own way. Not a man to emote, nor someone who seemed to care much about anything in life except his music, Christopher de Freitas nonetheless considered himself to be a decent person. And a brilliant musician – although not all would agree. An Early Music specialist, he had studied classical guitar at the Royal College, then the lute. His madrigal singers were internationally famous among Early Music enthusiasts.

Nancy had met him when he came to the Royal Northern College of Music – where she was studying piano – to give a lute masterclass. Not that she was interested in the instrument as such, but her fellow student, Oliver, was, and she was interested in Oliver. But he was quickly forgotten as Nancy became mesmerized by Christopher's penetratingly blue eyes – which lighted frequently on her as if he had singled her out for special attention – his mastery of the instrument, his fluent exposition of Renaissance music and madrigal forms. By the end of the two hours, she was hypnotized. Afterwards she had gone up to thank him.

He had given her his card. 'If you're ever in London, look me up. I have a concert at the Cadogan Hall in June. I can get you tickets, if you like?' It was posed as a question, although she felt he assumed she would 'like'. His confidence was absolute.

'You could have told me earlier,' she said now, as if she were speaking from outside her body, looking down on the middle-aged pair in their tidy, middle-class kitchen. No shouting, no drama, all perfectly polite, as she added, 'I wouldn't have bothered with supper.' Her body was screwed so tight, she seemed capable only of such inanities as she waited for him to go.

'Right . . .' her husband muttered, still hovering, as if he were reluctant to leave, *whereas the exact opposite must be the case,* Nancy thought. *He must be desperate to get this scene over with, to escape his intolerable guilt. Desperate to lie with relief against Tatjana's ample bosom.*

That was the last word spoken in their thirty-four-year marriage.

Better than a note on the kitchen table? Nancy wondered, after three-quarters of a bottle of Rioja on an empty stomach, gazing at the vegetables still sitting forlornly on the work-top – like her, rejected, deemed not fit for purpose. Numb with shock, she didn't cry. And after the whole bottle of wine and a couple of large shots of Christopher's Glenfiddich, she realized through the drunken haze that she'd known for some time, like a painful bruise she couldn't touch, what was going on between her husband and Tatjana Liepa.

CHAPTER ONE

Four years later

What the hell are you supposed to wear for a line-dancing evening in a Brighton pub? Nancy asked herself, as she flicked through the rail of clothes in her cupboard, vainly searching for an outfit for her friend Lindy's sixtieth. Lindy had not been helpful.

'Oh, doesn't matter, wear jeans and boots or something,' she'd said airily. But Nancy's jeans were M & S jeggings – not even distant cousins to authentic Levi's – her black boots better suited to a day's work in a building society office than stomping the boards to a Dolly Parton song.

All the clothes that used to fill her wardrobe when she was still Mrs Christopher de Freitas – sleek dresses and velvet jackets, black evening trousers, silk tops and beaded handbags – were long gone to the charity shop in Aldeburgh, and she didn't miss them one bit.

I'll look like someone who's wandered in from one of Mother's bridge evenings, she thought, ripping off a frumpy light-blue cotton shirt she'd tried on because it was sort of denim-coloured. *In fact, I dress more like my mother with every passing day.* Which thought had her slamming her wardrobe shut and running downstairs, out of her cottage, across the gravel to the bigger house.

'Hiya.' Ross, her son-in-law, grinned as Nancy came into the kitchen, a curved, two-handled blade poised in his hands, the chopping board in front of him covered with a mound of bright green herbs. Beside him was a bowl of uncooked grey prawns, another of broccoli stems, a smaller one with chopped garlic, a bottle of soy sauce and a shiny red chilli. Nancy smiled back, wondering if she ever saw him when he wasn't attached to a knife and surrounded by ingredients. He had his own restaurant, the Lime Kiln, three miles away, and even when he wasn't there – like today, Saturday – he still did nothing but cook every moment he was awake.

'How's it going?' he asked, turning to skim the sharp metal blade back and forth at high speed across the herbs. Overweight, broad-shouldered and around six feet in height, he had shaved the last vestiges of his hair, leaving a gleaming dome, which seemed to heighten the beauty of his huge brown dark-lashed eyes, the fullness of his mouth and his strong, jutting chin. Pale from too much time indoors, if he wasn't handsome he was charismatic, with a loud voice and a ready smile. Nancy liked him a lot.

'Not well,' she said, shifting Bob, the cat – female, but her granddaughters had insisted on the name – and flinging herself down on the faded green sofa, strewn with a bright and diverse set of cushions. 'Is Louise upstairs? I need to find an outfit . . . I'm going line dancing.'

Ross's eyes widened and he guffawed. '*Line dancing?* You're kidding me. Wouldn't have thought that was your thing, Nancy.'

'It isn't, but it's Lindy's sixtieth birthday party. What can I do?' In fact it wasn't the dancing that bothered Nancy – she loved dancing on the rare occasions when she got the chance. It was the party itself, any party, that wasn't Nancy's 'thing'. Unlike her ex-husband, who seemed able to enter a room full of complete strangers and instantly bond with them, Nancy found socializing like pulling teeth, the low-grade panic never quite going away. And she'd barely been out in the years since the split. At first after Christopher's defection she'd retreated, shut the doors of their white-painted Suffolk farmhouse on her friends and made endless excuses, which became increasingly implausible, to avoid their company, until they'd given up trying. Then, when she'd moved to the cottage just north of Brighton, three years ago now, teaming up with Louise and Ross, she had known no one with whom to party.

Before Ross had time to answer her, there was a shriek from the TV room. Hope, nine, and Jazzy, six, came barrelling into the kitchen with shrieks of 'Nana, Nana!' and threw themselves into her arms.

Clutching a large glass of Pinot, pressed upon her by Ross, some salted almonds inside her, Nancy plonked herself down on her daughter and son-in-law's bed. Hope was already eagerly rummaging in her mother's drawers and cupboards.

'Look, Nana,' she exclaimed, her large brown eyes – inherited from her father – alive with the drama as she reached on tiptoe and yanked down a shimmery gold knitted bolero jacket that would have been better suited, in Nancy's opinion, to one of Hope's Barbies than either her or Louise. 'This is perfect for a party.'

'Umm . . . Maybe a bit . . . shiny?'

Louise chuckled at her mother's expression. 'Impulse buy,' she said, tossing a fringed leather jacket in butter-coloured suede at her. 'Perfect, no?' She turned to rummage along the rail again. 'I've got some denim dungarees here somewhere . . . but maybe that's a bit more farmhand than cowboy.'

Jazzy pulled her thumb out of her mouth. 'Nana can't wear *dungarees* to a *party*,' she said, her tone shocked. She was sitting beside her on the bed, watching operations carefully with her round blue eyes.

'What about these?' Louise, nodding agreement, brandished a pair of jeans. 'These are better. They should fit and they're real Levi's.'

Her daughter took after Christopher in appearance: small-boned, slim, with well-defined, almost sharp features. She was shorter than her mother by about two inches, very like her father, with his deep-blue eyes. Only Nancy's thick, previously dark-brown hair seemed to have survived the genetic inheritance, and Louise didn't make the most of it, pulling it back in a short, severe ponytail. But she had a sort of gamine quality that Nancy knew men found attractive, and a charming smile that instantly softened her darting, nervy expression.

'Go on, try them on,' Louise was urging.

'Now? Maybe I'll take them home . . .' Nancy was embarrassed in front of the girls, who were gazing disapprovingly at their mother's choice of garments.

'No, come on. I want to see what you look like. Shoo, girls, let Nana change. I'll call you when she's ready.'

Once the girls had gone – she could hear them giggling outside the door – Nancy undressed to her T-shirt and knickers and pulled on the jeans and jacket. The jeans were a bit short and a bit tight around her post-menopausal midriff, but the jacket fitted perfectly. She eyed herself in the long mirror on the bedroom wall, Bob rubbing against her legs as she stood there.

'See? You look brilliant.' Her daughter grinned at her from the other side of the bed. 'Very C and W.'

'C and W?'

'Country and western, Mum. Get with the programme!'

'Ha! Of course.' She twisted sideways in the mirror, twitching her fringe on her forehead, her pure silver-white hair falling in a thick bob to just past her chin, accentuating her strong cheekbones and wide grey eyes. For a second she had a tantalizing glimpse of her younger self as she twirled in her daughter's clothes. 'I had a panic earlier that I was beginning to dress like Mum.'

Louise laughed. 'Could be worse. Granny always looks incredible.'

'Yes, but she's eighty-four! I have the exact same M & S jeggings as she does.'

'You and half the country.'

Nancy sighed. 'I think I panicked because the other day she pointed out that I'm the same age as she was when Daddy died. And I thought she seemed so old at the time.'

'You're not old, Mum. Sixty is the new forty,' Louise said briskly, shutting down Nancy's worries as she always did. Her daughter spent a lot of time in a state of anxiety herself, and perhaps couldn't cope with it in Nancy too. Nancy found it disconcerting sometimes, but perhaps it was better not to dwell on things she couldn't change. It was just the creeping fear, new to her, that the rest of her life was already mapped out, that she would follow her mother's example of safe, female company – notwithstanding Dennis, a septuagenarian fancy-man her mother's friend had recently taken up with – filling the time left with bridge and Noël Coward, fancy cakes, cruises and Marks & Spencer, en route to the grave. Because although Frances had an enviable life for someone of her age, she seemed permanently discontented, disappointed at the way things had turned out.

'Found them!' Louise, who had been scrabbling in the bottom of her cupboard, waved aloft a pair of ankle boots with small heels and pointed toes in light-brown suede, metal studs decorating the zip line. 'These are almost cowboy.' She handed them to her mother. 'They don't quite match the jacket, but no one will notice that.'

'Will they fit?'

'Have a go. I've worn them a lot so they're quite stretched.' She watched Nancy struggle into the boots. 'Fantastic. Come in, girls, come and look at Nana.' She eyed her up and down. 'You're so classy, so elegant, Mum. You look good enough for any line-dancing party.'

CHAPTER TWO

The pub was loud with a country song, although it wasn't one Nancy recognized. She was late, havering right up until the last second about whether or not she would go.

Wearing her daughter's clothes did nothing for her confidence. Not only did she feel a fraud – 'mutton dressed as lamb', as her mother would say, her voice heavy with censure – but the boots had pinched her toes even on the short walk from the pub car park and the jeans' waistband had created a small but unattractive bulge beneath her white T-shirt where it dug into her flesh.

Pull yourself together, she admonished herself, straightening her shoulders and taking a deep breath as she spotted Lindy in the crowded space, standing with a group of women by the bar. She was clutching a bottle of lager, dressed in outrageous denim shorts, a tasselled leather waistcoat over a white-cotton vest and the alligator-skin cowboy boots she'd told Nancy she'd bought in Denver thirty years ago. She looked amazing, about twenty-five, with a large Stetson clamped over her long blonde hair.

'Woo-hoo, Nance! Thought you'd chickened out!' Lindy shrieked, throwing her arms round her friend. Nancy had met Lindy at the school gates, picking up their grandchildren – Toby was in Hope's class – and a friendship had developed, fuelled by Lindy's voracious appetite for any form of culture. Cinema, literature, music, theatre, dance, you name it, Lindy would buy tickets.

Nancy handed her a birthday present. It was a silver bangle with a small turquoise in the centre that she'd found in a little shop in the Lanes.

'Darling, you're so kind. I didn't want everyone spending money on me,' Lindy was saying, bending to put the wrapped box and card into a large bag at her feet. 'I'll open it later – it's too crazy in here.' She stood up again. 'Now, who do you know?'

Monica, Jessy, Alison, Rosanne, Suzie and Precious were introduced and two more whose names she didn't catch. The only one Nancy had met before was Alison, an old friend of Lindy's from college. They had all gone to see a Terence Davies film, *The Deep Blue Sea*, which had been playing at the Duke of York's in Brighton. Nancy remembered being carried away by the soundtrack, a heart-rending Samuel Barber violin concerto, but Alison had seemed reserved, hard to talk to.

The women were pretty well oiled already so Nancy had some catching up to do. But she was relieved to see that Lindy's guests were wearing a mish-mash of outfits – just two with hats, three with authentic boots. Only Lindy really looked the part . . . and some.

'What will you have?' Rosanne, Lindy's teacher at the art class she attended in Lewes, asked Nancy.

She settled for a Budweiser, preferring wine but not wanting to get drunk. She was driving home.

'Okay, girls . . . listen up! I'm Jim Bowdry and I'm your host for the evening.'

The tall man dressed as a cowboy waved their birthday group over to a cordoned-off area on the opposite side of the pub, which had a small, black-painted plywood stage built against the end wall, supporting speakers, a stereo deck and a set of drums pushed into the far corner. An open laptop currently balanced on one of the speakers. Nancy was relieved the dancing was about to start, preventing the need for any more small talk. She was on her second beer and was beginning to feel mellow. The women, it turned out, were a good crew, unpretentious and lively – even Alison had thawed with a drink inside her.

'Right.' Jim stood in front of them adjusting his mic, which was attached to a headset buried beneath his worn silver-white Stetson. 'Who's done this before?'

Only four hands went up, one of them Lindy's, and Jim grinned. 'So many line-dancing virgins . . . Ooh dear, it's going to be a long night.' Which remark was greeted with drunken laughter. 'Don't worry about getting it right. We're just here to have some fun. And remember the old Japanese proverb: "We're fools whether we dance or not, so we might as well dance." '

It was clear this was well-rehearsed patter, but the proverb – if it was indeed a proverb and not something Jim had made up for the occasion – tickled Nancy and she couldn't help laughing as she caught his eye.

Lindy, standing next to Nancy as they formed two lines, whispered, 'Hmm, like the look of our friend. That outfit makes him all macho, as if he's just about to wrestle a steer to the ground or whatever cowboys do.' The wink she shot Nancy was positively lascivious. 'Know what I mean?'

Nancy grinned, but she felt slightly out of her depth. It was literally decades since she'd had such an exchange about a man.

Yet she did like the look of Jim. He was probably around her age, above six feet tall, his thick, iron grey hair – with a pronounced widow's peak – tied back in a short ponytail. His dark eyebrows were set over bright blue eyes, which seemed permanently amused, a strong, slightly crooked nose and well-defined lips. He reminded her of a more rugged, less effete, version of the actor Terence Stamp.

'We're going to start with some basic moves,' Jim was saying. 'I'll demonstrate first, then talk you through it. It's not rocket science, we'll have a routine going in no time.'

Nancy thought that was unlikely, faced with ten or so tipsy women in their sixties, most of whom had never performed a line dance in their lives, but she was prepared to give him the benefit of the doubt. He'd done this before; he should know.

'First, the grapevine, very simple . . .' He stood for a moment, facing them, his thumbs hooked into his jeans pockets, moving to the country song playing on the sound system. 'Step to the right, left foot behind, step out, feet together and tap.' He moved slowly, did it again to the left, still slowly, his body graceful and fluid. 'Now you try.'

The group, with varying degrees of commitment, performed the move.

'Great! Now a bit quicker . . . to the right, left behind, right foot, tap. Step to the left . . .'

Jim beat time to the music on his thigh and counted them in as they followed his lead. After a while he added other steps, turns, jumps, scuffs and taps, 'Back, back, back, back, now turn it out to the left, step to the right, grapevine . . .' changing the song on the laptop to suit dances with exotic names such as the Electric Slide, Bootscoot Boogie and Tush Push, which spoke for itself. He stood with his back to them, guiding them, calling out the steps into the mic, his lean frame swaying provocatively.

It was hot in the small space, the air close, music high volume, the rest of the pub filled to bursting with the Saturday-night throng. Nancy could feel the perspiration damp on her face, but she was loving every minute of the dancing.

'Oops!' Lindy, giggling and flailing in her shorts and boots, collided with Nancy, which prompted Precious, on Nancy's right, to crash into her, domino-style.

Jim turned to see what was happening. 'Need some help?' he asked Nancy, coming to stand between her and Lindy. With his hand on her arm, his body close, he began to coax her back into the steps. 'Jump . . . feet together, heel, toe, tap . . . You're good,' he said, his words suddenly sounding so intimate in that crowded room. She didn't dare look at him.

'Bloody left and right . . . never could tell the difference. You're going too fast!' Lindy gasped, flapping her arms as she headed in the wrong direction again and crashed into Jim and Nancy. Jim, laughing, held her up and again his eyes met Nancy's over Lindy's head. Nancy felt an unfamiliar bubble of pure joy as she laughed with him.

'All right for you, teacher's pet.' Lindy pulled a face at Nancy as Jim stepped to the front again and turned his back. 'Luurve his butt in those jeans,' she went on, too loudly, only inches from his ear. Nancy cringed as Jim turned, a wry grin on his face, and began instructing them in the Macarena, a less hectic dance that mostly involved arms and hips.

'That was so much fun.' Lindy, still breathless, was propped up on a high stool, her Stetson lying on the bar in front of her, her bare tanned legs looking enviably taut and muscled – Lindy worked out like most people breathed. Alison and Nancy were the only ones left now: it was after midnight and the others had gone home when the dancing finished. Jim was over by the stage, putting away his mic, removing his hat, brushing back the hairs that had strayed from his ponytail, wiping the sweat from his face with a red spotted hanky. He had slowed the tempo of the music now, and Kris Kristofferson was singing 'Sunday Morning Coming Down'.

'Jim's going to join us for a drink.' Lindy's eyes were fixed lewdly on their host as he walked towards them, mouthing the chorus to himself.

'Mind if I nip out for a smoke?' he said, as he joined the group. 'Won't be long.'

'What will you have to drink?' Alison asked.

'Oh, er, Heineken would be great. Thanks.' He disappeared into the night, delving into his shirt pocket for his cigarettes as he went, his boots ringing loudly on the wooden floor in the near empty room. Nancy was disappointed. She hated smoking.

'He is *mine*,' Lindy intoned drunkenly, shimmying her hips as she watched him go. 'He is *so* totally mine.'

Alison rolled her eyes. 'Leave him alone, Lindy.'

'Why should I? He doesn't have a ring on his finger and he definitely likes me.' She giggled. 'But, then, what's not to like?'

'I've had such a great time,' Nancy said, quickly changing the subject. 'I haven't danced in ages.'

'Me neither,' Alison said. 'I thought it was brilliant.'

And Nancy thought she looked unusually flushed and happy. Alison was an educational psychologist, a small, intense woman who, Nancy felt, seldom relaxed. Her husband, Nick, had died in his forties from some heart problem and she had never remarried.

When Jim returned, bringing with him cold air and the trail of tobacco smoke, Lindy pulled an empty bar stool close. 'Here, sit down and talk to me.'

Jim politely accepted, inching the stool a bit further back before settling. He picked up his beer and took a long, thirsty draught. Nancy thought he seemed a little nervous of Lindy's flirtatiousness, but he must surely be used to it in his line of work.

'So you enjoyed your birthday?' he asked her. He had a gravelly voice – probably from all that smoking, Nancy decided – with the undertone of amusement she'd noticed earlier.

'I just *adored* it, darling,' Lindy replied, laying a proprietorial hand on his arm, 'even if I can't tell my right from my left.'

'You did well . . . You all did, considering most of you hadn't tried it before.'

'Ha! Don't think so. I was rubbish.' Lindy reached out and drew Nancy to her side, wrapping her arm round her waist. 'Now, Nancy here, she's a natural.'

Jim glanced at her and smiled.

'It's easy if you follow everyone else,' Nancy said, then looked quickly away as she felt the heat rising to her cheeks. She hoped he wasn't still gazing at her. But when she turned back his blue eyes were fixed on her face. *Stupid bloody woman*, Nancy berated herself silently. *The first man to look at you properly in years and you have to go and blush.*

'I found it quite hard to keep up, though,' Alison was saying, and Nancy sighed with relief as Jim's attention was diverted. 'If I lost my concentration for a second it all fell apart.'

'It's just practice,' he said. 'Once you get used to the steps your feet do them automatically.'

'Mine don't.' Lindy wiggled her boots in the air, showing off her legs but wobbling dangerously, clutching the bar for support.

'Do you do a lot of these evenings?' Nancy asked Jim, interrupting Lindy deliberately. The booze was really getting to her friend – she was blinking in the slow, inebriated way of all good drunks, fading fast, her speech more and more slurred.

'Nope, not many. I'm mainly a singer. Country music.'

'A singer?' Lindy twitched back to life, nearly knocking over her bottle of beer. 'Wow, I *luurve* singers. Are you published . . . no, that's not right . . . recorded?' She laughed. 'You know what I mean.'

Jim smiled. 'Yeah, have been. But not for a while now.'

'Wow,' Lindy said again, the single syllable drawn out to its maximum capacity. She gave him a playful shove. 'Go on, then, give us a song.'

'Haven't got my guitar.'

'Shouldn't stop you. Come on, *pleeease*. One teensy tiny little song, just for me? Sing a Johnny Cash or something. It's my birthday! You can't deny a birthday girl her wish.' She batted her thick black lashes at him. 'That would be *sooo* mean.'

Jim shifted awkwardly on his stool. 'I'd love to, but it'd be rubbish without my guitar.'

Lindy blinked at him, her expression darkening. 'Oh, don't go all precious on me, darling.' Her tone was suddenly imperious as she made the effort to haul herself upright. 'I hired your services. If we want you to sing, isn't it all part of the package?' She stared at Jim as if waiting for him to burst into song.

Nancy froze and glanced quickly at Alison, whose eyes were wide with dismay. This was a side to Lindy – obviously drink-fuelled – Nancy hadn't witnessed before.

Jim just raised his eyebrows. 'Why don't you come to my next gig, Lindy? Then you can hear me at my best.' The accompanying smile was so winning that Lindy's expression relaxed.

'Yeah . . . yeah, might do that,' she said.

'I think it's time to get you home.' Alison moved purposefully to Lindy's side and took her arm, which her friend immediately shook off.

'*Noooo!* It's way too early! It's my birthday, for God's sake. I'm going to . . . stay up all bloody night.' And with that, Lindy slid gracefully off her stool and landed in a heap on the pub floor, her bare limbs concertinaed beneath her.

Jim helped Alison get Lindy into her car. They had persuaded her to drink some water and the barman had made her a strong coffee, which she'd immediately thrown up – luckily making it to the Ladies first. She was still barely conscious.

'You don't think we should take her to A & E, do you?' Alison asked them, after they'd loaded Lindy into the front seat. 'I've never seen her this bad before, even at college.' Her small face was pinched with concern.

Nancy looked at Jim, thinking maybe he had more experience of this sort of problem, but he shrugged. 'Not sure that'd help.'

'Won't she just sleep it off?' Nancy suggested. They were standing beside Alison's blue Mondeo in the semi-darkness of the empty pub car park, the night air bitingly cold after the warmth of the bar. She glanced through the window at their sleeping friend, whose head was slumped on her chest, blonde hair trailing across her face, hands hidden in the sleeves of her leather jacket.

'But what if she vomits in her sleep and chokes?' Alison asked.

'She's got a point,' Jim said.

'What will A & E do, though? Won't she just lie on a trolley for four hours and then be sent home?'

'Well, I don't feel comfortable leaving her alone. I'll take her home with me.' Alison frowned. 'You hear the most awful stories . . .'

Nancy remembered Lindy saying that Alison was a major worrier, her life a perpetual series of what-ifs. 'Do you want me to come too?' she offered, and was relieved when Alison shook her head.

'Thanks, I can manage.' She sighed. 'It was a really good evening. Sorry if Lindy was a bit rude,' she said to Jim.

Jim held his hands up. 'Just the drink talking.'

Nancy and Jim watched Alison drive away. Then Jim bent to pick up his black backpack from the tarmac. 'How are you getting home?' he asked.

'I've got the car. That's mine.' Nancy pointed to her Golf, sitting in glorious isolation at the far edge of the car park.

'You okay to drive?'

'Fine. I only had a couple of beers.' She shivered in the April cold, drawing Louise's thin suede jacket tighter round her body. Her feet hurt in her daughter's boots. 'Can I drop you somewhere?'

Jim hesitated. 'Uh, no . . . Thanks, but I'll walk, night air will do me good. It's not far.'

Nancy was relieved. She felt suddenly shy and awkward with the handsome man beside her in the darkness. She wanted to say something clever or funny, something that would renew the bond she'd felt with him earlier in the evening, but her mind was a blank. 'If you're sure . . .'

He nodded, hefting his bag onto his shoulders. But they seemed frozen to the spot.

'Listen, it was great to meet you,' Nancy said, holding out her hand. 'You made it a really fun night.'

He smiled, taking her cold hand in his large warm one, his handshake firm. 'Thanks. Great to meet you too, Nancy.'

As she caught his eye, Nancy had a strange feeling that the world was slowing down, as if Jim's gaze had placed her in the calm eye of a storm. A police car speeding down the road, blue lights flashing, siren blaring, jerked her back to reality and their hands dropped.

'I'm doing a gig next Saturday – not here, it's a club up near the station. If your friend was serious about hearing me sing . . .' Jim dug a card out of the back pocket of his jeans and passed it to her. 'It's all on here. If she calls me, I can arrange comps.'

Nancy took the card, which she glanced at but couldn't read in the darkness without her specs. 'Thanks.'

'Not sure if country music is your thing.' He shot her a questioning look. But she didn't reply. She was cold and tired, overwrought by the evening and the look that had just passed between her and the stranger. She was finding it hard to know what she thought about anything at that precise moment. Was the card specifically for Lindy? Or was she included in the invitation? They seemed to be standing unnaturally close for people who had barely met and Nancy moved back slightly, almost as if she needed to get some perspective.

'I love all music,' she said eventually. She was surprised to hear the passion in her statement. Not because it wasn't true, but because she had felt the need to share it with Jim.

It elicited a smile. 'Yeah, me too.'

There was a pause. 'Bye, then,' she said, turning towards her car.

Once inside it, she fired up the engine, eager for some warmth, but she didn't drive away immediately, wanting Jim to have a chance to get away, thus avoiding the awkwardness of passing him on the pavement, maybe having to wave, or at least having to decide whether or not to do so. She didn't want to see him again tonight. He had exhausted her.

CHAPTER THREE

Jim was bursting with excitement as he turned left out of the car park and made his way across town, the like of which he hadn't felt in years, perhaps decades. Nancy. He rolled her name across his tongue. Nancy . . . *Nancy*. He had known as soon as he set eyes on her, walking into the pub tonight – so diffident, so late, with that charmingly apologetic smile – that she was different. It was as if she'd been cast in brighter colours than the other women, defined by stronger lines. He had felt a jolt to his very soul when their eyes had met for the first time.

As he walked he sang softly to himself another Kristofferson song. It was actually a break-up song, but he'd always loved it, 'For The Good Times'.

This is what it feels like to be alive, he thought, slowing his pace as he took the route along the sea road towards his small Kemptown house, enjoying the cold wind that blew through him, like a message from the universe that things were about to change. He had no desire to get home while there was still a chance that Chrissie might be up. *Will Nancy come next Saturday? Did I make it clear I wasn't really asking her friend, just using her as an excuse?* He cursed himself silently for not being more forthcoming. But, then, he'd only just met her – he didn't want to frighten her away by coming on too strong. She seemed quite a reserved woman, not like her friend, the birthday girl.

If I'd asked Nancy outright to the gig, she'd have run a mile, he decided, raising his voice and singing into the night air, the notes of the song creating such an intense sadness that it seemed to squeeze his heart almost to a standstill.

But then he changed his mind. *No, I've messed up. She'll just give the card to her friend and I'll never see her again. I don't even know her last name, or where she lives and I can hardly ring Lindy and ask. She'll think I'm a sleaze or a stalker or something.*

Not that he cared whether he was seen as any sort of reprobate, if it meant he met up with Nancy again. He reached inside his leather jacket and pulled out his pack of Camel Blue – he was trying to give up, fooling himself that the light version might help. Bending over and cupping his hand against the wind, he lit the cigarette, drawing the smoke deep into his lungs, the nicotine washing through him, soothing his nerves even though the process made him cough.

Chrissie was up. Or, at least, lying half asleep on the sofa in the basement sitting room/kitchen, covered with an old knitted blanket, made of multicoloured squares, which had been intended for the refugees in Darfur or Iraq or some such place, until Chrissie had decided she liked her handiwork too much to give it away. She raised her head when she heard him, and blinked sleepily.

'How'd it go?' She pulled herself into a sitting position, stretching her arms languorously above her head and letting out a slow yawn, curling her short legs neatly under her – Chrissie had an almost feline quality. She was pretty, with green eyes in a small, freckled face, hair the colour that Jim had always compared to

Golden Shred marmalade – not yet faded although she was in her mid-fifties – cut boyishly round her head, accentuating her Cupid's bow lips and dimpled chin.

'Okay.'

Chrissie frowned. 'That's it? Just "Okay"?'

'I thought you'd be in bed by now,' Jim said, by way of a reply, still paused on the lowest stair as if he were not fully committed to coming into the room.

'I would have been . . . In fact I was, but some idiot drunk started banging on my window demanding to be let in. Tosspot thought he lived here. He wouldn't take no for an answer until he'd woken the whole sodding neighbourhood.'

'Hope you didn't let him in.'

'Do I look stupid? But it's hard convincing someone they're wrong through a locked door.' She yawned again, folded the blanket into a square and laid it over the sofa arm. 'Wasn't till Jared from number twelve threatened him with something horrible if he didn't shut the fuck up that he pushed off. But by that time I was wide awake.'

Jim didn't want to be there talking to his wife. With each word that passed between them, the euphoria he'd been revelling in since he'd left Nancy in the pub car park dwindled, melting away as if it had been a mirage, to leave him cold and depressed. It felt like the comedown from the drugs he'd experimented with when he was young and reckless. 'Hope he doesn't come back,' he said.

Chrissie scowled. 'Thought I'd get more sympathy than that. What's wrong with you tonight? Aren't you going to make me a cuppa and tell me the gossip?'

Which was what he often did when he came home late from a gig. Jim shook his head. 'Nothing's wrong. I'm just bushed.'

He pulled his jacket off and slung it over his shoulder. 'Night,' he called, as he headed upstairs to his bedroom, which looked out over the tiny paved garden at the back of the terraced house. His wife's room was on the ground floor, her window giving directly onto the street, hence her vulnerability to the passing drunk.

Jim's living space, his sanctuary, where he spent most of his time, was two bedrooms knocked together, which, with the landing and small bathroom, took up the whole of the first floor. He had converted it after their son Tommy had left home to do some incomprehensible coding job with an IT company in Edinburgh. Half was his sitting area, through which you had to walk to get to the bedroom. A large brown leather armchair, smooth with age, took centre stage, flanked by a G Plan glass and teak rectangular coffee table he had bought in the seventies when he'd had some money. The sanded wooden floorboards were partially covered by a rug from Mexico, now faded, but originally bright red, turquoise and yellow. He propped his guitar in the corner, next to a metal music stand and an electronic keyboard. The guitar itself, a Gibson Acoustic, which he'd had for more than thirty years, was his alter ego, his muse. Jim couldn't imagine his life without it.

He sat down, pulled off his boots and threw them into the corner. Then he reached for the bottle of Jim Beam he kept on a metal pub tray on the coffee table, poured a small measure into a Duralex glass and glanced around the room he loved. Sheet music lined the skirting, in low towers, with piles of books – Ed McBain a particular favourite, biographies of almost anyone – while the walls sported various framed posters, including Bob Dylan, Mama Cass, Joni Mitchell, a Hank Williams from the forties, and Nina Simone, a rare one, from a civil rights concert in the sixties.

Leaning back in his chair, he sipped the bourbon slowly, eyes shut, savouring the moment. He would have killed for a smoke to accompany it, but he was being strict with himself. No smoking inside, which even he had to admit made his room a much pleasanter place to be and reduced his ciggie count by about 80 per cent. He was gearing himself up for quitting – it just never seemed to be today.

I'm being daft, he told himself, as he pondered the evening and Nancy. *It was just one of those strange connections that happen sometimes. She probably didn't even notice me.* But he couldn't shake off the sense of destiny he had felt when he'd looked into Nancy's grey eyes for the first time. He definitely wasn't imagining it – his nature wasn't fanciful – and he'd never felt it with other women, not even Chrissie when they'd first met.

Chrissie. The thought of his wife downstairs immediately depressed him. What the hell were they going to do? They had become trapped together, immobilized by financial considerations. It wasn't healthy. Yes, they got on okay now, they had learned to be civil, which was a big improvement on the past. But they lived pretty separate lives, and hadn't been together as man and wife now for three years.

Jim had fallen apart the day he'd discovered her latest infidelity. Twenty-three years together – during which time she had strayed at least twice before, by her own admission – but the last straw was the morning she'd casually told him she was leaving. Bags packed, no argument. It had been going on for months, Chrissie told him, her and that little shit Benji. And him being so bloody matey with Jim whenever he walked into the pub. That was what had driven Jim insane, the humiliation. Probably half the pub had known what was going on and were sniggering behind his back.

He had loved Chrissie, been faithful to her even though he'd regularly been hit on by girls at gigs. He knew they were turned on by the music, the performance, not really by him, but he'd had chances and never gone there, because of the family.

Nearly a year she had been away, and they hadn't spoken, not once. Tommy had tried to make them, but Jim was stubborn, and still hurting. Then when Benji had messed her around – no surprises there – two-timing her with some bit of fluff behind the bar, Chrissie had come running home, thinking they could carry on as if nothing had happened. Same as last time.

Jim liked to think of himself as an easy-going guy – which he had been in the past – and he had stopped hating her quite quickly. But Chrissie wouldn't accept that she had finally broken him with Benji, broken *them*. She made him feel he was being old-fashioned, unreasonable in not taking her back. And maybe he was. But that didn't change the fact that he would never be able to make love to her again without seeing Benji's stupid face leering up at him.

For a while he had tried really hard to get past what she'd done. Now he'd stopped trying and just accepted he probably never would. It was more peaceful that way. And he and Chrissie got on a whole lot better. Except that recently she had been making subtle overtures to him again. Staying up, like she had tonight, with some excuse, real or imagined, wanting him to snuggle up with her on the sofa for a cup of tea and a cosy chat. He'd gone along with it too. Part of him kept fantasizing that they could be happy together. But he wasn't sure he loved her any more. Not in the way he had, or the way he should.

And after tonight, meeting Nancy, he knew he wouldn't in future. Nancy was it. He would see her again, even if it meant brazenly soliciting that dotty friend of hers and dragging them along to one of his gigs. The thought galvanized him. He leaped out of his chair and grabbed his guitar. He'd have to put on a sensational performance next Saturday, just in case she showed up. For the next couple of hours he strummed quietly, testing out the best order of songs, examining the words for significance, finding pieces that showed off his talent. When he finally fell into bed, he was certain that if Nancy pitched up, he could, bottom line, get her attention. He was, after all, a performer. The rest would be in the lap of the gods.

CHAPTER FOUR

'Oh God oh God oh God, Nancy. I feel like I've totally disintegrated. I'm dust.' Lindy groaned softly.

Nancy laughed. 'That bad?'

'It's not "bad", darling, it's bloody dire. I can barely see straight, there's someone racketing around my head who's obviously trying to demolish Palace Pier, and my liver is hanging from the chandelier, winking at me.'

'I didn't know you had a chandelier.'

Another groan. 'Nor did I till I saw my liver hanging from it.'

'Ha-ha! Alison was on the verge of carting you off to A & E, you know.'

'I do know. Bless her, she took me home with her, slept on the sofa. Second mile, eh?'

It was late on Sunday morning and Nancy was getting ready to go across the drive for lunch with the family. She heard Lindy sip what she imagined was a strong black coffee. 'I hope you had a good time,' she said.

'I enjoyed every single second, darling. Fantastic end to my sixth decade. Go out with a bang, eh? I just wish I'd stopped drinking about two hours before I did.'

Nancy heard the rustle of sheets, another groan.

'Will you tell me what happened, exactly?' Lindy mumbled. 'Ali refused to be specific. She just said I got wobbly and she took me home. I can't bear the thought that I humiliated myself in front of the beautiful Jim.'

Nancy paused. How much does she need to know? she wondered. She decided to leave out her friend's rudeness – Jim hadn't seemed to take offence. 'It wasn't too bad. You just slipped off your stool and landed in a heap on the floor.'

'Oh, God, the very worst. Is there anything sadder than an old woman falling down drunk?'

'You did it very gracefully,' Nancy added, and they both laughed.

'Jim must have been disgusted,' her friend's voice sounded suddenly tired. 'I'll never be able to look him in the eye again.'

'He was fine with it, Lindy. He didn't seem at all surprised. He must have seen people keel over a hundred times before in his line of work.'

'Yeah, well, doesn't make it any better. And he was so cute. I'd love to hear him sing. Wouldn't you?'

Before she answered, Nancy eyed the card that Jim had pulled from his jeans pocket. It was sitting on the kitchen table in front of her. It had been a distraction all morning, like a reflection that keeps catching the eye. She'd got home last night, tired out and dying to get into bed, but had lain wide awake in the darkness, remembering the fleeting frisson between them.

After the last four celibate years, Nancy knew that she was particularly vulnerable to male charms. Since Christopher's rejection, she had rarely spoken to a man, even less flirted with one: she had buried herself and her pain in her roles as daughter, mother, grandmother, and music teacher. Anyone could have looked at her as Jim had, with those bright blue eyes – questioning, full of humour and charm, but also delivering an unmistakable invitation – and she would have fallen for him. *He could have been the creature from the Black Lagoon*, she thought, *and I would still have been putty in his hands.*

'Are you up for it?' Lindy was asking. 'Shall I give him a bell and find out when his next gig is? I have a hazy memory of him telling me a date. Just can't remember when it was.'

'He gave me his card for you.' Nancy bit the bullet. 'I've got it here somewhere. He said he'd get us comps for his next show if we want. I think it's on Saturday.' She cringed: she had already checked out his website and knew all the details of his next four performances.

'Great! You'll come with me, won't you? I know it's not your thing, but I can't go alone and Alison doesn't have much sense of humour when it comes to chasing men.'

'Sure. I love any live music.'

'It's not the music I'm going for, darling.' Lindy chuckled. 'So he wanted me to have his card, did he? Good sign, no? Means he wasn't totally put off by my trolleyed-old-lady act.'

'It was your sixtieth,' Nancy reminded her friend.

'Please don't mention the dreaded six-oh ever again,' Lindy moaned. 'Send over the info and I'll call him.'

Louise and Ross's kitchen was a place of high drama today. That was how they liked it, Ross playing the lead as he rushed about preparing lunch: oven and stove-top at full heat, pans, dishes and cutlery banging, taps running, knives chopping, corks popping, his deep laugh booming at full volume, the room filled with a delicious meaty aroma. Louise played front-of-house, laying the table, filling glasses, making sure everyone had what they needed.

Today there were other guests – including Ross's trainee chef Jason and his girlfriend Kyla, another local couple – as well as Frances, Nancy's mother, and the girls, making ten round the table. Nancy was feeling under-slept and fragile from the night before and could have done with a quiet sandwich at home. But, living next door, she could hardly escape without lying, and Ross took rejection of his food rather personally. So Nancy sat with her mother on the sofa and let the others organize the feast.

'You look tired, darling,' Frances commented, as soon as Nancy sat down. 'I hope you're not coming down with something.'

Trust you to notice. Through her irritation, Nancy realized how fragile her mother seemed, although she was as pretty and immaculately groomed as always, the pure white pixie cut framing an unlined face, with pale-blue eyes and a still-full mouth made up with tea rose lipstick. Her tiny figure was dressed today in a grey linen dress, a light-blue cashmere cardigan and a silk scarf patterned with blue roses. These days, she seemed a little thinner every time Nancy saw her. She made a note to mention it to Louise: whenever she tackled Frances about it, her mother would brush her off with an airy 'I don't know what you're talking about.'

'I had a late night. I went to a friend's sixtieth.'

Frances's face lit up. 'Ooh, a party. What fun. Which frock did you wear?'

Louise, busy laying the table, caught the conversation. 'Not a frock, Granny. Mum was line dancing in a pub in Brighton. She wore my jeans and suede jacket and those ankle boots you like with the studs. She looked great.'

Frances raised her eyebrows. 'Gracious. That sounds a bit . . . eccentric. Sixty, did you say?'

Nancy saw the familiar mixture of bafflement and censure on her face. She was always falling short of her mother's expectations. Even when she had been tidily married to Christopher, Frances had managed to imply – without saying as much – that Nancy wasn't quite up to snuff as the wife of a high-profile musician. The divorce had proved her right.

'How did it go, Mum?' Louise was asking, as she paused with a handful of cutlery.

'It was good fun, actually,' Nancy said. 'The dancing was brilliant. Unfortunately Lindy got hopelessly drunk and had to be carried home, but that was only at the end. She's feeling very sorry for herself this morning.'

'Poor Lindy,' Louise said, laughing. 'Who took the dancing?'

'A guy called Jim. He's a country and western singer.'

As she spoke she felt Jim beside her, saw his eyes resting on her face. The memory made her catch her breath. Lindy had probably already rung him and organized the comps so he'd know they were coming. Nancy would rather have bought the tickets anonymously from the website, but it was too late now. What was she getting herself into? Her friend had made no bones about fancying the pants off Jim. Could she sit and watch while Lindy came on to him all night? And if the boot were on the other foot, how would Lindy react to Jim paying Nancy attention? It seemed destined to end in tears.

She shook herself mentally and tried to focus on the people around her, taking the glass of wine that Kyla handed to her and listening to the eulogy Ross was giving on this particular Chilean blush rosé. But it was hard to concentrate.

If Lindy fancies him, she can have him, she told herself. *What would I do with a man, anyway?* The question made her smile.

'What are you grinning at?' her mother asked, her eyes full of suspicion.

'Nothing,' Nancy said. 'I just had a great time last night.'

Which did nothing to alleviate her mother's clear misgivings.

'You're much too old to be getting drunk, darling.'

'I wasn't drunk,' she said quietly. If she had been, it would have been the perfect excuse for being so taken with Jim Bowdry. To avoid any further comment from her mother, Nancy looked out of the window. The girls were running up and down the lawn, each holding a long, floating scarf belonging to Louise above their heads like kites, the flimsy material billowing satisfactorily in the spring breeze. Jazzy's long blonde hair swung behind her like a cloak, while Hope's summer skirt belled around her skinny body, both of them shrieking with laughter. Bob sat by the flower border and looked on, turning her head from side to side as if at a tennis match, hypnotized. Nancy smiled. *I love those two so much*, she thought, glad she'd got to know them properly while they were young. *I have all I need*.

The succulent, still-pink roast beef and feather-light Yorkshire puddings had been polished off, as had the crunchy, sugary-sharp rhubarb crumble and thick cream, scraped from the sides of the white china bowls, followed by hot, strong espresso in flowered china demi-tasses. Now, most of the party, shooed out of the kitchen by Louise, had gone through to the sitting room and were lounging around the wood-burning stove, reading the Sunday papers and chatting. Hope and Jazzy had disappeared upstairs, leaving Nancy and Louise to clear up the remains of lunch.

'Don't you think Granny is looking more and more like a skeleton?' Nancy asked, as she soaped a glass and rinsed it under the tap. 'She never eats a thing these days.'

Louise thought for a moment. 'She barely touched her lunch. But that's nothing new – she's always been terrified of calories.' She rolled her eyes at her mother. Frances's obsession with her looks had always bemused Louise.

'Yes, I know she's obsessed, but she's never been this thin before. Do you think there's something wrong with her?'

'You mean cancer?' Her daughter was never one to mince her words.

'Well . . . I suppose it had occurred to me. Unexplained weight loss . . .'

'Persuade her to see the doctor, Mum. No point getting all het up about something that might not be true.'

'No, okay, I'll try.'

'Cup of tea?' Louise asked, the subject apparently closed.

'Love one.' She put the last glass upside-down on the tea towel placed on the draining board and dried her hands. 'By the way, I'm going out with Lindy again next Saturday night.'

'Great. What are you doing?'

'Oh, just a drink.' Nancy wasn't sure why she didn't mention Jim's gig. But it was too late now.

'It's good you and Lindy are friends. I like her.'

Nancy heard a patronizing edge in Louise's voice, as if she were in a position to sanction her mother's friendships. Perhaps she worried – more than she let on – that Nancy had become too isolated since the divorce.

'How's the restaurant doing?' she asked, to change the subject.

Her daughter pulled a face, sucking her bottom lip under her teeth. 'Yeah . . . okay.' She clammed up, turning away to get the milk out of the fridge.

The Lime Kiln had struggled in the four years it had been open. Its position didn't help, outside the village along a busy road; it depended on word-of-mouth, and there wasn't enough of that. But Nancy had always thought that the real reason for its lack of clientele was the 'fine dining' status upon which Ross insisted. That meant an air of seriousness about the towers of ingredients, which had been smoked, seared, salt-baked, or even cooked 'three ways' just to confuse matters. All very *Masterchef*, very modern, but also very pricey and, in Nancy's opinion, appealing to a limited market, which might have existed if Ross had established his reputation, but he hadn't, even though he was a talented chef. Nancy thought he would be better off making his menu more casual, more user-friendly and a lot cheaper. She had never dared suggest this to Ross, but had put her thoughts to Louise, only to find that her daughter agreed with her.

'You know Ross, Mum, stubborn as the day is long,' Louise was saying, her voice dropped to a whisper. 'He believes it will happen with time – that if he just hangs on in there people will come.' Her daughter sighed. 'And sometimes I believe it too. Then I see the accounts and I panic.' She suddenly looked close to tears. 'It's impossible to talk to him about it any more. As soon as I start he just gets annoyed with me.'

'Oh, Lou . . . Come here.' Nancy wrapped her daughter in her arms. This was a rare moment of weakness in Louise. She seldom opened up to her mother, especially about her relationship with Ross. 'I'm sure things will improve. It's the beginning of the summer – there'll be more weekenders, more holidaymakers looking for a treat . . . and you've got that lovely terrace at the back if the weather picks up.'

Louise pulled away, wiping her eyes and nodding in a mechanical way that told Nancy her words had been of little comfort. Maybe she'd heard them too often from Ross.

'Yes,' Louise said. 'Maybe.' She glanced at the clock. 'I suppose I'd better get Granny home.'

'I'll do that,' Nancy offered, her heart going out to her beleaguered daughter. 'If I don't keep moving I'll snooze, and then I won't sleep tonight.'

Frances was silent on the way back to her small terraced house in Hove. The journey took little more than twenty minutes, but she was nodding off by the time they arrived. Nancy stopped on a yellow line just down from the house and walked her to the door. 'Can I come in for a second, Mum?'

Her mother looked as if this were not a particularly welcome suggestion, but she ushered Nancy inside.

They stood awkwardly in the small hallway, until Frances waved towards the sitting room. 'Would you like some tea?'

'No, it's okay. I just wanted to talk to you about something.' They both sat down, Frances in her armchair by the fireplace, Nancy on the faded chintz sofa. The room was cluttered with heavy furniture from her parents' old house in Shrewsbury. Frances had insisted on keeping it when she'd moved south after Kenneth, Nancy's father, had died, but it made the room stuffy and cramped. She cleared her throat. 'I'm worried about how thin you're getting, Mum.'

Frances's face stiffened. 'What do you mean?'

'You've lost quite a bit of weight recently, don't you think? I just wondered if you're feeling all right.'

'I'm absolutely fine,' her mother said firmly.

'Are you eating properly, though? Because every time I see you, you just nibble at stuff. You never seem to finish a meal.'

Frances gave an irritated sigh. 'I'm old, darling, in case you hadn't noticed. People lose their appetite when they get to my age. I haven't a clue why, but I'm sure you could find out if you wanted to.'

Nancy steeled herself. 'Maybe, but are you eating *enough*?'

'I eat what I want.'

'So you don't have any pains, indigestion, difficulty in swallowing, that sort of thing?'

Her mother frowned. 'What is this? The Spanish Inquisition? No, I don't have any of the grisly symptoms you suggest. Now, please, I'm tired, and if all you came in for was to nag me about my diet then I'd rather you went home.' Her mouth, still carrying faint traces of tea rose, was pinched into a thin line.

Nancy shrugged. 'Okay, Mum. But, please, if anything's bothering you, you'll tell me, won't you?'

'Of course. I always do, don't I?'

Which, Nancy realized, was probably true, especially where illness was concerned. Frances was not above exploiting minor complaints as evidence of the rank unfairness of life, particularly of *her* life. 'Right. I'll see you on Thursday.'

Frances, gracious in victory, got up to see her daughter off. 'Thank you so much for bringing me home, darling,' she said, submitting to the brief hug that Nancy offered with warmth. Her mother was such an annoying woman most of the time. Demanding, finicky, self-centred, always expecting her daughter to drop everything and be there as soon as she asked – as if Nancy had no other life – then suddenly grateful and sweet, which always threw Nancy and made her feel intensely guilty. Her mother was, after all, vulnerable by virtue of her age. But perhaps the guilt, thought Nancy, was part of Frances's plan.

When Nancy got home, she went straight to her computer, which sat on a table in the far corner of the sitting room, looking out onto the garden. She wanted to hear the song that Jim had played after the dancing. She knew it was Kris Kristofferson, but she couldn't remember which one, and although she had recognized the tune from a long time ago, the title escaped her. Something about Sunday morning . . .

It took no time to find the song on YouTube, a site to which Heather, one of her music students – a twenty-four-year-old aspiring actress – had introduced her so that they could both study performances in the fifties musicals Heather wished to emulate.

She spent the next hour scrolling through a variety of Kristofferson songs, but the one that kept pulling her back was a seventies recording of 'For The Good Times'. It was about a break-up and the notes wrung her heart as she sang along. But it was not for Christopher that her heart broke. Far from it. It was a sudden and desperate yearning for her lost youth, the freedom of desire . . . And particularly for the opportunities she had never taken, closed down as her life had been back then in the pursuit of her single-minded passion for music. Tears trickled down her cheeks as she looked at Kristofferson's youthful beauty. It reminded her that hers, too, was now gone.

She felt a surge of resentment at Christopher for hijacking her – so easy in light of her youthful infatuation and awe – using her to smooth his own path to success, blinding her to what was happening in the rest of the world with his disdain for anything unrelated to his universe of Early Music. His passion was his work, not his wife and daughter. It was all about control, containment, precision, focus. And, looking back, it seemed as if she had employed only a minute fraction of her energy and vivacity. Now, when she was free to dance, to sing a country song loudly, even to fall in love, it was too late. *I am old.*

She went through to her beloved piano – a Steinway baby grand in a beautiful rich walnut that Christopher had bought for her when they got married – as she always did when she needed solace, and picked out the song she had just heard. The room was peaceful, empty, except for an old brown sofa against the wall, a table piled high with sheet music, a music stand, a piano stool and the instrument itself, upon which rested a metronome in a wooden case. She liked it that way, with no distractions from paintings or knick-knacks.

After a while she reverted to what was familiar and began to play the hauntingly beautiful second movement of Beethoven's Pathétique sonata. The soft, reflective notes seemed to match her mood.

Suddenly she was laughing.

God, what am I like? Sitting here sobbing indulgently for my youth, blaming poor Christopher, drooling after a man on a video who must now be in his late seventies! It's all Jim Bowdry's fault. He's unsettled me and made me want something I can't have.

But what that something was remained elusive to her tired brain.

Then, as she played on, the answer came to her. She yearned to feel properly alive again, to feel the blood rushing through her body, on fire with a passion that consumed her.

Saturday dawned, and with it, Nancy's nerves. *Maybe I should cancel tonight*, she thought, as she sat at the kitchen table with a boiled egg and some coffee. It seemed too complicated. For a start there was the perennial problem of what to wear. And did she want to encourage the sort of emotional disruption she had experienced last weekend? It had taken her most of the week to recover. Nor was she certain her friendship with Lindy was strong enough to survive Jim. Better to cry off and settle back into the life she had made for herself. It was a good life. She didn't feel brave enough for anything more challenging.

But even as she talked herself out of an evening listening to Jim Bowdry playing country music, she knew beyond a shadow of doubt that she would go, that she wouldn't miss it for the world.

'You know Grandy, Nana. Is Tatjana his wife?' Hope asked, as they sat at the kitchen table playing the children's version of Monopoly, waiting for Jazzy to find the die, which had fallen off the table a moment ago when she'd thrown it.

'They aren't married. He just lives with her.'

'Why doesn't he live with you?' Jazzy asked.

'They got divorced,' Hope told her sister authoritatively, before Nancy could reply.

Christopher had made a rare appearance in the girls' lives the previous weekend, taking them to Palace Pier on Saturday afternoon, with Tatjana in tow. Since the divorce, Louise's relationship with her father had been almost non-existent. She was still furious with him for leaving Nancy, had no interest in making nice to Tatjana and claimed she'd be happy never again to see either of them. It had only been Nancy's careful diplomacy over the years that had engendered a minuscule thawing in her daughter's attitude to Christopher, which, Louise insisted, was solely for the sake of Hope and Jazzy.

But the day, by all accounts, had not been a success. Christopher, completely inept with children and probably thoroughly nervous with his granddaughters, had tried to curry favour by feeding them a toxic mix of candy-floss and ice cream, Smarties and hot dogs, then allowed them to go on the cup-and-saucer ride, prompting poor Jazzy to throw up ignominiously on the boards of the pier.

'They kept arguing,' Hope was saying.

'Who did?'

'Grandy and Tatjana. She was cold and she didn't want to go on any of the rides. She said hot dogs were bad for us.'

'I don't like her,' Jazzy said, her large blue eyes sliding over Nancy's face, then looking away, perhaps not sure she was allowed to express this opinion.

'Why not?' Nancy asked, trying not to show how pleased she was by this information.

'She's mean,' Hope replied for her sister. 'She told Jazzy to stop crying when she'd just been sick and she had sick down her coat and all over her shoes.'

'Well, she doesn't have children. Maybe she didn't understand.'

'I bet *she*'d have cried if she had sick down her trousers,' Hope stated.

Nancy laughed, picturing, for a moment, the glamorous singer dripping in vomit. 'You're probably right. Now, come on, Jazzy, concentrate. Do you want to buy Pizza Party?'

'It's two million,' Hope said, giving her sister an evil grin. 'You can't afford it – you've only got one million left.'

Jazzy glared at Hope. 'It's not fair. Hope's got all the money. She always wins. I hate 'Nopoly.' She slid down from her chair and stomped off towards the stairs.

'Jazzy! *Jazzy!* Come back! We can't play without you,' Hope yelled, face crumpling with frustration. 'It's not fair!' She echoed her sister. 'She always does that when she's not winning.'

'She's only six, Hope. It's hard for her.'

Nancy's phone went. *That'll be Louise.* She snatched it up from the table. It was after six and Louise had said she'd be back by five. Nancy had to get changed and be at Brighton station to meet Lindy at seven-thirty. They were going for a drink before the gig.

'Mum, there's been a bit of a disaster. Jason dropped a knife and somehow gashed the back of his leg. It won't stop bleeding. I think it needs stitches, so I'm going to have to drive him to A & E.'

'Oh dear.'

'I won't stay with him, but it leaves Ross short-handed and I'll have to help out.' There was a sigh at the other end of the phone. 'I'm so sorry, Mum, I feel terrible – I know you're going out, but what else can I do? It's our busiest night and I'll never find a babysitter at this late notice. Would you mind staying with the girls? I hate to ruin your evening.'

Nancy felt a leaden thud of disappointment in her gut, but she took a deep breath. *I'm a grown-up*, she told herself. *I can't cry 'unfair' and stomp upstairs*. 'Of course I'll stay. Poor Jason, I hope he's all right.'

She heard her daughter exhale loudly. 'Mum, you're a saint! Thanks so much. I don't know what I'd do without you. I'm so sorry about Lindy. Will she mind?'

'I'm sure she'll be fine,' Nancy said. 'I hope the evening goes well.'

'Thanks. I'll call when I'm on my way home.'

'Oh, bloody great,' Lindy said, not sounding fine at all. 'Aren't we just the slaves to our grandkids? I'd have done the same for Toby in a heartbeat, but we shouldn't be asked. We've got our own lives. God, it's not as if we haven't put in the time over the years.'

Nancy heard her banging a cupboard or a drawer – her friend had probably been getting ready when she'd called. 'I'm as disappointed as you are. I was really looking forward to it.'

Lindy laughed. 'Yeah, well, I guess my lust will have to wait. Shame, though. These things have their time and if they don't work out the moment passes.'

Nancy said quickly, 'He's got another one on Saturday week – I checked his website. We should give it one more go, don't you think?'

CHAPTER FIVE

Jim's evening hadn't started well. When he'd gone to get himself a ham sandwich and a cup of tea before he left for the club, Chrissie had been making bread, pounding the dough on the wooden table, flour flying up in a cloud around her face. Her speciality was a chewy dark rye cob, which threatened to pull his teeth out but tasted delicious. She paused when she saw him, rubbing the end of her nose with the back of a floury hand. 'What time are you leaving?' she asked.

''Bout seven. Set's not till nine.' He began to fill the kettle, but when he turned, she was still staring at him.

'You look good.'

Part of him was pleased. He'd got his black shirt on with the thin white trim and stud buttons and his nearly threadbare 501s – his all-time favourite jeans. He knew he would weep for a month when they finally fell into dust on the bedroom floor. He'd dressed for Nancy, though, not his wife.

Chrissie, who had gone back to pulling, folding and pummelling the clay-like dough, said, 'Thought I'd come with you tonight. I like the Blue Door.'

Jim froze, teabag poised above his mug. 'You can't.'

She turned, frowning. 'What do you mean, I can't?'

'I mean I'd rather you didn't.' He knew this would be the red rag to the bull. Chrissie could kick off with much less provocation than this, but it had to be said.

'Ooh, would you now?' Her green eyes seemed to be cranking up, like the sparks on a Catherine wheel.

Jim put his teabag down and faced her. 'Listen, Chrissie. We aren't married any more. It's not right that you come to my gigs as if we are. It's confusing.'

'Confusing to who?' she demanded.

'Well, me, for starters.'

'"For starters", as you put it, we *are* still married, like it or not. And I've got as much right as the next person to come to a club and listen to you sing if I want to.'

'I know you have,' he tried to keep his voice reasonable, 'but I don't want you to any more. I think we should sort this thing out, Chrissie, once and for all. Do something about the house. Start afresh, the pair of us, like everyone else does in our situation.'

His wife's eyes narrowed. 'Hmm, I see. You've found someone else. Is that it? You don't want me queering your pitch.'

Jim turned away. She knew him way too well. 'I haven't, as it happens. But I'd like to. Wouldn't you?'

'I thought you'd been a bit offish recently. Who is she?'

'She isn't anyone.'

When he looked at Chrissie, there were tears in her eyes. *Oh, God*, he thought. *Please, not this again*.

'Are you really saying you don't love me any more?' She was hugging herself, like a child, tears making her eyes huge and luminous. But Jim was unmoved. It was a performance she'd been putting on since she came back after the Benji fiasco, and although he knew part of her believed every word, the rest of her was just using it as a weapon to manipulate him into doing what suited her best. He knew, however, that as soon as Chrissie found a new lover, she would behave exactly as she pleased, with no consideration whatsoever for him. Just like last time.

'Yes, that's what I'm saying,' he said, and he was surprised at the conviction behind the words.

Chrissie now began crying in earnest. Between the sobs, he caught some of her words: 'Twenty-six years . . . Tommy . . . just one mistake . . .' But he'd heard it all before. And it wasn't 'just one', was it?

'Listen, I've got to go.'

He felt like a total shit leaving her there, sobbing her heart out, but if he'd so much as touched her, she'd have been in his arms and trying to kiss him. And he couldn't bear that.

Shaken, he went upstairs without another word, hastily grabbed his guitar and left the house. It was drizzling, but he didn't care: he was just relieved to be away from her. It was his fault. He hadn't made himself clear. He'd let things drift because he was lazy and couldn't be bothered with the hassle of selling the house, which he loved, and finding some dismal bedsit – which was all he'd be able to afford if he stayed in Brighton – where he'd end his days drinking too much and having fights with the neighbours over his music.

As Jim strode along the streets parallel to the sea, towards the station, head down against the rain, his only focus was Nancy. Would she come? Her friend had been adamant that they would. But the thought of seeing her again made him almost shake. He always had a stiff whiskey before a gig, just to take the edge off, but tonight, what with Chrissie and the thought of Nancy, he decided he might have a couple.

It's just a fantasy, he thought as he walked, trying to calm his nerves. *You'll see her again and you'll wonder what all the fuss was about.*

The Blue Door was in the basement, attached to a pub, within three minutes' walk of Brighton station. The club ran live music events two or three nights a week and Jim liked playing there because it always drew a good crowd – often a spillover from the pub upstairs. His small but loyal following was guaranteed to bring in at least thirty-plus punters on any given night, but his gigs at the Blue Door usually upped that to much more.

'Hey, Steve.' Jim reached across the bar, immediately on the right as you walked in, and shook the manager's hand.

The walls were whitewashed brick, the dark ceiling a crisscross of tubular metal light-fittings shedding a bluish glow across the area below. Tonight there were wooden pub tables and chairs in the space between the bar and the stage; for bigger bands the floor was cleared to allow standing room. Sometimes his gigs would be like that, when he had the boys with him and they were billed as the Bluebirds, Jimmy P on bass, Mal on drums, but Mal was ill, some virus thing, and they hadn't played together for months now. Jim missed them: Jimmy P was a genius with harmonies, his tenor a perfect match for his own growly baritone.

'How's it going?' Steve asked. He had a blond man-bun and black-rimmed, rectangular specs, his grey T-shirt sporting a photo of Freddie Mercury – ironic, Steve had assured him, when Jim had reminded him that Steve loathed Queen.

'Okay, I suppose.'

Steve laughed. 'Don't sound so sure. Chrissie coming tonight?'

The manager, although probably twenty years younger than Jim's wife, made it no secret that he lusted after Chrissie – in a respectful sort of way. Which was why she liked the club and had wanted to come tonight, Jim suspected.

'Nope.' Jim settled himself on a bar stool and asked for a whiskey, ice, no water. 'So how many have we got?'

He had played to as few as four people, and as many as a couple of thousand – it was all the same to him, performance-wise. He wanted anyone who'd bought a ticket to have the best of him.

Steve glanced at the book beside the till. 'Pretty good. A solid thirty-plus sold, but then there's the pub lot to come. You always pull in the crowds, Jim. That's why we keep asking you back.' He gave Jim an arch smile.

'Yeah, right. You got the two comps I asked for?'

Steve nodded. 'Name of Tooley?'

'That's right.' He put his glass down, pointed at it. 'I'll be back for that. Just going to set up.'

There was a good buzz as Jim settled on his high stool, adjusted the mic, played a G chord and fiddled with the peg for his E string. He'd already tuned the guitar backstage, but it gave the audience time to settle down, and him to get into the zone. He scanned the seats for Nancy and her friend. No sign of them so far, but it was only just after nine, and they'd probably lost their way or something. Jim took a deep breath and smiled.

'Hi, everyone. Good to see you all. I'm Jim Bowdry and I'm going to start with a song made famous by one of the legends of country music. It's Don Williams's "My Best Friend". Hope you enjoy it.'

The first song felt a bit flat to Jim's ear, although the punters clapped enthusiastically at the beginning and the end. He, however, was letting his nerves get to him. Usually, as soon as he started singing, the music would take over, he'd be carried up into his performance, lose time, so that when it was over it seemed like barely a minute since he'd started. But not tonight. Nancy was stealing his breathing space. He needed to know she was there, to begin to play to her, but there was still no sign as he peered into the semi-darkness of the club.

He played his fifteen songs, then an encore of 'Help Me Make it Through the Night', which he took slowly – it always got them going.

As he stepped down from the small stage, wired from his performance and dying for a ciggie and a drink, he was immediately accosted by Terri, one of his biggest fans – almost at stalker-level – who never seemed to miss a gig. She was middle-aged and overweight, but knew more about country music than anyone he'd ever spoken to.

'Liked the Dierks Bentley, Jim. Great to hear some decent modern stuff with the old favourites,' she said.

'Yeah, it's a good song. Not too pop for you?' He grinned slyly.

She pulled a face. In their frequent exchanges, Terri seldom failed to mention the dire state of modern country, to her mind hijacked by pop to provide a watered-down version of the true faith. 'Not with you singing it,' she said, smiling up at him flirtatiously.

He patted her arm, thanked her for coming, and ordered a drink from Steve as he passed him on the way to the stairs. 'Just going for a smoke,' he said.

As he stood outside on the wet pavement in the city darkness, he took a long slow breath of night air, trying to quell the overwhelming disappointment that had been building since the end of his act. He'd been so sure he'd see her again, that they had some shared destiny. *Dumbass*, he thought. *She didn't come. She's not interested. All in your stupid head, mate. End of.*

CHAPTER SIX

'What are you asking me for?' Nancy asked. 'It's Louise you should be talking to.'

It was early in the morning, not yet seven, and Christopher had woken her with his call. He regularly got up at six and it had never occurred to him that the rest of the world might not follow suit.

'Yes, I know, and of course I will. But I wanted to get your advice first. It's not as if Louise and I have much of a rapport at the moment.'

Well, whose fault is that? Nancy thought, slipping effortlessly into the bitchy 'wronged-wife' mode she loathed and for the most part had avoided. But to her ex-husband she said evenly, 'I'm sure the girls would love to be bridesmaids, but it depends on Louise.'

'You think they would?' His voice brightened. 'Because Tatjana wants the whole church thing, bridesmaids, the lot.'

'Wow. Sounds a bit challenging.'

Their own wedding had been at the Marylebone town hall, with a lunch afterwards for twenty people. It had been Christopher's choice – he had been preparing for a concert tour in Scandinavia but said there would never be a better time, he was always so busy – and Nancy hadn't minded. In fact, she'd been glad not to have to go through all that palaver. But Frances had probably never forgiven her.

He had the grace to laugh. 'Yes, well . . .'

Nancy said nothing, just smiled to herself.

'So I was wondering if you'd be kind enough to have a word with Louise? Sort of pave the way? She can be so spiky, and I understand it's been difficult for her. But it is four years now and I do feel she could make a bit more of an effort with Tatjana.'

Sensing from Nancy's silence, perhaps, that he'd unwittingly strayed onto dangerous ground, he hurried on: 'I really want Louise and the family to be there, obviously. I just don't want to create any extra tension. Would she come, do you think?'

'I can't speak for Louise, Christopher. But you're making a mistake if you hope my paving the way will help. She'll think you're being a wimp.'

'A *wimp*?' her ex-husband spluttered. 'Is that how she sees me? I'm trying to do the right thing here for everyone. I hardly think it's fair to accuse me of some sort of weakness.'

Nancy had to stifle a giggle. She could just picture his face, his mouth all pruny at the insult. 'Hold on a minute. She hasn't accused you of anything yet. But you know our daughter. She's nothing if not straight-talking. My advice to you would be to stop apologizing. Just tell her you'd really like them all to be at the wedding and see how she reacts.'

'Hmm . . . You think that's the best way to handle it?' There was a suspicious edge to his voice, as if he were worried she was selling him down the river.

'I do . . . By the way, I hope you're inviting me too.'

She couldn't help herself. But Christopher had never been big on humour.

'I – I thought you wouldn't want to—'

'Joke.'

His laugh was forced. 'Of course. I knew that.'

'Well, if that's it . . .' Nancy was suddenly bored with the conversation.

'Are you all right?' Now he'd got her on a rare phone call, he seemed to want to linger. 'How are things?' But she knew if she said anything but 'Very good, thank you,' he wouldn't want to hear.

So she said just that, which had the merit of being true, then added a quick goodbye.

Putting the phone down, she realized that, for the first time, Christopher hadn't upset her. The thought of his chocolate-box wedding just made her laugh. She almost felt sorry for him, so clearly at the mercy of Tatjana's whim – and it must be horrible to be at odds with your daughter like that.

Later, Nancy welcomed Heather, her first student of the day. She taught piano to seven altogether, all women. The girl was musical and keen, a pleasure to teach. So different from her eleven o'clock, Sally, who, despite good sight-reading skills and a definite ability at the keys, was a depressive, which came through in the heavy, plodding style with which she attacked the music. But that morning even Heather felt like an effort. Nancy was going to Jim's next gig in two days' time and could think of little else although, over the intervening days, his image and the memory of the connection she'd experienced with him had faded. *Have I exaggerated the whole thing?*

'Nancy?' Heather was smiling at her. 'You were miles away.'

'Sorry . . . sorry,' Nancy tried to focus, noting the girl's bright pink Lycra top stretched over large breasts, the full, fifties-style floral skirt, the silver trainers, the swinging blonde ponytail and thinking how great it would be to feel so confident, so carefree.

They worked for a while on 'Love Me Tender' – Heather was developing a good repertoire of Elvis songs, fifties musicals, the Everly Brothers. She had no interest in playing classical music, although she'd trained in it at school.

'Right hand, F sharp seven chord . . . A sharp, C sharp, E, F sharp . . . Love me . . .' Nancy prompted, singing the melody as Heather stopped and repeated the phrase.

'Aww, love this song,' Heather said, with a grin of satisfaction, adding, 'You've got a good voice. Do you sing?'

'Only in the bath,' Nancy replied. Not true, but her years with Christopher and his group of professional singers had silenced her public voice.

'What should I do?'

Louise had come with Nancy the following day for her weekly coffee with Frances in the small, artisan-style cafe on Church Road – a converted butcher's shop that still had the white-tiled walls – which sold delicious coffee and sublime cakes. Her mother, Nancy knew, loved it when Louise joined them: she was very fond of her granddaughter and seemed a lot livelier that morning, somewhat allaying the fears Nancy harboured about her health.

'Honestly, darling, aren't you making a bit of a meal of it? You can't punish your dear father for ever.' Frances, as usual, took Christopher's side.

Louise frowned. 'I'm not punishing him. I just don't feel like being nice to that bitch, who ruined Mum's life.'

'Language!' Frances said.

'Well, she is a bitch, Granny. She knew Dad was married and she didn't give a toss. What would *you* call someone who did that?'

Nancy watch her mother's lip curl slightly.

'Trollop?' Frances said, making them both laugh.

'Seriously,' Nancy interrupted, 'I'm not saying it'll be easy, Lou, but maybe this is the moment to mend some bridges. For your and your father's sake. It's just one day.'

Louise groaned. 'God, Mum. Not you too. Dad only wants me and the girls there as a trophy, to save his public image. Otherwise everyone will ask where we are.'

Nancy thought there was some truth in this. 'Fair enough, but I think he also wants you to come because he loves you and he hates the rift between you.'

Louise was silent.

'The fact is, darling,' Frances said, after another of her minute nibbles of caramel tart, 'Tatjana isn't going anywhere. You're stuck with her.'

When Louise just looked sullen and didn't reply, Frances asked, 'What does Ross think?'

'That we should go. Everyone thinks we should. He says I'm being petty if I don't.'

There was a long silence during which they all bent their heads to the cakes and stirred their coffee, the atmosphere round the little table thick with the unsaid.

'If you don't go,' Frances said eventually, 'you risk alienating your father for ever.'

The words, although spoken softly, sounded harsh, but Nancy agreed with her mother. Christopher had a huge ego: he had never taken kindly to rejection of any kind.

'And you won't win, dear,' Frances went on. 'When it comes to a man choosing between the woman he loves and his family, he'll choose the woman every time.'

Louise looked at her, aghast. 'Seriously, Granny? You're saying if push comes to shove Daddy would choose Tatjana over me and the girls?'

Frances, both eyebrows raised now, nodded. 'I'm afraid so.'

Louise looked at her mother. 'Mum? Is that right?'

Nancy considered the question. 'He wants both, of course,' she said slowly. 'But I suppose Granny is right. If you make him choose he's not going to dump Tatjana, is he? He's obsessed with her.'

She saw Louise's face harden. 'I don't know why I'm even asking. He never, *ever* put me first.' She looked at Nancy. 'Or you, Mum. It was always him, him, him – him and his bloody music.' She shook her head angrily. 'Well, Tatjana's welcome to him. I'm not going to the wedding. I'm not going to expose my children to that bitch. Or fake some sort of rapprochement just so as he can look good in front of his poncy friends.'

Frances laid her hand over her granddaughter's. 'Don't make any rash decisions, darling.'

By Saturday, Nancy had almost resigned herself to the fact that something would stop her going out. Either the girls, Louise or her mother. There would be a drama and she would feel obliged to respond. She thought of Frances's assertion that a man would always choose love over family and wondered if that were true of women. Probably less so, she decided, because women tended to be more involved with their offspring from the start.

Nevertheless, she got dressed early, plumping for the dreaded black jeggings – they looked good on her slim legs and Jim wouldn't know her mother wore them too – and a round-necked black

T-shirt with the faint outline of a butterfly drawn stylishly in off-white across the front. It was the trendiest piece of clothing she had, bought from a stall in a London market about five years ago because the proceeds would save some rainforest somewhere and she had been charmed by the young guy's passionate sales pitch. Jim had only seen her in her daughter's clothes, and she worried her own would seem old and dowdy by comparison.

She had also had her hair cut, trimmed a bit shorter to 'give it more body' according to Tess, her hairdresser, and it did look better at chin length. Nancy never wore much makeup – mostly from laziness – but she was lucky to have inherited her good skin from Frances. Tonight, however, she was at pains to smooth a thin layer of foundation and blusher over her cheeks, brush mascara across her lashes and add a berry-tinted lip balm to her mouth. She considered eyeshadow, but her efforts were usually clumsy and she might end up looking worse rather than better.

I can't compete with Lindy anyway, she thought, pulling a face in the mirror as she surveyed what she considered, with some surprise, to be not such a bad result. She shimmied, did a little side-step, copying a move Jim had taught them the other night, and felt a fizz of excitement in her gut.

As she was leaving the house, Louise and the girls were returning from a play-date. Hope jumped out of the car and crossed the gravel to kiss her grandmother. 'Wow, Nana, you look really pretty,' she said, eyeing her up and down in the disconcerting way of children.

'You've got lipstick on.' Jazzy pointed to her mouth, clearly intrigued.

'You do look great, Mum,' Louise added, making Nancy blush.

People rarely said she looked good, maybe because she didn't most of the time. But she coloured as much for the reason she was doing it as for the compliment itself.

'Where are you going with Lindy?'

'Oh, just a pub in Brighton.'

'Enjoy yourself, then. Don't be late back!'

The girls, still staring at her as if she'd sprouted wings, watched her walk to the car until Louise shouted at them to come inside. Nancy remembered the childish thrill of seeing her mother all dressed up, ready to go out to a dinner party with her dentist father. The waft of scent and face powder, the swish of taffeta, bright lips and shiny nails, hair curling in a neat perm, a fox-fur stole around her shoulders. She herself was a poor substitute, but her grandchildren had seemed rapt anyway.

Lindy looked amazing, as usual, in a black pencil skirt, white T-shirt, silver-link belt, trendy ankle boots and black leather jacket. Her wrists sported a quantity of bangles – including, tactfully, the turquoise one Nancy had given her – her nails a shiny French manicure, her long blonde hair tousled around her face. She might have looked cheap, but she didn't. *More Goldie Hawn*, Nancy thought, feeling about eighty. If Jim had to choose from looks alone, it would be no contest.

They were early, it was only just gone eight, but it was raining again and Lindy hadn't wanted to wander about finding somewhere else to drink.

'We can get a good table near the front,' she'd said, 'maybe catch up with Jim before he goes on.'

Nancy felt cold and hungry, her stomach a mess of nerves. She should have had a sandwich before she'd come out, but she had been so busy tarting herself up – time clearly wasted in the light of Lindy's stellar efforts.

The club was murky, with a dim blue glow from what looked like tin cans dotted about the concrete ceiling. There were only about ten people so far, sitting at the small tables, mostly in pairs, the stage lit up at the far end, a microphone and stool waiting for Jim.

'Do you think more people will come?' Nancy whispered, although the sound system was playing so loudly, even Lindy had trouble hearing.

'Hope so. Might be a bit embarrassing with only this lot.' Lindy ordered two glasses of white wine and asked the tall man behind the bar if Jim had arrived.

He glanced up at the clock, then shook his head. 'Should be here in a minute. Usually pitches up before eight.'

They chose a table, Lindy determined to sit as close to the stage as possible, despite Nancy's objections. There was a slightly awkward atmosphere in the room as they waited for other people to arrive and the gig to start, the two women sipping their cold wine and making small talk above the noise of the music.

'So you managed to escape another babysitting drama,' Lindy said.

'Yes, although I wasn't sure I would until I was actually in the car.'

'It's not fair, really. Your daughter shouldn't expect you to drop everything at a moment's notice. Mine's the same. Even if I'm working, Cheryl thinks it's okay for *me* to take a day off work, rather than her, if there's a problem with Toby.'

Lindy was retired from her job as an events organizer, but she worked in an antiques shop in the Lanes three days a week.

'Louise isn't usually like that,' Nancy said.

'No? Well, maybe that's because you don't get out much.'

Nancy laughed. 'True, but she'd respect it if I did. Last time was an emergency – she didn't really have a choice.'

'Ah, it's always an emergency.' Lindy nodded wisely. 'But, hey, we love to be needed, right? I don't begrudge it . . . not most of the time, anyway.'

Nancy's reply never materialized because she caught sight of Jim's figure crossing the room behind Lindy's chair, heading towards a door on the far side, next to the stage. The room had filled and he didn't notice them as he walked through, head down, clutching his black guitar case. Nancy found she was holding her breath, and her face must have shown it because her friend twisted sharply to see what she'd been staring at. But Jim had disappeared behind the door.

'What?' Lindy demanded.

'Nothing . . . I thought that was Jim – it was Jim. He went through that door.'

'God, Nance, what are you like? Why didn't you say hello?'

Nancy felt embarrassed and stupid. 'I – I don't know . . . I wasn't sure it was him and then he'd gone.'

Lindy sighed with frustration. 'Oh, well, we can catch up with him later.' She wriggled her skirt down and crossed her legs. 'Now, I want him to see me sober tonight, so promise you won't let me have more than two glasses.'

Nancy tried to laugh, but the sound that came out was more like the yelp of a strangled cat.

'Are you all right?' Lindy peered at her.

'Fine, thanks. The wine went down the wrong way.' She was drinking too quickly: most of her large glass had already gone.

'I didn't mean that. It's just you seem a bit jumpy tonight.'

'Do I?' Nancy tried to look baffled. 'I suppose, as you say, I don't get out much.'

Lindy laughed, reaching down to adjust the metal tag on her boot zip. 'Relax, girl. Let your hair down. Music, wine, cute cowboys . . . Just enjoy the moment and forget about all the other bollocks in your life.'

'I'll try,' Nancy muttered, wishing she had never come. The brief sighting of Jim had reminded her that he was, in fact, a total stranger, made familiar only by her fantasy projections over the intervening days since they'd last met. And here she was, sitting with bloody Goldie. What chance did she stand even if they did get to talk to him afterwards?

CHAPTER SEVEN

Jim was in a bad mood. Again. It had been his default position since the night he'd realized Nancy wasn't going to turn up to hear him sing. He and Chrissie had been at loggerheads, which didn't help, because he had bitten the bullet and got two estate agents round to value the house. She was, quite reasonably, freaking out. He was freaking out too. And they couldn't manage to talk about it without resorting to accusations and tears.

'You're lying to me,' Chrissie had said that evening, standing, arms akimbo, in the hall outside her bedroom, just as he was preparing to leave for the gig. It was only half an hour since the second agent had gone, after poking in cupboards, making notes on her clipboard, asking all kinds of ludicrous questions. Chrissie looked as if she'd been crying and her Golden Shred hair was sticking up at all angles. 'You've got someone else and you're not telling me.'

He said, 'I haven't got anyone else. I swear.' Which was true as far as it went.

'So why are you trying to get rid of me all of a sudden?' Her voice was raised, tinny, pained.

'You know why,' he told her wearily. Because they'd had the

same conversation almost every time they'd seen each other in the past few weeks.

Then she came close to him, put her arms round his waist, laid her head against his chest. 'Oh, Jim,' she said, 'you know I never meant to hurt you.' She looked up at him with her green cat eyes, 'Benji cast a spell on me, that's all I can tell you. I wasn't myself.' She reached up to drop a light kiss on the corner of his mouth, as if she didn't quite dare kiss him full on the lips. 'You know I love you . . . I've always loved you.' Her eyes filled with tears. 'There's never been anyone else for me.'

Jim heard himself let out a deep sigh. Wouldn't it be easier to just go with it, forget Benji, be her husband again in the proper sense and keep the house they'd lived in for more than twenty years? Wasn't he too old for all this disruption? And while Chrissie would be able to get a mortgage on a new place – she was only fifty-five and worked for the council in the environmental health department, monitoring food safety – he was self-employed and over sixty. They'd laugh him out of court if he tried to borrow money.

He and Chrissie had rubbed along pretty well for a long time until Benji, he wouldn't deny that. But he had never felt a soulmate thing with his wife. It was more a sort of surface compatibility, easy and mostly thoughtless, good sex being the glue that had held them together. Now, as she cuddled up to him, he realized he felt only an age-old familiarity with the shape of her body, the smell of her skin, the girlish tone of her voice. He didn't feel love or even much tenderness, just the memory of both. This shocked him. Was he the cold-hearted bastard she had recently taken to calling him?

Carefully disengaging himself from her arms, Jim picked up his guitar. 'We've got to move on, Chrissie.'

And she just stood there dumbly, eyes wide with hurt, as he drew his leather jacket round him and walked out into the rain.

Now, guitar in hand, he took a deep breath and opened the door to what Steve liked to call the Green Room, but which was in fact a cupboard with a mirror and a chair, just room enough for the artists to change but no good at all if you had cat-swinging in mind. He hadn't arrived in time to grab a drink this evening, because of Chrissie's meltdown, so his nerves were jagged.

Climbing the three rickety wooden steps to the stage and settling on the high stool, he hoisted his guitar onto his lap and adjusted the mic, did his usual fiddling with the E string, then cast his eye over the evening's audience. There was a good crowd again, which lifted his mood. This venue was becoming a home from home, the management, Steve had said, pleased with the take at the bar from the slightly older punters with deeper pockets who followed Jim; students tended to hang on to one miserable pint for the whole night.

And there she was. Jim did a double-take. Was he imagining it? No, it was definitely Nancy and her blonde friend. He realized he should speak, suddenly conscious of the room silent and waiting. Swallowing hard, dragging his gaze away from the two women at the table, he strummed a couple of chords to fill the time until he felt he could find his voice. But the name of the first song escaped him. What the hell had he decided on as an opener? And why did she have to sit so close, right in his eye-line?

'Evening, everyone,' he finally croaked, managing a smile that swept across the tables and included Nancy and Lindy. 'Great to see you all. I'm going to start with an old favourite of mine . . .' and out of the blue a song title sprang to his lips, hardwired as they all were into Jim's very genes. It wasn't the one he had planned, he still couldn't remember that, but it was unfailingly popular. 'Written by Don Schlitz and made famous by Kenny Rogers, I'm sure you all know it well.'

There was a smattering of applause and a couple of whoops from the crowd as he picked out the first D chord of 'The Gambler' and was surprised to find the words flowing easily along with the music. He didn't look at Nancy.

All through the set, instead of running the order he'd decided on earlier, he felt his way to the next song, instinctively choosing numbers that meant something to him, songs he could sing from his heart. Was she enjoying it? How would he know? On the occasions when he dared to glance her way, she seemed as if she was, but then she was way too polite to look bored. Lindy, on the other hand, was getting into the music with her usual zest, clapping along, singing the lyrics to the ones she knew, swaying and stamping her feet. Not to mention catching his eye whenever he gave her the chance.

Jim finished with a song he'd written himself, 'Don't Pretend You Love Me', which had been a minor hit with the Bluebirds back in the early eighties, but had made some real money for him when a cover version a decade later had sat in the top ten for weeks – house money, as it turned out. He still got trickles of cash from the song, even today.

'*I know you want to mean it, but your eyes tell the lie . . .*' He sang the last mournful chorus and his fans in the audience whooped enthusiastically until he did an encore. But the only person he cared about was Nancy. It seemed crucial that she appreciated his song. She could never be attracted to him if she didn't like his work.

Stepping down from the stage, clutching his guitar, he felt his heart hammering in his chest. Post-performance adrenalin mostly, but this evening it was more intense.

'Darling, you were sensational!' Lindy stood in front of him, her arms wide as she moved in to kiss both his cheeks. She smelt strongly of a musky perfume he recognized from somewhere as she pressed her breasts against his chest.

'Hey,' Jim said. 'Glad you could make it.'

'Nancy's here,' Lindy said, dragging him by the arm to their table.

He smiled at Nancy, who was sitting on the edge of her chair, and reached across to shake her hand, which felt cold to the touch, just as it had in the car park.

'Hi . . .' she said.

'Sit, sit!' Lindy ordered him. 'I'll get you a drink.'

'No, let me,' Jim insisted, wanting a breathing space to collect his thoughts.

'Absolutely not!' Lindy was pulling out a chair. 'You've just given us an amazing performance. The least I can do is buy you a drink.'

A girl was hovering, obviously wanting to speak to him. She was young, curly dark hair springing untidily around her face. Jim hadn't seen her before.

'Sorry, I'll just . . .' He began to move away to talk to the girl, propping his guitar against the stage as he went.

'What'll it be?' Lindy called, and he told her a Jim Beam, please. He'd almost asked for a Maker's Mark, he knew Steve kept some, but it was more expensive and he didn't want to take the piss.

All the time he was listening to the girl telling him that she'd done a cover of his song and she'd love him to hear it, could she send him a link, he was aware of Nancy at the table behind him. She hadn't had a chance to say whether she'd liked the set or not.

Lindy, who had placed herself close to him on the other side of the table, was holding court, telling him, with impressive authority, that she thought the American singer Tyler Farr was quite clever to have made the tricky journey from country to rock and back again without losing his integrity.

'It certainly works for him,' Jim said, wanting Nancy to join in the conversation, but realizing she wasn't being given much of a chance.

'I like my country traditional, me,' Lindy said, 'but Farr keeps that gritty, wounded thing going at the same time as making the sound bigger and richer. And he's sexy, of course, which helps.'

Nancy was sitting quietly, sipping her wine, as they talked on. Jim had hardly had a moment to glance her way for the last half-hour, but when he did, he would catch her eyes on him before she looked quickly away. He was embarrassed by Lindy's monopolizing of the conversation and couldn't fail to notice her hand constantly straying to his white cotton shirt sleeve when she was making a point. But the bourbon was relaxing him and it was hard not to be enthusiastic as he talked about the subject he loved. *I hope she doesn't think I fancy Lindy*, he thought, remembering those agonizing moments from his youth when the girl he'd had the hots for had chosen his mate instead.

Lindy finally got up to go to the ladies, leaving him alone with Nancy. He raised his eyebrows slightly, gave her a smile. 'Wow, your friend really knows her stuff,' he said, nodding towards Lindy's retreating figure.

'Yes, I hadn't realized she was such an aficionado.'

There was silence.

'Can I get you another drink?'

He saw her check her glass.

'Uh, no . . . I'm all right, thanks.'

Another silence.

'I thought after the other week that I wouldn't see you again.' He leaned forward, his voice low, probably inaudible above the thumping sound system, but he didn't want to shout. He held her gaze, his eyes doing the work for him, determined to make Nancy understand that it was her he fancied, not her friend.

'I had to babysit my granddaughters,' she said.

Jim nodded. 'Didn't matter. I wasn't sure it was your thing anyway.'

He saw Lindy emerging from the ladies on the far side of the room.

'No, no, I really loved it,' she was saying, her words hurried as if she wanted to finish before Lindy reached them. 'I think you have a beautiful voice . . . and you make the songs so emotional. They really mean something.'

'Thank you.' Jim, hearing the sincerity in her tone, leaned back and gave her a dazzling smile. 'Thanks very much.' He got up as Lindy arrived, pulling her chair out for her.

Lindy sent him off to get some more drinks, and from the bar he could see the two women whispering across the table together. God, he felt drained. Could he put up with any more of Lindy's outrageous flirting – the legs flashing, the hand on his arm, the frequently tossed hair? The more he didn't respond in the way Lindy clearly wanted, the more she seemed to ramp up the seduction. He wished she'd stop. It was humiliating. She seemed an intelligent woman, good company – she didn't need to behave like that to get a man's attention. Jim had never enjoyed that level of come-on, especially not now, when all he wanted to do was spend quiet time with Nancy, see if there was really anything there or if he'd imagined it.

Reluctantly, he took the drinks back to the table. He thought Nancy seemed uneasy as he sat down and wondered what Lindy had said to her behind his back. But he didn't have a chance to find out because Lindy took up where she'd left off, and Jim's attention was once more hijacked.

'I think I might call it a night.' It wasn't particularly late, but Nancy, pushing her chair back and standing up with intent, had clearly had enough.

'You're going?' Lindy said, pulling a face. 'It's barely eleven-thirty.'

Jim thought she didn't look very upset that her friend would be leaving. He made a quick decision. 'Yeah, I ought to be heading off too.'

'No! Come on! What's wrong with you guys? The night's still young.' Lindy took hold of his sleeve as he tried to get to his feet. 'Please . . . stay for one more drink.'

Jim gave a laugh in an attempt to soften the blow of his refusal, gently extricating his arm. 'No, it's been great, Lindy, but I've got to be up early.'

'On a Sunday?' Lindy pouted.

'Yeah. I have to be . . . somewhere.' It was true, but he knew he hadn't sounded convincing.

'Where? What's so important that you can't stay another half-hour with me?'

I can see why she was such a successful events manager, Jim thought. *She just doesn't take no for an answer*. Lindy had spent the last half-hour telling him about her work, the people she'd met, the situations she'd negotiated, the toughness needed to bring off an international conference, a festival, a rich man's party.

'London, if you must know,' he said. 'Meeting friends.'

Lindy waved her hand dismissively. 'You can sleep on the train.' She yanked his arm again, but he kept moving, teeth gritted, and turned to pick up his guitar.

'Gotta go, Lindy. We should meet up another time.'

Lindy gave a theatrical sigh, but her face looked resigned as she gathered her bag from the floor. 'Oh, okay, have it your own way. Bloody party-poopers. Nobody has any stamina, these days.'

Jim heard Nancy give a self-conscious laugh, obviously aware of her friend's mood as Lindy stood and gulped down the remains of her wine, then followed them as they made their way between the tables.

Outside it was still raining.

'Bugger,' Lindy muttered. 'I'm going to get fucking soaked.' They all stood in the shelter of the pub doorway, Lindy holding her large black leather bag over her head. She hadn't said a word while they waited for Jim to return from the Green Room with his guitar case, the two women standing in stony silence.

'Shall I see you to your car?' Jim asked.

'God, no. I'm a big girl.' She gave a forced laugh, leaning in to give Nancy a peck on the cheek. 'Night, darling. You be all right getting home?'

'Yes. Night, Lindy.'

'Call me tomorrow, yeah?' Lindy turned to him briefly. 'Thanks for a great evening.' She didn't attempt to kiss him or shake his hand as she took off, almost running along the wet pavement, into the night.

'I think we pissed her off,' Jim said, as they watched her go.

Nancy nodded. 'Lindy loves to party.'

Neither of them moved. Reluctant to say goodnight, he watched the drizzle, feeling the cold night breeze that had sprung up while they'd been inside, conscious of Nancy's presence beside him.

'Can I give you a lift? You can't walk home in this,' she said eventually.

Jim hesitated. 'Nah, I'll be fine . . . It'll be out of your way.'

'How do you know?'

He grinned. 'Guess I don't. Where are you heading, then?'

'North, towards Ditchling.'

'I'm east, Kemptown. So definitely out of your way.'

'I don't mind.'

And that seemed to settle it. Jim just nodded and they set off in silence towards her car.

He waited while Nancy removed a bottle of water and a newspaper from the passenger seat and threw them into the footwell in the back before he got in. The Golf seemed a very cramped, intimate space with the darkness outside and the rain blurring the windows. Neither spoke as she manoeuvred out of the parking space. He felt as if he were holding his breath.

'Tell me which way to go,' she said.

He directed her across town. As it was Saturday night there were still a lot of drunken revellers about – students mostly, by the look of them – despite the rain, but Nancy and Jim continued in tongue-tied silence.

'Left at the next one.' Jim realized with dismay they were almost at his house. 'Here. Just drop me at the corner.' They hadn't said a word the whole way and he was kicking himself. This woman was about to drive off into the night and he hadn't made any sort of a move.

'Thanks for tonight,' Nancy was saying, turning to him, her face lit by the yellow glow from the streetlamp. She didn't turn the engine off, just kept the car idling by the kerb as the rain fell heavily on the windscreen.

Jim nodded. 'Thanks for the lift.' He knew he sounded wooden and moronic, but he couldn't seem to do a damn thing about it.

'Night,' she said, as he got out and dragged his guitar case from the back seat.

'Night,' he said, through the passenger door, then shut it firmly and stood for a second in the pouring rain as Nancy began to pull away. But suddenly he was galvanized. Running along the sopping pavement to keep up with the car, he banged on the wet roof. The car stopped immediately, the window wound down and Nancy was peering up at him.

'Did you forget something?' she asked.

Jim rested his hand on the open window. 'Umm . . . Just wondered if you fancied going for a coffee some time.' He could feel the rain cold on his head, trickling down his collar as he waited for her to reply. He sounded as if he wasn't bothered whether she accepted his invitation or not, nonchalant in a way he had not intended. It seemed for ever before she spoke.

'I'd like that,' she said, from the depths of the car, and he let his breath out in one long continuous flow, giving a low chuckle as he gave the car a soft thump of triumph. She was smiling, too, and he wished fervently that they were back in the bar, having another strong drink, and that he was looking into her eyes, letting her know he was interested.

'I've got your card,' Nancy was saying, before the window wound slowly up again and she was gone.

Soaking wet now, Jim still stood on the corner, watching the car disappear up the hill. Then he slowly crossed the street and made his way to his front door, very quietly inserting the key in the lock, glancing anxiously at the curtained window behind which his wife should be sleeping, hoping he wouldn't wake her.

CHAPTER EIGHT

'You look very perky, Mum.' Louise had knocked on Nancy's door the morning after Jim's gig.

Nancy smiled at her. She didn't feel 'perky' as such, since she'd hardly slept a wink trying to decide when to phone Jim and what she should say to Lindy. 'Do I?'

'So the pub was fun?'

'Umm, yes. Lindy's friend was singing. Country music. The guy from her party.'

'Is he Lindy's boyfriend?' Louise sat down on one of the kitchen chairs and picked up a stray flake from a croissant Nancy had warmed up for breakfast, popping it into her mouth.

'No, they met when she hired him to do the line dancing. Coffee?' Nancy waved a mug she'd taken from the rack. 'Just made it.'

Louise nodded. 'Thanks, Mum. I've got the morning off – Ross has taken the girls swimming . . . Bloody miracle, although I didn't give him much choice, to be fair.' She took the cup Nancy offered. 'So, tell me about this singer.'

'I don't know much about him, but Lindy says he's sort of Willie Nelson meets Kris Kristofferson. He has a beautiful voice.'

Louise frowned. 'Ross loves country music. He's taken me to a couple of festivals over the years. Can be a bit cheesy, no?'

'I'm sure it can. But the good ones seem to sing about what matters . . .' She paused. 'You know: love, death, broken hearts.'

'Bit like madrigals, then,' Louise said, straight-faced.

'Oh, God, no!' Nancy laughed. 'But I suppose, in fact, there is a vague comparison. The modern-day equivalent, perhaps, but I wouldn't suggest that to your father. He'd have a fit.' She sat down opposite her daughter and poured two cups of coffee. Bob had come in with Louise, and was now prowling around the kitchen, lapping at the water Nancy always left for her in a bowl by the fridge. 'Have you told him yet?'

Louise's face dropped. 'I don't know how to, Mum. I can hardly ring him and say, "I'm not coming to your sodding wedding because I can't stand your trollop" – as Granny so brilliantly puts it.' The look she gave Nancy was resigned.

'You're sure it's not easier just to go?'

'Easier in almost all respects, yes, definitely. And it would get Ross off my back. But I know I'd just puke seeing her and Dad all smug and loved up. It's so bloody embarrassing the way she paws him all the time. Fathers aren't supposed to have sex, for God's sake.' She laughed at herself.

Nancy, clutching the thought of Jim close, didn't reply as she wondered whether her daughter's rule extended to mothers too. She was pretty sure it would.

'It's Nancy . . .' Her heart was hammering so hard against her ribs that she was sure he must be able to hear it at the other end of the line. She had waited until what she considered a respectable time, just after six, to call.

'Hey . . . Nancy.' His reply was low, cautious, and suddenly she wished she hadn't bothered. It had taken her the whole of Sunday to pluck up the courage and now it sounded as if he wasn't keen to speak to her.

'I said I'd give you a call.'

There was the sound of a door closing.

'Yes, yes . . . I didn't know whether you would or not.'

Still she heard the hesitation in his voice. 'Is this a bad time?'

'No . . . no, it's good. Umm . . . great to hear from you.'

Nancy pulled a face, her gut clenching with disappointment. *I'm too bloody old for this*, she thought. 'You don't sound like it is.'

He didn't reply at once. Then he cleared his throat. 'You have no idea how happy I am to hear your voice.'

Taken aback, she found herself grinning inanely. 'Oh . . . well . . .'

'Are we on for coffee, then?'

'I am, if you are.'

'Tomorrow, Monday? I can do absolutely any time, dawn till dusk and beyond.'

She laughed. 'Playing hard to get, eh?'

'Treat 'em mean and keep 'em keen,' Jim replied. And now they were both really laughing, although there was nothing particularly funny in what they'd said.

A minute after she'd hung up her phone rang. She was still buzzing from her conversation with Jim and she answered it without checking the screen, thinking it might be him calling back. 'Hello?'

'Hi, Nancy,' Lindy said. 'Thought perhaps you weren't speaking to me after last night.' Her friend's voice held a rueful note.

Nancy laughed. 'Why wouldn't I be speaking to you?'

'Because I behaved like a brat when you said you were both going home.'

'Oh, that. I understood. Nothing worse than a party-pooper.'

'Yeah, I got it that *you* wanted to go, but Jim's a performer, for Christ's sake. He must hang out into the small hours all the time. I suppose I was pissed off because it meant he wasn't into me.'

Nancy was just about to reply, when Lindy went on, 'But maybe he's one of those guys who takes a bit of time to warm up. Maybe he's been burned in the past or something. Because I really got the impression he liked me, the night of my party.'

Tell her, a voice in Nancy's head insisted. *Tell her now. It'll be much more difficult later.*

But Lindy kept talking: 'I mean, I didn't buy it at the time, but he *could* have been getting up early. And I'm not going to give up on someone that cute without a fight. He seems to do gigs most weeks. Are you up for another? It'd be a bit sad if I went on my own.'

'Umm . . . okay.'

'Don't sound so enthusiastic!' Lindy laughed. 'You enjoyed it last night, didn't you?'

'Yes, yes, I did.'

'Well, then.' Nancy heard the sound of running water. Lindy never just talked on the phone, she was always doing something else at the same time, her phone crunched between her ear and her shoulder. 'Listen, I'll give you a bell when I've got some dates.'

Nancy cursed herself for being a wimp. Now she'd have to lie, invent a scenario, say that she bumped into Jim in Brighton, totally out of the blue, and that he'd asked her for a coffee, something like that. But Lindy was pretty robust where men were concerned – she never seemed short of offers – and she would move on quickly, Nancy told herself, as she went to take the macaroni cheese ready-meal out of the oven, smiling at the thought of her son-in-law's horrified reaction if he saw the culinary depths to which she had sunk.

The coffee shop was full, the small space cramped and steamy. People milled about the counter waiting for takeaways, all the tables occupied; a low buzz of conversation filled the air. Nancy spotted Jim in the corner by the window, an empty coffee cup on the red Formica surface in front of him, his ponytailed head bent to a newspaper. It was a shock to see him again, almost as if she hadn't really believed he would be there, or that she was actually meeting him.

He looked innately cool, whatever he was doing, and Nancy suddenly felt intimidated. As she squeezed between the tables, her stomach began to flutter, making her feel queasy. She had spent a sleepless night torn by a mixture of dread and expectation. *It's a coffee, no more*, her rational brain insisted. *He's a man and you fancy him*, her heart countered. Whatever the reality, when she had bumped into Louise on the drive earlier, she hadn't mentioned Jim, as if there were something shameful in meeting up with him.

He looked up as she reached him, his face instantly creasing into a smile as he got to his feet. Nancy held out her hand and he took it, shaking it formally, neither making any attempt at a cheek kiss.

'Hi . . . Great you could make it,' he said, still standing, seeming suddenly tall and awkward. 'Sorry it's a bit clubby in here this morning,' he added, noticing Nancy's problem: a large man lounging at the table behind, concentrating on his laptop. He moved her chair. 'Usually doesn't fill up till later on a Monday.'

She waited while he went to make their coffee order, trying not to stare at him as he did so. It was clear he was a regular because the girl behind the counter chatted to him, laughing at something he said as if she knew him well, although Nancy couldn't make out anything of their conversation.

'Did you find it okay?' Jim asked, into the silence that settled over them once he had brought back Nancy's cappuccino and his own black Americano.

'Yes, but the parking's a nightmare.'

'That's Brighton for you.'

Nancy couldn't think of a single bloody thing to say, so she stirred the chocolate-sprinkled foam into her coffee, head bent, praying for inspiration.

'I'm not used to meeting strange women in coffee shops,' Jim said, eventually, amusement behind his blue eyes, as it had been that first night. 'And I'm not great on small talk, I'm afraid.'

'We're doomed, then,' Nancy said. 'I'm rubbish too.'

'So tell me something that isn't small – about yourself, for instance. That should keep us going for a while.'

Nancy felt flustered at the request and almost too wound up to begin the tale of her life. Jim was very disconcerting, the way he gazed at her. Those eyes of his seemed to know her before she'd said a single word.

'God, where to start? I'm sixty-one, divorced – my ex ran off with a blonde Latvian diva four years ago. Only child, father a dentist, dead twenty years now, mother still going. I live next door to my daughter, son-in-law and two granddaughters, eight and six, no pets, although Bob, my daughter's cat, almost lives with me. I trained to be a concert pianist but married a musician with an ego instead.' She stopped, shrugged, winced privately at her words, which now seemed terminally dull and slightly bitter. 'Your turn.'

'A musician?' He grinned. 'I knew it.'

'Knew I was a musician?'

'No, knew you were a kindred spirit.'

'I'm not a performer, like you. I just play for myself and teach a bit.' He seemed to be waiting for her to continue. 'But I couldn't live without it,' she added, almost as if he had pulled the words out of her.

'Me neither. Music is my life.' Jim let out a slow breath. 'Hard to imagine how people get by without it.'

Nancy gave a small laugh. 'I know what you mean, but my son-in-law, Ross, feels just as passionate about food. Cooking is his life.'

Jim considered this. 'More useful than music, I suppose. 'Fraid my skill in that area runs to peeling the cellophane off a cottage pie for one.'

'Or a macaroni cheese.'

'Yeah, that too!'

She watched Jim pick up his cup, cradling it in his palm instead of using the small handle. His hands were tanned, with long, tapering fingers, a small crescent-shaped scar clear beneath the first knuckle of his right hand.

'Your turn now,' she said, tearing her gaze away.

Jim pulled a face, tucked a stray hair behind his ear and sat up straighter. But it was a minute or two before he spoke.

'Right. Well, I'm sixty-four, separated for three years. *My* ex ran off with a sleazy barman – not quite as upmarket as your diva. One son, Tommy, twenty-four, no grandchildren, no pets. One brother, Stevie, who runs a gîte in the south of France – with his partner, Pascal, until he died nearly two years ago. Parents both gone, father a master brewer. I'm a country singer-songwriter with a band called the Bluebirds. One hit about twenty years ago – no, much longer than that now. Teach guitar to anyone who'll hire me, and I've given up smoking.'

'That's great.'

'Which bit?'

'Well, I meant the smoking. Have you really quit?'

Jim gave her a sheepish grin. 'Sort of. More of a cutting-down situation, if I'm honest. But I put that in because I want it to be true. I'm sure you hate smoking.'

Nancy didn't state the obvious. Their conversation felt easy now, and she had the oddest feeling that, although she hardly knew the man, she could tell him anything. But she was also aware of an energy between them, a sort of flighty buzz of anticipation, which made her heart beat faster. Thoughts were flying around her head and she wanted to share them all.

She heard herself say, 'My ex is marrying the diva in September.'

Jim's handsome face creased into a frown. 'Are you upset?'

'No, no! I'm fine about it,' she said, but his eyes resting on her seemed to question her response. She sighed. 'Okay . . . I'm not really fine. I'd sort of got used to him being with her, but marriage puts it into a whole different league.'

'Had you hoped you might get back together?'

'No. Definitely not. I honestly do *not* want to be with Christopher any more.' She gave him a wry smile. 'I suppose I'm still miffed that he cheated on me, then dumped me.' She paused. 'And she is very young and beautiful . . . Sort of reminds me of my age.' Ridiculously, she felt tears building behind her eyes. She swallowed hard.

'It's tough, being cheated on, however old you are.'

Nancy heard the pain behind his words. 'The insult sort of defies reality, doesn't it? I mean, I am all right, I've got a good life now, but the hurt seems ingrained.'

'Yeah, you know you should move on – everyone tells you to.'

Jim gave a short laugh. 'And most of the time you feel as if you have. But it comes down to the spike in your gut that refuses to shift. No logic behind it.'

'Is your ex living with the sleazy barman?'

'No . . . Took the creep less than a year to start chasing skirt again.'

'But you didn't take her back?'

'I couldn't, Nancy. I just couldn't. She wanted me to, and maybe I should have been more generous, but every time I looked at her . . .' He shrugged and fell silent.

Neither spoke for a while.

'I reckon it's a case of "One false move and the kid gets it",' Jim said.

'Don't understand.'

'It's like the hurt is controlling us. Every time we try to get free, it holds us to ransom.'

She laughed. 'So what are we supposed to do?'

They stared at each other for a very long moment.

'Oh, I don't know. I expect we'll work something out,' Jim said, a wicked glint in his eyes that made Nancy feel suddenly very weak.

CHAPTER NINE

Jim said goodbye to Nancy at the cafe door. He had wanted to walk with her in the sunshine, but she'd said she had to get home for a music lesson – she'd seemed a bit flustered at the end. Now, as he wove his way along the narrow pavements, dodging the other pedestrians going about their daily lives in the busy town, he silently berated himself.

Why the bloody hell weren't you honest with her, you pillock? Why didn't you tell her you were still technically married, that you were living with your wife? But he knew the answer, of course. A woman like Nancy would have flatly refused to have anything to do with him if he'd said he was married. And explaining that he lived with Chrissie, but didn't live with her, would have sounded plain ridiculous. She'd just think, Yeah, right. Or, at least, *he* would, if she'd told him the same scenario.

God, she was gorgeous, though. He loved those intelligent eyes, which seemed totally grey one minute, then bright, almost gold another, like light falling on water. Chrissie's eyes were green, but they were always the same shade, never varied that he could see. And Nancy's smile – quite wry, a bit wary: it was clear she took no prisoners where bullshit was concerned. Perhaps got too much from her cheating ex. He loved the way her mouth lifted crookedly on one side. He'd made her laugh, which was a good sign, and they'd talked for hours, about everything on the planet, which showed they had something going on. He'd definitely detected a sexual buzz too, when she'd relaxed a bit. But, hell, what was the point in chatting her up when the whole thing would fall apart like a house of cards, as soon as she found out about Chrissie?

I'll tell her next time, he promised himself. Although they hadn't made any plans for a next time. Should he have nailed it, while she was there? Maybe he'd text her later . . . Or was that too keen? And did it matter if it was? They weren't kids, although right now he felt just as unconfident as he had back them. He groaned softly. *I don't know how to do this. I never did.*

He was experiencing an odd mixture of excitement and fear. Perhaps this moment was as good as any relationship ever got. This churning, this thrill, all unrealistic, nothing committed, nothing known, but the possibilities appearing to be endless.

It was way too early to say, obviously, but he had a feeling about Nancy, a feeling he knew was too premature to be anything but irrational, but was so strong as to be overwhelming. Maybe this time he could reach beyond the thrill, find something deeper and more satisfying than he'd ever had with Chrissie.

As Jim walked on, his head heavy with all the things he had to brave in order to disentangle his life from his wife, he badly wanted a cigarette. But he'd deliberately thrown out the two packets he'd had in the drawer and left his lighter at home. He was passing all kinds of shops where he could have bought more, but on the one-step-at-a-time principle his friend Jimmy P had banged on about when he'd given up the booze, he kept telling himself he could stop at the next, then the next, and he got home without buying any. Small triumph, but then his thoughts were a powerful distraction, even from nicotine. Nancy predominated, of course, but even she was being edged out by a fog of agents, lawyers, banks, surveyors, property websites and, worst of all, Chrissie's angst.

Yesterday, Sunday, had been hell. The same old boring row had started up at breakfast. Chrissie had made a plan months ago for them to spend the day in London, meet up with their friends Mick and Jen and go to a gig in Camden where one of Mick's friends was playing. Mick was a bass guitarist who had sometimes taken Jimmy P's place in the Bluebirds when Jimmy's drinking had got out of hand. He was a bloody good player, in Jim's opinion – quite brilliant at times – but his voice was lousy: he couldn't hold a tune to save his life.

Anyway, Jim had told Chrissie at breakfast that he wasn't going.

'Why not? Are you ill?' she asked, glancing up from the grim bowl of granola, seeds, yoghurt and banana she insisted on eating every morning. The radio was playing loudly – some chirpy schmaltz his wife seemed addicted to. He went over and turned it off.

'No. I just don't want to. You go, should be fun.'

She frowned. 'But they're expecting us both, and you love Micky. We haven't seen him in ages.'

He perched on one of the high stools that stood beside what Chrissie called the 'breakfast bar', although she always ate her breakfast at the table. 'That's the point. It's what I keep telling you. We aren't together, Chrissie. And we shouldn't keep pretending we are. Mick and Jen don't even know there's a problem. That's why they're expecting us both.'

His wife's expression darkened. 'What are you scared of, Jimmy?

We both went to Lisa's party a couple of weeks ago and I come to your gigs all the time. What's changed?' She'd stopped eating, but still held her spoon in her right hand, her eyes narrowing. 'Like you're suddenly terrified to be seen out with me . . .' When he didn't answer, she continued to stare. 'Who is she? Because all this bullshit about selling the house and getting a divorce . . . I know you. There has to be a woman involved.'

Jim couldn't help but remember asking Nancy to drop him off at the end of the road so that Chrissie wouldn't spot her, him creeping upstairs like a thief, feeling as if he were cheating on both women. 'It's not bullshit.'

'Well, it is from where I'm standing. I've told you a million times, I hate the idea of selling this place. And spending God knows what on lawyers to get a divorce when neither of us is planning to get married again seems totally daft. Unless . . .' she raised her eyebrows '. . . unless I'm right, of course.'

Jim didn't know what to say so, ill-advisedly as it turned out, he said nothing. Chrissie slammed down her spoon, got to her feet and leaned over the table towards where he sat, her pale skin pink with rage, her white cotton dressing-gown gaping open, exposing her small breasts.

'You have, haven't you? You sneaky fucking bastard, you've been seeing someone behind my back, haven't you? Jim, answer me! Haven't you? Christ, you lying, lowlife bastard.'

Jim got up too and, keeping his voice as even as possible, he said, 'You talk as if I'm cheating on you, Chrissie. I don't know whether you've noticed, but we haven't had sex since you came crawling home after Benji dumped you. That's not a marriage, not in my book anyway. So I don't need your permission. I can do what I bloody well like.'

Her green eyes filled with angry tears. 'I don't believe you, Jim. I don't believe you don't love me any more.' She stood up and tugged roughly at the tie on her dressing-gown, yanking the material off her shoulders, letting the robe slither to the kitchen floor. Standing before him entirely naked, hands dropped to her sides, head held defiant, slim, toned body, smooth-skinned and youthful even at her age, she seemed painfully, heart-achingly vulnerable.

'This is the body you promised to worship, Jim. To love and to cherish till death us do part.' She raised her hands and planted them on her hips, relaxing her body into an altogether more sexual pose, thrusting her small breasts towards him, bringing her lips together into a pout. 'And I know you want me. You're just too fucking stubborn to admit it.'

She began to walk round the table towards him and Jim was horrified to realize that he was, indeed, aroused. Sex had always been their thing and her nakedness instantly evoked the intensity of their past lovemaking, the way she had moved beneath him, her legs wrapped tight around his body, the taste of her nipples on his tongue, the charming way her lips turned pinker after orgasm. And it had been so long.

He didn't move or speak as she came closer, pressed her body against his own and raised her face, her green eyes alight with desire.

'Kiss me,' she whispered. 'Go on. You know you're fucking dying to.'

CHAPTER TEN

Louise leaned on the bar in the Lime Kiln, a cup of espresso in her hand. The restaurant was a single-storey Sussex-flint building, with square casement windows that let in little light, set back from the road with a pretty paved garden behind that looked onto a field and the Downs beyond. It was an idyllic setting, which had previously been a small pub till Ross and Louise had taken over the lease five years ago. The décor, chosen by Louise, had an airy, contemporary feel: cream walls on which hung colourful pen-and-ink drawings of marine life, large mirrors, flagstone floor, a big brick fireplace, wooden tables and azure scatter-cushions on the driftwood-grey banquettes and tub chairs. Ross had objected at first, saying the whole thing was too beachy and not serious enough for his style of cooking. He wanted a more severe, black-and-white interior–starched tablecloth look. But Louise wasn't having it. 'This is the Sussex Downs. People want beachy – they want to relax.'

It was early. Louise had just dropped the girls at school, and Ross was still in his blue T-shirt and jeans, loading wine bottles into the glass-fronted, floor-level cooler that ran along the wall separating the bar from the kitchen behind.

'Something's up with Mum,' Louise said.

Ross stopped what he was doing and waited for her to go on.

'She's . . . different. Can't put my finger on it, but she's being sort of weird.'

'Haven't noticed. Weird in what way?' Ross's dark eyebrows came together as he put the bottle of Meursault he was holding onto the bar, giving his wife his full attention.

'Well, she's not listening most of the time, as if something's on her mind. And she keeps looking at her phone. Then the other morning when I asked her where she was going, she actually blushed and stumbled out some lame story about meeting Lindy.'

'She could have been meeting Lindy.'

'She could, but she wasn't. It was a lie, I absolutely know it.'

Ross chuckled. 'Hmm. Maybe she's got a bit on the side.'

'Ross!' Louise was genuinely shocked.

'Why not? She's an attractive woman, your mother. And your dad's got his totty.'

'Mum? With a boyfriend? Really?'

'Don't see why you think it's so impossible, Lou. She's only sixty, or close . . . No reason she should stay single for the rest of her life, is there?'

Louise was silent. It had genuinely never occurred to her that her mother might meet another man.

'Have you asked her?' her husband said.

'Uh, no . . . No, of course not.' She frowned at Ross. 'Do you really think she's seeing someone? It would certainly account for her strange mood.'

'Maybe she's been on Tinder.'

'Oh, for God's sake, Ross. Can you honestly see my mother doing that?'

Her husband shrugged. 'I think you're in denial about her. Everyone does it these days, why not your mum?'

'But . . . isn't it dangerous? I mean, what sort of men would she meet online? They could be anyone.'

Ross went back to stacking the bottles in the cooler. 'So could your average guy in a wine bar. You're sounding like you're *her* mother, not the other way round. Probably best to ask her, though, before you jump to any conclusions.'

'Yeah . . . It's tricky, though. How would I put it?'

'Christ, Lou, she's not the bloody Queen. Something along the lines of "Are you seeing someone?" should do it.'

'Okay, okay, don't tease. It's just that me and Mum don't have that sort of relationship, where we talk about sex and stuff.'

He roared with laughter. 'No need to mention sex at this stage, love. In fact, better you don't mention it at any stage, I reckon.'

Louise finished her coffee while Ross tore up the empty wine boxes and took them out to the recycling bin at the back of the restaurant. *Mum, with a lover?* She didn't like the idea one bit, any more than she'd liked her father shacking up with Tatjana. She hoped Ross had got it totally wrong.

Louise waited till after the lunchtime service before she tackled Ross. There was usually a moment, after all the punters had gone home and Jason and Maja – the Polish waitress they had just taken on – were cleaning up, getting the place ready for evening service, when she and Ross would sit at the table nearest the bar and debrief with a cup of Lapsang and one of Ross's famous orange shortbread biscuits. At those times he was like a performer coming down after a show, buzzing with what had gone right, what had gone wrong, eulogizing about a new dish, relaying diners' comments and whispering any foolishness that Jason or Maja had committed – Ross being the perfectionist he was, there was always something. She had rung her mum and asked her to pick up the girls from school today: there was a serious discussion to be had and she didn't want to have to rush off.

She watched Ross wipe the sweat from his forehead with a palm as he sat down heavily, throwing the blue cushion onto one of the other chairs.

'Not a bad turnout for a Thursday,' he said, pouring tea for them both.

'No . . .'

He looked at her questioningly. 'Do I sense a "but"?'

'I've been on the books all morning.' Louise had trained as an accountant, but had given up her job with a Brighton firm when Hope was small, opting to run the business side of their restaurant instead.

Ross held up his hand. 'Please, Lou, not now. Can't deal with another bloody moan about profit margins.'

'Well, you'll have to. It's bad, Ross, really bad. I keep having to hike the prices – even the lunchtime deal – because you're spending way too much on high-end ingredients. People are opting for the cheaper dishes. I checked. It's fishcakes, salads, mackerel, et cetera, and orders for two starters. They aren't going for the lobster and turbot, the beef fillet.'

Ross shrugged his big shoulders. 'They never spend as much at lunch. But what do you expect me to do? Buy crap ingredients? That's hardly the way I'm going to build my or the restaurant's reputation.'

'Of course I'm not. But there's got to be a balance or soon you're not going to have a restaurant at all.'

He raised a sceptical eyebrow. 'I don't believe you, Lou. You're scaremongering because you're so fucking cautious and you want to control me. Look at today. All right, we weren't full, but it was lunch and we did at least thirty covers.'

'Twenty-one.'

'Really?'

'Yup.'

'Well, as I said, it was lunch and a Thursday. Tomorrow will be better.'

'I've checked the bookings and so far it's not.'

'For Christ's sake! What do you want me to do? I can hardly go out and drag punters in off the street.' His large eyes were boring into her, and all she could see was resentment.

Louise felt close to tears. She didn't actually know what her husband should do. 'You could stop blaming me, for starters. I don't understand why you're not worried. We've been open nearly four years, and we should be showing a profit by now, even if only a small one. Instead we're just bumping along the bottom.'

He wouldn't look at her, his jaw rigid.

'Ross?'

Finally he met her gaze. 'You've never believed in this venture, have you? Or in me.' His voice was cold. 'Right from the start you've been nothing but gloom and doom – this is too expensive, that won't work, you can't do the other. Negative, negative, negative. You'd much rather I'd stayed safely at Maison Verlet, no? Kept my cushy salary, let someone else take the risk.' He began twisting the napkin that lay in front of him, his hands seeming to strangle the starched white cloth.

Louise gawped. 'That's so bloody unfair, Ross. I've supported you one hundred per cent, put every ounce of effort into making it work. You know I have.' Her heart was thumping in her chest. 'But I also know that opening a restaurant is risky. Around a third fail in the first few years. And I don't want that to be us. That's why I'm nagging you.' He still wouldn't look at her. 'But, hey, if you think I'm a negative influence, then I'll back off. You can run it yourself. I'll get another job.'

There was no way on earth Louise wanted to do that, but on the other hand, the effort of banging her head against a brick wall was exhausting her. She hated the strain the business was putting on her marriage. And people always needed accountants.

Ross's head shot up. 'Don't be ridiculous, Lou. You know I can't manage this place without you.' He reached across for her hand, which she quickly removed to her lap. 'Listen, I'm sorry.' He gave a long sigh. 'I'm worried sick, you know I am. I didn't mean what I said. I know how much you've supported me. I just hate the thought of compromise. It's all about the quality of the ingredients, you know that. If I let my standards slip, I'm dead in the water.'

'Of course I understand that. But you're so stubborn about the suppliers. At least two of them are rinsing you, big-time – Johnsons for a start – but you won't let me shop around and find cheaper ones.'

The argument rumbled on between them and didn't address the real issue that was at the heart of the problem. But Louise didn't feel able to open up the subject about what sort of food they should be serving right now. She knew, with both their tempers frayed, that she would have to find another time to broach that. But broach it she would.

When she got home, her mum and the girls were sitting outside on the striped swing seat. The sun was out, but it was not particularly warm. Jazzy, regardless, was wearing her ballerina dress, her legs bare, Hope was curled up next to her grandmother, carefully nibbling the chocolate off a Jaffa cake to get to the orange jelly centre. Both girls rushed up to give her a hug.

'We've done our reading,' Hope said, when she saw Louise eyeing the biscuit. One, after homework, was their allowance: she was strict about sugar. She had to be, because Ross would feed them all sorts of rubbish, from sugar sandwiches to pancakes and syrup, to marshmallows and beyond – it reminded him of his childhood, he said.

Nancy smiled as she swung gently back and forth.

'Thanks for picking them up, Mum,' Louise said. 'Please, Jazzy, stop it, will you?' She heard the snap in her voice as her younger daughter dragged her by the hand and tried to make her dance.

'Fancy a cuppa?' Nancy got up.

While the girls played in the garden, Hope doing somersaults on the blue plastic mat Louise had laid out, Jazzy pirouetting across the grass, fairy wand in hand, Louise sat down in Nancy's kitchen and burst into tears.

CHAPTER ELEVEN

Jim had rung Nancy the evening after they'd met at the cafe.

'Hi, Nancy?' he'd said, his tone tentative. 'It's Jim.'

As if she didn't know. Just the sound of his deep voice set her pulse racing. The call had taken her by surprise. She had thought he might ring in a couple of days, maybe. Would she phone him if he didn't? She wasn't sure of the current etiquette. The young seemed not to talk to each other: they texted or Facebooked or tweeted or whatever, but didn't lift the phone for a real chat, which must make for a good deal of misunderstanding, she thought, dreading the day when her granddaughters were old enough to have mobiles.

'I'm trying to be super-cool, as you know, so I left it a whole afternoon before I called you,' he said.

'Is it only an afternoon? Seems like a hundred years.'

After the joke there was an awkward pause.

'What do we do now?' Jim asked.

'Not sure.'

'We could have another coffee . . . or go up a notch and risk an evening drink?'

'Whoa, fast work.'

'I could do Thursday . . .'

'Umm, Thursday is good.' Nancy didn't need to think: she knew she wasn't going out that week. Or next week, or the week after, for that matter.

'Great. I'll find somewhere to go. Are you okay coming into Brighton, or shall I come up your way?'

'Brighton is easy for me,' she said, not wanting to be in the local pub where some of Louise's friends might see them.

Now it was Thursday. She checked the kitchen clock. She and Jim had arranged to meet at a wine bar in town at six-thirty, but it was already five forty-five and Louise and the girls were still there. Nancy had felt obliged to offer to do supper for Hope and Jazzy, as her daughter was still upset, although Louise had said little since the girls had come in from the garden.

I'd better text him, she thought, searching for her phone. She had been going to have a shower and get ready in a leisurely fashion, calm her nerves, but she would barely have time to change now.

'What are you looking for, Mum?' Louise was asking.

'My phone . . .' She searched her handbag again, pulling out supermarket vouchers, her bus pass, a purse laden with change, a brush, earphones, a biro without the top, a small notebook, an old tissue, lip balm. No phone.

'I'll call it,' Louise said, bringing out her own mobile from the back pocket of her jeans. But there was no responding ring tone.

'I must have left it in the car.' Nancy was beginning to feel flustered. She didn't want Jim to think she wasn't coming. She went outside and found the damn thing in the well beneath the dashboard. Before going inside, she quickly texted Jim: *Got caught up, can we make it 7?*

When she looked up from the screen, Louise was watching her, standing at the open front door. Nancy knew she probably looked shifty as she pressed 'send'.

Once they were inside again Louise, who had begun to clear up the supper plates, turned to face her. 'Mum, I wanted to ask you something.' She paused, and Nancy waited uneasily. Her daughter's tone was unusually hesitant. 'Umm, it's just you've been a bit odd recently. And Ross wondered . . . well, I did too . . . if perhaps you were seeing someone. Like, a man.'

Nancy held her breath. *No point in beating about the bush,* she told herself. 'Well . . . it depends what you mean by "seeing". I've had a coffee with someone.'

Louise's eyes widened into an amazed stare. 'Oh, my God! Ross was right.'

Hope was sitting with her sister on the other side of the room, watching a programme called *Horrible Histories*. 'What was Daddy right about?'

'Nothing,' Louise said quickly, then muttered, 'That child has ears like a bat's.'

Nancy nodded, trying to assess her daughter's reaction to what she had said.

'So who is he?' Louise lowered her voice, one eye on the sofa.

'The country singer I told you about.'

'The one at Lindy's party?' Louise's face took on a knowing look. 'So when I asked if he was Lindy's boyfriend, he was really yours. And you never said a word!'

'He's not my *boyfriend*, Lou. I told you, I've had one coffee with him, on Monday . . . but I'm meeting him for a drink this evening, so I should get a move on.'

Her daughter looked a bit put out. 'Tonight? Oh. Well, I'd better take the girls home then.'

'You don't mind, do you?' Nancy asked.

'Mind? No, of course not. Why would I? I'm not your keeper. But you could have told me, Mum. I feel as if you don't trust me.'

Nancy winced inwardly. Louise was so confusing, had been all her life. She seemed tough and certain most of the time, but underneath lurked a wealth of insecurities. Ross had dealt her a mean blow, accusing her of not being behind his venture. The worst thing being, as Nancy knew all too well, that there was probably some truth in what he'd said. Louise was risk-averse by nature, and without her husband egging her on, she would never have contemplated opening a restaurant in a million years. But having done so, she had worked like a Trojan to make it successful.

'Of course I trust you,' she said. 'It's just there was nothing to tell you till now. I've had one coffee with him, that's all. I hardly know the man.'

'But you've been *thinking* about him longer than that. I've seen it in your eyes, Mum. That's what I meant by you being odd. And you lied to me on Monday when I asked where you were going.'

Nancy sighed. 'I know I did and I'm sorry. You caught me on the hop and I was a bit embarrassed, that's all.'

'Listen, you'd better get on or you'll be late,' Louise said, her tone softened. 'Come on, girls. Nana's going out so we have to go home.'

'*Nooo! Pleeease!* We've got to watch the end of this,' Hope shrieked, eyes glued to the television. Jazzy just sat sucking her thumb, leaving it up to her big sister to sort things out.

'They can go on watching while I get changed,' Nancy said, just as her phone pinged with a text. Under the beady eye of her daughter, she read Jim's message and couldn't help smiling: *I'll wait till the end of time. Or 7, whichever sooner. x*

Louise raised an eyebrow. 'No, come on, you two, home. Have a good time, Mum. I look forward to hearing all about it in the morning.'

Which was exactly why Nancy hadn't wanted her daughter to know about Jim.

The wine bar was half full when Nancy arrived in the large, dark-walled space, with black-and-white architectural photos, a marble bar along the back, high round tables and stools and a long window onto the lane, which stretched at right angles to the sea. The atmosphere was cool, the clientele young – she and Jim were the oldest by decades, she reckoned. Jim was sitting on a padded stool at the bar, talking to the barman.

As Nancy went to greet him, she noticed the clock above the bar said seven twenty-five. 'God, I'm so sorry. Seems like it *was* the end of time, rather than seven o'clock.'

Jim got up and gave her a single kiss on her cheek, which threatened to undo her. His skin smelt delicious, clean, something woody, perhaps cedar, his thin blue cotton shirt soft beneath her fingers. There was not even a hint of cigarettes, she noted.

'Your friend here thought you might have stood him up.' The young barman grinned mischievously. His dyed black hair stuck up in long spikes from his head, reminiscent of an eighties punk.

'Thanks, mate. Give away my darkest secret, why don't you?' Jim rolled his eyes. 'What'll you have, Nancy? Sid here may be indiscreet, but he makes a mean cocktail.'

'A cocktail? Uh . . . What are you having?'

'Me, a Perfect Manhattan. Whiskey and vermouth, God knows what else.'

'I'll have one of those too, then,' she said quickly, even though she had no idea what it might taste like. She was keen not to shilly-shally in front of Jim, but her cocktail repertoire was limited to the odd lunchtime Bloody Mary – Christopher only ever drank Glenfiddich or good red wine, about which he was a tiresome, indefatigable snob.

Jim, carefully balancing the brimming drinks, led her to a window table. 'This okay?'

She nodded as they perched on the high stools and raised their chilled glasses.

'Here's to new beginnings,' he said, with a smile.

The Perfect Manhattan was cold, smooth and sweet on Nancy's tongue, with a slightly astringent aftertaste.

'Bit like cough mixture?' Jim asked, when she didn't comment immediately.

'Mmm . . .' It was, but it was also delicious and she wanted to down the lot to calm her nerves. 'So sorry I was late,' she said, 'I got caught up with the grandchildren, then had to explain to my daughter that I was meeting you for a drink.'

Jim raised his eyebrows. 'Was that a problem?'

'Not really. But Louise – my daughter – was a bit put out because I lied the other morning, when we had the coffee. I said I was seeing Lindy.'

'Why did you lie?'

She shrugged. 'I don't know. It was stupid. I suppose I didn't want her knowing about something that might not be something, and making a big deal out of it.'

'Sounds fair enough.'

'Yes, but I shouldn't have lied.'

'We all do sometimes . . . Sort of seems easier in the moment, then we live to regret it.' Jim looked away and she wondered what lie he was regretting.

'And Louise hates my ex Christopher's girlfriend. At least, she hates the fact of her. She doesn't really know her personally.'

'So, a touchy subject, then.'

Nancy shrugged. 'I haven't been out much since the divorce, and never with a *man* before.'

Jim chuckled. 'We're a dodgy breed, no question.'

There was a brief silence between them. The bar had filled up, the early summer light from the window starting to fade to shadow. Nancy's nerves were easing, either due to the strength of the Manhattan or because Jim seemed so relaxed in the warm, dark bar. Now there was just a pleasant fluttering of excitement in her gut, an anticipation that she hadn't experienced in years. 'It's different for you,' she said. 'Men's sell-by dates are longer – or that's the perceived wisdom. But there's an "eugh" factor about women of my age dating. We're sort of seen as past it.'

Jim raised his eyebrows, said nothing, the laughter clear behind his eyes.

She felt momentarily disconcerted. 'You know what I mean. I suppose I feel . . . self-conscious maybe. You, for instance, could hit on someone half your age and nobody would turn a hair, but if I came on to Sid over there . . .'

Jim's face dropped. 'Are you saying I'm too old for you? That you really want a toy-boy?'

They both started to laugh.

'You look so beautiful,' Jim said, which made her stop laughing at once, taken aback by the unaccustomed compliment, a slow heat creeping across her cheeks. She turned to look out of the window.

'Sorry.' He gave a small frown. 'I . . . Hell, why apologize? It's true.'

'Thank you.' Nancy's mother had taught her from a young age that it was very rude to shrug off a compliment: 'If someone says something nice to you, Nancy, you must respond. Be gracious and thank them. It's the height of rudeness not to.' But she felt flustered rather than gracious as she met his eye. He was still staring at her, his gaze suddenly alive with desire. She couldn't look away, but the previous panic slowly gave way to an answering thirst, her body overwhelmed by a wave of almost brazen sexuality. For a moment she gave into it, wallowing in the powerful current that seemed to have sparked between them, her heart dancing in her chest.

'Hmm . . .' Jim said, shaking himself and getting to his feet as if he were as thrown as she. 'Don't know what Sid put in that drink.' He grinned. 'Same again?'

She nodded, not trusting herself to speak. It was a relief that he had gone. It gave her time to catch her breath.

When he returned, the atmosphere lifted, the conversation taking on a deliberately lighter, safer tone. But the aura of that spark hung between them, like a tantalizing background glow.

'How's Lindy?' Jim asked later. They had finished the second Manhattan and were sharing a bag of plain crisps, which Jim had torn open and placed on the table.

Nancy felt distinctly light-headed. 'She's . . . I haven't talked to her this week.' But as she spoke, Nancy remembered guiltily a text from Lindy a couple of days ago that she hadn't replied to, her head so full of Jim Bowdry. 'She was suggesting we come to your gig on Saturday.'

'That'd be great. I can introduce you to the Bluebirds – the band. I haven't played with them in a while; Mal the drummer's been off with this sort of ME thing, but he says he's okay now.'

Nancy didn't reply for a moment. Then she said, 'The thing is . . . I think I've stepped on Lindy's toes as far as you're concerned.'

Jim looked at her questioningly.

'She had her eye on you.'

'I did notice. So was she annoyed when you told her?'

'I haven't. Not yet.'

'Right.' Jim grinned. 'Seems you've kept me very quiet on all fronts.'

'It's not like that.' Nancy felt defensive, but it was true, she hadn't wanted to share even the thought of Jim with anyone. It seemed too new, too private, too uncertain. 'It's just so underhand, sneaking a coffee and now a cocktail with someone you know your best friend fancies. But I can't find the right moment to tell her.' She knew she sounded cowardly and wished she hadn't mentioned it. 'And I didn't know what might happen.'

'Between us?'

'Yes.'

Jim shook his head. 'I can't imagine Lindy'll be crying into her porridge because it didn't work out with me. She's not short of offers, I imagine, an attractive woman like her.'

'No. But it's the same problem I had with Louise. I didn't tell her upfront. She'll think I'm a right bitch going behind her back like this.'

'So don't tell her. Just come to the gig on Saturday and I'll leap on you and snog you to death in front of the whole room. Then she'll think I'm a mad bastard and want nothing more to do with me.' He chortled.

'Ha! Not sure I fancy being snogged to death.' She sighed, overwhelmed by guilt again. 'Why does it have to be so complicated?'

'You could just ring her and explain,' Jim said reasonably, clearly amused by her predicament.

She never had a chance to reply, because there was a sudden rumpus behind them. A tall, swarthy youth with a bull neck and tattoos covering both forearms had a jumpy, ferret-faced redhead by his T-shirt, lifting him off the ground and snarling into his face. 'You fucking dickhead. You bloody little ponce. Think you can fucking come in here and make like nothing's happened? I should fucking kill you.'

'Come on, Frankie, let him go. He's not worth it,' a friend was trying to drag the big lad off, pulling at his arm, then the waistband of his jeans. But Frankie, livid with rage, just batted him away with his elbow and continued trying to strangle the redhead.

As Nancy watched in horror, a couple of the boy's friends attempted to step in, tugging uselessly at his body in a bid to yank him free as they yelled at his attacker. But Frankie lashed out and hit one on the side of his head, making him stagger against a table and fall over. Everyone in the bar was on their feet now, backing away from the fight, which was only a yard or so away from where Nancy and Jim were sitting. Over the heads of the crowd she could see Sid on his mobile, presumably calling the police, and a girl next to her was capturing the scene on her phone, presumably to post later on Instagram.

'Go. Wait for me outside,' Jim said, pushing her towards the door. But she hadn't got far when she saw Jim stride across to Frankie and plant himself inches from his face, the victim's carrotty head between them.

Very calmly, his deep voice loud so as to cut through the shouting and screaming, he said, 'Let him go, lad. Right now. *Right now, I said.*'

The swarthy youth seemed to do a double-take. He frowned and dropped the redhead, who was quickly pulled out of harm's way by his mates, his face as red as his hair. He was complaining loudly, his voice hoarse and reedy from the choking.

Frankie turned his attention to Jim. 'And who the fuck are you?' he snarled.

Jim didn't flinch. 'Just get out of here before you do any more damage.' When the lad didn't move, he came closer. 'I said fuck off. *Go.*'

For a moment the lad's eyes, bloodshot and dazed from alcohol, glared at him threateningly, but Nancy could see the fight had gone out of him. With one more louring look in the direction of his victim, he swung round and lurched towards the street, monitored closely by his friend, who had a hand firmly clamped to Frankie's shoulder. As soon as the lout was safely off the premises, the remaining customers burst into spontaneous applause, those nearest to Jim clapping him on the back and congratulating him.

Jim waved a hand at Sid, who was still looking distinctly nervous behind the bar. When he got level with Nancy, he took her hand and made for the exit. 'I said to get out,' he muttered, as they walked along the pavement. 'You have no idea how quickly those things can get out of hand. Only takes one moron with a knife.'

'You were great in there.' Nancy was in awe of Jim's authority, the calm way he'd dealt with what was clearly a violent character.

'He was just a lad who'd had too much to drink.' His face was still showing the tension of the past five minutes. 'So, where to now?'

'No idea,' she said, not caring at all as long as she could hold his hand a while longer, feeling its strength and warmth.

'There's a little Italian a couple of streets away. Fancy a pasta?'

'Have you dated much since you split up?' Nancy asked, as they sat eating their bowls of spicy *penne all'arrabbiata* in the bustling, old-style Italian cafe Jim had led her to.

Jim shook his head. 'Nope. Nobody at all.'

'Really?' She was amazed.

'Do I seem like the Casanova type?' He looked almost hurt by the suggestion.

'No . . . It's just you must meet a lot of girls, women, at your gigs, who come on to you.'

'Doesn't mean I fancy them, though.'

'I suppose not.'

'Is Chrissie with someone else?'

'Not that I know of.' Jim clearly didn't enjoy talking about his ex-wife, because the tone of his reply shut down any further enquiry. She wondered if he still had feelings for her.

Later, they stood in silence outside the restaurant waiting for the taxi Jim had ordered – she had drunk too much to drive home and would have to pick up her car in the morning. Nancy welcomed the cool April breeze on her hot cheeks and took deep breaths of the night air. She felt dizzy and tired – it had been a rollercoaster of an evening.

'Talk tomorrow?' he said.

'I might see you on Saturday.'

'I hope so.'

A constrained silence had descended on them as they prepared to say goodbye, as if neither knew how to end the evening. Then he took her hand again.

'I'd so like to kiss you,' he said quietly. 'But not here.'

She nodded, her heart somersaulting as his eyes bored into her and she felt the flash of desire again, like a physical presence between them.

The taxi driver leaned out of the window of his cab. 'Bowie?'

'I wish,' Jim joked, before opening the rear door for Nancy.

'Mum?' Nancy was woken the following morning by a call from Louise. 'Listen, would you be able to take the girls to school for me? The alarm's gone off at the restaurant and Ross is halfway to Worthing to see a supplier.'

'Umm. . . Sure.' Disoriented, she checked the clock. Seven forty-five. Hope and Jazzy had to leave at eight-fifteen to be at school for the eight-thirty 'kiss-and-drop'. She tumbled out of bed, her head throbbing, her mouth dry as a bone, and grabbed a pair of jeans, a T-shirt, a teal cotton cardigan. As she pulled on a pair of canvas slip-ons she remembered. Panicking, she ran across the drive to her daughter's house. Louise was in the kitchen, buttering brown toast on the breadboard, the girls sitting at the table in front of bowls of Shreddies and glasses of orange juice, already in their school uniforms.

'I forgot, I don't have the car,' Nancy said. 'I had to leave it in Brighton last night.'

Louise's eyebrows rose. 'Right.'

'Hi, Nana,' Hope said, through a mouthful of cereal.

'Hi, darling.' Nancy waited for her daughter to respond.

'Well, nothing you can do about that,' Louise said eventually. 'Come on then, girls, we'll have to go right now.'

'But I haven't had any toast,' Jazzy wailed.

'You can eat it in the car,' their mother said.

Neither child moved.

'I said, *come on*! I've got to deal with the alarm at the restaurant. Go and get your shoes on. Hurry up!'

'What about our hair?' Hope asked, looking a little nervous of her mother's mood.

'I'll do it.' Nancy went to grab the brush and ponytail holders from the box on the ledge by the front door.

'I don't want a ponytail. I want slides at the sides.' Jazzy winced as Nancy drew the brush through her heavy blonde locks.

'It'll have to be a ponytail this morning, darling. I don't have slides.' Her granddaughter looked as if she were about to protest but, apparently sensing the tension, decided not to.

Louise stomped off to gather up the girls' blue satchels, anoraks, and Hope's swimming bag, while Nancy tussled with the knots and shrieks until both girls looked tidy enough for school.

'See you later,' Louise muttered, as they all piled into the family hatchback.

Nancy watched the car pull out of the drive, then trailed back to her cottage. She made herself a strong cup of coffee and drank a large glass of water. Her head was throbbing in a most uncharacteristic way. It had been years since she'd had a hangover. *It's not my fault*, she said to herself. *I wasn't to know the bloody alarm would go off*. But she still felt unaccountably guilty.

As she sat at the table in a daze, hands wrapped round the coffee mug like a security blanket, she went over the evening in her mind. *Jim . . . Jim*. She rolled the sound over her tongue. *What a perfect name*. And he had been so cool, so courageous, tackling that lout as if he were just a naughty kid – which he probably was, of course. But, as Jim had said, it could have turned nasty.

She remembered his last words, 'I'd like to kiss you,' and felt her tired body tremble delightfully at the thought. What would it be like, kissing Jim Bowdry? Nancy hadn't kissed anyone except Christopher for thirty-plus years. She chuckled to herself, imagining what her ex-husband would have done, faced with a fight in a bar. He'd have been out of there like a greyhound out of a trap. But maybe that was unfair, because so would most normal men.

Sighing with wonder at her feelings for Jim – an infatuation as intense as any teenager's – she went upstairs to have a shower.

CHAPTER TWELVE

The boy, Tanner, worked hard, Jim had to give him that. He got the fingering right, or mostly right, read music well and could now change between chords with fewer hiccups. But he lacked musicality, which was the one thing Jim couldn't teach him. He found himself silently urging Tanner on as he played, willing him to let go, to forget the actual notes and get in touch with the magic that would lift his music beyond the mere plodding of note follows note, chord follows chord.

'Good . . . good,' Jim said, as the boy finished playing 'Take Me Home, Country Roads'. He was a good-looking lad in a quiet, pale sort of way, eighteen, and dead set on becoming a musician – John Denver his hero and role model – once he'd finished college, where he was studying some media bollocks that Jim knew would get him nowhere, certainly not into a job. 'You know the words?' he asked.

Tanner nodded. Jim had been trying to persuade the boy to sing for weeks now.

'Go on, then.' He smiled encouragingly as Tanner blushed, his pale adolescent skin betraying him.

Tanner shook his head. 'Can't.'

'Can't? Or won't?'

The boy gave a sheepish smile. 'S'pose it's "won't".'

'Okay, but how's it going to work when you want gigs, you not singing?'

'Someone else can sing, can't they?'

'Yeah, they can. But they can probably make a stab at playing guitar too. So where do you fit in? You're limiting your options.'

The boy slumped over his guitar.

'Give it a go. It's just me,' Jim urged, wondering if maybe the key to unlocking the boy's talent lay in his voice.

And finally Tanner nodded, took a deep breath, placed his fingers on the guitar strings. He started badly, his voice hoarse and quivering all over the place, but as he settled into the rhythm, the sound got stronger. It was perfectly on key, but still tight and small. When he finished, he gave Jim a smile of pure relief.

'See, that wasn't so bad, was it?'

'Dunno, you tell me,' the boy replied.

'You've got a good voice, you just need to use it,' Jim told him. 'In fact you'd be better off finding a singing teacher, instead of coming to me.'

Jim's mobile rang just as Tanner was leaving. He grabbed it from the table, hoping it was Nancy. But it was Greg, the estate agent.

'Good news. The couple who saw it on Wednesday have made an offer. Ten short of the asking price, but I'm sure we can get them up. They seem keen and there's no chain. We *love* first-time buyers.'

'Great,' Jim said, when *fuck* was what he actually thought. 'So what do we do now?'

'I tell them you reject the offer, see what they come back with.

Brinkmanship, Mr Bowdry, it's all brinkmanship. See who blinks first.'

'Well, I'm in no hurry, so it's not going to be me.'

'Just what we want to hear,' said Greg. 'I'll get back to you soon as.'

Jim groaned softly. Here we go, he thought. Another row with Chrissie on the slate. But it was also good. The sooner he put some distance between him and his wife, the more comfortable he'd feel around Nancy.

He sat for a moment, phone in hand. Since the previous Sunday – a week ago now – when Chrissie had dropped her robe on the kitchen floor and come on to him, relations between them had been sticky to say the least. He cringed at the memory of her body pressed against his own, the challenge in her eyes as she'd dared him to kiss her, his almost default desire to do so. He'd gone so far as to lay his hand on her naked back, slide it down her smooth skin to her buttock, as he always used to. He'd heard her soft intake of breath, her own hand reaching down to touch him. It would have been so bloody easy. But the thought of Nancy had stopped him. Even in his dumb, unthinking state of arousal, he'd known he couldn't face her again if he gave in to Chrissie's manipulation. But when he'd gently disentangled himself from her arms, she'd had a major meltdown. He'd had to leave the house to escape her rage.

Now he waited for her to come home from work with trepidation. He'd been teaching all day and was knackered, but he knew he had to tell her about the offer on the house.

'Okay,' Chrissie said, seeming surprisingly sanguine at his news as she kicked off her navy court shoes and lay back on the sofa in the kitchen, closing her eyes.

Jim had made her some tea to smooth his path and got out the ginger nuts. He handed her a mug and offered her the biscuits. 'If we accept their offer, it'll all start to happen,' he said. 'We'll have to set a date for moving out.'

Chrissie rolled her eyes at him. 'Like, duh!'

'Just warning you.'

'Yeah, Jim, I do know what happens when you sell a house.'

'So what are you going to do?'

Chrissie gave him a dark look as she dunked the ginger nut in the hot tea, sucking the liquid from the biscuit before biting off a chunk and chewing it slowly. 'Like you care,' she said.

'Of course I care,' Jim said. And he did. But a part of him was dying to be free of her.

'Care that you're finally getting shot of me,' she said, as if she could read his mind.

Jim sighed. Why was he trying to be nice to this woman? The relationship had run its course months ago, maybe years. It was just a technicality now, separating their lives. But she was still his wife.

'I spoke to Tommy yesterday,' Chrissie was saying. 'He thinks the same as me – that you've got another woman.'

He loved his son very much, but Chrissie had always spoiled him, treated him more as a friend than a son. Jim knew he should make more effort with the boy, but they had so little in common and they barely saw each other these days. Tommy's only focus seemed to be computers and making money. He was very successful at both, apparently. His son wasn't much of a country music fan either, his tastes running more to the likes of Kanye West.

'He says you're behaving like a total bastard.'

Jim raised his eyebrows. 'He said that?'

'Not those exact words, no. But he's really pissed off with you, chucking me out onto the streets like this. He says I should go up to Edinburgh and start again. Leave you to stew in your own juice.'

Jim doubted very much that his son had said any such thing. He was a kind, mild-mannered boy, even if he did normally take his mother's side about the marriage. But, then, what kid wants his parents to split up?

'Would you do that? Go and live in Scotland?'

'I might. He says I can stay with him for a bit, while I get on my feet. His new flat is gorgeous, he says, in Leith Docks. I'm going up there soon, check it out.'

'Yeah, he told me about the flat,' Jim said, just to point out that he did talk to his son occasionally. 'Won't you miss your friends if you move all that way?' Chrissie had barely been out of Brighton since the day she was born.

She gave an exaggerated sigh, her green eyes wide with self-pity. 'Probably. But this town's no good for me any more. Crap job, no one to love. I need to get away, make a fresh start somewhere before it's too late . . .'

Christ, she's beginning to sound like a bad country and western song, Jim thought, repressing a smile. He made a mental note to call his son later, make it right with the boy.

CHAPTER THIRTEEN

Lindy answered the phone on the second ring. 'Hi, Nance. Thought you'd died. What's up?'

'Sorry . . .'

'Just wanted to check we're still on for Saturday.'

'Looking forward to it,' Nancy said, her guilty heart beating twice as fast as it ought, but she wasn't going to wimp off again. 'Funny thing . . . I was in town the other night and I bumped into Jim. We went for a quick drink.' Her words came out in a rush.

Oh, what a tangled web we weave, when first we practise to deceive, Nancy heard her mother's warning, delivered repeatedly, with much finger-wagging, from early childhood. It's not exactly a lie, she told herself, cringing at her own denial. More of a true outcome arrived at by a false route.

'No! What a coincidence. Where were you?'

'Near the Lanes.'

'Why didn't you ring me? I'd have joined you.'

'You look after Toby on a Thursday, don't you?'

'I didn't have to this week. Cheryl's yoga teacher's on holiday.'

'Ah, well . . .'

'God, I'm *sooo* jealous. Tell me about it.'

'There was this fight in the bar that Jim had to break up.'

'Sounds like my man,' Lindy said approvingly. 'Did you talk about me?'

'I said we were coming to his gig on Saturday.'

'Did he sound pleased?'

'He's looking forward to us meeting the band.'

What is wrong with you, Nancy de Freitas? She considered herself an honest person, but since meeting Jim she had done nothing but duck and dive with her friends and family. Was what she was doing really so embarrassing, so shameful?

'If his band mates are up to Jim's standard, we're in for an interesting night,' Lindy remarked, and they said goodbye.

Louise had been decidedly frosty with her mother since Friday morning. Nancy had gone over to apologize when she heard her daughter's car pulling into the driveway later in the day.

'Did you sort the alarm out?' she asked, following Louise into the kitchen.

'Yes.' Louise dumped her large tote onto the worktop and went to fill the kettle.

'Sorry I couldn't help. I'd had a bit too much to drink and couldn't risk the car.'

Her daughter turned to her mother with a worried frown. 'Was that wise?'

'I was just being careful – you know what the Sussex traffic cops are like,' she replied.

'I didn't mean that. I meant was it wise to get tanked with someone you hardly know.'

'I wasn't "tanked", as you put it. We'd just had a few glasses.'

She handed Nancy a cup of tea. 'Mum, you've got to be careful.

You don't know this guy from Adam. Anything could happen if you're not in control.'

'I said, I wasn't drunk. It's called socializing. It's what people do. And Jim is a nice man.' Nancy was irritated by her daughter's patronizing attitude.

'Maybe he is. But you haven't seen him often enough to make that call. Perhaps you should meet up during the day, take it slowly, avoid the booze.'

'I'm not a child, Lou, and I think I'm a pretty good judge of character. Jim's not some sleaze-bag trying to get his leg over.'

'Mum!'

'Well, you're making out I'm a vulnerable child.'

Louise's expression lightened. 'Yeah, okay, sorry. I do sound like your mother, don't I? Ross said that the other day.' But her grin quickly faded. 'It's just you haven't dated since before you met Dad. You have no idea what a horrible world it is out there and how many people would love to take advantage of a person like you.'

Nancy wasn't sure what her daughter meant by 'a person like you' – she was probably referring to her age – but she knew it wasn't really personal. This was Louise's world-view, danger lurking round every corner. 'I promise I'll be careful. If I go on seeing him, I'll bring him home for you to vet.'

Louise looked a bit sceptical at the idea, and Nancy realized she didn't have much faith in her mother's relationship – if it could be termed that – having a future.

'They look exactly as I thought they would,' Lindy whispered to Nancy, when they saw the other members of the Bluebirds. Drummer Mal was small, wiry and intense, but also pale from his recent illness. His shock of frizzy grey hair stood out from his head and his bare arms, one with a tattoo, under the leather waistcoat were muscled. Jimmy P was altogether more chilled. Overweight and sweaty in a baggy white T-shirt, with a faded transfer print of Jimi Hendrix on the front, he seemed to be in his own world, his head mostly bent to his guitar, but occasionally offering a lazy smile to the fans in the audience.

Nancy was intrigued by his friends, but her enjoyment of the evening was marred. She was so looking forward to seeing Jim again – she'd thought of nothing else – but she couldn't relax, constantly aware that she was compromising her friend's dignity.

Lindy had insisted on getting a bottle of Pinot, 'instead of wasting money on singles,' and Nancy – against her daughter's best advice – had found herself piling into the wine. Now she was beginning not to care what happened. She just wanted the evening to be over.

After the set – which had gone down well with the small audience – Jim brought his friends over and introduced them to her and Lindy.

'Glad you liked it,' Jimmy P said to them, collapsing into the pub chair with a pleased grin. 'Just lime and soda for me,' he told Nancy, when she asked what he would like to drink.

'Sorry, ladies, love to stop and chat,' Mal said, not taking the stool Lindy had pushed towards him, 'but the missus only let me out if I promised to get home before the stroke of eleven.'

Jim laughed. 'Don't want to upset Sonia.'

Mal nodded vigorously, brown eyes wide with assumed terror.

'Pumpkin's definitely a better option,' Jimmy P agreed.

Jim followed Nancy to the bar and waited while she made the order. She glanced nervously back to the table. Jimmy P and Lindy didn't seem very engaged with each other.

'So what did you tell her?' Jim whispered.

Nancy groaned. 'I said I'd bumped into you and that we'd gone for a drink.'

'So you chickened out.'

'Basically, yes.' She paid for the drinks, which the barman had placed on a tin tray.

'Cue, rampant snogging?' Jim moved closer and she could smell the clean, woody scent of his aftershave.

'Don't!' Nancy, feeling slightly hysterical, cast an eye in the direction of her friend. 'I can't do this any more,' she said.

At that moment, Lindy did turn, her gaze searching through the crowd around the bar until her eyes alighted on Nancy and Jim. She gestured impatiently as if to say, 'What the hell's taking you so long?' and Nancy pulled herself together.

It was clear now that things were not going well between Lindy and Jimmy P. Nancy could feel the awkwardness between them as she and Jim sat down. Jimmy P looked a bit spaced out, Lindy bored.

'Thought you two had done a runner,' she said, tight-lipped.

Jim moved to sit by his friend, on the far side of the table from Lindy.

'Hey, come over here,' she said, waving at him with one hand and putting the other on the chair next to her to prevent Nancy sitting there, just as Nancy remembered doing when she was at school.

Jim hesitated.

'Lindy? I need to talk to you for a minute,' Nancy said, avoiding Jim's eye.

Lindy frowned. 'Now? Okay.' She got up and followed Nancy to the ladies, which was across a courtyard behind the pub, a cold outhouse with a corrugated-iron roof and two cramped stalls that smelt acrid with disinfectant.

Nancy waited till they were in the shed, then faced her friend. Lindy shivered, clasping her arms around her body and leaning her bottom against the small basin. 'What?' Her tone was impatient. 'Hope this isn't going to take long – stinks in here.'

'I haven't been honest with you, Lindy,' she began hesitantly. 'I . . . When I took Jim home the other night, we agreed to meet for coffee. And then we had a drink. I didn't bump into him.'

Lindy looked puzzled. 'Okay.'

'And I should have told you,' Nancy ploughed on, desperate for some sort of response. 'But I really like him.'

Lindy's puzzled look turned into a frown. 'You "really like" him?'

Nancy nodded, anxiety cramping in her stomach.

'Why didn't you tell me?'

'Because it's a shitty thing to do, going after someone your friend fancies.'

Lindy bowed her blonde head, shivered, but didn't reply. *Christ*, thought Nancy, *say something*.

When she looked up, she said coolly, 'I just wanted to fuck him, darling, I didn't want to marry him.' She wasn't smiling, her large eyes stony. 'You're fucking welcome to him. But next time don't humiliate me like this. That *is* shit.'

'I'm sorry,' Nancy whispered.

Lindy stared straight ahead, lips pursed. Nancy didn't know what to say, what to do. The place was freezing and the disinfectant was sticking in her throat, making her want to gag.

Then her friend's face cleared. She shook her head and began to laugh. 'Fucking hell, Nance, wouldn't have taken you for a man-snatcher.'

'Wouldn't have taken myself for one, either.'

Lindy was peering at her. 'So you really like him, eh?'

Nancy nodded weakly.

'Well, you go for it, darling, have some fun. I'm so over the man.' She gave Nancy's arm a semi-friendly thwack which actually stung Nancy's bare flesh. 'Wait while I have a pee – this place gives me the creeps.'

They strolled along the dark pavement, Nancy and Jim. He carried his guitar case in one hand, held her hand tight in the other as they made their way towards her car, parked in the next street. Free at last from the stifling atmosphere in the pub, and her equally stifling guilt about Lindy, Nancy's heart lifted with excitement as she walked beside him, smelling the salt on the cool wind from the sea.

'She was pissed off at first,' Nancy told him. 'Said I'd humiliated her. Then she admitted she only wanted to fuck you, not marry you.'

'Ha! Just toying with my affections, eh? You women are always complaining about being objects of lust – you'd think she'd have more respect.'

Nancy laughed. 'You can hardly talk about respect! You were planning to snog me to death, just to make a point.'

She heard Jim chuckle in the darkness. 'Yeah, but I got the short straw, didn't I? Not only have I been cruelly toyed with, but I didn't get to snog you either.'

Nancy couldn't help feeling a surge of happiness as they joked together. Christopher, although clever and knowledgeable about a host of things, had seldom made her laugh.

'Are you really okay to drive?' Jim asked, as they reached her car.

'I'm fine. I had a few glasses at the beginning of the evening, but then I went the lime and soda route, like Jimmy P.'

'Yeah, he's being a good boy, Jimmy. You should have seen him when he was on the sauce. He was a proper mess.'

'He doesn't say much.'

'No, never did. But he's got perfect pitch and can sing any harmony without even thinking. That's enough for me.'

'You'll have to tell me the way to your house again,' Nancy said, as she pushed the key into the ignition.

But Jim had other ideas. He reached across and took her hand as it rested on the steering wheel and brought it to his lips. For a moment she was very still, then she turned to him. He placed his hand on her neck, his thumb grazing her chin as he stroked her gently, his gaze never leaving her face. She stared back, losing herself in his eyes, her pulse mounting. She was barely breathing as he leaned forward and kissed her softly, first a light flutter on her cheek, then full on her lips. His mouth was warm against her own, his kisses not forceful but sure and perfectly at home, as if he'd been waiting to kiss her his whole life.

They seemed to enter a zone where they floated together, barely moving, the charge between them, as they kissed, electrifying her until she could hardly bear it. When they finally pulled back, she was trembling so hard, the throb in her groin so intense that she thought she might come in a second if she touched herself.

Jim looked as shell-shocked as she felt. 'Wow,' he muttered.

She let out a long breath, not able to speak.

'I think we must have done this before,' Jim said.

'In a previous life?' she joked.

'Maybe. God, Nancy.' He took her hand again and held it tight between his own. 'Does it get any better than this?'

'What should we do now?'

'Hmm . . . Well, apart from the obvious, the second best thing might be a nightcap somewhere? . . . I don't want you to go yet.'

It was nearly two in the morning when Nancy arrived home. Jim had taken her to a narrow, wood-panelled bar, with soft lighting and jazz playing on the sound system – it was clear that he knew the owner well. Sammi, in his sixties, perching proprietorially on a bar stool, had dyed, slicked-back wavy hair to his collar, a black shirt and heavy jowls. He squeezed them into a corner at the side of the crowded bar, the seats obviously kept for his mates.

Jim had put an arm around her shoulders and drawn her against him. And there they had stayed, sometimes talking, sometimes silent. Nancy, revelling in the intimacy, found she was still stunned by the level of desire triggered by their kiss. Time passed without them caring, and even though it was so late when they finally parted, it was almost painful to tear herself away.

Now she turned very, very slowly into the drive, lights off, terrified that she would wake her family. But the perfidious gravel had a mind of its own, the crack and snap beneath the tyres like gunshots in the darkness.

As she crept towards her front door, one eye on the windows of the big house, the clouds parted and she gazed up at a full moon, round and silver-white, the nimbus spreading across the night sky like a silken veil. For a moment she stood and stared. The magic of the heavens, to Nancy's overwrought soul, seemed to mirror the magic of the hours she had just spent with Jim Bowdry.

But before she'd had time to unlock her door, her phone shrieked into the night. She fumbled in her bag, the security light above her door flashing a horrible brightness across the drive, and finally answered it. 'Hold on,' she whispered to Jim.

Once inside, she put the phone to her ear again. 'Sorry, I was trying to get into the house without waking the entire family, but it was like a bloody *son et lumière* out there. No way will my insomniac daughter have slept through it.'

Jim laughed. 'Oops! Didn't mean to cause trouble.'

'Don't worry, I'd already banged the car door, crunched the gravel, dropped the keys and cursed loudly. So the phone was just the icing on the cake.'

'Just wanted to say goodnight,' he said softly.

Nancy sighed. 'Goodnight, Jim. Missing you already.'

'Missing you too.'

At first Nancy didn't know what had wakened her. But as she came to she realized it was rain, pounding on the skylight above her bed. A design fault, she had often thought, in the otherwise imaginative conversion.

It was early still, so she lay in bed, luxuriating in thoughts of the previous night, picking over everything Jim had said, her own replies, their shared laughter and, most of all, the physical thrill of his touch. *Everything*, she thought, *seems somehow exceptional this morning – the duvet is particularly cosy, the pillow particularly soft. Even the rain on the window looks prettier, the light struggling to break through the May clouds more beautiful*.

Then a thought struck her: *I am in love*. And the admission threatened to overwhelm her. Not because she doubted it, or doubted Jim, but because of the sheer, ridiculous improbability of the situation.

CHAPTER FOURTEEN

Jim felt like a criminal as he looked right and left, then entered the premises of Butler & Sitter, Solicitors at Law. It wasn't that he was hiding anything exactly: he'd told Chrissie weeks ago that he wanted to divorce. But she'd been so crazy recently that he'd thought he'd see the lie of the land before he brought the subject up again.

Andrew Sitter was in his fifties, Jim calculated, a plump, pale, untidy man in a bad suit with about four half-drunk mugs of coffee making rings on top of the piles of paperwork littering his dusty desk. It wasn't reassuring.

'So, let me get this straight,' Andrew said, pushing his rimless glasses up his nose after he'd settled Jim and himself with yet another mug of coffee to swell the ranks on the desk. 'You and Christine are living together in the same house, but you have your own rooms, do your own shopping, eat meals apart and never have sex. You have separate bank accounts, no dependants and you do no joint socializing.'

'Umm, well, we occasionally socialized . . . but I've stopped that now. And she lets me eat the bread she bakes. But that's it.'

'She bakes bread? Wow. I wouldn't have divorced my wife if

she'd baked bread. Or even if she'd bought some occasionally.' His pudgy face took on a bleak expression. Then he continued: 'You say the infidelity happened over three years ago?'

'About three years. She came back just over two years ago, but we haven't lived together . . . properly since.'

'Hmm.' Andrew scratched his nose. 'And she's not contesting it?'

'I don't think so.'

'It's quite an important point, her contesting it or not, Mr Bowlby. You need to know.'

'Bowdry, and I do know. Chrissie won't contest it.'

'Do you own your house?'

'Yes.'

'Jointly?'

'Yes.'

'Children?'

'One, but he's left home.'

'Pensions?'

'Not me, but she probably has.'

'So you'd need a financial order.'

'Would I? Couldn't we just divvy it up the middle?'

'That's what a financial order will do.'

'But will it cost more, having one?'

Andrew sighed. 'Yes, a bit. Listen, are you in a mad hurry to get married again?'

'No, not really.'

'Well, I'd suggest you sell the house and live separately, divide all your assets, bank accounts and so on. When you've lived apart for two years or more, file for divorce online. You can get all the information on the government website. It's the cheapest way for an uncontested divorce if you're worried about money. And if you aren't in a rush to marry someone else.'

'Talking yourself out of a job?'

Andrew smiled. 'Something I do a lot of. I'm just not sure that you need a divorce, Mr Bowdry. You and your wife seem to get along quite well, considering.'

'But I don't want to be married to her any more.'

That seemed to amuse Andrew Sitter. 'Common problem, I'm afraid. Look, I'll take you on if you like, but it's always more tricky proving you're living apart when you aren't. Can cause hassles if the judge is a stickler, is all I'm saying, and therefore cost more money.'

Jim sighed. 'The bread issue, you mean. Okay, well, thanks for the advice. I'll go away, think about it and get back to you.'

He was glad to be out of the stuffy office and began to walk quickly along the pavement, heading for a coffee with Mal across town, but needing time to think. Walking always helped him think.

The solicitor was right, he supposed. He didn't really need a divorce just yet. Whatever happened with Nancy wouldn't involve marriage . . . at least, not yet. But it irked him that he would have to stay married to Chrissie for another *two years*. Seemed like a lifetime. And that lifetime might be with Nancy, if the universe was on his side. Wouldn't it be strange to be with Nancy and still married to Chrissie? He didn't know if it would matter or not.

I've got to sell the bloody house, he thought. Once that's sorted, I can manage the rest. God, he'd so longed to take Nancy home last Saturday. It was way too soon, of course: someone like her would never leap into bed with a man she'd only known a few weeks. Although, when he thought about it, they'd virtually had sex in the car – that kiss felt as if they had. He still ached from it, as if a physical memory of her lips had been seared on his brain. It would be months, or weeks at least, before they completed on the house. Would he have to wait that long before he took Nancy to bed? Because it sounded as if the disapproving daughter in the house next door to Nancy's might be a bit of a passion killer for both of them.

Mal was sitting hunched inside a leather jacket that seemed too big for him now, with the weight he'd lost.

'Hey.' He grinned as Jim sat down.

'How're you doing? Good to see you out again.'

'Good to *be* out,' he said, but Jim could see he wasn't sure that it was.

Mal already had a mug of tea in front of him and the remains of what looked like a sausage roll, so Jim ordered a black coffee for himself and told his friend what the solicitor had said.

'Looks like you've got yourself in a bit of a hole, with this Nancy woman.' He sucked his teeth. 'Should have told her right off, you numpty.'

'Don't you think I know that?' Jim snapped, on edge. 'But it's too bloody late now, isn't it?'

'Never too late to be honest.'

'She'd run a mile. Even the solicitor bloke wasn't convinced I should get divorced because Chrissie still lets me eat the bloody bread she bakes.'

Mal laughed, a series of short barks that, as usual, drew the attention of the people at the next table. 'Does sound a tad cosy to the uninitiated.'

'Come on. You know Chrissie. She's great in lots of ways, but I just don't want to be with her any more. You'd have chucked Sonia out years ago if she'd behaved like Chrissie.'

'Ha, wish she'd give me the excuse,' Mal said. But Jim knew that, although Mal liked to pretend he was henpecked and put upon by his fierce wife, he would never leave Sonia in a million years. 'Problem with you,' Mal went on, 'is you're too bloody soft. You should never have let her back after that prick in the bar. I told you at the time.'

Jim sighed. 'Yeah, I know you did. But I wanted her back then. Or thought I did. It was only when she was there and promising me she'd never *ever* do it again, that I discovered I didn't believe her.' He shrugged. 'I did try, Mal, you know I did.'

The friends were silent, both men's expressions registering gloom, although for entirely different reasons.

'Truth is,' Mal said eventually, 'you haven't lied. You're as good as divorced. So next time you see Nancy, just drop it into the conversation like there isn't a problem. Something along the lines of "Much as I'm dying to take you home and jump your bones, Nancy, my love, the ex lives downstairs and it might prove tricky." '

Jim couldn't help laughing. 'One snag. She isn't my *ex*.'

Mal shook his head. 'No. I get it. Don't know what to say, mate.'

Jim, who hadn't held out much hope that his friend would come up with a solution, just nodded. All he could see was Nancy's beautiful face, the quiet, almost shy expression in those amazing eyes. And the hurt and anger that would replace the shyness when she found out she hadn't been told the truth.

'What about Tommy?'

'Haven't spoken to him yet. I can't tell him about Nancy till Chrissie knows, or about the solicitor. Chrissie says he's pissed off about the house business, but I reckon she's just using him to wind me up. Wouldn't be the first time.'

'So talk to him, Jim. Don't let her get to him first.'

'Yeah.' Jim felt almost sick at the tangle of half-truths he had constructed and didn't need a lecture about his son as well.

'Me, I'd have gone for her friend,' Mal said thoughtfully. 'She's a bit of a knockout, that one.'

'Not my type,' Jim said. He looked hard at him. 'I'm serious about Nancy, Mal. Really serious. I think I love her.'

Mal's eyes widened. 'No kidding!'

'That's why I don't want to fuck it up.'

'You know what they say . . .' he began to sing the first line of 'Love Hurts' in his scratchy tenor.

'By that token . . .' Jim countered with a Kris Kristofferson number, 'Loving Her Was Easier'.

The two girls at the next table were giving them funny looks.

'Could be worse, I suppose,' Mal said vaguely.

'How?'

'Dunno, but it could always be worse, couldn't it?'

Jim grinned. 'Yeah, Mal, I suppose it could.' Which, if he thought about it, was true. He was in love, he'd said it now, it was official, and things could really be a whole lot worse.

CHAPTER FIFTEEN

Frances was crying again. She didn't understand why: she had never been someone to give in to tears. But recently she'd been experiencing this horrible sense of dread, which crept up on her at odd times when she was alone. It was like a soft, dark cloak descending, suffocating her and making her guts turn to water, her heart trip over itself in a race to nowhere. She felt as though she were about to die, and she had no idea what to do when the feeling overtook her. Taking deep breaths helped, but sometimes she was in so much of a tither that she couldn't even do that: her lungs seemed to shrink to a tiny section up round her throat and she despaired of getting the next breath.

She was just recovering from an attack now, as she sat in the sitting room at two in the morning, huddled in her quilted pink dressing-gown, a cup of tea on the table beside her, her toes freezing in the towelling mules she wore in summer. She had turned on the television for company, and settled on an episode of *Minder*, keeping the sound very low. She'd never liked the programme, even back in the early eighties, but George Cole and his roguish antics had always made Kenny laugh. The thought brought another tear to her eye.

Picking up her mug, Frances took a sip of tea. Just a tiny one, because she'd been having trouble swallowing recently. Even when she did force something down, she'd get terrible indigestion. Nancy had noticed, of course, but Frances dreaded fuss so she'd said nothing, swatted off her daughter's concern. She'd go to Dr Henderson soon, but on her own terms. Otherwise there would be a whole family hoo-hah and everyone would get involved – dear Louise worried for Britain. It was probably just the usual.

'You must expect this sort of problem at *your age*,' her doctor had been telling her for years. Frances didn't see why she should. Was it entirely necessary for her knees to give out, her fingers to swell and skew with arthritis, her heart to need statins, her ears to buzz continuously with tinnitus? Couldn't someone do something? She often envied Kenny, getting out when he had – she was still furious with him for leaving her to suffer on her own.

The pain in her stomach was like a sharp, pricking cramp, which came and went in pulses as soon as the hot tea went down. Frances held her breath; she felt sick. The house was chilly, but she certainly wasn't going to turn on the heating, not in May. What she needed was a hot-water bottle, but she didn't have the strength to get up and organize it.

How tired she was of being alone. She was jolly good at pretending otherwise, of course, what with the bridge club and the theatre, trips to galleries and those endless dreary gardens to which her friends seemed so addicted. Good at pretending she had a great life. And she did do an awful lot more than most people of her age, because she knew she'd go mad if she didn't. But the other week, when she'd been over for lunch with the family, she'd had this overwhelming desire just to stay put, never go home, never move from that ghastly green sofa with Bob curled up by her side, sleep in Nancy's slope-roofed spare room, with the delightful blue-flowered curtains, let others sort out her life for her.

Now the thought of that alternative life gave her a moment of yearning as she idly watched George and his sidekick Dennis Waterman crazy-running along the pavement, fleeing some dodgy villain in a sharp suit, George holding onto his trilby for dear life. She wondered how many older people like herself were sitting there, dreaming of the exact same thing. Thousands, surely. It wasn't natural to be alone at her age. In the past she would have been expected to live within the bosom of the family, pass down all the wisdom she'd gleaned in her life – not that she could think of what that might be right now.

Nancy might welcome not being alone, Frances thought. She didn't seem to go out much. *I could keep to myself, 'maintain my independence'* – that patronizing phrase always used about her age group – *go out with my friends just like I do now, not bother Nancy when she has pupils. The spare room is just big enough for me to have a television up there.* Louise and the girls were across the way, so if she and Nancy were driving each other mad she could divide her time between them, not burden anyone. Her friend Joyce had just sold her cottage and moved into an adorable 'granny-annex' next to her son's house. And Joyce had a pretty tricky relationship with her daughter-in-law at the best of times – Frances wouldn't want to live so close to that bossy girl. So if Joyce could do it . . .

She sighed, knowing she would rather die than ask Nancy to take her in.

The next thing she knew, light was pouring through the sitting-room window, the birds chirping away noisily at their dawn chorus. Looking at the clock on the mantelpiece, she saw it was nearly five-thirty. Her whole body was like ice and aching with stiffness. She felt nauseous, but when she tried to get up, her limbs wouldn't respond. The familiar panic began to take hold.

Breathe, she told herself. But it wasn't working and she felt the bile rise in her throat. Bending over, gasping for breath, she threw up on the carpet, tears streaming down her face as she retched and retched, bringing up only liquid and mucus, but unable to stop.

When she finally lay back on the flowered sofa cushions, wiping her mouth with an old tissue she found in her dressing-gown pocket, she knew she needed help. Reaching for the phone she rang her daughter.

'Mum . . .' Nancy's sleepy voice held a tinge of irritation.

'Sorry, darling . . . so sorry. . . I'm not well . . . Can you come?' Frances forced the words through her parched lips.

'What is it? What's happened?' Nancy no longer sounded sleepy.

'I've been sick . . . I don't know . . .' The effort of holding the phone seemed too much for Frances and she felt a new wave of nausea sweep over her. 'Please . . .' She hung up and retched again, looking in dismay at the slimy mess on the carpet.

It seemed a lifetime before she heard Nancy's key in the door.

'God, Mum, what happened?'

Nancy was by her side: she was safe. She lay back and closed her eyes, clutching her daughter's hand as if for dear life.

The next thing she knew she was tucked up in bed, warm and clean, a hot-water bottle against her side, a glass of water on the night table, the yellow plastic washing-up bowl on the floor beside the bed, a nasty taste of bile still in her mouth. She reached for the water and took a sip, then pulled the duvet tighter around her shoulders.

'You're awake.' Nancy's anxious face appeared at the door. 'How are you feeling?'

Frances gave her a wan smile. 'All right, I think. I must have eaten something.'

Nancy sat on the bed beside her, gently took her hand. 'What did you have for supper?'

'Umm . . . an egg . . . bread and butter. A couple of biscuits.' The egg bit was a lie, and the bread and butter, but she had nibbled at least half of a digestive with her tea.

Her daughter frowned. 'Maybe it was the egg.' Her eyes widened. 'I hope it's not salmonella.'

Frances shook her head. 'I'm sure I'd be much worse if it was. I don't feel sick any more.'

'No, well . . . Dr Henderson is coming this afternoon, anyway.'

'Oh, darling. You shouldn't have bothered him. I'm fine now.'

'Are you, Mum? You look dreadful.'

Frances raised her eyebrows.

'You know what I mean.' Nancy said, getting up. 'Can I bring you anything? A cup of tea?'

'No, thank you. But if the doctor's coming, can you pass me my brush and face cream, please.'

CHAPTER SIXTEEN

'I'm sorry, Jim, I can't meet this morning – Mum's ill. I'm round at hers and I can't leave her.'

'No, of course not. What's the problem?'

'She's been vomiting and she seems terribly weak. The doctor's just left.'

'What did he say was wrong?' Jim said.

'Didn't seem to have a clue . . .' Nancy lowered her voice, aware of her mother lying upstairs. 'I was so looking forward to seeing you.'

'Me too. Call me when you can – let me know how it's going.'

Nancy sat down on the sofa and wondered what to do. Dr Henderson had barely examined her mother, just taken her pulse and her temperature and Frances's word that it was something she'd eaten, but he did admit she was looking very thin.

'The thing is, Mrs de Freitas, your mum is getting on,' he'd said, cocking his scrubbed young face sympathetically at her, raising his blond eyebrows a little.

'She's only eighty-four,' Nancy replied, with a certain amount of asperity, which the GP seemed not to notice. In the past, she would have assumed doctors knew what they were talking about, but these days they all seemed to be twelve years old and her confidence was waning.

'Older people do suddenly get frail, not necessarily for any sinister reason.'

'Don't you think you should check her out, though? Do some tests?'

The doctor appeared to give this some consideration. Nancy could tell he was humouring her when he replied, 'We could. Listen, why don't you make an appointment for her when she's a bit better and we can see how things are looking?'

Which meant bugger-all.

'The doctor says you must make an appointment, Mum. Get things checked out,' she said, the next time she went upstairs.

'Of course, darling,' Frances replied, waving a hand dismissively at her daughter.

Nancy stayed the night, scrunched up on the spare bed, which was high, narrow and metal-framed, the mattress as stony as Brighton beach, in the small spare room full of old boxes and too much heavy dark furniture – like the rest of the house. The room smelt damp, but Nancy couldn't open the window as the security key was missing.

What would happen, she wondered, if her mum wasn't better in the morning? A small knot of panic began to form as Nancy lay in the chilly darkness. She knew what she should do, of course. Take Frances home with her. There was room. But she felt herself resisting the suggestion with every selfish fibre of her being. Jim. She wanted Jim.

They had met again earlier in the week, for lunch in a village pub on the Downs. It had been a beautiful day and they'd sat outside at a creaky weathered-wood picnic table, overlooking the fields and hills, just talking and talking, every tiny bit of information exchanged seeming like a delectation that made them both smile idiotically. He'd put his arm round her shoulders as they walked back to the car, drawing her close.

'That kiss . . . ' he said softly, 'blew my mind.'

She looked up at him. 'Mine too.'

'Too many people around, too much light,' he said, desire sparking up his blue eyes, his face almost touching hers so that she could feel the warmth of his skin. She was on the point of asking him back to her house, but she remembered it was half-term and the girls had friends over for a play-date.

If she took in her mother, that would be that. She certainly couldn't imagine canoodling with Jim on the sofa while her mother was in the house.

Maybe next time we meet in Brighton, Jim will ask me over to his place, she thought. *Maybe I should suggest it. He might be afraid I'd think he was coming on too strong if he did.* It wasn't just the sex. Nancy knew that was a big step and it made her twitch just thinking about it – and the implications. But it would be so good to be alone with him, in a private space, to have the chance to make a choice.

She hugged her cold body and watched the dawn light slowly filter through the cotton curtains, fighting the overwhelming sense of claustrophobia that seemed to be settling over her life.

'She's still very weak,' Nancy told Jim later, 'although she hasn't been sick again. But I can't leave her here alone. She wouldn't be able to cope.'

'So you'll stay for a few days?'

'That, or take her home. Louise is coming over in a minute and we'll decide what to do.'

'It's hard, when they get so they can't manage on their own.'

'Did you have that?'

'My gran, Mum's mum, lived with us for years. She came after she broke her hip and never left. Drove Mum nuts most of the time, but it was the right thing to do, I suppose.'

Nancy sighed. 'That's what's worrying me. My relationship with my mother works best in sound bites – specifically coffee or lunch. Long term, we'd kill each other.'

'Hey, don't get ahead of yourself. She might not be that bad . . . You sound exhausted, Nancy.'

'I didn't sleep, the bed's crap.' It was so comforting to hear Jim's voice, to know he really understood, that she felt quite tearful. It was a long time since she'd been able to lean on someone. Christopher was never really interested in her problems, unless they specifically affected him.

'Call me later,' he was saying. 'And if there's anything I can do . . .'

'I don't think we should move her,' Louise said, as they faced each other across Frances's small kitchen, each with a cup of instant coffee, bottoms propped against the units. 'She seems too frail.'

Nancy didn't reply at once. Then she said, 'I suppose I'll have to stay with her.'

Louise looked stricken. 'Oh, Mum. I'd help, but I've got the kids home this week, and the restaurant.'

'I know, Lou. I wouldn't expect you to. It's just so depressing here. I hate this house and I was never cut out to be a carer. Don't have the patience.'

Her daughter grinned. 'Remember when I had chicken pox and you kept on saying it was just a rash from those nylon shirts I had to wear for school? You were in denial because you didn't want me off school for weeks.'

'Me and all the other mums.' She laughed. 'But you're right, illness isn't my forte.'

They were silent for a moment.

'Would you really want her at home, then?' Louise asked.

'I just thought it'd be easier in some ways. I could get on with stuff . . .' she paused, 'and at least I'd sleep.' She was feeling scratchy and raw from her restless night.

'And we could help out a bit more.'

Another silence fell, broken by her mother's voice calling from the bedroom. Nancy heaved herself upright, tipping the remains of her tasteless coffee down the sink, rinsing the mug and standing it upside-down on the draining board. 'Coming, Mum.'

Jim wrapped his arms round Nancy as they stood in the narrow hall of her mother's house. It was late and her mother was asleep upstairs. Nancy had been there for three days now, and although Frances seemed better and had been up for much of the afternoon, Nancy still didn't feel she could leave her alone. But she was going stir-crazy, stuck in that tiny house with nothing to do, no piano to soothe her frayed nerves.

She looked up at Jim – the ceiling held an energy-saving bulb that shed a meagre acid light on them.

'That's better,' he whispered, as he held her close.

She didn't reply, just closed her eyes and luxuriated in his embrace, his warmth, the fresh scent of his skin, the frisson of sexual excitement his nearness evoked making her head spin with pleasure.

She pushed him into the sitting room and shut the door. Jim raised an eyebrow. 'Alone at last,' he said, grinning suggestively.

'Except for Mum upstairs,' Nancy said, but she didn't resist when he pulled her down with him onto the chintz-covered two-seater.

'She's asleep, no?' Jim murmured, stroking her fringe back from her face.

Nancy could hardly breathe. 'She is, but she could wake up at any moment and stagger downstairs.'

'We'd hear her,' Jim said, bending to kiss her, his mouth seeking hers with an eagerness that matched her own, his tongue sending almost unbearable shivers of desire through her body as they drew closer, his hand now against her breast, fingers fluttering across her nipple until she was ready to faint. She no longer cared about her mother in the room upstairs, she was no longer aware of anything except Jim's hand between her legs, stroking her thigh beneath her cotton skirt, moving upwards, his mouth still pressed to hers, sending her body into a frenzy that clamoured for more.

Then she heard her mother.

'Nancy . . . Nancy . . .'

They froze, then dissolved into silent laughter, Nancy still shaking from Jim's touch. Taking long breaths to calm herself, she pulled her clothes back into place, flicked her rumpled hair behind her ears and assumed a solemn expression as she stood before Jim.

'Do I look okay?' she asked.

Jim looked up at her as he lay back on the sofa. 'You look bloody gorgeous.'

She laughed. 'I mean do I look normal?'

He frowned as he considered this, but was unable to control his grin. 'Hmm . . . you look as if you've just had sex, if that's normal.'

Nancy punched his shoulder as her mother's voice, more impatient this time, called again.

'She'll know I've been up to something,' she said, as she opened the sitting room door and called, 'Coming, Mum.'

'She'll never expect in a million years that you've been having sex on her couch.'

'I'd never have expected it either.' Nancy hurried upstairs, still trying to smooth her hair and compose her features.

Her mother was sitting up in bed, seemingly wide awake.

'Isn't it late?' she asked, eyeing Nancy's clothes.

'Quite, but I wasn't tired,' Nancy lied.

'I hope your bed's comfy enough. That was your father's when he was young.'

'It's fine, Mum. Did you want something?' She didn't get too close to her mother, worried she would smell Jim's scent on her.

'No, I just thought I heard something . . . a sort of thump. I was worried someone was downstairs.'

That would have been Jim's boots hitting the floor, Nancy thought, repressing a smile.

'Just me. Now you snuggle down, Mum, and get some sleep. You've got your water there on the side. And I'm here, you don't need to worry.'

Frances's face relaxed and she shuffled down the bed, pulling the duvet round her shoulders, only the top of her head with its rumpled white pixie cut visible above the sheets. 'Thank you, darling. I do appreciate your looking after me like this.'

'Shall I turn the light off?'

'If you wouldn't mind.'

Nancy moved round the bed and fumbled with the stiff brass safety switch, which resisted her attempts, until finally she succeeded.

Her mother's head turned on the pillow and Nancy had a sudden desire to drop a kiss on her pained face. But she knew Frances would hate that.

'Sleep well,' Nancy said softly, into the semi-darkness, and waited for a moment to make sure her mother's eyes were closing.

Jim was exactly where she'd left him, leaning back against the sofa cushions, his long legs and grey-socked feet stretched out in front of him, crossed at the ankles. She sat down next to him.

'Is she okay?' Jim asked.

'Bit twitchy. She thought she heard a thump and had forgotten I was here, I think.'

'Must be miserable, getting to the stage where the smallest thing frightens you. Hope I'm dead before I get like that.'

'Yeah. Everyone's always telling us to exercise and eat lots of vegetables so we can live for ever, but no one's found a way to make it fun.'

He put his arm around her and she dropped her head gratefully onto his shoulder. 'We've got to make the most of this time *now*,' he said, suddenly passionate. 'Or before you know it we'll be like your mum, jumping at shadows and totally dependent.'

Nancy shuddered. 'Should I take her home, do you think? Just bite the bullet and have her come to live with me?'

'I haven't seen her, Nancy. I don't know how bad she is.'

'She isn't "bad" as such, just weak. But I'm not sure I'd cope, being her carer twenty-four/seven.'

She felt him shrug. 'Depends. Might be easier than having to worry about her at a distance.'

But, Nancy wanted to say, *what about us?* The words remained trapped in her throat.

They sat together in silence, the room feeling suddenly chilly and depressing.

'I suppose I ought to get home,' Jim said, although he didn't move, just brought his hand up to Nancy's cheek, resting it there. It felt blissfully warm and tender. 'You won't be able to get away for a while, then?'

Nancy sighed. 'I can always leave Louise to babysit, if Mum's at home. But, yes, I suppose the next week or so might be difficult.'

He gazed at her. 'I miss you as soon as I leave you.'

'I miss you too.' She smiled. 'Feels like I'm sixteen again.'

'It was never as good as this when *I* was sixteen,' Jim said. 'It was just lust then, mostly unrequited. My mate Marty always got the crumpet. He looked like the back end of a horse, but that didn't stop him. Girls fell over themselves to get his attention.'

'Can't believe they didn't fancy you, Jim,' Nancy said. And she couldn't.

'Ha, nice of you to say, but I was shy and a bit geeky back then. I never knew what to say to a girl.' He grinned. 'Not like with you. I can't shut up when I'm with you.'

'I . . .' Nancy stopped, took a breath. 'Next time maybe we could go to yours? If Mum's at home . . .'

There was an unexpectedly heavy silence and Nancy felt Jim tensing.

'Or not, if you don't think that's a good idea.'

When she looked up at him he was frowning.

'I'd love to take you home more than anything, Nancy,' he said, his voice oddly vehement. 'I'm bloody dying to. But Tommy's staying for a bit . . .'

'Oh, okay. Doesn't matter.'

He gave a heavy sigh, as if the world rested on his shoulders. She wondered if there were problems with his son, but as he didn't volunteer any more information, she didn't ask. 'It was just a thought,' she said.

'Do you think she'll need to stay long?' Lindy asked as they stood waiting for their grandchildren in the school playground. It was the sort of primary school most parents dream about, set behind a pretty village green, shaded by a huge oak tree in a quiet corner of East Sussex, the head teacher a dynamic, no-nonsense woman who knew every child by name and insisted on her own high standards for everyone, from teachers and children to parents and grandparents. And woe betide anyone who stepped out of line.

'I don't know. She seems to have perked up in the last week, but she's still not eating much. I don't think she'd manage on her own.'

Her mother had been in the spare room for nearly ten days now, and this was the first time she had left her for more than an hour or so. Louise was at home and had said she would keep an eye on her grandmother while Nancy went into town, then picked up the girls.

'God, Nance, bit of a problem for you if she can't go home.' Lindy looked her usual glamorous self, in a navy jersey dress, which clung to her curves, chunky silver necklace and patent leather wedge heels.

'I know.' Nancy felt weary even discussing it. 'She's no trouble, really. She sleeps a lot . . . It's just . . .'

Lindy raised her eyebrows, laid a sympathetic hand on her arm. 'You don't have to tell me, darling. I was super-crap at being sweet to my mum for more than ten minutes, God rest her soul.'

Nancy laughed. 'I thought I would be too, but she's so vulnerable, my heart goes out to her.'

'Hmm, you're a way nicer person than I am, then.' Lindy dragged Nancy further away from the group of mums who were beginning to gather. 'But let's talk about the real issue here.' She dropped her voice. '*Our Jim*. You've gone suspiciously quiet on the subject. I want all the goss.' She grinned expectantly at Nancy, a lewd look in her eye.

'Well . . .' Nancy hesitated, knowing Lindy wouldn't settle for anything but the full monty, and she was not about to give her that. 'We've been seeing each other quite a bit. Or, at least, we were until this last week.' She didn't add that she'd just had coffee with Jim because it had been an oddly uncomfortable meeting and she hadn't yet worked out why.

'Woo-hoo! So, bonking and the lot?'

'Ssh! No, no bonking.'

'*No bonking?* Why ever not? Is something wrong with him?' Lindy interrupted her in a stage whisper.

'There's nowhere to go with Mum at home.'

'Why can't you go to his?'

'His son's staying, apparently.'

Lindy frowned. 'Sounds a bit of a lame excuse. Hope he's not dragging his heels for some other reason.'

'Like what?'

'Well, he's older, Nance. Maybe he's got a problem in that department and he's nervous of putting you off.'

'What on earth are you talking about?' Her friend's face had taken on a concerned expression.

'Impotence is very common in the over-sixties. Especially for smokers. Something about shrinking blood vessels . . . Not sure of the details.'

Nancy was almost shocked by her friend's suggestion. Not least because she'd thought, after this morning, that Jim might be hiding something. 'Jim is definitely not impotent,' she hissed, glancing around to check that no one was listening.

But Lindy just laughed. 'Ah! So things have gone a bit further than you're letting on, Miss Prim Nancy.'

'You're incorrigible,' Nancy muttered, her cheeks suddenly flaming as brightly as a beacon set to warn off enemy ships.

'Ooh, enjoy, darling.' She waved as she saw Toby coming towards her. 'Call me later and we can arrange a meet-up. We haven't been out in an age. All very well for you with your gorgeous fella, but what about me? You've got to help me find another Jim.'

'Can we get a cupcake on the way home, Nana?' Hope asked tentatively, when they had piled themselves and all their bags into the Golf. There was a cupcake shop cunningly situated just outside the village along the route home, and occasionally Nancy gave in and treated the girls.

'Why not?' she said, to a chorus of delighted shrieks from the back seat. She knew Louise might be irritated, but she felt like one herself. She was still unsettled by Jim's behaviour. He'd seemed so moody and tense, not fully engaged, with none of his usual amused and flirtatious smiles. But when she'd eventually asked what was wrong, he'd practically bitten her head off.

'Nothing,' he'd snapped, then obviously realized he'd been rude, because he added, 'Sorry, Nancy. Things at home are difficult at the moment.'

'With your son?' she asked. But he hadn't really replied, just shaken his head and glowered at the table. And she'd felt this huge tension sitting between them, like an explosion waiting to go off. He was troubled by something, and she'd thought he was on the point of blurting it out, whatever it was, he was silent for so long. But in the end he just looked up at her, his eyes full of misery.

'I want it all to be perfect, Nancy,' he said.

And she hadn't been able to reply, her breath trapped in her chest, her heart racing to beat the band.

'Can I have the Smarties one?' Jazzy pointed to her favourite.

Nancy nodded. 'Please.'

'Please,' echoed Jazzy.

'Hope?'

Her elder granddaughter was wandering along the line of cakes, head on one side, lost in an ecstasy of indecision. 'I can't decide between chocolate buttons and sprinkles.'

Nancy picked the most lurid one for herself, a chocolate/toffee concoction with about three inches of buttercream covered with chocolate drizzle and chunks of chocolate, guaranteed to give her a sugar high into next week. She needed it.

They sat on the bench outside the shop, Nancy between the two girls, for the short time it took them all to devour the cupcakes.

'Nana . . .' Hope licked a smear of buttercream from her thumb and didn't look at Nancy as she asked, 'Did you and Grandy fight?'

'Yes, I suppose we did, but not very often. Why?'

'So you didn't stop being married because you argued?'

'It wasn't anything to do with that.' Nancy replied. 'I think we just ran out of steam. Marriage is complicated, darling, people change.' She knew she wasn't making much sense, but she wasn't sure how much an eight-year-old would understand. Jazzy, she noticed, had gone very quiet, her large eyes fixed on the waxed paper shell that had held her cake.

'Why do they change?' Hope asked, persistent, as usual, in her enquiry.

'Well, lots of reasons.' Nancy was suddenly clear about where this was going. 'Have Mummy and Daddy been arguing a bit?'

'Not a bit,' Jazzy mumbled, as Hope sent her sister an angry glare.

'Oh dear. Tell me.'

Neither child spoke, just sat with ducked heads.

'Hope?'

When her granddaughter raised her head, tears were welling in her brown eyes. 'They shout at each other every night, Nana. It wakes us up.'

'Oh, darling.' Nancy put her arm round Hope. Jazzy was staring at her sister.

'They sound like they hate each other.' Tears trickled down Hope's cheeks, as fast as she wiped them away. 'They won't get a divorce, will they?'

'It's scary,' Jazzy put in. 'They fighted last night and Dada sounded really angry and made Mummy cry and scream.'

Nancy drew Jazzy into her embrace too. 'That's horrid for you. But all people argue, darling. You two fight all the time, and sometimes you sound very angry . . . And you cry too.'

'Not like that,' Jazzy said.

'No, I understand. Grown-ups fighting can sound really scary,' Nancy said. 'But Mummy and Daddy love each other very much, you know. They're both working so hard at the moment, to make the restaurant really good, and I think they're exhausted and a bit scratchy – you know how you get when you're tired.'

'So they aren't going to get divorced?' Hope persisted.

'No, definitely not,' Nancy said firmly, hoping she was right.

The two little girls went silent and she felt them relax a bit in her arms. But she was far from relaxed herself.

When she got home, her mother was upstairs taking a nap, her daughter dozing on the sofa downstairs, covered with the green throw, her face pinched with tiredness.

'Ross made her some chicken broth, which I gave her for lunch,' Louise told her later, as they sat with a cup of tea. She still looked crumpled and drawn. 'She ate some and I've left the rest in the fridge for later. But she seems so tired.'

It was overcast and muggy, a storm brewing, from the state of the coal-black sky and the thunder flies hovering in the air. The girls went outside to play chasing games in the garden, buoyed up, no doubt, by the half-ton of sugar they had just consumed.

Nancy nodded. 'I've made an appointment with Dr Khan on Friday. That GP she's got is useless. There's definitely something wrong.'

Louise nodded. 'How are you coping, Mum?'

'Not so bad.' That was what she said when anyone asked, even though it wasn't true. But if she'd told them what she was really feeling – even her daughter – they would have thought her the biggest bitch on the planet. What had been keeping her going, allowing her to be kind to her mother and deal with the trauma of having someone else in her space, was the thought of Jim. And today those thoughts seemed under threat. She longed to be alone to work out what might be wrong. But she wasn't going to phone him and ask.

In the silence that followed, Nancy glanced quickly outside to check the girls were out of earshot, then said, 'Lou, the girls are worried. They've heard you and Ross fighting at night.'

Louise's eyes widened. 'What? They'd sleep through World War Three.'

She told her daughter what the girls had said.

When she didn't immediately reply, Nancy asked, 'What's been going on?'

Louise sighed. 'Nothing, Mum. Honestly, it's not that bad. Yes, we have been arguing a bit recently. He gets back late, we're both knackered and the whole restaurant thing kicks off.'

Nancy looked her straight in the eye. 'Be honest with me. The girls were definitely not making it up.'

Louise sat hunched at the table, clasping her hands so tightly that her knuckles paled.

'Okay. I suppose it has been a bit full-on this past week. We lost a supplier because I refused to pay his exorbitant prices and Ross went ballistic. Maja left suddenly, as you know, and the girl who's replaced her is worse than useless. Then the bloody toilet in the ladies was blocked – the last fucking straw.' The look she turned on Nancy was despairing. 'And each time there's a problem, Ross blames me.'

'That's not fair.'

'I know, but I give as good as I get, I suppose. We can't seem to help winding each other up at the moment.'

Neither said a word for a while.

'You can't have the girls thinking you're getting a divorce, Lou. You and Ross should sit down with them and explain, reassure them.'

'You're right – although getting a divorce doesn't seem like such a bad idea right now.'

'Don't joke, Lou—' Her mobile interrupted her.

'Hi.' Jim's deep voice sounded tired. 'Sorry about earlier. I was in a foul mood, but I shouldn't have taken it out on you like that.'

'It's okay,' she said, aware of Louise's eyes fixed intently on her face.

'Is this a good time to talk?'

'Louise and the children are here for tea.'

'I'll call back later, then,' he said, and was gone.

'Everything all right?' Louise asked.

'Fine,' Nancy said firmly.

'You should ask him round for lunch on Sunday. I'm dying to meet him.'

'I'm not sure. Maybe it's a bit soon.'

'Soon for what? I'm only suggesting lunch.' Louise grinned. 'We won't bite, you know. And Ross could do with some male company.'

'Okay, well, maybe I'll ask him later.'

CHAPTER SEVENTEEN

Jim waited until he heard Chrissie go out before he phoned Nancy again. His wife had taken a sickie today, especially so she could break the bad news.

'I don't want to sell the house,' she'd said. 'I've told the agent to take it off the market.' Her tone was defiant.

They were in the kitchen, as usual, the only place they ever met, and it was gone ten. He had a student at ten-thirty, so her timing wasn't great: they couldn't have it out properly before Brian – a bloke Jim's age who fancied a retirement hobby – was punching the bell upstairs. As a result he'd given a crap lesson, hardly able to concentrate for the ramifications.

'You can't do that,' Jim told her.

'I can. I own this house too. You can't do anything without my permission.' She was unusually calm, which unnerved him.

'But you said – you said you were okay with it.'

'Well, I'm not. I love this house. I don't see why you should push me out just because you've got a new tart you want to shack up with.'

'She's not a tart.' Jim had told Chrissie about Nancy a couple of days before, thinking he should be honest with at least one of the women in his life. And that had been his mistake. Although his wife had suspected for a while that he had someone else, the fact of it did not go down well. And this was her revenge.

'Whatever. Phil at work says you have no right to sell it if I don't want to.'

Fuck Phil-at-work, Jim thought. *Busybody should keep his nose out of other people's affairs*.

'You'll have to get a mortgage, then, buy me out,' he said. 'Or what am I supposed to do? Stay shackled to you for the rest of my life?'

'Is that how you see it? "Shackled"? Bloody arse you've turned out to be, Jim Bowdry.'

'Yeah, yeah,' he said. 'But that doesn't alter the fact that we can't live together any more, Chrissie. You must see that.'

But whether she did or not, she was clearly enjoying her moment of power over him.

'Well, I'll just have to divorce you,' he said eventually, after a lot more spiteful wrangling. 'Make it legal. I didn't want to do that yet because it's expensive and neither of us has much to spare, but there's nothing else for it.'

He'd thought that might do the trick. Chrissie was notoriously close with money. But she'd just shrugged.

'I won't have to pay.' She glared at him defiantly. 'Do your worst, Jim. I'm past caring.'

Which obviously wasn't true, or she'd have sold the house, as they'd agreed, and got on with her life.

So then, to cap it all, he'd gone and been rude to Nancy. He'd felt almost sick, seeing the surprise on her face when he'd snapped at her. He wanted to spill the whole thing out, get it over with there and then. But he just couldn't bring himself to say the words.

As soon as he'd got home, he'd phoned Andrew Sitter and made another appointment. The solicitor didn't seem surprised to hear from him so soon. But what upset Jim was that there was no prospect in view of getting shot of his wife any time soon. Divorce took an age, and the deeper he got in with Nancy, the worse the betrayal would seem.

So it was with reluctance that he picked up the phone now, the lie looming huge in his central vision. She answered at once.

'Hi, Jim.'

'Okay to talk?'

'Yes. Mum's gone to bed. God, what a day.'

'Do you want me to come over for a bit?' he asked. Nancy had not invited him back to her house yet. Because of her mother, he assumed.

Nancy sighed. 'Thanks for the offer, but I'm tired. I think I'll just get an early night.'

He listened as she told him about her daughter's problems. 'Is this son-in-law of yours a bit of a dick?'

'No. Selfish, maybe, obsessive. My daughter's not always easy.'

'He's not being violent, is he?'

'God, I hope not. Lou was playing it down. Insisted it wasn't as bad as the girls were making out.' He heard her sigh again. 'It's difficult, living so close, being so involved with them all. I don't want to create a situation . . .'

'Families, eh?' he said, and she gave a soft laugh.

'Yes, always something. How's it going with your son?'

'Fine.'

'Is he staying for long?'

Jim didn't know how to reply. He'd forgotten what reason, if any, he'd given for Tommy being at home in the first place. 'He hasn't said.' He winced, still hoping that somehow this tangled mesh of untruths would quietly smooth out, like a shiny satin ribbon, and leave him free to follow his dream.

'By the way, you've been asked for lunch on Sunday,' Nancy was saying.

'With the family?'

'Yup. Louise and Ross, the girls, Mum. Could be others – Ross likes a crowd. Can you cope?'

Jim laughed nervously. 'Not sure. Especially after what you've just told me. Sounds like a bit of a hornets' nest.'

'That's my family you're calling hornets!'

'Ha. Sorry.' He paused. 'Would you like me to come?'

'I would . . . and I wouldn't.'

'Helpful.'

He heard her chuckle. 'I would, because I'd love you to meet them, and them you, obviously. And see the house, see where I live. And I wouldn't, because everyone will be looking you over, assessing you.'

'And you're worried I won't measure up?'

'God, no! It'll be awkward, that's all I'm saying. But we'll have to do it some time, I suppose, if we're . . .'

He didn't dare finish her sentence for her.

It was pouring with rain on Sunday morning as Jim got into the car he shared with his wife and drove north out of the city. The torrential summer downpour pounded on the roof and sluiced the windscreen, reminding him that he should replace the worn wiper that was screeching uselessly back and forth across the glass. He hardly used the car, but Chrissie never bothered with any maintenance, just left it to him.

He did not consider himself a nervous person, socially speaking, but now his stomach was knotted with anxiety at the thought of being scrutinized by Nancy's family. He didn't know a lot about her previous husband – she didn't talk about him much – but it was clear he was a highly educated classical musician of some standing. What was the family going to think of a broke country singer who did gigs in pubs and clubs and taught guitar to make ends meet? He couldn't imagine they would welcome him with open arms. But, worse, would seeing him through her family's eyes change Nancy's view of him?

He found the address too early. He didn't want to burst in on Nancy, so he drove around, parked beside a gate to a field and listened to music on his iPod for twenty minutes, which did little to soothe his nerves. He'd had a late gig the night before and he was tired. '*Shit*,' he said out loud, banging the steering wheel angrily. *Pull yourself together, Jim Bowdry*. A ciggie would steady him – since the row with Chrissie, he'd lapsed a bit, had a few – but there was no way he could meet Nancy reeking of smoke.

His phone rang. Tommy. He'd left a few messages for his son, and now, although he wasn't really in the mood, he knew he had to take the opportunity to talk to him.

'What's going on, Dad?' Tommy asked, after a brief greeting. His son's voice was light, bewildered rather than accusatory. Taking after his mother, Tommy was a slim, pale boy, with his mother's marmalade hair. Good-looking but a bit nerdy, he'd gone through his childhood without causing many ripples, his mother always the main act in the family. 'Have you really hooked up with someone else?'

'Yes . . . Yes, I suppose I have.'

'Would have been good to hear it from you,' Tommy said mildly.

'I know. Sorry, I should have called sooner. I'm afraid I've made a bollocks of it with everyone.'

He heard Tommy chuckle. 'Yeah, seems you have. Mum's going mental.'

'You know we haven't been . . . together for a long time, me and your mother. Not in a proper way.' He wasn't sure how much Tommy really understood about his parents' marriage, most of his information gleaned from Chrissie.

His son was silent for a moment. 'Tell me about this woman, Dad.'

'Nancy, her name's Nancy. I . . .' He stopped. How to tell his son that he loved someone other than his mother? 'She's . . . Well, I hope you'll meet her soon. She's my age, a pianist . . .' He couldn't think of anything else to say about Nancy without seeming to compare her to Chrissie. Now he was beginning to understand why Nancy had had such trouble telling her daughter about him. Tommy didn't speak, so he went on, 'I'm very fond of her, and—'

'Okay, Dad,' Tommy interrupted. 'Don't want to slip into the too-much-information zone. Well, Mum's just going to have to suck it up, I guess. But go easy on her, eh? She sounds like she's on the edge.'

'Sure. But you know your mum, Tommy, she likes a bit of a drama.' Which was obviously the wrong thing to say because there was an immediate harrumph from his son.

'For God's sake, Dad, you can hardly call breaking up a "drama".' Tommy's voice was suddenly spiky. 'That makes it sound totally unreal. It must be mega-stressful for Mum, especially at her age, being on her own. Okay for you, you've found someone new, but Mum's losing everything.'

Jim wanted to remind his son that he hadn't started this, that his mother's infidelity was the problem here. But instead he said, 'I know it's hard for her. It's hard for us both.'

'Maybe,' Tommy conceded reluctantly, 'but you still have to look after her. Even though you're splitting up, you have to make sure she's okay. Promise me, Dad.'

Jim promised. 'Tommy, I'm sorry about all this. Sorry for not being in touch. Been a difficult time, but no excuses.'

'It's okay.' Tommy's voice was kind. 'Just call me once in a while, yeah?'

They said goodbye on a subdued note, and Jim knew he could have handled things better. But that, he thought, as he saw the time and realized he was now late, seemed to be the story of his life.

By the time he pulled into Nancy's drive, he was feeling headachy and uncertain. If he'd had any choice, he'd have turned tail and fled.

The sight of Nancy coming out to greet him, however, brought a smile back to his face. She put her arms round him.

'So glad you're here,' she said.

'Sorry I'm late,' he whispered, casting an eye towards the big house. 'I'm scared to death.'

She laughed up at him, her grey eyes so loving that a bolt of absolute joy ran through his body, banishing all his worries about Tommy and the lunch ahead.

'Just be yourself,' she said, eyeing him up and down, clocking his black jeans – new for the occasion – his pressed white shirt with the black trim and buttons, his leather belt with the ornate silver buckle depicting a praying cowboy he'd got aeons ago from a guy he'd met in Memphis. 'You look great.'

He grinned. 'Should do, took me long enough.'

It started well. Ross, Jim saw, was larger than life as he manically stirred the contents of a vast steel paella pan with a huge wooden spatula, a jug of stock in his other hand, sweat pouring from his face, his laugh reverberating round the hot kitchen.

'Grab a glass, Jim, great you could come. Try this lovely little Rioja Blanco I found online, unless you'd prefer red, of course,' he said, bashing Jim on the back in welcome. 'At last, a man to rescue me from this sea of women.'

'Yeah, you're *so* hard done by,' Louise countered good-naturedly.

Jim took his first sip of the delicious wine, grateful that everyone appeared to be in a good mood. Even Nancy's mum looked better than he'd expected – and beautifully turned out – given Nancy's gloom about her condition. Although he thought she was eyeing him with a certain amount of suspicion.

It was quite a while later – and a couple of glasses of Rioja, another of a very palatable Tempranillo – that they were finally seated, the luscious paella posed in the middle of the farmhouse table like a guest of honour, vibrant with colour: saffron yellow, orange, pink, the shiny black of the mussel shells and green of the scattered parsley, pale lemon wedges neatly lining the metal pan. Jim thought he might faint from hunger as the rich, pungent aroma filled the air. He hadn't eaten any breakfast in an effort to avoid the kitchen and his wife.

Louise was holding the long spoon towards him. 'Help yourself, Jim.'

He looked at how much the others had taken and fought against the desire to pile his plate to the ceiling.

'You're a country singer, Mum says,' Louise began, when they all had food in front of them. Jim couldn't see Nancy in her daughter: Louise's features were small and sharp – boyish almost – her eyes a wary blue, although he could see how attractive she was when she smiled.

'Umm, yeah.' He stopped, unable to think of anything intelligent to say. But Nancy's daughter seemed to be waiting for more and silence fell. He swallowed a piece of chicken, which suddenly seemed huge and unwieldy in his mouth, and tried again. 'I have a band, the Bluebirds, but mostly I sing solo, write songs. One of my songs made it into the top ten a while back.'

'Great – what was it called?' Louise was smiling encouragingly.

'Oh, you won't have heard of it,' he said.

'I will. I love country music,' Ross shouted from the far end.

' "Don't Pretend You Love Me",' he said.

'Wasn't that the Judd Brothers?'

'Well remembered. It was their cover that made it into the charts. But I wrote the song.'

'Wow, good one.' Ross beamed. 'Louise hasn't a clue what you're talking about. She thinks country and western is cheesy and cheap, don't you, love?'

Jim saw her mouth tighten.

'I haven't really listened to much,' she said.

'Don't worry, most people won't admit to liking it, even if they do. Sort of a guilty secret,' he said.

'I'd be quite happy to say I liked it if I did,' Louise said, with a stiffness that surprised him.

'I'm sure you would,' Jim said, realizing his response echoed Louise's acerbity more than he'd intended. He saw her frown, but his head was heavy with booze and he suddenly couldn't think entirely straight. Casting a look at Nancy, he saw that her expression was tense.

'I didn't mean . . .' He tailed off as Louise got up from the table and fetched a glass jug of water from the fridge.

'You know Nancy's husband has his own madrigal group, the Downland Singers?' Frances, who had barely said a word up until then, was sitting next to Jim. Now she turned her gaze on him, a slight challenge in her faded blue eyes.

'I'm not married to him any more, Mum.' Nancy spoke up from across the table.

The old lady ignored her. 'They really are marvellous. You should listen to them some time.'

'I don't imagine Jim is particularly interested in madrigals, Granny,' Louise said.

'Can't blame him for that,' Ross muttered, glancing at Jim and raising his heavy eyebrows a fraction in brotherly solidarity, then turning away to concentrate on serving second helpings of paella.

'I'm interested in any form of music.' Jim addressed this to Louise. 'But you're right, I don't know much about madrigals.'

'Jim has a beautiful voice.'

He gave Nancy a quick smile, grateful for her support.

'Really? Well, you must sing for us one day.' Frances was gracious now and bestowed on him a queenly half-smile.

Christ, this is turning out to be a sodding train wreck, Jim thought. *Change the subject, man, just change the bloody subject*, he urged himself.

Ross held out his hand for Jim's plate.

'Fantastic food,' Jim said, reaching over to give it to him, at the same time knocking his glass with his elbow. It tipped over on the wooden table, spilling a sea of red wine across the surface and directly into Frances's lap.

'Bugger!' The word was out before he could stop it as he grabbed the glass and set it upright, bringing his pristine white cotton napkin down on the wine in a vain attempt to stop the flow. Frances had jerked her chair back, lifting the skirt of her cream linen dress to shake the liquid off, her face set, not uttering a single word.

'Bugger, bugger, bugger!' Jazzy repeated the word in a dreamy voice from the end of the table.

'Jazzy, stop it!' Louise's voice rang out across the room. 'That's a very bad word. You must never, *ever* say it again.'

Jim saw Hope's eyes widen with what appeared to be enjoyment and he shot her a desperate look. 'Sorry – I'm so sorry. It just slipped out,' he mumbled, as he continued to dab ineffectually at the spilled wine until Louise snatched the napkin from him and efficiently mopped the surface with a yellow cloth she'd brought from the sink.

'Are you okay, Granny?' she asked, through gritted teeth, ignoring Jim completely.

Jim looked at Nancy, expecting the worst, but was surprised to see her trying to repress a smile. It was all he could do not to grin back.

There was an uneasy silence.

'Think I'll check on the pudding.' Ross, face impassive, heaved himself to his feet, patting Jim on the shoulder as he went past, which must have infuriated Louise, because a second later she'd left her grandmother's side and was dragging Ross by the sleeve of his T-shirt towards the door. A door shut in another room, and there was the sound of muffled voices.

'I'm so sorry about your dress,' Jim said to Frances, to receive a small raise of the eyebrows in response.

Nancy got up. 'Shall we nip home, get that off you and in to soak, Mum?' she asked, as her mother continued to sit there in silence, the dark stain huge and accusatory on the light fabric.

Jim didn't know what to do or say to save the moment, so he kept silent and wished to God he'd never agreed to the lunch. He'd known it was a bad idea, and he was pretty sure Nancy had too, but they had both convinced themselves it would be all right.

He watched Nancy walk slowly across the gravel, her hand under her mother's elbow, leaving Jim alone with the two girls. They were staring at him expectantly, clearly intrigued as to what he might do next.

'It's not going well, is it?' he said, giving them an apologetic smile.

'Mummy gets cross with us when we spill things too,' Hope said.

Jazzy nodded. 'She says we should look what we're doing.'

'Your mum's right.'

'Do you play the piano when you sing?' Hope asked.

'I can play it . . . not as well as your grandmother, though. But no, I play guitar.'

'Can you sing "Let It Go"?' Jazzy was suddenly animated.

Jim frowned. 'I don't think I know that one.'

'You haven't seen *Frozen*?' The younger girl looked astonished. 'It's about this princess called Elsa who turns everything to ice and she hurted her sister by mistake, but they love each other in the end.'

'Sorry, I seem to have missed it.'

Hope shook her head at Jazzy in a slightly condescending manner. 'It's for children, Jazzy.'

'Sing me the song and I'll see if I recognize it,' Jim said, reducing both girls to embarrassed giggles. 'Go on.'

Jazzy frowned and shook her head, but after a minute Hope, looking acutely self-conscious and taking a deep breath, to Jim's delight began to sing.

She sang what Jim thought must be the chorus, with real passion, her young voice gaining strength to become clear and tuneful. After a minute or two, Jazzy joined in, waving her arms theatrically as a singer might.

When they stopped, both pink in the face, he clapped enthusiastically. 'Brilliant! That was brilliant, girls. Not an easy thing to do, sing unaccompanied.'

They were grinning from ear to ear now. 'We did it in a show at this theatre group we go to after school,' Hope told him. 'Jazzy's seen the film about a hundred times.'

At that moment, Ross reappeared and Jim heard Louise running upstairs. 'Sorry about that.' He stood by the work island and rubbed his hands together, offering a tense grin to his daughters and Jim. 'Who wants meringues and homemade strawberry ice cream?'

CHAPTER EIGHTEEN

'Oh . . . my . . . God.' Jim slumped onto Nancy's sofa with a long groan. 'Could I have fucked it up any more royally?'

Nancy giggled. It was after six and they had just got back from Louise's house, where they'd been playing a challenging game of Sorry with the girls for the last hour. Her mother had not returned to the party, saying she was worn out, and was currently watching television – at high volume – in her bedroom, with a bowl of broth and a ham sandwich on a tray for her supper. Louise had taken herself off for a long walk with a reluctant Ross; she had barely spoken to Nancy or Jim since the spilled-wine incident.

'Oh, I don't know, the girls clearly love you and Ross would, too, if he was allowed to.'

Jim brushed his hands across his hair. 'But Frances and Louise think I'm a nightmare.'

'Chucking wine in Mum's lap probably wasn't the best getting-to-know-you tactic.'

They laughed as Nancy sat down beside him and he took her in his arms.

'Then there was "Bugger!" '

'Yup, could have done without that as well.'

Nancy put her arm across Jim's chest and laid her head against his shoulder. She wanted to forget about the tensions in her bloody family.

'You know how it is. Things start to slide and then everything you do only makes it worse,' he said, his voice lowered.

Looking up at him, Nancy said, 'Louise is in a bad way at the moment, Jim. You just got in the firing line.'

'Hmm, not sure about that. Obviously things aren't so hot between her and Ross, but I think she took an instant dislike to me . . . Just didn't get me at all.'

'She's tough, my daughter. But she's fair in the end. She'll come round.' Nancy paused. 'In fact, I thought she might be quite well disposed towards you, considering the current fracas with her father and the diva.'

'I suppose she's right to be wary of someone who's after her mum.'

Nancy didn't reply. She was embarrassed and disappointed by her daughter's *froideur* towards Jim. She'd hoped they would get on – in fact, she couldn't imagine anyone not getting on with Jim, he was so easy-going, so charming. But he hadn't been at his best today, she accepted that.

'Too much bloody Rioja,' Jim was saying. 'Always a mistake to drink on an empty stomach. I'm sorry, Nancy, I feel as if I've let you down, made more problems for you.'

'Rubbish. It's just what happens with families, you must know that. What does your son think of you being with some-one else?'

'Uh, he's sort of on the fence. Very protective of his mother, like Louise, but he knows we haven't been close for years . . .' He stopped, looked suddenly disconcerted.

Nancy wondered what this ex of his was like to make him so jumpy every time the subject came up. She waited for him to go on, but he didn't, a tension similar to the one in the cafe descending on them both.

When Jim still didn't speak, his gaze distant, distracted, she pulled away from his arms, perching on the edge of the cushion so she could see him properly. The look he sent her was anguished.

'What is it? Has something happened?' She felt a crush around her heart.

'No, no, nothing's happened.' She could see him pulling himself together. But it seemed like an effort. 'You'd think us being together would be so simple at our age,' he said, 'but sometimes it feels as if we're buried in our past and can't get free.'

'What do you mean, exactly?'

He sighed, forced a smile. 'I just wanted your family to like me, Nancy. I'm frightened that if they don't you'll be put off me.'

She roared with laughter, relieved he was worrying about nothing more sinister. 'It would take a lot more than Louise's sniping to put me off you, Jim Bowdry.' She lay back on the sofa again, their bodies close.

Neither said any more for a while, but Nancy's heart was beating double time. 'Do you want to stay tonight?' She spoke impetuously, then held her breath as she realized what she was asking. She had thought of little else in the past few weeks, wondering what it might be like to make love again, to expose her ageing body to another man, to give herself to Jim in such an important way. Christopher had been her first and only partner, and his lovemaking had been a cautious, controlled manipulation of his own pleasure. He'd been very specific about what he did and didn't like, but rarely enquired about Nancy's desires. It was never passionate, not even in the beginning. She knew things would be different with Jim – even the kisses they had exchanged were light years away from her experience with her ex-husband. *There will never be a perfect time. Mum might be here for ever*, she thought, as she waited, trembling inside, for Jim to reply.

Jim seemed to have gone very still. 'What about your mother?'

'She's in the attic.'

They looked at each other.

'What do you think?' Nancy asked, her heart kicking against her ribs. 'We don't have to . . . you know . . . do anything.' She suddenly felt very bold.

Jim laughed, pulling her hard against him. 'No, but then again . . .'

They drank some beers Nancy had in the fridge and she cooked a cheese omelette, serving it with a green salad. But although they ate the meal together at the kitchen table, neither was concentrating on the food. Nancy felt as if her whole body were suspended, as if she were holding her breath for a very long time, making her light-headed, giggly. Jim was animated too, his gaze constantly finding hers, drawing her in, flirting with her as she was with him, his blue eyes bottomless and hungry. It felt as if they were caught up in a feverish tempest, exclusive, just the two of them, her mother forgotten, the family forgotten, the rest of the world ceasing to exist.

Food dispatched, Jim reached over and took her hand, raised his eyebrows a little. 'Ready?' he asked her softly. They got to their feet and tiptoed to the stairs.

He held her hand as they paused on the landing to listen, but there was silence from Frances's room above, the television no longer blasting through the house. Without a word, they made their way along the corridor to Nancy's room. It was a large, light space, windows on two sides as well as the skylight, although now it was dark outside as Nancy drew the heavy grey-blue patterned curtains along the wooden rail. She had kept the furnishings plain, the room containing only the essentials: a white-painted built-in wardrobe, bed, padded bucket chair, a rag rug on the bare wood floor next to the bed and a table in the corner on which was a mirror and the meagre ranks of creams and cosmetics that constituted Nancy's face care. On the bed there was a beautiful tartan rug from the fifties in faded blues, greens and pinks that she had picked up at an antiques fair the previous year. Nothing in the room remained of her marriage, for which, at that moment, she was extremely grateful.

They stood at the end of the bed staring at each other, neither seeming to know what to do next.

'Are you absolutely sure about this?' Jim whispered.

She nodded without hesitation, unable to speak, suddenly cold and shivery.

He pulled her to him, traced his finger along her lips, brushed a strand of hair off her cheek so gently so that she could barely feel his touch, yet every cell in her body responded as if to a clarion call.

Jim was hesitant, almost as if he didn't believe it was finally safe to continue, but when their lips came together it was as it had been that night in the car: there was a certainty, an absolute rightness, which washed away any doubt.

'Let me look at you,' he said, pulling her T-shirt up until she lifted her arms and it was over her head and flung to the floor. He hooked the straps of her bra off her shoulders, pulling them down to reveal her small breasts, his hands cupping them as he bent to kiss first one nipple, then the other, his tongue teasing her skin until she was ready to explode.

Coaxing her back onto the bed, he hurled aside the rug and the duvet, then knelt in front of her, rhythmically running his fingers along her body from top to toe, dropping soft kisses on her thighs, her stomach, her breasts, her neck and upwards to her lips again, his mouth seeking hers with increased impatience.

'God, you're beautiful,' he muttered.

But all she could do was moan with pleasure, the recent fears about her figure, about her age, about her ability to allow another man full rein with her body seemed irrelevant now as she undid the buttons of Jim's shirt, drew his jeans down over his buttocks, felt his hard smoothness in her hands.

For a while they did little else but revel in the closeness of their naked bodies, an endless kiss holding her spellbound, almost in a trance, so that when they began to make love, it felt like an extension of that caress, part of the all-consuming desire that had existed between them from the start.

Then, suddenly, it was over. Jim's erection sank to nothing and a minute later he rolled off her uttering a low groan.

'What is it?' she asked, thinking he might have heard her mother call. She felt flushed, almost dizzy from the unaccustomed sex and lay there weakly, waiting for him to reply.

'Sorry . . . I don't know what happened.' He covered his face with his hands.

'It doesn't matter,' she said quickly.

'It does! It bloody does!' Jim had hauled himself up and swung his feet to the floor, his naked back all she could see of him as he sat on the far side of the bed.

She reached out and stroked his skin. 'It doesn't. Come back to bed . . . please.'

He turned his head, a strand of grey hair, come loose from the ponytail, flopping across his face. She smiled. 'Come on,' she urged, and he finally lay down again, pulling the duvet over their nakedness.

The silence was heavy with Jim's angst. 'It's not been my day,' he said. Then rolling on his side to face her, he added, 'I haven't had sex for so long, seems like I'm out of practice. I'm so sorry.'

'Stop, Jim. I've told you, I don't mind.'

'But I ruined everything. The first time . . . I've been imagining this for so long . . . It was supposed to be perfect.'

She lifted her head to kiss him lightly on the lips. 'It's been a stressful day,' she said. 'Doesn't help having Mum along the corridor.'

He smiled, his face clearing a little. 'No, but . . .'

Nancy put her finger to his mouth. 'But nothing.'

'I should probably go,' he said.

'No, please. Stay with me. Let's sleep together. Don't run away.'

For a long while they lay in the darkness in each other's arms, neither saying a word. Nancy's body gradually came down from the interrupted sex and she found her eyes closing, the nearness of Jim's body, so loving and warm, allowing her to drift off into a much-needed sleep.

She awoke a long time later, in the half-light of the summer morning, to Jim's hand running up between her legs. They didn't speak this time, there were no lingering kisses, but the sex was fierce, almost greedy, unfinished business that, if anything, made this coming together all the sweeter. And when it was over, they both lay on their backs, smiling like idiots.

'That was perfect,' Nancy murmured.

'This sounds like a cliché, but I never imagined I could feel like this about anyone.' He rolled over to look at her. 'You literally take my breath away, Nancy.'

She felt unexpected tears gathering behind her eyes. 'It is the strangest thing.'

'Had I better get going?' Jim whispered, as he cradled her in his arms. 'I'm not sure I can deal with your mother over the cornflakes.'

'If you leave now, you'll wake everyone, including the girls. That gravel is the most treacherous on earth.'

He laughed. 'What shall I do, then?'

'Well, we could go to sleep again and see what happens. Mum never gets up early. I take her a cup of tea about eight usually.'

'Louise and the children will see my car when they go to school,' he said.

'So they see it. We haven't done anything wrong, Jim.'

'Yeah, but I don't want to antagonize your daughter any more than I already have.'

'Too late,' Nancy said, realizing she didn't give a fig about any of it at that precise moment. She was buzzing with a hazy contentment. 'Come here and stop worrying,' she said, pulling his tall body once more into her embrace.

'I heard that man leaving this morning.' Her mother's mouth was set in a dangerously disapproving line when Nancy went in with her morning tea. Frances was sitting up in bed, propped against the pillows, a very old Dick Francis, pages yellowing at the edges, open in her hand.

'I'm sorry he disturbed you.' Nancy steeled herself. Now Jim had left, the euphoria was fading and tiredness scratched at her eyes. For a moment she felt like a naughty child, but her body purred like a woman, delightfully bruised by Jim's lovemaking. She still couldn't quite believe that she had managed to let go to that extent, to find such a powerful sensuality within herself. Jim's touch had made it so easy.

'Hmm,' said her mother. 'I hope you know what you're doing.'

'I'm going to boil you an egg,' Nancy said, turning to leave the room. There was no mileage in having the discussion about Jim her mother so obviously wanted. 'I'll bring it up.'

'No need,' Frances replied, in a martyred tone. 'I shall be down in a minute.'

Nancy plodded downstairs, her nerves jangling.

When her mother appeared, already dressed, about twenty minutes later, it was clear there was an agenda from the chilly smile she offered her daughter and the way she held herself unusually straight and stiff, every muscle in her body denoting opprobrium.

'I think I should go home today,' she said, as soon as she was seated and Nancy had placed the egg and crispbread her mother liked in front of her.

'Because of Jim?'

'No. I just feel I would like to be at home. I'm not ill any more and there's no need for me to be here.'

'Mum, please, you don't have to go.'

Frances offered a brittle smile. 'I know I don't, darling. But I feel I should.'

'This is because of Jim, isn't it?'

Her mother shook her head. 'How you run your life is your own business, Nancy. You're far too old for me to be telling you what you should do.'

'But you don't approve.'

There was a long silence while Frances spread a thin layer of butter on the crispbread, carefully taking it all the way to the edges. When she finally looked up at Nancy, her eyes were cold. 'This man. You barely know him. He drinks too much, swears in such a rude way in front of the girls . . . He's hardly in Christopher's league, darling.'

Nancy held her breath and tried to control the kick of rage that felt like a physical pain in her gut. '"Christopher's league"? Meaning a man who thinks it's okay to have an affair with someone half his age, then run off and leave me after thirty-four years of marriage?'

Frances raised her eyebrows. 'That isn't what I mean, and you know it.'

'I know that you're being snobbish, Mum. Your remark about the madrigals yesterday proved that.'

'Well, Christopher is a highly talented and sophisticated musician, you can't deny it.'

'So what? Christopher left me, Mum! *He left me*. He isn't my husband any more because *he walked out on me*.' She couldn't help raising her voice.

'I'm sure he had his reasons.' Her mother spoke softly.

Flabbergasted, Nancy was catapulted back to childhood. She knew she had never been the daughter her mother wanted. But no child could ever have lived up to her impossible standards because Frances's mantra was always 'Be the very best', not 'Do your very best'. There was a difference.

'It doesn't matter now,' Nancy said tiredly.

But Frances hadn't quite finished. 'I know you've been terribly hurt by Christopher, and obviously I don't approve of what he did. How could I? But that doesn't mean you should settle for just anyone. I'm only saying this because I'm worried about you, darling.'

When Nancy said nothing because she was afraid of what she might say, Frances added, 'I'm sure Louise would agree with me about this Jim fellow.'

And when Nancy still stayed silent, Frances got up from the table. 'I'll go up and pack my things, if you wouldn't mind running me home later.'

Nancy sat alone in the kitchen, exhausted with anger. She should have been relieved that her mother wanted to go home, but she wasn't. Things had been aired that it would be hard to forget, but Frances was old and ill, whatever she said, and Nancy couldn't imagine how she would manage on her own. So she felt hideously guilty for provoking her mother's departure, the guilt sitting alongside a dull knot of anger, anger that was both historical but also spiky raw, a painful reminder of what her mother really thought of her.

But fall out with Frances she could not, so she took a deep breath and dragged herself upstairs.

'Please, Mum. Don't go. It's stupid.'

'I'll be fine, darling.' Her mother's face had softened, perhaps thinking back on what she'd said. 'You've been wonderful, but I really would like to get home.'

Nancy had no idea whether she meant it or not, but she didn't argue, just went back downstairs to phone Heather, who was due for a lesson at ten-thirty.

CHAPTER NINETEEN

'Dad, hi.' Louise groaned inwardly. The last person she wanted to talk to this morning was her father, but she hadn't bothered to check the phone display before answering: she was involved with a massive list of ingredients she needed to order for Ross.

'I hadn't heard back about the wedding, Louise. Did you get our invitation? We sent them out a couple of weeks ago.'

'Our', 'we': she was already annoyed. And also annoyed with herself that she'd forgotten, in all that was going on, to write back with her fake excuse.

'Uh, yeah, I got it. Sorry, we've been so busy, I haven't had time to reply.'

She heard him breathing at the other end of the phone.

'I'm really hoping you can come,' he said.

Louise had worked out the lie weeks ago, the one about her friend in Scotland getting married the same weekend, but now the moment had come, the lie wouldn't.

'Dad, listen.'

'I don't know if your mother told you, but I was hoping that the girls might like to be bridesmaids.'

'Oh. No, she didn't.' This lie seemed to have no problem slipping out.

'So would that be fun?'

Fun? she thought. *Fun? Is he kidding?* She hesitated. Now she was actually talking to her father, she found herself not wanting to be cruel. 'Dad, look . . . I don't think it's such a good idea for us to come.'

A moment's silence at the other end. Then he said, 'Oh. Why not?'

'I don't know . . .'

Christopher's tone hardened. 'Has your mother put you up to this?'

'No! Of course not. In fact, Mum said we should go.'

Her father gave a heavy sigh. 'Louise, I know you're still angry with me, and I'm not stupid, I understand why, I do. But Tatjana and I are getting married. Nothing is going to change that.'

She waited.

'I just really wish you and the girls . . . and Ross, of course, could be with us on the day . . . It would mean so much to us.'

Louise doubted very much that it would mean a single thing to the bloody trollop he was marrying, but her father's quiet, almost humble request, struck a chord. He was never humble. 'You say you understand, Dad, but can you imagine what it will be like for me, watching you canoodling with a woman who isn't my mother, doing the whole white wedding bit like some dumb twenty-year-old? Like Mum never existed?' She kept her voice even, but she knew the choice of the word 'dumb' would wind him up.

He didn't answer at once, but when he did his response sounded tired. There was no anger or irritation in it. 'I know it's been hard for you.'

'It still is.' Louise felt the pain of her own intransigence. 'Let it go,' everyone had told her repeatedly. 'He won't change.' And she knew that to be true. 'Listen, I don't know if we'll come. I need to think about it.'

'It would mean the world to me if you were all there, Louise. You're my family.'

Which, Louise had to admit, was true. *Tatjana might be his wife*, she thought, *but the girls and I are his proper family.* 'I'll ring you back,' she said, 'let you know, one way or the other.'

'Wonderful.' Her father obviously thought he'd said enough to persuade her to come. And he was right, he had. She would go, whatever it cost her, because she believed him when he said it would mean so much to him. But there was no way the girls would be bridesmaids to Tatjana. That was a step too far.

Ross poked his head round the door of the small office at the back of the restaurant. 'Did you get everything?'

'Almost.' She saw he was just about to say something, but he stopped and just nodded. They had had a long talk the night before. Louise had told him about the girls hearing them fight and he had been, predictably, horrified and ashamed. So they had agreed to a truce for the time being. A truce Louise was already finding hard to keep: she'd checked the bank account earlier. 'That was Dad. I've sort of said we'll go to the wedding.'

Ross moved into the room and closed the door behind him. Kim, the girl who came to clean, was hoovering the corridor. 'Right. Well, that's probably a good decision. Are you okay with it?'

She shook her head. 'Not really. But he badly wants us to come. I didn't have the heart to pretend we were busy.'

Ross laughed. 'Trouble with you, Lou, is you're too honest.'

'Anyway, Mum obviously doesn't care any more. Did you see Jim's car still in the drive this morning?'

'Yeah . . . I wondered about that.' Ross had left for Shoreham harbour at crack of dawn to choose the fish for a bouillabaisse he was planning, so she hadn't had the chance to speak to him earlier.

'I think she's gone mad,' Louise said. 'He's dreadful.'

'That's a bit harsh, love. Seemed like a good guy to me.'

Louise glared at him. 'Good for a couple of pints and a bit of male bonding down the pub on a Friday night, maybe, but certainly not good enough to be with my mother. He was drunk!'

'He wasn't . . . not really. He was just enjoying himself.'

'Do you think . . . do you think they were having sex last night?' Louise's question was tentative.

Ross chuckled. 'Well, that's usually the reason a man stays over in a woman's bed, love.'

'It's not funny! It's disgusting. And with poor Granny probably listening to the whole thing upstairs.'

'I'm surprised he could get it up with her in the attic. It'd certainly put me off my stroke.'

'Ross! That's my mother you're talking about.'

Ross was bent over at this point, his big shoulders shaking, wheezing with suppressed laughter. Louise wanted to kill him. 'I think it's brilliant,' he said, when he got his breath. 'Your mum's clearly into him big-time, I saw those looks they were giving each other over the paella. She deserves some fun, don't you think?'

'Not with that man.'

'You're such a prude sometimes, Lou,' Ross said mildly. 'Being someone's mum doesn't stop you having sex, you know.'

Louise raised her eyebrows. 'Really? Could have fooled me.'

Ross's face darkened. 'Christ, you certainly know how to hit a man below the belt.' And with that he turned and stamped out, slamming the door behind him.

Left alone, Louise laid her head on her arms on the desk. She shouldn't have said that to Ross, she knew it. But her father was bonking for Britain and making a public display of his affections, her mother had allowed that dreadful cowboy to spend the night, and her own husband hadn't been near her in ages – literally months. What was the world coming to when her ageing parents were having a better time in the sack than she was?

Her sex life with Ross had been good until after Jazzy was born. But it had been a difficult birth, high forceps, loads of stitches – Louise hadn't been able to sit down without a rubber ring for weeks afterwards – and she'd found sex very painful for a long time. But they'd got back on track and things were almost normal till last winter, when Ross had seemed to lose interest. He'd said he was tired, that he was under too much strain, which was certainly true, but Louise sensed there was something else. Not some*one* else, she didn't think for a minute he was having an affair – he wouldn't waste valuable time that he could be spending on food-related issues – but he exuded a sort of new hostility towards her. Maybe she was being paranoid, but she felt as if Ross were punishing her for something. She had given up trying to seduce him: it was just too humiliating each time he fobbed her off. But that, added to all the other frictions between them at present, was not helping her temper.

Her phone rang again. This time it was her mother. *Why won't they all just leave me alone?* Louise thought, before exchanging a weary greeting.

'I thought I'd let you know that Granny decided to go home today,' her mother told her.

'Oh, why?'

Her mum sighed. 'We had a bit of a fight. I think she just wants to be in her own house. I tried to persuade her to stay, but she was determined. You know what she's like when she sets her mind to something.'

'Certainly do. What was the fight about?'

'Nothing, really. It's probably good she's gone. Any longer and we'd be bound to rub each other up the wrong way.'

'Will she be all right on her own?'

'I don't know . . . We'll see. Anyway, I've settled her in and I'll go back and check on her this evening.'

'Right.' Louise wanted to ask about Jim. Wanted to find out if the row between Nancy and Frances had really been, as she suspected, about him staying over. It made sense. Granny hadn't liked him either. But Louise hated the thought that her mother might not tell her the truth, so she didn't probe further.

As she put the phone down, tears of frustration trickled down her face. She prided herself on being strong, but she'd always been able to turn to her mother for help and advice. Now this bloody man was threatening to come between them. How could she be close to her mother if neither of them was willing to be honest about Jim Bowdry?

CHAPTER TWENTY

It was late afternoon before Nancy was able to phone Jim. She'd spent all day settling her mother, shopping for food – in the vain hope she might eat something – warming the place up, changing the sheets, then nipping back later to make sure she was all right. Her mother had been very quiet, but she seemed glad to be home. Nancy had cancelled the appointment she'd made with her own doctor for Friday. She'd have to contend with the twelve-year-old half-wit instead.

'I've arranged for you to see Dr Henderson on Thursday,' she'd told Frances, who was sitting on the sofa covered with a soft throw, looking very cosy, almost asleep.

Her mother's eyes sprang open. 'Is there any need, darling? I'm perfectly all right now.'

'He wanted to check you out. He was worried about your weight, Mum.'

Frances shook her head in irritation. 'There's no point in my going to see the doctor so he can tell me I'm thin. I know I am.' She gave an exasperated sigh and closed her eyes again.

'He wants to find out if there's a reason why you are,' Nancy said, but her mother pretended not to hear and Nancy didn't want to upset her again.

Now she was back home, and although she was enjoying the solitude, she was very uneasy about her mother.

'She's so bloody stubborn,' she told Jim. 'I know she knows there's something wrong, but she refuses to do anything about it.'

'Well, I suppose it's her life.'

'You're telling me I should do nothing? Not bother to get her checked out? Really?'

'I'm not telling you anything . . . but maybe she doesn't want to have tests and scans and ops and shit. It's her call.'

'So I just leave her to die.'

'Hey, Nancy, don't get upset.'

She swallowed hard, wiping the tears from her cheeks. 'It might be something simple, something that could be fixed without too much trouble. And then she'd be fine again.'

'It might.' Jim sounded dubious.

'We had a fight, about you staying over. That was why she huffed off home.'

'Ah. I'm sorry about that.'

Nancy sniffed. 'Don't be. It was wonderful.'

Jim was silent for a moment. 'Seems tough that you're paying for it now, though.'

She listened to him breathing, gave a long sigh. 'Will you come over tomorrow?'

'Love to.'

'We'll have the place to ourselves.'

'Fantastic. I've got a student at four. I'll come after that.'

They said goodbye and Nancy felt calm for the first time in a while. The sound of his voice, the tenderness she'd heard in it, his concern for her and her problems, was like balm to her soul. Still holding the phone, she leaned back against the sofa cushions and closed her eyes.

Her phone woke her. Glancing at the clock she saw it was nearly seven. She must have been dozing on the sofa for a couple of hours.

'Lindy, hi.' She struggled to sit upright, her neck stiff from the awkward angle at which she'd been lying. She was cold – it had been such a rubbish summer so far.

'How are you?' Lindy sounded a bit strange.

'I'm fine. You?'

'Yeah, good.' Her friend paused and Nancy waited for her to go on. 'Just wondering if I could pop round.'

'Now?' It was the last thing Nancy wanted.

'Just for a few minutes. I'll be up your way in about twenty. There's something I want to talk to you about.'

'Yes, of course. Come in and have a glass of something.'

'I won't stay long.'

Nancy didn't ask what Lindy wanted to talk about, but she felt a certain uneasiness as she waited for her friend to appear. Lindy was always rushing about so it was perfectly possible that she was passing, but she had sounded unusually grave when she'd said she wanted to talk. Perhaps she needed a favour. But Lindy didn't beat about the bush. If there was something she wanted Nancy to do for her, she'd come right out and say it.

Nancy went upstairs and washed her face, brushed her hair, put on a clean T-shirt and some lip balm. She'd been on the run all day and she felt sweaty and tired still, despite the snooze. But then, she thought, with a small smile, she hadn't slept much last night. The row with her mother had sidetracked her, but now she sat on her bed and remembered. It seemed nothing short of miraculous the way she felt about Jim . . . and the fact that her feelings appeared to be reciprocated. It wasn't just sex, fantastic as that was between them: they could talk too, never stopped. She reckoned she'd said more to Jim in the two months they'd known each other than she'd said to Christopher in thirty-plus years of marriage. Still smiling to herself, already dreaming about seeing him tomorrow, she heard Lindy's car in the driveway and went downstairs to greet her friend.

Lindy immediately gave her a big hug. Then, without more ado, she took hold of Nancy's arms and guided her backwards, down onto a kitchen chair.

'Darling, I've got something to tell you and you're not going to like it.'

Frowning, Nancy stared at her. 'What do you mean?'

'Can I get us both a glass of wine first?' Her friend was already moving towards the fridge, where she found a bottle and unscrewed the top. 'Glasses?'

Nancy pointed to the cupboard above the dishwasher, her heart beginning to pound.

'Right,' said Lindy, sitting at the end of the table, next to Nancy and handing her a glass. 'Now, there's no easy way to say this. Jim's married.'

Nancy stared at her. 'He was . . . but he's divorced now.'

'No, he's not. He's married and still living with his wife.'

Nancy felt a fluttering in her chest and realized she was trying to breathe. 'That's rubbish. They separated three years ago when Chrissie ran off with some barman.'

Lindy did not take her eyes off Nancy's face. 'No, Nancy. They live together in a house off Sutherland Road. Fact.'

'I don't believe you. Who told you this?'

Lindy leaned back and let out a weary sigh.

'It's a long story. Chemmy, my boss at the shop, knows Jim because his son, Tanner, does guitar lessons with him, at his house.' She pursed her lips, eyeing Nancy with real concern. 'Tanner's met Chrissie, darling, she often opens the door to him.'

'Chemmy told you this? Why? Why were you talking about Jim?' She felt confused, as if her head were filled with sand. She couldn't work out what to focus on first.

'Okay. It happened like this. I was at work and my boss was there. Tanner dropped by on his way home from his lesson.' Lindy stopped, checked Nancy's face. And seeing whatever she saw, she reached over and took her hand, gave it a squeeze. 'You want me to go on?'

Nancy nodded dumbly, quickly removing her hand.

'So Tanner was chatting to his father, saying that Jim had been encouraging him to sing and that he thought he might do some singing lessons as well as guitar. Chemmy wasn't best pleased about that because, of course, he'd be the one funding the lessons and he hadn't been too keen on his son becoming a musician in the first place. Anyway, I heard all this and asked, "Is that Jim Bowdry you're talking about, by any small chance?" '

Nancy took a gulp of wine. It tasted sharp and too cold and she put the glass down hard on the wooden table.

'Tanner said it was, and I said, "What a coincidence. I know him and my friend is dating him." ' Then Chemmy said he thought Jim was married. Turns out Chemmy's sister-in-law works with Jim's wife at the council. God, small world, eh?'

When Nancy didn't respond, Lindy went on, 'It was Chrissie who'd suggested Jim as a guitar teacher for Tanner.'

Nancy's brain was spinning. She couldn't make head or tail of what Lindy was talking about. Tanner, Chemmy, a sister-in-law with the council . . . She shook her head. 'I don't understand.'

Her friend took a long breath. 'No, well, I don't blame you.' She topped up her glass. 'But, Nance, it makes sense, no? You said Jim's never taken you back to his, which is odd – or, at least, I think it's odd after all this time. If he were on his own, wouldn't that be the first place he'd take you? Especially with all your family crowding in on you over here.'

'He said his son was staying.'

Lindy raised an eyebrow, and didn't reply.

Nancy tried hard to marshal her thoughts, trawl back over the many conversations she'd had with Jim. *Did he actually say he was divorced?* 'He never wanted to talk about her,' she said, remembering the tension when she'd brought up his family.

Lindy just nodded.

'But he definitely said they were separated. He always refers to her as his ex.'

'Well, looks like she's not.'

'You don't know that for certain.' She didn't think that even she believed what she was saying, so she stopped and stared straight ahead, at the jumble of colourful felt-tip and painted images, pinned to the fridge with magnets, that the girls had done. None of it made sense.

'Lucky you hadn't got around to the bonking bit yet,' Lindy, ever practical, suggested.

'We did. Last night.'

'Oh, darling.' Lindy frowned, mouth tightening. 'Bastard.'

'He's not a bastard,' Nancy blurted out. 'You've met him, Lindy. Jim's not a bastard.'

'I must say, I didn't have him down for one.'

'There's got to be some explanation,' Nancy said.

'What are you going to do?'

'Ring him, I suppose. Find out what it is.'

Jim answered on the second ring. Lindy was long gone. She had been reluctant to leave Nancy alone, although Nancy had assured her that she'd be fine. In the end she'd virtually had to push Lindy out of the door, desperate to be alone and away from her friend's kind but pitying gaze. Then she had just sat for a long time as the summer light faded, baffled by what she had heard. She plumbed her brain, searching for deceit in Jim's eyes, his words, his touch, but she could find none. He was loath to discuss his ex-wife – wife? – but that seemed fair: she didn't much like discussing Christopher.

And the fact that he hadn't asked her home . . . If his son was there, why would he?

'Hey, Nancy,' Jim's deep voice made her heart flutter.

'Hi.' She swallowed hard. She was not going to cry.

'I've been walking around in a daze,' he was saying, 'after last night.'

She took a deep breath, batted his words away. 'Lindy came round just now. She told me that you're married and still living with your wife.' The words sounded aggressive, rude. She immediately wanted to retract them. There was a stunned silence at the other end of the line. 'She works for Tanner's father.'

'Right . . .' she heard Jim whisper.

'Is it true?'

'Nancy . . .'

'Is it true, Jim?'

She heard him sigh. 'Yes, I am still married to Chrissie. And yes, she does still live in the same house. But we haven't lived as a married couple for three years, just as I told you.'

'You told me you were separated.'

'We *are*. We live in different parts of the house. She lives downstairs, I live upstairs. We have nothing to do with each other, I swear.'

'Lindy says that Chrissie was the one who recommended you to Tanner. And Tanner says she often opens the door to him. That's not exactly nothing.'

'She opens the door because her room is closest. And, yes, I suppose we talk sometimes. God, Nancy – you've got to believe me that it's totally over with her. We haven't had sex or anything, we barely speak – we haven't for years, not since Benji.'

Nancy heard the desperation in his voice. 'Then why didn't you tell me?' The question was the only one she really wanted answered. It wasn't Jim's circumstances that tore at her heart, it was that he'd lied to her so comprehensively.

'I – it was bloody dumb of me, but when we first met I thought if I said I was still married and living with Chrissie but not living with her it would sound wrong and you wouldn't believe it was over. Men always say that just to get their leg over. You'd have run a mile.' He paused. 'You would, wouldn't you?'

'Why aren't you divorced, if you've been separated for three years?'

'Money. It costs a lot to get divorced. And before I met you, it didn't seem important. Neither of us was with anyone else.'

They both fell silent.

'I'm so sorry, Nancy. I've been kicking myself for not telling you the whole story right from the start. It's been tearing me apart. There were a couple of times when I nearly did, but then I thought you'd just walk . . . and the longer I left it, the bigger the hole I'd dug got.'

She didn't answer. She didn't know what to think.

'But this doesn't change anything. Certainly doesn't change how I feel about you, Nancy. Please, please, believe me. My wife means nothing to me any more. Nothing. And she knows that. Our relationship is totally non-existent. We've just never bothered to sort out the technical side.'

'Doesn't change anything?' Nancy was stunned. 'How can you say that? Of course it changes things. It changes everything. You're a married man, living with your wife. You lied to me.'

Jim emitted a low, agonized groan. 'Nancy, please, will you let me come over, explain to you properly, face to face?'

She wanted nothing more, in that moment, to see him, to lie in his arms, for him to tell her it didn't matter until she believed him. 'No. Don't come over.'

'But . . . we've got to talk about this. We can't let it ruin things. I've filed for divorce now – I saw the solicitor yesterday. It's only a matter of time . . .'

'I've got to go.' She put the phone down without saying goodbye.

It was as if the world had gone very silent. She shivered, feeling disoriented. Christopher's betrayal, although shocking at the time, was somehow in character, and her connection with him had faded to an almost perfunctory state by the time he'd left. But Jim . . . Jim was her soulmate. Jim was . . . Jim was . . .

Louise was on the doorstep just before eight. 'Mum, hi.' She peered at her. 'God, you look rough. Did you have a bad night?'

Nancy nodded, waiting for her daughter to state her business.

'I've sent you a couple of texts, but maybe your phone is off?'

'Yes.' She had turned it off soon after her conversation with Jim because he kept calling and she couldn't bear it.

'Only I wondered if you wanted me to pop in on Granny this morning, or if you're going to.' She looked round to check the girls' progress. Hope was standing on the gravel, strung about with her school paraphernalia, staring at something on the ground. 'Hope, *get into the car* . . . I could drive by after I've done the school run if you're not.'

'Thanks, Lou. I was planning to go anyway this morning. I'm sure you're busy.'

'Well, let me know if you want any help.' She began to turn away, then changed her mind. 'Maybe you ought to go back to bed, Mum. You don't look too hot.'

'I'm fine.' She was dreading telling her daughter about Jim. She knew, word for word, what Louise would say, Frances too.

As she shut the front door, Nancy remembered she was still in yesterday's clothes. She hadn't been to bed, hadn't changed or washed since her phone call with Jim. She wasn't sure if she'd slept – she must have: the hours had passed quickly enough. But she had barely moved from the sofa all night, her mind in a fog of bewilderment.

She knew that Jim had told the truth. She believed that his relationship with his wife was over – or at least she told herself she did. But the foundations of their relationship had shattered into shards, like broken glass. She didn't even dare touch it because she knew it would hurt too much. All she could do was tread gingerly over their time together and try to understand where she had gone wrong, why she had trusted him so completely on such little evidence. And if he could love her so apparently sincerely while concealing this huge lie, what else might she uncover if she looked?

CHAPTER TWENTY-ONE

At seven o'clock that morning Jim, head splitting, was so angry that he didn't know what to do with himself. Angry with himself, first and foremost, for being such a prick and not telling Nancy the truth. Then, in descending order, with Chrissie, just for existing, with Lindy for sticking her nose in where it wasn't wanted, and finally with Nancy's priggish daughter, who was probably denouncing him to Nancy right now, reinforcing her notion that he was a thoroughly bad lot.

Nothing he could do about it, either. He hadn't slept for a single moment, just sat tonking back the whiskey, berating himself and cursing the world. The five or so calls he'd made to Nancy immediately after they'd talked had all gone straight to voicemail, and he didn't leave a message because he'd said it all. He couldn't lose her – he just couldn't handle that. He could still feel the softness of her skin beneath his fingers, smell the freshness of her hair, see in his mind's eye the smile she had given him after they'd made love, so tender and open, so trusting.

Andrew Sitter, his solicitor, had said that, with the best will in the world, a divorce when the other party was dragging their feet might take four or five months. Longer even, depending on how quickly the 'respondent', i.e., Chrissie, returned the papers. Knowing how stubborn his wife was capable of being, that might be decades. Five months! And if she wasn't prepared to sell the house, God knew how long it might take before he was really, properly free – in Nancy's terms. By which time she would probably have moved on, found someone else.

I have to talk Chrissie round, he kept telling himself. But he knew that would be an uphill task, because she held all the cards now. And would it make any difference in the end? Nancy was upset because he'd deceived her, and that wasn't going to change even if his circumstances did. His head was heavy with despair, frustration and too much bourbon. If only he could see Nancy, he knew he could explain so that she'd understand. But if those relatives of hers got to her first, he was lost anyway. Should he doorstep her? But the humiliating prospect of having the door slammed in his face or, worse, not opened at all, turned his guts to water.

He took up his guitar again – he'd hugged it like a comfort blanket most of the night – and spent the next hour in an unsatisfactory fugue, picking out songs he half finished, strumming mindlessly, finally slamming his instrument onto the desk and storming downstairs, desperate for a cigarette. Who cared now, if he smoked or not?

Meeting Chrissie in the kitchen, he glared at her. She was peacefully eating her birdseed breakfast, reading a magazine, the radio wittering some moronic advert, sun pouring through the glass door that led into the garden, which she'd opened onto the summer morning.

'Somebody die?' she asked, eyeing Jim's dishevelled, unshaven appearance with raised eyebrows.

'Pretty much.' He headed outside for a smoke.

'Fall out with the fancy-woman, did we?' Chrissie's smug voice followed him outside. It was sodding irritating how well she always read him. He didn't answer until he'd had a sufficient hit of nicotine to quieten his nerves. Then he went inside to make a cup of coffee, spooning a large quantity of grounds into the glass cafetière, boiling the water, filling it only half full so that the brew would take the skin off his throat with a bit of luck.

Taking a steadying breath and sitting down opposite his wife, he said, 'I filed for divorce yesterday.'

Chrissie's eyes widened slightly. 'Without telling me?'

'I did tell you.'

'No, you didn't. You told me you'd have to get a divorce if I didn't agree to sell the house. You didn't tell me you were actually going to do it.'

Jim clenched his hands round the brown pottery mug. 'Well, I have. The solicitor is lodging the petition this week, so you'll be getting some papers to sign in a week or two.'

Chrissie munched away. 'And if I decide not to sign them?'

'You have to, within a week, Andrew says, unless you're going to defend it – which isn't easy these days, he says.' He felt the kick of the coffee on top of the nicotine and the sleepless night, then experienced a surreal moment when he saw himself saying what he had said and Chrissie reacting to it, as if it were a play he was watching. 'You should get a solicitor yourself,' he added.

'Spend money I don't have?'

Jim didn't reply. Chrissie earned a good salary from her job at the council, but to hear her you'd think she was practically on the streets. 'We need to do it, Chrissie. You know that.'

He waited for the denial, waited for the tears. But his wife just shrugged. 'Suppose we do,' she said mildly, almost making Jim choke.

He looked at her closely. Had something changed? Not wanting to rock the boat, he said nothing, waited for her to speak. But she didn't, so he said, 'Obviously the house'll be sold when the divorce comes through.'

She nodded, put her spoon in her empty bowl, reached for her mug of green tea and swirled the contents gently, a faraway expression on her face. 'Obviously.'

The look in her green eyes seemed almost lazy this morning. When had he seen that look before?

'I've been thinking,' she said. 'We should probably get the bloody thing on the market again. I don't want to live here without you. Be weird.'

Jim held his breath. 'If you're sure, I'll ring the estate agent, shall I?'

'Could do.'

Then Jim remembered when he'd seen that look before. After sex. It had first alerted him to Benji. Well, not Benji himself, just the fact of a Benji. 'Have a good time last night?' he asked, controlling his smile, which felt like it might overtake his whole body – like he might become his smile, as the Cheshire Cat had.

Chrissie gave him a sharp look, then turned away quickly, but not quickly enough to prevent Jim seeing the faint blush that coloured her pale, freckled skin. *Oh, my God*, he thought. *I'm right*.

'Not bad, as it happens,' she said, almost coy.

'Phil came through, did he?' He hadn't known he'd known until he said her co-worker's name.

And Chrissie actually laughed. 'Christ, Jim. We know each other so bloody well, we'd make a great married couple.'

For a moment both were silent. He saw a shadow pass across his wife's features and felt a stab of sadness. Because he knew, in that moment, that their marriage was finally over. A marriage that had been very good at first, then okay for a while, then not so good when she'd started to stray, but no worse than many other couples put up with the world over. Suddenly he wanted to hug her, hold her close one last time and tell her he'd loved her, really had loved her, once. But he didn't do it. The truce was too new, too tenuous, and Chrissie was capricious to say the least. One false move on Jim's part and she might revert to her tantrum-self. So he sat very still.

She stood up. 'Better get on,' she said, taking her bowl and cup to the sink and rinsing them under the tap.

Jim, back in his room waiting for his ten-thirty, had initially felt euphoric, knowing that Chrissie and he were finally on the same page, that he could push on with the divorce, sell the house without her opposition, without any more hysterics or nastiness. But gradually, as he sat there, he saw it didn't make much difference to his situation with Nancy. She didn't trust him, end of. And she had only just started to recover from being lied to and betrayed by that pompous ex of hers. His mood slumped and he found himself singing a Keith Urban song, 'Stupid Boy', loudly and angrily, strumming the strings until they might snap. Almost wanting them to. It just summed up all he felt about his folly.

He picked up his phone for the hundredth time, hoping against all rational belief that she would have called. But there was only a text from Mal asking when they could meet up. He wasn't going to call again, but he tapped in a quick text to Nancy. She would read that – she couldn't help it: it would be there on her screen. *I'm sorry. I've messed up, but that doesn't change my feelings for you. xxx* He looked at the words for a moment, amended them to *I'm so sorry. I know I've messed up badly. But my wife and I ARE separated in all but name. xxx* Then he stared at it some more and amended it again to *I'm sorry. xxx* When he finally pressed 'send', he had lost hope that his message would change anything.

CHAPTER TWENTY-TWO

Nancy did read the message and it didn't change anything. She knew he was sorry. But it prompted her to ask herself, *Wouldn't I have done the same thing?* She sat in her parked car, making no move to get out and check on her mother. *Wouldn't I have lied just a little if I'd been in his situation with his wife? As he said, I'd have run a mile if he'd told me he was still married, still living with her.*

She walked reluctantly up the path to her mother's door and let herself in. There was a stale, unused smell to the place.

'Mum?'

Frances called back from the sitting room, 'In here.'

Nancy, even in her mood of despair, was cheered by her mother's appearance. Dressed with her usual care, she was wearing makeup for the first time since her turn and was looking surprisingly chipper, her reading glasses perched on her nose, the *Daily Telegraph* open in front of her, a half-empty mug of coffee on the table beside her.

'You seem much better,' Nancy said, sitting down in the armchair opposite.

Frances smiled almost smugly, peering at her. 'More than can be said for you, darling. Are you coming down with something?'

'No, I'm fine, just didn't sleep very well.'

Her mother studied her some more and seemed about to say something, but she stopped. Then started again. 'Were you seeing that man again?'

'I wasn't, although it's none of your business if I was.' Tiredness did not allow her to be gentle.

'If he's making you ill, it is.' Her mother's reply was equally sharp.

'Well, I'm not seeing him any more, so you don't need to worry, Mum.'

Frances frowned, clearly not knowing what to make of her remark. 'Has something happened?'

Nancy detected a note of concern in her mother's question, which surprised her somewhat and she let her guard down, tears welling behind her eyes as she said, 'He's married, Mum, and still living with his wife.'

'No!'

'Not in the way you think. They live in different parts of the house and don't have sex or anything but, still, he lied to me, implying they were totally separated.'

It felt good to let it out, instead of having the miserable monologue tramping round and round her head.

Frances tutted. 'Men, honestly. Why do they find it so hard to be truthful?'

'I don't think it's only a male problem, is it?'

'Oh, definitely, darling. Men . . . what's the word? . . . compartmentalize. But they never work out that mistress will sooner or later meet wife, work colleague will speak to boss, statement in red follows spending too much, heart attack follows bacon sandwiches. They jog happily along until someone comes and joins up the dots.'

Nancy couldn't help smiling at her mother's most uncharacteristic philosophizing. 'Maybe you're right. But you were lucky. Dad was never like that.'

Frances raised her eyebrows sardonically. '*All* men are like that.'

Even though her mind was so preoccupied with Jim, Nancy was just about to ask her mother what she meant, but Frances had already pushed herself up from the sofa, taken her glasses off and folded the paper neatly.

'I'll get you a cup of coffee, darling,' she said, and the moment was lost.

'That's enough, Hope.' Nancy held out her hand for the spoon that her granddaughter had been licking, previously covered with golden syrup.

'Can I put the oats in now?' Jazzy was holding out the chrome bowl from the scales, piled with the oats, waiting to tip it into the pan.

'Nana said *I* could do that,' Hope said, trying to snatch at the bowl. 'You did it last time.'

'*Nooo!*' shrieked Jazzy, clutching it to her chest, as Hope pulled at the rim.

'Stop it, you two, or neither of you will do it.'

'But you said, Nana . . .' Hope's huge brown eyes were turned reproachfully on her grandmother.

Nancy laughed. 'Come on, Jazzy, hand it over.'

Jazzy scowled and banged the bowl onto the table. 'Let me, I want to stir it,' she said, as soon as the oats were in with the butter and syrup, grabbing at Hope's wooden spoon. But her sister was too quick for her and pulled away.

Nancy sighed. This was supposed to be fun, not a battleground. 'Let Jazzy have a go, Hope,' she said. 'I'll get another spoon.'

'Jim said he'd teach us how to play the guitar,' Jazzy said, as they flattened the oat mixture into the square tin with the back of their spoons.

'And to sing in harmony,' Hope added.

'Did he? Well, we'll see,' Nancy said.

'Does that mean no?' Hope asked.

'No, it means let's see if that works out,' she said, her heart heavy.

She was completely exhausted. She had stayed with her mother until it was time to pick the girls up from school. Frances had been in a good mood, kind to Nancy in her triumph at seeing Jim off. But Nancy just wanted to sit in a corner and cry. Or ring Jim. Or see Jim. Or make love to Jim. Did it really matter that he had lied to her?

'Nana?' Hope was staring at her, a slight frown on her face.

'Yes?'

'Are you all right?'

'Of course I am, why wouldn't I be?' she said, but tears were sliding down her cheeks. Shocked, she wiped them quickly away, giving her round-eyed granddaughters the brightest smile she could muster. 'I'm just a bit tired today,' she said, by way of an excuse that even she thought lame. But the girls seemed willing to accept what she said and didn't ask any more as they waited eagerly for the flapjacks to cook.

Louise, however, was not so easily fobbed off. When she came to pick up her daughters after tea, she shooed them out, telling them to go home and turn the television on while she 'had a quick word with Nana'.

'He's married?' she said, as soon as the coast was clear. 'I spoke to Granny.'

'Right. News travels fast.'

'I can't believe it, Mum. What a—'

'Please, Lou, can you not go down that route? I'm not in a good way and I can't deal with you telling me what a bastard he is, or that you never liked him, or that you told me so. Okay?'

Louise pursed her lips in silence.

'Even though all those things may be true,' Nancy added.

Her daughter's look was of concern – just like Lindy's – as she said, 'I'm sorry it didn't work out for you, Mum.'

'No, well, it wasn't likely to, I suppose. Not at my age.'

'Don't say that. Your age has nothing to do with it. It's just Jim wasn't right for you. You've had a lucky escape.'

Nancy wished she'd added 'lucky escape' to the things she didn't want her daughter to tell her. Hearing it set her teeth on edge.

'How did you find out?' Louise was asking.

'Lindy told me.' Nancy opened the dishwasher and began loading in the bowls and tins, pans and spoons they'd used to make the flapjacks.

'Wow. Lucky she did when she did. You could have got in much deeper.'

Nancy stood up and faced her daughter. 'Please. Can we not talk about it?'

Louise shrugged. 'Okay, but you shouldn't feel too bad. It's the first time you've gone out with somebody since Dad and it wasn't very likely you'd meet the man of your dreams without kissing a few frogs first.' She smiled encouragingly at her mother. 'See it as a trial run.'

Could she be any more insensitive? Nancy wondered. 'I really liked Jim,' she said quietly.

And something in her tone must have alerted Louise because she came round the table, laid a hand on Nancy's shoulder and stroked it up and down, peering into her face. 'Sorry, Mum. I'm being tactless. I'm just so relieved.'

'I'm glad somebody is.'

Louise frowned. 'Don't be like that. I – I was worried about you, that's all. I thought you were moving too fast and that he wasn't with you for the right reasons.' Her daughter's blue eyes were painfully honest in their gaze.

'Right reasons?'

'You know,' Louise seemed embarrassed now, 'not in it for the long term.'

Nancy couldn't meet her eye.

'He lied to you, Mum. And it was a big lie. You'd never be able to trust him again.' Louise banged her point home with a relentlessness of which her father would have been proud.

'I think I'll go up and have a bath now,' Nancy said, to get rid of her daughter. One more comment about Jim's unsuitability and she would be tempted to slap her.

'Good idea,' Louise said, clearly oblivious to the distress she was causing. 'Thanks so much for looking after the little terrors. Hope they behaved themselves.'

'They were perfect. Take the rest of the flapjacks.' Nancy pulled a section of clingfilm from the roll in the drawer by the sink and laid it over the white plate, stretched the sides taut, then handed it to Louise. 'I won't eat them.'

That night Nancy slept like the dead, unable to think about Jim for one more minute. But when she woke up the next morning, she found herself trapped again by the conundrum she faced: could she ever trust him?

She dressed in grey tracksuit bottoms and an old T-shirt – she wasn't planning to go anywhere. After two cups of coffee and a bite of toast – she couldn't face the rest – she spent the morning at the piano. The smooth touch of the ivory keys and the swirl of sound she created were comforting. The music took her out of herself, stopped all thought as her tired brain began to relax into the deeper vibrational resonance. After a while she found she could breathe again, come back into herself, sense a modicum of calm.

A call from Lindy interrupted the peace. 'How are you doing, darling?'

'I'm all right.' Nancy tried to sound normal.

'Listen, I've got a couple of things to sort out, but they won't take long and I'm free after that. Why don't we meet for a coffee in town?'

'Not sure,' Nancy said. 'I've got a student at four.'

'Four's a lifetime away. Shall we make it one-thirty at that crazy place with all the kitsch décor? On Ship Street – it looks like a fifties junk shop.'

'No. Honestly, Lindy, I've got stuff to do. Maybe another time.'

But Lindy wouldn't go away. 'Stuff to do, like pining for Jim Bowdry? Not a good plan. Come on, Nance, get your arse into town and I'll cheer you up. I owe you.'

They sat outside against the back of the brick building at a wobbly wooden table, which looked as if it had once been a door, on random chairs – Nancy's a wicker garden one, with a red flower-patterned cushion on its seat, both badly in need of repair. The early June sun was bright and hot, and both women wore sunglasses. Lindy's were ostentatiously Chanel with diamanté and pearls on the arms, Nancy's fifteen pounds from Boots.

When they had coffee in front of them and Lindy a large slice of chocolate cake, Nancy began picking over the Jim saga with her friend, trying to make sense of it. Lindy listened for a while, then cast a sheepish glance at her. 'I feel so bad for telling you. It was none of my bloody business. I should have kept my mouth shut.'

Nancy shook her head. 'I had to know.'

'Yeah, but Jim'd probably have told you sooner or later and then he'd have had a chance to explain himself.'

'It doesn't make any difference, Lindy. He still lied to me the whole time we were together.'

Lindy sighed. 'Have you talked to him since?'

She nodded.

'But you didn't believe his story.'

'I did, actually. But that doesn't help much.'

'Why not?'

'I suppose my worry is that he's not over his wife, even though he says he is. It's weird that they've gone on living together for so long if they're completely over each other, don't you think?'

'How long is it?'

'About three years. Who does that?'

'Hmm. . . What did Jim say about it?'

'Money, and the fact that neither of them was with anyone else.'

'Well, that's not impossible . . .'

'But why weren't either of them with someone else?' Nancy sipped her coffee and realized it was probably a mistake: she'd already had too much caffeine for one day and not enough food to soak it up. 'Is the real reason that they still love each other?'

Lindy laughed. 'I don't think you can deduce they still love each other just because they haven't found anyone else. It's hard out there.'

'No, but . . .'

'Say they do, why on earth would Jim be chasing after you?'

'Maybe they don't know they still have feelings for each other. People often use affairs, subconsciously, to sort out their marriages, don't they?'

'I suppose, but you're not making sense, Nancy. If Jim was using you to get back with Chrissie, why would he care that you'd found out? If that were the case, he'd just walk away, not ring you umpteen times and send texts saying he's sorry.'

'Christopher was off like a streak of lightning as soon as he'd 'fessed up about Tatjana.'

'Exactly, because he was in love with someone else. But if your relationship had broken down and there wasn't anyone else, he might have stayed around making you both unhappy.'

Nancy thought back to her marriage. They hadn't made each other unhappy, precisely, but it had been years since they'd taken real pleasure in each other's company. However, it had never occurred to her to leave.

'So you don't think it's odd, them still being together?'

'I didn't say that,' Lindy backtracked. 'I think it's unusual, but I don't think you can read into it that Jim is still in love with his wife.'

'He was obviously very cut up when she cheated on him.'

'Yeah, that's probably what killed it for him. Men don't get over infidelity nearly so easily as women.'

Nancy felt too tired to think. 'Should I give him the benefit of the doubt?'

Lindy rubbed her nose with the palm of her hand, jangling the multiple silver bracelets on her wrist. 'Can't answer that, Nance. Depends if you feel he's worth the risk.'

'The risk being that he might run out on me . . .'

Her friend nodded. 'A risk every single person in a relationship has to take.'

'I'm too old to be breaking my heart.'

She studied Nancy's face for a moment. 'Are you really telling me you'd rather you'd never met Jim, even if it didn't work out?'

'No, of course not,' Nancy had no hesitation in replying. The thought of not meeting Jim was almost more painful than the thought that she might never see him again.

As she left the cafe, Nancy found herself looking about, wondering if she might bump into him. She hoped she wouldn't, because she looked like shit and because one glance from those magic blue eyes of his and she'd be lost. And although it would make things much simpler just to fall into his arms and forget about the ex-wife, she also knew that things between them had changed for ever. So she hurried along the narrow streets, back to where she'd parked her car, head down, her heart not steadying until she was safely on the road, driving north out of the city.

CHAPTER TWENTY-THREE

Frances smiled at the doctor. He really was very sweet, even though Nancy said he was useless. She didn't mind if he was useless, though, because she hadn't wanted to see him in the first place. This was the third time her dear daughter had made the appointment. Frances had managed to slide out of the first two, claiming she wasn't feeling well enough. But it was tricky: if she said she was feeling too ill, then Nancy would get the bloody man round to the house anyway.

'Mrs Havers . . .'

Dr Henderson was saying something and she tried to listen. He'd been poking and prodding her for the last ten minutes and it hadn't been pleasant. Her clothes felt all askew now and she longed to be at home and in peace.

'Mrs Havers,' he was trying again, 'I'm a bit concerned about the tenderness around your tummy. I'd like to take a closer look, see what's going on. How do you feel about a few tests at the hospital?'

Idiot man, she thought. *Does he think I haven't graduated to the word 'stomach' yet? As for how I 'feel' about having tests . . . how the hell does he think I feel? Of course, I'm simply dying for it, I can hardly wait to sit for hours on one of those blue plastic chairs in some dreary NHS waiting room with rows of half-dead people staring at me, only to be told I have some ghastly disease they can do nothing about.*

'What tests?'

'Well . . .' He put his head on one side again. *Is there something wrong with his neck?* 'There's a sort of scan called an endoscopy. We put a wee tube into your stomach with a camera on the end and look around, check things out. It doesn't hurt at all.'

Frances glanced round at Nancy. It ought to be her seeing the doctor, she thought. Since that ghastly man had told her those lies about his wife, her daughter had got steadily paler and more miserable. She was worried about her. But it never did to rush into things where men were concerned. Especially when it involved sex. They were just too unreliable in their needs. She had never liked sex much. Hadn't really seen the point of all that heavy breathing and thrashing about, all that . . . mess. Kenny hadn't seemed to mind that she'd closed that door after Nancy was born. But then, of course, he'd made his own arrangements later on with little Miss Butter-wouldn't-melt Julie, his devoted dental nurse, who had a bottom the size of three buses. Frances hadn't minded, really. It was just sex and Kenny was always very discreet. She knew he adored her.

'I know what an endoscopy is,' she spoke tartly to the doctor, 'and I don't want one.' *Wee tube? Who was he kidding?* Her friend Barbara had had one and said it was more like a garden hose, that the Valium they'd given her hadn't worked and she'd gagged so much they'd had to give up. Said her throat was sore for a fortnight. She shuddered at the thought.

'Mum, that's silly. You must get it checked out.'

'There's nothing wrong with me,' she asserted, not for the first time.

'You've just told me you don't feel like eating much,' the doctor said, 'and you say you get pain sometimes, a lot of indigestion. Why don't you let us take a little look? Then maybe we can fix it.'

'Fix it? How would you do that?' She knew for absolute certainty that she had stomach cancer. She'd known it for a while. The symptoms were exactly the same as poor Richard, Joyce's husband, had suffered – she'd asked her about it the other day.

'Well, it would depend on what the problem is,' Dr Henderson's reply was distinctly cagey. 'We can't know what to do until we've found out what's wrong.'

'I don't want any tests.' As Frances said this, she felt the anxiety building, her heart fluttering at twice its normal speed. *Please don't let me have another of my turns*, she thought, concentrating hard on her breathing. *In, out, in, out, big breaths.*

Nancy had reached out and taken her cold hand. 'Please, Mum. Please don't be stubborn about this. If there is something wrong that can be easily treated, make your life better, why wouldn't you want to do it?'

'You're assuming it can be easily treated,' she said to her daughter.

'Well, yes. Until we know otherwise.'

She saw Dr Henderson let out a sigh. *Another recalcitrant patient taking up his precious time, he's probably thinking. His fault. I'm only allowed eight minutes, and he's already wasted ten prodding my stomach and asking damn-fool questions.*

'Why don't you go home and have a wee think?' he said, with another of his patronizing smiles.

'Couldn't you just go ahead and book the endoscopy?' Nancy was asking him. 'Then my mother can decide while we wait for the appointment to come through.' Her face was drawn and anxious and Frances felt a pang of guilt for the distress she was causing her daughter. But she was not having the tests.

'I can't do that without Mrs Havers's consent.'

Nancy was staring at her with beseeching eyes. 'Let the doctor book it, Mum. Please. You can always change your mind later.'

Suddenly Frances felt too tired to argue any more. 'Oh, all right,' she said. 'Go ahead. Do your worst.'

Both of them beamed at her as if they were about to give her a gold star. She felt relieved that they would stop nagging her now. The endoscopy appointment would be weeks away, and a lot could happen before then.

'Well done, Mum,' Nancy said, smiling for once, as they made their way back to the car, parked behind the surgery.

'Don't congratulate me too soon,' she said.

Nancy didn't reply, just opened the car door for her and waited while she got in.

'Shall I stay for a bit?' her daughter asked, when Frances was comfortably settled on her sofa at home.

'No, no. You get off. I'm sure you've got a lot to do.' She wanted to be alone. Nancy, if she stayed, would get all enthusiastic about lunch, then there would be the battle to eat enough to stop her niggling. And she needed to think, to make a decision about the cancer.

Frances was not afraid of being dead. If the God she prayed to every Sunday turned out to be real, he'd scoop her up. And if he wasn't, she'd just cease to exist, which was fine by her. But the process of dying was a worry. She had always promised herself that she would never be a burden on her family. However nice it might seem to give in and do as everyone told her, she knew that neither

Nancy nor Louise had the stomach for nursing her through nasty ops and the long recovery from chemo, any more than she did for having them. And although it had been wonderful to be looked after in her daughter's home, have everything done for her, Frances could feel the tension her presence was causing. Nancy had been nothing but kind and helpful, but she had sensed a permanent air of forbearance about her, and Frances suspected she was screaming inside. Frances herself, faced with her own mother coming to stay indefinitely, would certainly have been screaming, and it wouldn't only have been inside.

CHAPTER TWENTY-FOUR

It was twenty-seven days since Nancy had last spoken to Jim – she'd counted them. But it felt like a lifetime. His number still came up on her phone, although he never left a message and the calls were dwindling as the days went by.

She found herself thinking about him almost every minute of every day: she went to sleep wondering how he was, woke up from dreams full of jumbled images of his face. The worst thing was that everyone assumed her liaison with him was over, done and dusted, big smiles of relief all round. And this had put a real strain on her relationship with Louise in particular, because her mother, although of the same opinion as Louise, no doubt, had never raised the subject after that first row.

'You know what, Mum? You ought to join a gym or something,' Louise said now, as she stood with her mother in the garden, hands on hips, watching as Nancy deadheaded the roses and cut back the bamboo shoots that had strayed from the original shrub in the corner of the garden, springing up in all the wrong places as the summer had worn on.

It was hot for a change, the miserable weather earlier in the season giving way to a few days of cloudless blue skies. Louise had taken the other pair of secateurs from the canvas bag on the lawn and was searching for something to snip.

'Those, over there.' Nancy pointed with hers towards some fronds of ivy poking out through the hedge to the side of the house.

'Did you hear what I said?' Louise asked, pushing her sunglasses up her nose with the back of her hand. She was wearing shorts and a skimpy yellow vest – Nancy thought she looked much younger than her thirty-three years.

'Join a gym.' She paused in her task of breaking up the long stem of bamboo she'd just extracted from the back of the rose bush along the fence. 'Why would I want to do that?'

Louise laughed. 'Usual reasons. Get fit. Meet people.'

'I am fit. I do yoga twice a week on my iPad, walk the cat.'

'Ha-ha. It's just there's a new gym opened on the way to the restaurant. I popped in and it looks very glossy and hi-tech. I thought you might enjoy it.'

'I can't think of anything more horrible than sitting on seats wet with other people's sweat and pulling weights up and down to deafening disco music.' She sounded more snappish than she'd intended, because she knew what her daughter was trying to do. It was along the lines of all the other suggestions she'd made – oh, so subtly – since the split with Jim. These had ranged from a cookery course Ross's friend Mark was starting in Lewes, to a film club in Brighton, to a rambling group that went up on the Downs every weekend.

Louise said nothing as she pulled at the ivy, stacking her pile of shoots neatly on the grass.

'Listen, Lou, I know you mean well, but please stop. I'm perfectly happy as I am.'

Her daughter turned to her, wrenched her glasses from her face. 'Really? Can you honestly say you're "perfectly happy"? Because you don't seem it. You've been going around for weeks looking as if somebody died.'

'Thanks.'

They were facing each other across the lawn. 'I assume it's that whole business with Jim, but you have to move on. I mean, you'd only been together for five minutes.'

Nancy felt her body stiffen with umbrage. Don't react, she told herself. And in truth she didn't know how to respond.

'Granny's worried too. She was the one who suggested you should get out more – like she always tries to. Keep busy.'

'Oh, for God's sake.' Nancy could no longer contain herself. 'Can you both stop treating me like some half-wit who doesn't know her own mind? For a start, you have no idea what Jim meant to me. And second, if you think a few evenings drinking warm wine with some film anoraks in Brighton is going to change anything, you've got another think coming.' She suppressed the desire to shout and scream and rip into her poor daughter.

Louise looked taken aback. 'Well, hey, sorry for caring.' She bent down, picked up her pile of cuttings, dumped them in the bag Nancy had placed in the middle of the lawn and stalked off towards her house.

Nancy sighed. 'Lou!' she called half-heartedly – she had no real desire for Louise to turn round. She sat down on the swing seat, pulled off her gardening gloves and laid them beside her. Riven with guilt, she knew she would have to go and apologize. Louise was only trying to help. But it was so hard to keep hearing how Jim was merely an unfortunate lapse – an insignificant one at that – when he was etched onto her very soul.

As she swung back and forth in the sunshine, summoning up the strength to go in and talk to Louise, she saw Ross pulling into the drive. Not wanting to have to speak to him, she got up, putting on her gloves again, but he waved and came across the lawn. 'Hi, Nancy. How's it going?'

She thought he looked more cheerful than previously and wondered why. Louise kept telling her that, despite the summer, nothing much had changed at the restaurant.

She smiled at him. 'Not great – just had a set-to with Lou.'

He frowned. 'About?'

'Two guesses.'

'Not Jim again.'

She nodded.

'What did she say?'

'Nothing really, just that I should move on.'

'Hate it when people say that.' He gave her a sympathetic grin and lifted the nearly full bag of cuttings, took it over to the green bin on the edge of the drive and emptied it, pressed the leaves down and slammed the lid. When he came back with the bag, he said, 'How do you feel about the whole thing?'

His question disarmed Nancy. No one had asked her that. They had just pontificated about what a rotter Jim was and what a narrow escape she'd had. 'I feel like I've lost an arm,' she said quietly, and watched as his eyes widened.

'That bad, eh?'

'That bad.'

'I didn't know.' He looked a bit furtive. 'This is heresy, obviously,' he said, dropping his voice, 'but have you thought of maybe seeing him again? I mean, if he means that much to you, perhaps you should try and work it out.' He pulled the corners of his mouth down, raised his eyebrows. 'Dumb idea?'

'He lied to me,' she said, the tired old phrase like sand in her mouth.

Ross shrugged his big shoulders. 'Sounds like he did it for a good reason.' He paused. 'Listen, I liked the guy, for what it's worth. And everyone fucks up, don't they? Louise'll kill me for saying this, so please don't dob me in, but what have you got to lose by giving him another go?'

'My heart?'

'Sounds like you've lost that already,' he said, then patted her shoulder and walked off, hands deep in the pockets of his khaki cargo shorts.

It was as if someone had lifted a heavy lid and let the light into the darkness. Nancy sat back down on the swing seat. What harm *could* it do, as Ross had said, just to see Jim again, talk to him? Because nothing, she thought, could be worse than the misery she was currently experiencing. And if, when she saw him, she decided they couldn't work it out, then so be it. At least she would have given it her best shot.

She found herself smiling like a mad woman as she got up from the seat again, put away the gloves and secateurs, stowing them with the leaf bag inside the tiny potting shed. Should she ring or text him?

By the time she'd found her phone, lying on the tiled shelf in the bathroom upstairs, she'd decided a text was the least stressful course of action. Because he might have 'moved on', to use that hateful phrase. He might be pissed off with her and have lost interest. It was at least nine days, she knew to the hour, since his last message.

The silence had tortured her almost as much as the previous calls, each one of which had pulled her right to the edge. But to hear rejection – or, worse, indifference – in his voice now would send her over that edge. Trembling, she sat down on the bed and tapped into the phone: *The cafe, ten o'clock tomorrow? Nancy x*

Then she sat for an age before pressing 'send'.

It was nearly midday, a Thursday. Did he have students on Thursdays? She wasn't sure. Maybe he was away, out with his mates. Maybe he wouldn't reply for a hundred other reasons.

She waited. She paced. She tried to play the piano. She leafed through the magazine Louise had left on the kitchen table, which had the details of the film club, page turned down, she was so anxious for her mother to join. She took the washing out of the machine and went to hang it on the whirlybird clothes dryer at the side of the house. And all these actions were punctuated by anxious glances at her mobile, which she knew quite well would ping loudly – and, indeed, twice – to alert her to any incoming message. Nothing.

Gradually, as the afternoon wore on, hope faded and her previously feverish mood was replaced by a leaden deadness of spirit, which stole her energy so that she could do nothing but lie on the sofa in a heap and close her eyes.

Nancy slept, she woke, she checked her phone, still clutched in her hand.

Can't wait, xxx it said, and tears spilled down her cheeks.

Nancy was planning just to talk to Jim. Hear his side of the story. She told herself she at least owed him that. *If there is ever going to be closure*, she thought, *I need to have this conversation*. But the lengths she went to, in the choice of her clothes, the washing and styling of her hair, the carefully applied makeup, gave the lie to her rationale.

Arriving at the cafe where they had first met for coffee, she saw she was ten minutes early. So she walked round the block, wandered up narrow alleys, then spent a few minutes in Boots, picking up random lipsticks from the tester-bar. The weather had turned cooler and a layer of grey cloud on the horizon did not bode well. She wished she'd brought a sweater, her bare arms in the white T-shirt goose-bumping with cold. And all the while, as she glanced yet again at her watch only to discover barely two minutes had gone since she'd last checked, her heart was fluttering in her chest, her empty stomach churning with anticipation, with apprehension.

It seemed like a lifetime since they had last seen each other on the morning he had made love to her, laughed with her as he crept out early to avoid her mother and Louise. What would he say to her now? She, who had so callously refused to answer his calls and texts. They had reason to be angry with each other, but anger was way down the list of emotions Nancy was experiencing as she finally pushed open the door to the cafe, on the dot of ten.

The place was not busy – only three tables occupied – and Jim was not there. Dithering as to where she should sit, she settled at a window table near the door, positioning herself facing the entrance, then dithered as to whether to order a coffee or wait. Maybe he wouldn't come, she thought, even though it was only four minutes past ten. She sat down, waited, got up, ordered a cappuccino, took it back to her table, picked up a copy of yesterday's *Racing Post*, which was lying on the window ledge, and read some baffling piece about bloodstock without understanding a word. Nine minutes past ten. The coffee had been a good idea, the caffeine reacting well on her nerves. But Jim was seldom late . . .

Then the door burst open with a jangle of the bell and Jim charged in, breathless, eyes wild as he glanced around the room. When his eyes rested on her, he seemed relieved and apprehensive in equal measures. Nancy half rose to greet him, shocked by his sudden presence.

'God, Nancy, I'm so sorry. I had to let the estate agent in and he was late.'

They stood on opposite sides of the table, both wired to the hilt, staring, barely knowing what to do or say.

'It's fine,' she said. She thought he looked thin, worn, not his usual confident self as he took off his leather jacket and hung it on the back of the chair, revealing a familiar denim shirt.

As he hovered, glancing at her half-full cup, Nancy felt her previously defended heart melt. When he met her gaze, she smiled. Uncertain, he smiled back as she came round the table. Then he opened his arms and she felt the warmth of his body against her own, the press of his arms on her back as he pulled her into his embrace. She inhaled the familiar scent of his woody aftershave, felt the cold metal studs of his shirt against her cheek. Almost internally, she heard him sigh and closed her eyes. When she finally raised her face to his, he had tears in his clear blue eyes.

'I thought I'd never be lucky enough to do this again,' he said softly.

'Me too.'

Loath to disengage, they finally drew apart to let someone by in the cramped aisle. As she stood there, the strain of the past month fell away, along with the reason for it, leaving Nancy feeling physically without strength. She sat down, never taking her eyes from Jim. He was smiling now, relief flooding his gaunt, handsome features.

'Another coffee?'

She nodded. 'This one's cold.'

She watched as he spoke to the girl behind the counter, took his battered wallet out of his back pocket, glanced round at her as he waited for his order to be ready as if he were worried she might vanish.

'How have you been?' he asked, after a long silence during which their eyes had quietly rested on each other, luxuriating in the miracle of being together again.

'I've been utterly miserable, if you must know.'

He laughed, an edge of hysteria in the sound. 'Not wishing to be competitive, but I can definitely trump you. I haven't breathed a single breath since I last saw you.' He was smiling, keeping it witty, but the words were obviously deeply felt.

'I was just so shocked . . .'

He nodded. 'I knew you would be. You have no idea how sorry I am.'

'It doesn't matter now.' She spoke the words without thinking, but she realized they were no less true for being impulsive. Her worry as to whether she could trust Jim had died when she'd first gazed into his eyes again. They were totally without guile, without deceit, which she had always known, even while also knowing he had lied to her.

'Doesn't it?' he asked, sounding anxious. 'Are you sure? Haven't I broken something between us?'

Nancy grinned. 'Perhaps the notion I had that you were perfect . . .'

'Ha! Shame that had to go.' His expression became serious. 'But I'm getting sorted, Nancy. The divorce papers are lodged with the court – Chrissie's agreed to sign them as soon as they arrive. And someone's made an offer on the house. Good one too. Seems they're in a bit of a hurry and want to complete four weeks from now.' He gave a small shake of his head as if he were in shock from the whole thing.

'And Chrissie's okay with it?'

'Yeah, bit of a turnaround there. She's hooked up with this guy at work. Makes all the difference.'

Nancy watched his face. 'How do you feel about that?'

Jim looked surprised at the question. 'It's nothing to do with me, who she's with, not any more. But having said that, I'm over the moon she's off my case . . . We should have done all this years ago.'

'Wow! It's been a busy month,' Nancy said.

'Getting stuff organized stopped me going round the bend pining for you, Nancy. The thought that I'd lost you was driving me nuts. It would have been the most stupid thing I'd ever done. And I knew my cause wasn't helped by your family thinking I'm a real-life version of Sideshow Bob.'

She laughed. 'Well, they still think that. Not sure how I'm going to sell you to them this time.' She didn't want to think about her daughter's reaction when she told her about Jim. 'But it's my life.'

'You would think so,' Jim said.

'Where will you go when the house is sold?' she asked. 'It's so soon.'

He shrugged. 'No idea. Rent something in the area, I expect.

Can't afford to buy around here on my share of the takings. I'm checking online, but the places I've seen so far are rubbish.' He glanced outside – the sun was shining again, the black cloud dispersed. 'Anyway, I don't want to think about it right now. Come on, let's go and get some fresh air. It's suffocating in here.' Jim jumped up and she followed. He took her hand as soon as they were on the pavement. 'The sea?' he asked, and she nodded happily.

CHAPTER TWENTY-FIVE

Louise sat across from her husband in the Lime Kiln, exhausted after Friday evening service, both of them with a glass of red wine on the table in front of them. The restaurant staff had gone, so they could finally talk in peace, without concerning themselves that little ears might be picking up their every word.

'Wouldn't your mum help?' Ross, still in his chef's whites, face flushed from the kitchen and the wine, put forward this suggestion as if it were the obvious thing to do.

Louise frowned. 'You don't get it, do you? How can we ask Mum for money – which she probably doesn't have, by the way – to bail us out when the restaurant's prospects are so dire?'

'Dire? Christ, Lou, could you be more negative?'

'Don't make this about me, Ross. Honestly, at this rate we won't get through the winter.'

'It's July, for fuck's sake. Winter's aeons away.' Ross took a large gulp of wine, his face dark with annoyance. 'You really do pick your moments. I've just done fourteen hours of hard graft in that kitchen and you expect me to focus on the sodding accounts?'

'So when is a good time, then? You don't want to talk about it in the morning because you're working out the day's menu. After lunch you're knackered, before dinner you're preoccupied, after dinner you're knackered again. And we can't talk in the house because we can't be civil and the girls will hear. Ditto your rare days off. When the fuck *can* I talk to you about the fact that our business is going slowly down the Swanee?'

To her shock, Ross leaned across the table and grabbed her wrists, squeezing them as if he wanted to break her hands off. 'Shut up, woman. Just shut up, will you? Fucking on and on you go about bloody money. You don't give a toss about the food, or my reputation as a chef. All you care about is money, money, money.' He brought his face close to hers and she was unable to pull back because his grip was so tight. His dark eyes looked so murderous her heart jolted in her chest. 'Just *shut the fuck up*!' he shouted, then slumped in his seat, running his big hand over his baldness, eyes shut, a look of utter exhaustion on his face.

Louise, shaken, didn't say a word, just got up, rubbing her wrists where he had gripped her, tears welling in her eyes. As she turned to go, she heard Ross say, 'Lou . . . Lou, please, I'm sorry.' And he was beside her, his arm going round her shoulders, trying to pull her into his embrace.

But now she was rigid with fury. 'Get off me.'

'Please . . . God, I don't know what got into me. I'm just so tired.'

At his words, Louise rounded on her husband. 'You're tired?' she hissed. 'So tell me something I don't know. I'm fucking sick of hearing it – how tired you are, how hard you work, how much you care about your precious, precious food, your precious fucking reputation. None of it is any excuse for what you just did to me.'

Ross looked shamefaced. 'I was just trying to make you listen.'

'You attacked me, Ross. You hurt me.' She held out her arms to him, where the red marks of his hands were plainly visible on her pale skin. She felt anger spark through her body. 'And if you ever touch me again like that, I promise I will leave you.'

'Lou! Please don't say that. Look, I'm really, really sorry. I don't know what came over me. I'm worried too. I know you think I don't give a fuck, but I do, I do.' His brown eyes were full of pleading. 'This has been my dream ever since I was a kid. I can't bear the thought I might lose it.'

Louise had seldom been able to resist his little-boy-lost look, but her wrists were smarting and she was still in shock. 'We can't bury our heads in the sand any more, Ross. This is serious. It's not just the restaurant, it's the house too. If we can't meet the mortgage . . .'

They stood in the semi-darkness of the empty restaurant, the reminder of their failure and, indeed, their potential, all around them in the intimate layout of the square tables and tub chairs, the pictures on the walls, the wine in the racks behind the bar, the faint aroma of coffee that still lingered.

'What about your mother?' Ross said, his tone carefully non-confrontational.

Louise sighed. 'I can't ask her. She's in such a bad way at the moment because of the Jim fiasco. And, anyway, she's not rich. She can't afford the sort of investment we need to give this place a real chance.'

'Could you just sound her out, though?' Her husband, perhaps forgetting what he had just done, seemed shameless in his persistence. 'It wouldn't be good for her if we had to sell the house . . .'

Louise flicked the hangers listlessly along the chrome rail, barely taking in the dresses, shirts and jackets hanging below. She knew she should concentrate if she were ever to find a dress for her father's wedding, but all weekend she'd been haunted by Ross's brutish behaviour, the hostile, contemptuous look she'd seen in his eye, as if he despised her. *Does he even love me any more?* she wondered. *Or does he see me and Mum merely as facilitators for his ambition?*

'What about this?' Nancy was calling to her, waving a cobalt-blue sleeveless dress with a lacy black overlay.

Louise nodded. 'Yeah . . . maybe.'

'Try it on,' her mother said.

This trip was at Nancy's suggestion, and Louise had been grateful for the olive branch. Since their set-to in the garden, she and her mother had barely spoken. But Nancy seemed happier this morning, and there was a light in her eye that Louise hadn't seen for weeks. *Thank God she's finally getting over that bloody man*, she thought.

'And this one.' Nancy held up a paler blue wrap dress in a clingy material, also sleeveless.

'Hmm . . . bit short?'

'Nonsense. You've got good legs.'

Louise, struggling for some enthusiasm, took both dresses from her mother and made her way to the changing rooms.

'Show me.' Nancy's voice floated in to her from outside the cubicle as she put on the second.

Louise pulled back the curtain and held her arms out, checking her mother's face to gauge her reaction, but Nancy was staring at her wrist, not the dress. 'What have you done to your arm? That's a horrible bruise.'

Louise pulled her hand quickly across her body. 'Oh, that. I caught it on the edge of one of the tables at the restaurant a couple of nights ago.' She managed a laugh. 'Bloody place will be the death of me.'

Her mother was eyeing her carefully and Louise turned away, showing off the back of the dress.

'So you like this one?' Nancy asked.

'It's okay.'

Her mother laughed. 'It would look even better without the doomy expression. Listen, let's buy the damn thing and get out of here, find somewhere for coffee. If you don't like it when you get home, you can always bring it back.'

And when she continued to stand there, vacantly, in the pale blue dress, Nancy pushed her gently into the cubicle and pulled the curtain across.

Catching sight of the clock on the cafe wall, Louise saw she was late. She gave her mother a hug, then hurried off to the car park on Cannon Place. The silver Micra was on the second level, and as she approached from the lift, she began to feel for her car key in her bag, then to search her pockets. Then, frantic now, her bag again. Nothing. Anxiety building, she took a deep breath and told herself to calm down. She crouched and tipped the contents of her capacious tote onto the concrete floor of the car park, running her hand around the now empty interior. No key. No bloody key. She wanted to cry. Nothing in her life worked properly any more.

But Louise was practical by nature. She thought for a moment, then texted Ross. He'd be furious – lunchtime service with only that idiot girl, Evie, to cope would not be a pretty sight. But he'd have to suck it up until she could get there. Ross didn't respond, so she called her mother. Maybe the key had dropped into one of the shopping bags, which Nancy had offered to take home. But her mother was on the phone.

After a second try, she gave up, shovelled the stuff back into her bag and raced back to the cafe, hoping to God that Nancy was still there. With a sigh of relief, Louise saw her through the window, talking and laughing, one arm hugging herself, her expression alive, animated and – Louise had no problem finding the word – flirtatious.

As soon as she saw Louise, however, her face changed, as if she'd been caught out doing something naughty. She waved through the glass and quickly ended the call as Louise entered the cafe.

'Lou! What's wrong?'

'Just lost my bloody car key, haven't I? I thought it might have dropped into one of the bags.'

For a few minutes the two women rummaged around in the carriers. But the key was not there.

'Maybe it fell out of your jeans in one of the changing rooms.' She had tried on dresses in at least four different shops. She shook her head in despair.

'Come on, I'll drive you,' her mother said, getting up and gathering the bags together. 'You can sort it out after lunch.'

As they drove out of town, Louise shot a glance at her mum. 'Who were you talking to when I came into the cafe? You looked very merry.' She asked only to hear her mother confirm what she'd already worked out: Jim.

CHAPTER TWENTY-SIX

Jim had just finished the last teaching session of the summer. Which was a relief and also a worry because it meant no cash for the next month – an annual problem. But he wouldn't have had time to teach anyway. Now he sat cross-legged on the Mexican rug on the floor of his sitting room, a brown cardboard box in front of him in which he was slowly placing CDs. Not until they had gone through careful scrutiny, of course, but he would never play them now, he knew that. All his music was on his iPhone – or in his head. Still, it was hard getting rid of such a huge collection, but Mal had told him there was money in it. For reasons that escaped Jim in this download world, there were people out there who would pay good money for CDs. And every penny counted right now, with deposits to find and moving costs.

He and Chrissie had both had their heads down in the past few days, with only three weeks till they signed their house away, both filling endless black plastic bags for charity shops and the dump, trying to make a hole in the decades of hoarding – or not even hoarding, just putting things in cupboards and forgetting they were there. There was a quiet resolve in their task and they came together as they hadn't for years, laughing at things that reminded them of a past when they were happier together, arguing about who should keep what, talking about their plans.

This Phil-at-work guy is obviously making her happy, Jim thought, not without the odd pang of residual jealousy as he imagined them together. He couldn't help it. The scorching pain he'd experienced over her affair with Benji had never entirely faded; like any burn it had left a scar. While no part of him wanted to be with Chrissie any more, and every part was pleased she had found someone else, he couldn't help noticing her sleepy, contented expression when she got back from Phil's place some mornings in time to change for work.

Aware suddenly that the wooden floor was rock-hard and his limbs were stiff from sitting on it, Jim got up with a groan, chucking the CD he was holding – a Tom Waits album from the eighties that he'd never really liked – into the box.

He stood for a moment, looking out of the window onto the gardens at the back, still almost in shock that he had got his life back. Hourly he relived the moment when Nancy had come round the table and he'd put his arms round her. The delicious warmth of her in his arms, her body melting into his own. An almost painful heaven. But right, so right. Whatever it was they had going on between them, it felt as if it was meant to be.

He was the luckiest guy in the world that she'd decided to forgive him. But things were still tricky. She hadn't told her daughter or her mother yet. And he wondered what might happen when she did. To him, Nancy seemed beleaguered by her family. All of them had problems of one sort or another, and all of them seemed to look to poor Nancy to solve them. Which seemed unfair at her age, when she'd finished with all the parenting stuff years ago. He didn't want his presence to add to her woes, but if they were going to be together – which he was utterly determined they would be – then something had to give.

He reached for his phone.

'Hi, Jim,' Nancy answered immediately.

'How's it going?'

They had met for a drink the night before, and both had been aching to make love again. But Nancy had not felt it prudent to have him stay overnight before she'd told her daughter about them, and Jim wasn't comfortable with Chrissie's presence, so they had just sat in the pub near Nancy's house, arms round each other, feeling like exiles from their own lives.

'Well, I told Louise we were back together. At least, she worked it out.' She told him about the wedding outfit, the lost keys, her daughter spotting her on the phone to him.

'How did she take it?'

'Not brilliantly.''

'What exactly did she say?'

He heard Nancy take a long breath. 'Oh, just stuff about you not being someone who could make me happy, it being a mistake . . .'

Jim felt a shaft of anger in his gut. 'She's got me all wrong. It's not fair, judging me from one meeting.'

'I think Lou would have found fault whoever you were, Jim. She's just trying to protect me, I suppose.'

Hmm, is she? Jim thought it more likely that Louise just didn't want her mother's attention taken away from the family unit. Didn't want to share her. Maybe she was also worrying that Jim was after her mother's money.

'What did you say to her?' he asked, his voice neutral, anxious not to be seen to criticize her daughter.

'I said that I heard what she was saying, but it didn't change how I felt about you.'

'And how did she respond to that?'

'In a resigned on-your-head-be-it sort of way. I felt bad for upsetting her on top of all she's coping with at the moment.'

'But you weren't upsetting her, Nancy. You were just getting on with your life.' He spoke calmly, but he wanted to yell with frustration at Nancy's attitude.

'Yes, but you know what I mean.'

He did and he didn't. 'Do you want to meet up tonight? Sounds like you could do with some fun.'

'Can I call you later? I want to get this thing with Lou sorted or I won't be able to relax. I'm giving the girls their supper, so I'll see her around six. Is six too late?'

'Listen, I'm sitting here sorting a mountain of ancient CDs. No time is too late.'

'I'm so sorry about Louise, Jim. It must feel horrible to be seen as a *persona non grata* by my family when you haven't done anything to deserve it.'

'Doesn't feel great but I've only myself to blame. I should never have had that second glass of Rioja.'

'Ha, it's always the second glass,' Nancy said. 'By the way, have you found somewhere to live?'

'Might have. It's just a studio, but it's quite big, high ceilings and very light, top floor of a conversion not far from where I am now. Think it'll do.'

In fact it was way more than he wanted to pay, but most of the places were so depressing – basements or damp or dark, cramped or shabby, or all of the above and nowhere he would dream of bringing Nancy – that he'd decided his mental health was worth the extra money. Trouble was, the place didn't come free until three weeks after he had to move out. But, hell, he'd worry about that later. Worry about everything later.

Putting his mobile away, Jim sat for a long time in his armchair, considering. How was he going to bring Louise and her grandmother round? He couldn't be anyone but himself – which had always been good enough till now – and he wasn't about to try. But would Nancy get tired of the conflict? Tired of being stuck in the middle, and finally blame him?

CHAPTER TWENTY-SEVEN

'There's no point in talking about it again,' Louise said, and Nancy winced at her daughter's expression, rigid with censure.

The girls were outside, lying lengthwise on the swing seat in the warm summer evening, giggling as they annoyed each other by kicking and pushing and rolling around, but enjoying every minute.

Nancy and Louise were inside, standing by the sink, watching the children as they played. 'We have to talk about it, Lou,' she said. 'If I'm going to see Jim, he'll be around here, maybe staying the night. You can't pretend it's not happening.'

Louise, arms crossed tight over her chest, raised her eyebrows and looked away. 'You get on with your life, Mum. I'll get on with mine.'

Nancy reached over and stroked her hand down her daughter's bare, tanned arm. 'Come on, darling. That's silly. We practically live in the same house – we can't afford to fall out.'

Louise sighed, and finally met her mother's eye. 'I know . . . and that's the last thing I want. Your support is the only thing that keeps me going, Mum.' She sighed again. 'But I really have a problem with Jim. He's been nothing but trouble so far and I don't understand why you're giving him a second chance.'

'I can see how it looks from your perspective, but you don't know him. You've only got that one lunch to go on, which was disastrous. But he's a good man.'

'Apart from lying to you about his marriage.'

'Yes, apart from that.'

A tense silence ensued, during which neither of them moved.

'I'm going to give it a try, Lou. I've taken note of your warnings, but I want Jim in my life. And if it all goes pear-shaped you can say, "I told you so." '

Louise didn't reply, so Nancy went on, 'I would love it if you could give him a second chance too.'

Her daughter stared at her for a very long time, then replied, 'Okay.' Just that, the clipped syllables forced between stubborn lips.

'Thank you,' Nancy said. She offered a smile, which Louise reluctantly returned. 'Friends?'

'Oh, Mum, of course friends.' Louise stepped forward and gave her a hug. 'Just be careful, please. He looks like a heart-breaker to me.'

'Well, he has broken my heart, but in a good way.' She pulled back and looked her daughter in the face. 'This isn't a casual thing, Lou. I really have feelings for him.' She couldn't quite bring herself to say the word 'love' to her daughter.

But despite the absence of the actual word, there must have been something in her tone that Louise picked up on because her eyes narrowed with suspicion and her lips pursed, as if she were preventing herself from speaking. She said no more, neither good nor bad, and Nancy had to be satisfied with that.

Nancy went to pick up her mother for the endoscopy early on Thursday. She was feeling a little fragile because Jim had stayed the night and they had made love, talked, made love again for hours, both of them so starved of each other that they couldn't draw back, wouldn't let go. Sleep had not happened until the early hours, and they had woken to Nancy's alarm clock with a sense of disbelief and a smile on their faces.

Now Nancy felt as if she were walking on air, a pleasant bruised dizziness accompanying her every move. She prayed her mother would not cause trouble about the hospital visit, the thought of which filled her with dread. Would Frances be able to cope with a tube being pushed down her throat?

But her mother wasn't ready. Still in her dressing-gown, tired and washed out, the usual cup of coffee by her side, she was watching morning television at ear-splitting volume. 'Oh, hello, darling,' she said, when she saw her daughter.

'Mum, have you forgotten?'

'Forgotten what?'

'The hospital? You've got an endoscopy booked for ten o'clock. We should leave in about forty-five minutes.'

Frances waved a hand dismissively, a familiar gesture, which didn't bode well. 'I rang them yesterday and said I wasn't well enough,' she said.

'You cancelled it?'

Frances dragged her eyes from the television, where an excitable presenter was fawning all over a woman of around Nancy's age, wearing black bat-wing false eyelashes and what looked like a wedding dress.

'I thought I'd told you, darling.' She held a hand to her forehead. 'I'm so sorry, bringing you all this way for nothing, but I could have sworn I told you.'

Nancy didn't believe a word of it. She should never have left the hospital letter with her mother.

I won't nag her, she thought, as she made herself a cup of coffee. *If she doesn't want the problem investigated, I must respect that*. But the conclusion did not sit easily with her. There was still the faint chance that whatever ailed her mother was treatable, although as she watched her slowly wasting away week after week, she knew it was very faint indeed. And on top of that thought was the renewed fear about how she would look after her mother when she became too ill to cope.

'Me and the boys are doing a gig at a small festival in Derbyshire on Saturday,' Jim said, as they had supper a few days later in the pub near Nancy's house – it had become their favourite haunt. Old and beamy and dark, the high wooden bench seats were cosy when it was rainy and cold. Outside it had a beautiful garden overlooking the Downs where they sat when it was fine. Tonight a summer storm was in progress, the thunder rolling back and forth overhead and they were snug inside. 'I was wondering if you'd like to come.'

'Saturday?' Nancy queried, immediately worrying about her mother. Louise wouldn't be around. She and the girls had left for their bucket-and-spade holiday at the weekend to stay with her friend Sarah at her seaside cottage in Brixham.

'We'll go up in the morning and come back Sunday,' he was saying. 'There's only one snag.'

She looked at him questioningly. Jim had stayed almost every night in Louise's absence. And although she hated to admit it to herself, it was a relief to have a break from her daughter's censorious eye. Nancy was enjoying her freedom.

'Camping.'

She laughed. 'Right!'

'No point spending on a B & B when we're up half the night.

And Mal's big on camping, he's got all the gear. It's bloody uncomfortable, but you don't sleep anyway.'

'Umm . . .' Nancy knew she sounded dubious, but it was only her mother stopping her.

'Not convinced?' Jim was laughing. 'Not blown away by the thought of a mildewed tent and a blow-up mattress in a muddy field in the pouring rain? You've obviously led a sheltered life.'

'Ha,' she said. 'It's true that I've never been camping. Maybe I should give it a try.'

'Is that a yes?' He looked triumphant and leaned across the small pub table to plant a firm kiss on her mouth, as if that sealed the deal.

On Saturday morning she went to see her mother again. She was unfairly angry with Frances for needing her, thinking wistfully of Jim heading north to the festival without her. Because although she had agreed to go with him on the spur of the moment, when she'd thought about it, she'd known she would just worry. Jim had been kind about it, he'd said he understood, but she knew he was disappointed at her volte-face. So she was morose and snappish with Frances, until her mother, frowning, asked, 'Is something wrong, darling? You don't seem in the greatest of moods this morning.' Then her eyes narrowed. 'I hope that man isn't causing trouble again.'

Up till now Frances had made no comment on the fact that Nancy was seeing Jim again. Nancy had been surprised: it wasn't like her mother to pass up the chance of a lecture. 'If you're talking about Jim, no, he's not causing any trouble at all.'

Frances raised her eyebrows, but didn't reply.

'He's gone to a music festival with his band. They're performing tonight.'

'And you're not going with him?'

'It's in Derbyshire.'

Her mother's expression took on a faraway look. 'Your father and I used to love live music, as you know,' she said. 'We went to all the festivals . . . Cheltenham, Three Choirs, Aldeburgh . . . Glyndebourne, when we could afford it.' She smiled at Nancy. 'I know you think it was only your father who loved music, and I wasn't as keen as he was, of course, but a live performance is such a thrill. It'll never be the same again . . . just that moment, the whole occasion . . .' She lapsed into silence.

Nancy was amazed. She had always thought her mother went along to those events on sufferance, because that was what a wife did in those days. Her father had indeed been the acknowledged music fanatic, everything from Bach to Andrew Lloyd Webber, and the house was always alive with it. It had been he who drove Nancy's playing as a child, leaned over her as she practised, stopped her riding a bike in case she damaged her hands, ferried her to lessons, sat in the front row at school concerts, went with her to check out the various music colleges. He'd had such high hopes for her career until Christopher had stolen her away.

'I suppose it's not quite the same, country and western,' Frances was saying.

Nancy sighed. *Might have guessed she'd ruin it.*

She watched her mother press her head back against the sofa cushions and close her eyes. 'I think I might have a little nap now, darling. I'm sure you've got things to get on with.'

And suddenly Nancy decided she had. Checking that her mother had food in the fridge and that everything in the house was in order, she said, 'I'll come again on Sunday evening, Mum. Will you be all right?'

Her mother smiled and waved her away. 'Of course I will. Thank you, darling, you're very kind.'

As soon as she got home, she threw some things into an overnight bag and phoned Ross. 'Will you call Mum and just check she's okay this evening, please? I'll be home by lunchtime tomorrow, but if there's any problem, just ring me and I'll come straight back.'

'Sure, no worries,' Ross said. 'Feel a tad jealous. I haven't done a festival in a tent since I can't remember when.' She heard him laugh. 'Go, Nancy, have a great time.'

She laughed too, her heart bursting with childish excitement as she said goodbye.

CHAPTER TWENTY-EIGHT

'Probably the tent put her off,' Mal said, as he and Jim began to pitch the weathered green-canvas A-frame in which Jim would be sleeping. Mal, an old hand at tent-pitching, had already carefully laid out the canvas on a flat patch of grass in the field designated by the festival. It was a boiling hot August day and the journey up had been nightmarish, the M1 at a standstill south of Loughborough, in a van with no air conditioning, for what had seemed like hours. Jim was already exhausted and wished he was back home with Nancy.

'You think?' he asked, handing Mal a metal tent peg and watching him angle it at forty-five degrees, then bash it into the soft ground with his mallet. 'She seems so buried in her family responsibilities, I'm just beginning to wonder where I fit in.'

Mal handed him an aluminium pole. 'Stick that at the other end, mate. Make sure it's straight.' Jim did as he was told.

'What's the daughter got against you?' Mal stood back to survey his handiwork. 'Not like you to fail in a charm offensive, Jim-boy.' He chuckled, throwing his mallet onto the grass next to the bigger tent, where he and Jimmy P would be sleeping. 'You must be losing your touch.'

It was late afternoon before Jimmy P arrived. The field was packed with a huge variety of tents in all shapes and sizes – colourful blues and oranges, purples and greens, domes and inflatables, pods, a single tepee – festival-goers milling about in shorts and T-shirts, busily organizing their creature comforts in the sunshine before the night's entertainment began. It had been children's day and there were lots of families, some with quite small kids who shouted and laughed as they ran wild around the campsite, the smell of barbecue hanging on the warm air, a simple, jolly tune thumping from the covered stage set up in the field on the other side of the lane.

Mal had got both tents pitched, the ground sheets fixed, air mattresses pumped, the Primus stove and crockery unpacked, camping chairs unfolded. *Bloody faff*, Jim thought, *this camping lark*. He was already dreading a cold night on a wobbly air mattress in Mal's nylon sleeping bag – which, although slippery and sweaty, was clean, courtesy of Sonia's obsessive tendencies.

The three of them were finally able to relax, sitting in a circle around the stove. Mal had made green tea for himself, Jimmy P was nursing a Beck's – the alcohol-free variety, which he'd packed into a well-stocked cool-box in his boot – and Jim had a glass of whiskey on the grass by his bare feet, his hands occupied with his guitar, on which he was strumming the song list for the set.

'We sticking with "Walk the Line" after "Remember When"?' Mal asked.

'Rather have "For the Good Times" than "Remember When". Hate that song,' Jim said.

Jimmy P laughed. 'Yeah, yeah, so you say every time, but the punters love it.'

'They love "For the Good Times", too.'

'Want to watch we don't come across as a Kris Kristofferson tribute band,' Mal warned. 'If you want to end with "Help Me Make It", then I'm with Jimmy P.'

They bickered on, Jim picking out the tunes as they came up, singing a verse or too, harmonizing with Jimmy P. It felt good, sitting there with his friends, sipping his whiskey as the sun began to sink behind the Derbyshire hills in dusty amber shafts blurred with the smoke from numerous barbecues.

''Ey up,' Jimmy P's gaze was suddenly fixed on something behind Jim's back.

Jim watched Mal's eyes widen and a grin spread across his friend's face. He swivelled round and saw, to his amazement, Nancy threading her way through the tents, eyes darting from right to left as she searched for him. *Beautiful woman*, he thought, taking in her jeans, sandals, a simple white embroidered Indian-cotton tunic, silver bangles on her wrist.

'I love it that you came,' Jim whispered into Nancy's ear as he slung his arm across her shoulders, pulling her close. They were walking in the semi-darkness back across the field to the campsite after the gig. It was late, well after midnight, but groups of people were still lying on the grass around their tents in the glow of small lanterns, drinking, laughing, some smoking weed, judging by the sweet, pungent tang Jim detected, floating on the cool night air.

Mal and Jimmy P were still in the drinks tent, hanging out with the last stragglers, but Jim wanted to be alone with Nancy.

'They loved you,' she said. 'You were great, Jim. Honestly, I didn't want you to stop.'

He grinned with pleasure. 'Thanks. Now for the challenging part.'

Nancy stood looking down at the tent while Jim fiddled with the small lantern Mal had hung outside. 'I did warn you,' he said, noticing Nancy's uncertainty. 'Portaloos that way.' He pointed to a row of cabins on the far side of the field.

'Long way in the middle of the night,' she said, giving an embarrassed laugh.

'Yeah, but it already *is* the middle of the night. And you won't sleep a wink. We'll be up by six.'

They hovered, reluctant to squeeze themselves into the narrow interior of the tent, which was taken up entirely by the blow-up mattress.

'We've only got one sleeping bag, so I'll unzip it and use it as a cover . . . Lucky it's not cold.'

Ten minutes later they were lying on their backs, side by side on the chilly, slippery rubber of the mattress, still fully clothed under the nylon sleeping bag.

'Comfy?' Jim asked, turning on his side and moving his leg till it rested across hers, his arm over her body. He began to laugh and heard Nancy giggle in response. She had sat on the grass near the stage while he was playing earlier, her knees hugged to her body, her eyes so full of happiness it had almost put him off his performance. And nothing did that.

'Blissfully.' She just had time to say before he brought his mouth down on hers, his hand moving to feel the softness of her breasts beneath her shirt. He heard her gasp and felt her hand on his trousers, impatiently pulling at his belt with the kneeling cowboy buckle, which was a bugger to undo.

For a while they struggled with each other's clothes, kissing and caressing like hungry kids, gasping with laughter as they bounced on the mattress, trying to get sufficient freedom from their clothes.

The buzz Jim still felt from the show and the crowd's appreciation, the whiskey they had consumed afterwards, the fresh night air and the sense they were free from the shadow of Nancy's disapproving family, all added to the thrill of their lovemaking. Even the vagaries of the cramped tent couldn't dent it.

How long they made love, he had no idea, but when they finally lay back exhausted on the rubbery surface, in the now steamy air of the tent, he heard ragged clapping and cheering from outside, as if a performance were over.

Nancy looked at him in horror. 'Were we making that much noise?'

He grinned. 'Must have been.'

But as they lay there, in silence now, not wishing to make another sound to delight their impromptu audience, they realized with dismay that the air mattress was no longer bouncy, but gradually sinking, hissing softly as it delivered them to the cold, unforgiving ground.

'Oh, God, we've done for it,' she said, but neither of them could speak for laughing, which was interrupted rudely by Jimmy P's growl from the next-door tent.

'Any chance a fellow can get some shut-eye around here?'

Which did nothing to abate their mirth, although now they tried to smother it beneath the inadequate nylon fabric of the sleeping bag.

It was a long night. Nancy and Jim talked softly together, knowing sleep was unlikely. The ground was unyielding, there was no position Jim could find that made it easier. Sounds from around them punctuated the night as campers trailed back and forth to the loos – too much real ale consumed, no doubt – children cried, hard-core boozers stumbled past the tent talking loudly, a dog barked in the distance. But Jim, pressed against Nancy's back as he became aware her breathing had slowed into sleep, didn't mind any of it. He wanted to stay awake, experience every detail of that magic night, from the musty smell of the old tent, the tickling of Nancy's hair in his face, the post-coital purr in his loins, his lover's body sheltered in his arms, the pain as his hip pressed into the solid earth. But sleep began to blur the edges of his thoughts and he found himself drifting off just as dawn was filtering through the ageing canvas.

'I'm too bloody old for this,' Jim whispered grumpily, as he and Nancy crawled stiffly, in turn, out of the tent onto the wet, dewy grass, to be blinded by early-morning sunlight. It hurt his tired eyes and every bone in his body ached.

'God, me too,' she said, stretching her arms above her heard, face turned to the sun, dark circles under her huge eyes, her hair so gloriously dishevelled that, despite his screaming joints, he wanted to make love to her all over again.

There was no sign of Mal and Jimmy P, the flap on their tent firmly zipped shut.

'Tell you what,' he said, voice still not above a whisper. 'Let's get out of here. We'll go and find a strong cup of coffee and a decent washbasin.'

'It's early – the cafes won't be open for hours yet, not on a Sunday,' Nancy said.

'Well, we'll drive until we find one that is.'

CHAPTER TWENTY-NINE

'How lovely,' Nancy spoke brightly, despite the sinking feeling in her gut.

'We should be there in about half an hour,' Maria, an old friend from Suffolk, yelled over the Bluetooth transmitting from their car, although there was no need to shout: Nancy could hear the bad news perfectly well.

She was still tired from the festival weekend, tired from too much lovemaking and not enough sleeping, tired from the ongoing excitement and turmoil generated by Jim's presence in her life. Monday was going to be a rest day. Jim was busy packing for the move next week and they'd agreed he wouldn't stay over that night because Louise and the girls were due back. But now Maria and Hugo were descending on her.

Distracted, she raced upstairs, selected a pink shirt and a pair of clean jeans, glared at her hair in the mirror – it needed washing – pulled the bed together, raced back downstairs, cleared away the plates from breakfast, wiped the crumbs from around the toaster, swept the tiled floor, plumped the sofa cushions, threw away some dead roses Jim had picked from the garden, recycled a pile of newspapers and emptied the filter in the coffee machine. Bob the cat had slept the night in the armchair – her favourite spot – so she emptied the cat litter too. She had barely finished when she heard the crunch of tyres on gravel and went to open the front door.

Hugo Olorenshaw was a conductor, an old friend of Christopher's. Tall, very thin and pale, iron-grey foppish conductor-hair trailing below his ears, he was a restless, intense character whom Nancy had never found very comfortable to be around. It was as if he were constantly listening to something – music, she assumed – inside his head, his expression almost permanently distracted.

Maria, his wife, was an extreme contrast, so much so that Christopher had dubbed them the Sprats, after the 'Jack Sprat' nursery rhyme. She was small, plump and bosomy, her dyed-brown hair in an untidy French pleat, dressed today in a striped matelot T-shirt and, like her husband, jeans. But whereas Hugo's jeans looked too pressed, too clean, too formal even to pass for jeans, Maria's looked as if she'd slept in them for a month, unidentified stains and dog hairs from their dopy Cavalier King Charles spaniel – now careering round the garden – clinging to the crumpled blue denim.

'Darling, it's so wonderful to see you.' Maria gave Nancy a warm hug. 'It's been years.'

Had it? Nancy wondered and realized with surprise that Maria was right. When she'd first moved to Brighton, she had made the effort to visit her friends back in Suffolk. But she found she was pained by the careful editing in her friends' conversation concerning her ex, and couldn't settle when she was out and about in familiar haunts in case she bumped into Christopher and Tatjana holding hands – for example, on the high street. Aldeburgh was a very small town.

'We miss you,' Maria was saying.

They settled at the kitchen table with their coffee and some Jaffa

Cakes bought for the girls. Hugo immediately grabbed two and crammed them into his mouth, one after the other, munching fiercely as if he hadn't seen food in a week. Nancy saw Maria giving him a disapproving frown, which he ignored as he reached for a third.

'You know Sally's had breast cancer?' Maria said. 'She's okay now, but she had to have lymph nodes removed and all sorts. She's been quite low.'

Her friend spent the next half an hour filling her in about people who were no longer part of Nancy's life, some of whom, even in the short time she'd been gone from the area, were already fading from memory. Hugo chipped in occasionally to correct his wife on some small detail – a habit she remembered only too well from the years with her own pedantic husband. Neither, however, mentioned Christopher or Tatjana, although their presences prowled around the conversation until Nancy could bear it no more.

'So how is Christopher? This wedding seems a bit of a number,' Nancy said, keeping her tone light.

She saw the slight wariness that settled over Maria's open features. 'He seems fine,' her friend said noncommittally.

'Except for the baby,' Hugo put in. 'Christopher's not so fine about that.'

Nancy felt a jolt to her chest, as if someone had hit her. 'Baby?'

Maria, seeing her expression, looked as if she would happily kill her tactless husband right then and there. But Hugo, insensitive as usual to the atmosphere around him, sailed blithely on. 'You can't blame the silly old bugger. He's my age and he'll be dealing with a screaming infant, up half the night, paraphernalia everywhere. Quite ghastly if—'

'Hugo!' Maria's voice cut across him like a rifle shot.

'What?' he asked, bewildered.

Nancy was feeling dizzy. 'Tatjana's pregnant?'

Only now did Hugo frown with understanding.

'I thought Christopher would have told you ages ago,' Maria was saying, her kind face creased with concern.

'Ages? Why? How pregnant is she?'

'Not sure, must be at least four months, maybe more. That's why they're getting married.' Maria tutted angrily. 'You'd think he'd have had the decency to let you know before someone else did.'

'Sorry, Nancy.' Hugo was uncharacteristically humble as he fiddled with the handle of his mug, not meeting her eye.

'It's none of my business any more, thank goodness.' She spoke with what she hoped was a conviction she was far from feeling.

'Well, no, maybe not you,' Maria said, 'but Louise, certainly. Christopher says she's coming to the wedding. Was he going to wait for the poor girl to arrive and notice the bride's bulging dress?'

Nancy sighed. More stuff to upset her already tense and troubled daughter. But it wasn't just Louise. Nancy wasn't taking it particularly well herself. There was something so hurtful, so sneaky, so . . . *predictable* about them having a baby. Although, oddly, she hadn't predicted it. She'd thought Christopher would be too selfish, Tatjana too ambitious, but clearly he was a slave to her whims. Anything she wanted, she got.

Into the silence, Hugo said, 'I hope I haven't caused trouble, letting the cat out of the bag.'

'Well, of course you have,' Maria snapped. 'Maybe you should learn to think before you speak.'

'It's not Hugo's fault,' Nancy said.

'The old boy's bitten off more than he can chew.' Hugo gave her an apologetic smile. 'Should have seen her coming.'

Maria nodded in agreement.

'But he's happy with her, no?'

Hugo shrugged. 'He *was*. I'd say the gilt's worn off the gingerbread a bit recently. Better the devil you know, eh?' His wife harrumphed and got up, grabbing the empty cups and dumping them on the draining board with a bang. Then she said, in a lighter tone, 'Talking of seeing people coming, anyone on your horizon yet, Nancy?'

Nancy got up too, deliberately turning away from her friends to close the lid of the Kilner jar in which she kept the coffee, just in case she should blush. But the sudden thought, unbidden, of Jim's tongue flicking repeatedly across her nipple, sent a flash of pure lust through her body, which made her tremble, sealing her fate. She could feel the provoking heat flood, like a tidal wave, across her cheeks.

Lost once more in his own distractions, Hugo seemed unaware, but a small flicker of Maria's eyebrows, quickly gone, made it clear that her friend had definitely noticed. She gave Nancy a quizzical smile.

'Hmm,' was all she said, however, before hustling her husband out of the door and shouting for Solti, the dog, who was snuffling at something against the far fence and paid no attention whatsoever to Maria's call. 'Ring me,' said her friend, as she gave Nancy a goodbye hug.

'Nana! Nana!' Hope, followed swiftly by Jazzy, flung herself into Nancy's arms as she came through the door. Both girls looked so well, their hair bleached by the sun, their skin lightly tanned, their young faces purged of that exhausted end-of-term pallor. Jazzy ran to fetch a blue bucket full of shells and pebbles, which she dumped on Nancy's lap as she sat on the green sofa in their kitchen.

'So how was it?' Nancy looked up at Louise, as she sifted through the shells, showing suitable delight at Jazzy's collection of razor clams.

'It was great, Mum. We did nothing but go to the beach, swim, muck about in the sand, dig in rock pools, go for ice creams. Proper old fashioned bucket-and-spade holiday. Bliss.'

'I swimmed in the sea without wings, Nana,' Jazzy interrupted.

'Fantastic. Well done, darling.' She kissed the top of Jazzy's head, smelling the sweaty, salty tang of the sea in her thick blonde hair, then went to stand by the worktop as Louise filled the teapot. 'And the kids got on?'

Louise nodded. 'Sarah's two are brilliant. Zac's younger than Jazzy and can be a bit whiny, but on the whole they played beautifully, left us alone to read and chat.'

'So you got a proper break.'

'Yeah. It was perfect.' Her daughter's face fell slightly as she brushed her dark hair off her face. 'Too perfect. Didn't want to come back, to be honest.'

Nancy wasn't sure what to say. The secret of Christopher's baby was burning a hole in her tongue. She'd phoned him after Maria and Hugo had gone, but he'd been decidedly snappish. 'Don't lecture me, Nancy,' he'd said. 'Louise never picks up the phone, as you well know, so it's damn hard to tell her something as sensitive as this. What the hell am I supposed to do? Text her?'

'Okay, okay, keep your hair on,' she'd said, wearied by his lifelong commitment to blaming others. 'It's just not going to be a good look if you don't mention it before the wedding and everyone except Louise knows.'

'I'm not stupid, I do know that. I just haven't found the right time.'

Now Louise handed her a mug of tea and they sat on the sofa, her daughter pushing Bob onto the floor. As they did so, Louise's mobile rang.

'This'll be Ross,' she said, reluctantly pulling it out of her shorts pocket and glancing at the screen. 'Oh. No . . . Dad.' She held it for a moment, staring at the device. In the end she made a face and said, 'Better get it, Mum. He's probably ringing because he wants the girls to strew crimson rose petals in Tatjana's hallowed footsteps or some such bollocks.'

CHAPTER THIRTY

Louise had hoped that the ten days apart might have reduced the friction between her and Ross and give them both a fresh start, but quite the reverse was the case. Her husband was almost sullen with her when he eventually arrived home after midnight.

'Had a good time?' he asked, without enthusiasm, his face so dog-tired that Louise immediately felt guilty for the rest she'd had.

'It was great. The girls loved it.'

'That's good,' he said, immediately twisting the top off a bottle of red wine and pouring himself a large glass, without offering her one. His T-shirt was damp with sweat, his jeans bagging around his bottom as he threw himself onto the sofa in the kitchen.

'How did it go with Kyla?' she asked, making herself a cup of fennel tea. Jason's girlfriend had taken to stepping in at busy times and had offered to be on call while Louise was away. It was late and she was tired, but she hadn't wanted to go to bed without seeing her husband. And she needed to tell him about the baby. She still felt shaken by the news, although she couldn't explain why because part of her had been expecting it, despite her mother's predictions. But she sensed that this baby would push her one more step beyond reach of her father's affections. She always kept hoping that some miracle would happen to bond them closer, but it seemed that the exact opposite was the case now Tatjana stood in the way. This child of his mellow old age, she knew, stood a much better chance of securing his love than she ever had.

She saw Ross shrug. 'Yeah, okay, I guess. She's not trained, but she's a hard worker, I'll give her that.'

'And the bookings?'

Her husband was lying back, eyes closed, glass cradled in his big square hands. He didn't open his eyes to say, 'Didn't take you long to start nagging, I see.'

Louise, stung, just stared at him. 'I was only asking.'

'Yeah, yeah. "Only asking" so you can shake your head and tell me the whole thing's a disaster, right? It's been bliss not having to listen to the voice of doom for a few days.'

'And it's been fucking bliss not listening to your bloody whingeing, not facing calls from people we owe money to, not being blamed for every tiny fucking thing.' She took a long breath as she glared down at him slumped on the sofa. 'I wish I'd never come back.'

Ross, she saw, looked shocked. He sat up. 'Right. Well, maybe you shouldn't have. Maybe you should have stayed there, nice and cosy, with your little friend in her luxury cottage, doing fuck-all except gossip and whine about your useless husbands. Maybe I'm better off without you breathing down my neck.' His face was flushed, his voice heavy with sarcasm.

'If that's what you think, then maybe you should give it a try,' Louise said, her voice high with rage. 'Because I can't fucking do this any more!'

'Mummy?'

Louise jumped at the sound of Hope's voice, and turned to

see her daughter in the kitchen doorway, her face a mask of bewilderment.

Ross was on his feet in a moment, moving quickly across the room to scoop her up in her lilac-cotton onesie and hug her.

'Sorry, darling,' he said, burying his face in her shoulder. 'Sorry. Mummy and Daddy were just having a bit of a discussion about stuff. Nothing to worry about.'

Hope was obviously half asleep, but her eyes searched Louise's face anxiously over her father's shoulder. Louise came over and stroked her hand. 'Sorry we woke you. It's okay . . . Everything's okay.' She knew she sounded pathetic and unconvincing, but she had no idea what to say. She hoped the child was too sleepy to really understand what she'd just said to Ross. 'Go back to bed . . . Daddy'll take you.' She kissed Hope's cheek, smoothed her rumpled hair off her face, tried to give her a comforting smile. Hope just nodded tiredly as Ross carried her away.

When he came downstairs, both of them were subdued and neither spoke for a moment.

'We can't keep doing this. The girls have been upset enough already, hearing us fight.'

Ross looked sour. 'You started it.' He picked up his wine and took a long, angry gulp then turned his back on her, shaking his head slowly as if he couldn't believe what he was hearing. He walked across the room and threw himself down on the sofa again. Louise didn't have the energy to say any more. She raised a hand in defeat and left him there to stew.

Tiptoeing upstairs, she checked on both girls before climbing wearily into bed. There she lay tense in the darkness, dreading her husband coming upstairs, yet longing for it too, wanting somehow to resolve what remained so unresolved, hoping that Ross might have been suitably shocked by Hope's distress, that they might find a way to talk sensibly about the restaurant. And their marriage. The two seemed so inextricably entwined, both sinking in unison towards an uncertain end.

But Ross didn't come to bed. When Louise woke around five, her sleep restless and haunted, his side was still empty. Creeping downstairs, she found him where she had left him, horizontal on the green sofa, curled on his side, hands pressed between his knees, face slack with sleep, his bulk partly covered with the purple faux-fur throw the girls snuggled under when they were watching television. She stood looking at him, but didn't disturb him – she had no desire to witness the hostile expression she might see in his eyes if he opened them. So she crept back upstairs and lay in bed, frightened by the implications – they had never slept apart in the same house – until she heard Jazzy stomping sleepily to the loo just after seven. She hadn't even had the chance to talk about her father's baby.

CHAPTER THIRTY-ONE

Jim stood at the kitchen table, surrounded by brown cardboard boxes, staring at the piles of china stacked in front of him. He had no idea where to start. Chrissie was across the room, tackling the shelves on the Welsh dresser.

'So what's sex with Nancy like, then?'

Chrissie's tone was conversational as she wrapped paper round a large cup, but Jim knew not to be fooled, it could turn on a penny. He attempted a nonchalant laugh. 'Come on, Chrissie. Like I'm going to discuss my sex life with you.'

'I'll discuss mine with you, if you like. Phil's a bit of a perv. Likes the whole game-playing thing. You know, tying my—'

'Stop right there,' Jim interrupted, shuddering as if he'd swallowed something revolting. 'I don't want to know.'

Chrissie faced him, raising her eyebrows, a bold smile on her lips. 'You didn't used to be so squeamish. I remember a few discussions about stuff in the past that got you all worked up, like the time when—'

'Enough!' Jim bent his head to his task.

'You know this relationship with what's-her-name'll end in tears, don't you?' Her voice was soft, almost kind from across the room.

'She's just using you because you're handsome and a good fuck, Jimmy. Probably didn't get much of a seeing-to from her ex or something. But don't kid yourself she'll go the distance. Soon as the honeymoon's over, she'll be moving on to pastures new. Older women are like that – they don't want commitment. They want friends with benefits.'

Jim didn't reply immediately: he was experiencing familiar outrage at his wife's manipulations, and a deep fear that her words might hold water. Was she right? Was Nancy just playing with him?

Chrissie was looking smug, knowing she'd hit a home run, as he cleared his throat. 'I didn't know you were an expert on sex with older women. Is there something you haven't told me all these years?'

Which made Chrissie throw her head back and roar with laughter.

'*Touché*, Jim, *touché*! Glad to see you haven't completely lost your sense of humour.'

'Glad to see you haven't completely lost the will to wind me up,' he said.

With Chrissie's mood temporarily stabilized, and the talk safely off the subject of sex, they set to work on the contents of the cupboard, his wife lingering irritatingly over certain pieces of china, reminiscing about their provenance and the memories they evoked. She brandished a blue-patterned bowl: 'We bought this from that Turkish woman by the side of the road. She must have been a hundred and fifty if she was a day.' Then, holding up a white espresso cup, 'Do you remember Tommy getting his finger stuck in the handle?' If Jim had had his way, he'd have shovelled the lot into a crate and dumped it on the steps of the local charity shop – despite the notice in the window that asked him not to do so.

Finally they sat down with a cup of tea. Chrissie had gone quiet in the last hour. As she took the mug he offered she let out a long, melodramatic sigh. 'You and me . . . This is really the end, is it?' She blinked her green eyes at him sadly. 'Stupid, the whole thing. We'll both end up in scuzzy bedsits, you realize, all alone, getting old. Phil will dump me, Nancy'll dump you. And we could have been sharing this house we love, all cosy, looking after each other. Where's the sense in it?'

Jim wasn't going to engage in this cheerless scenario, not least because it was exactly what he feared most, and Chrissie, with her unerring knowledge of his frailties, knew it.

'When do you get into your place?' he asked.

'Pick up the keys Friday. Then I've got to get on and find somewhere to buy. You?'

'Staying with Mal and Sonia for three weeks till my flat's free.'

Chrissie grinned. 'Blimey, you won't last three days, let alone three weeks with Sonia. You'll have to put your head out of the window to breathe – you know how terrified she is of germs – and you'll be ironing your underpants, washing your plate up before you've even eaten your supper, bed before nine . . . Not a pretty sight.'

'Yeah,' he laughed, 'won't be easy, but it's kind of them.'

'Why doesn't Nancy want you at hers? Is it the snoring?'

'I don't snore.'

'Huh? Are you kidding, Jimmy? It's like lying next to a Flymo. I can hear it clear as day, even on the floor below.'

'That's such rubbish,' he said, hoping to God it was. Had he been snoring like a lawnmower next to Nancy? She hadn't complained. 'You and me haven't slept together in years. And I've given up smoking since we shared a bed.'

She gave him an evil grin. 'Doesn't make much difference, evidently. Something to do with the throat muscles getting weak because you're so old.'

'Yeah, yeah, give me a break, will you? If I believed all your guff, I'd shoot myself right now.'

'You know me, Jimmy. I tell it how it is.'

Later Jim went upstairs and settled in his chair with his guitar. He hadn't had the time to do much playing with all this moving crap and he missed the calming influence it had on him. But today he couldn't seem to play. He felt jumpy and unsettled. Creature of habit that he knew himself to be, he was finding it hard to cope with the upheaval. It wasn't just the move itself, or the time he must serve at Mal's house, under the neurotic eye of Sonia. It was Nancy. When he was with her, he believed it would all turn out fine. They would push through the hassles on both sides and end up together. He loved her and he was pretty sure she loved him. But when they were apart, he began to doubt. Was he just 'handsome and a good fuck,' as Chrissie had put it? Would Nancy tire of him soon? Louise had got back yesterday, and Nancy was already involved in her daughter's dramas again – in particular the baby her ex had conveniently forgotten to mention.

CHAPTER THIRTY-TWO

As soon as the front door was shut, Nancy and Jim moved into each other's arms and stayed that way for a very long time.

'Hello,' he muttered into her hair.

'Missed you,' she answered, giddy with his proximity.

They didn't bother with supper, just sat on the sofa with a bottle of wine and a bowl of crisps, Jim's arm round her shoulders, and talked, a flow of chatter, although they'd spoken on the phone during the week. It was as if lock-gates had been opened, equilibrium restored.

'Play for me,' Jim said suddenly, hauling Nancy up from the sofa. 'I've asked you a million times and you always refuse. Not fair, when I've played for you so much.'

She pulled a face. 'I will one day, promise.' Christopher had always made her feel so self-conscious about her ability. She didn't want Jim to be disappointed.

'No,' Jim said. 'Now . . . please, Nancy.'

The wine must have lowered her resistance because, reluctantly, she allowed him to lead her to the piano room, still clasping her hand. She sat down on the stool, adjusted the position.

'What shall I play?'

'Anything you like.'

She thought for a moment, and, not bothering with the music, laid her fingers on the keys and began to play Liszt's famous 'Liebestraum'. At first she was nervous, then forgot Jim was standing there, eyes fixed on her as she played, and got caught up in the lyrical love song. She fluffed the first fast cadenza – she hadn't practised it for a while now, and it needed a huge amount of practice – but by the second she was getting into her stride and made a better job of it. At the end of the five or so minutes, she stopped.

'Wow,' he said, his blue eyes misting. 'Wow, Nancy. That was so beautiful.'

Embarrassed, she said, 'It's Liszt, a love song.'

He nodded. 'Your playing is sensational.'

'Steady on. I'm not that good. Not any more. I don't practise enough.'

Jim frowned. 'Which just shows how brilliant you are.'

His approbation made her heart sing.

For a while Nancy played for him. He wouldn't let her stop. In the end she got tired of her solo performance and tried to persuade him to do a duet with her.

'Nope,' he said immediately.

'But you play the piano too.'

'Not like that. It would be like comparing a tin mug to Dresden china.'

'I love tin mugs.'

'Me too, but they aren't in the same league.'

That night, after they had made love, he hummed the melody of 'Liebestraum' to her in his husky baritone as they fell asleep.

*

'You don't have to go to Mal's, you know, you could come here while you wait.' It was early morning, but Nancy had been awake for a while, thinking.

There was silence from the other side of the bed, but she knew he wasn't asleep.

'No . . . no, I couldn't do that, Nancy.'

She thought Jim's voice sounded almost harsh in his refusal. 'Why not?' It was the first time she'd suggested it to him, but it wasn't a new thought. She'd been steeling herself to ask him ever since he'd told her about staying with his friends. But she knew the proposition held a significance deeper than the simple offer of a bed for three weeks.

'Because . . . because it would mean I was living here,' he said.

She turned over to look at him. 'And that wouldn't be good?'

He smiled. 'It would be great, Nancy. But what would your daughter think? And your mum? Won't they say we're jumping the gun, rushing into things?'

'It's what *we* say that matters, isn't it?' She waited to hear his response. The thought of him actually living with her was frightening, she admitted that, but he was spending most nights with her anyway, so would it make much difference?

Jim had rolled on his side, propping his head on his hand. 'Not sure. I don't want Louise kicking off, making me feel like some no-good gigolo.'

'Look, it's only until your new flat comes free. We spent most of the last week together.'

'Yes, but Louise wasn't around, and you always knew I had a home to go to. This'd be different, a real commitment. Three weeks is a long time.'

She laughed. 'Well, up to you. I'd love you to be here . . . but if you think it's too soon, I get it.'

Jim reached over and laid his hand gently against her face, his thumb tracing a pattern on her cheek. His grey hair had come loose from its ponytail during the night and it softened his face, made him look more vulnerable somehow. 'I love you, Nancy.'

Her eyes filled with tears at the unexpectedness of his words. He had never actually said it before. 'I love you too.' She felt the truth brush her heart, like a mother stroking her child.

They lay in silence for a while, holding hands, each lost in their own thoughts.

'Will you talk to your daughter, check out the lie of the land before we make a decision?'

'I will, but we both know she's not going to be keen. My feeling is that if she sees you about, gets to know you a bit, she'll relax, come round.'

'Okay . . .' Jim still sounded doubtful and she understood his circumspection. 'What about your mum? She might need to come back. And if I'm here . . .'

'Mum seems surprisingly all right at the moment. I saw her earlier and she was telling me about going to bridge again. Not sure what's happened, whether she's putting on a brave face so I won't nag her about the endoscopy, but I don't think that'll be a problem in the next few weeks.'

Jim fell silent again. Then, 'Umm, Nancy . . . *are* we jumping the gun, spending so much time together?'

'It doesn't feel that way to me,' she said slowly.

'It doesn't to me, either. But . . .'

'But you're worried we'll ruin what we have if we push it into different territory.'

He neither nodded nor shook his head, just waited.

'We're not spring chickens. We don't have the luxury of years of courting.' She paused. 'If it falls apart, it falls apart.' Her mind skittered away from the thought, but she knew what she was saying was true. No amount of cautious dating would make their relationship any more robust. It wasn't as if they were planning a family, starting a dynasty. At their age, they had only their own happiness to consider.

Lindy's eyes widened. 'Whoa! Moved in?'

'Only till his flat comes free . . . a month, tops.'

Nancy was at her friend's house with Hope, Jazzy and Toby.

The children, in their swimming costumes, were jumping and shrieking on the safety-netted trampoline in Lindy's back garden, their faces flushed and sweaty in the August sun, a blow-up pool full of water – now tepid, the surface covered with bits of grass, twigs and the odd fly – standing by for when it all got too much.

Lindy and Nancy were propped up on two padded calico loungers, mugs of tea in hand, watching the kids.

'God . . .' Nancy covered her eyes as Toby and Jazzy crashed into each other and fell in a laughing heap on the rubber matting. 'Is it safe, them all jumping at the same time?'

'Probably not,' Lindy said, 'but nothing any of us does these days is considered "safe", is it? There's got to be compromise.'

Nancy wasn't sure Louise would see a broken limb or concussion in such a sanguine light, so she called, 'Don't jump so close together – you'll hurt yourselves.' Which warning went totally unheeded by the three children.

'What's it like, having him there all the time?' Lindy was asking.

'Okay so far . . .' she grinned, 'but he only arrived two nights ago.'

Lindy nodded, but Nancy saw a frown forming on her friend's brow.

'So you're not actually going to live together yet?'

'He'll have his own flat. It's just it doesn't come free for a few weeks.'

'Right.' Lindy pursed her lips. 'Is he buying or renting?'

'Renting.'

'Hmm . . .'

Nancy glanced sideways at her. 'What?'

'It's just renting's not so permanent, is it? Suppose this flat falls through . . .'

'Why would a rented flat be more likely to fall through than a bought one?'

Lindy stretched out her tanned legs in their turquoise pedal-pushers, her immaculately groomed feet with their plum-polished toes glinting in the sunshine. 'I suppose it wouldn't . . .' She gazed at the kids as she spoke, as if she didn't want to confront Nancy.

'What are you saying, Lindy?'

Lindy expelled a breath sharply, swung her legs off the lounger and faced Nancy, propping her elbows on her knees, hands clasped, bending her head closer to her friend.

'You know I love Jim, darling, but all that stuff with his wife . . . I'm just wondering how well you know him. I mean, it's going to be quite hard to get rid of him if things don't work out and he's got nowhere to go . . .'

Nancy felt a hard stone of irritation forming in her gut, which she made a determined effort to breathe through, as her old yoga teacher in Suffolk used to instruct: 'Breathe the anger out,' she'd said to the class. 'Surround it with a gentle breath, then breathe it away. No force, no strength. *Whooo*, just let it go.'

'I'm sure we'll work it out.'

Lindy laid a hand on her arm. 'Don't be cross, Nance. I just always like to have an exit strategy in life. And I know you're pretty gone on Jim so you may not be thinking particularly straight.'

'Are you suggesting he's taking advantage of me?'

Lindy laughed. 'Such an old-fashioned expression! But, yes, maybe I am. Not that I think he's the type to hang on anyone's coat-tails, but men aren't good at being on their own. So it'll be great for Jim. He'll be snug as a bug with you looking after him. But once the sex thing wears off, are you really going to want him hanging around all day, strumming on that guitar of his, leaving the loo seat up, waiting for you to wash his underpants and getting under your feet?'

Nancy couldn't help laughing. 'God, Lindy, you paint a bleak picture. But you could be right. We might drive each other nuts. And if we do, it'll have to be Plan B.'

Lindy banged her palms on her thighs. 'Good. Well, I've had my say. And if things get ugly, just call me and I'll be round in a jiffy with my shotgun, see him and his guitar off the premises before the poor guy knows what's hit him.'

'You've got a shotgun?'

'Sure. It was Ronnie's, but he forgot to take it when we got divorced and he's never asked for it.'

Nancy chuckled. 'Do you know how to use it?'

'Of course I do. My dad was a poacher when he wasn't digging people's flowerbeds. I knew how to shoot before I was eight . . . He only poached rabbits and pheasant for the family to eat, though, not like the lamping that goes on these days – armed hoodlums in four-by-fours blasting anything that moves.'

A scream from the pool put an end to their conversation. Toby, it seemed, had picked up a dead wasp from the water by its wings and was waving it in Jazzy's face, rendering the child rigid with terror. Both women leaped to the rescue, but it was a while before the mayhem subsided, Lindy taking a dim view of her grandson's behaviour, Jazzy refusing to stop sobbing, Hope shivering in her swimsuit, grinning because she liked a good show, Toby stomping off inside, wet footprints trailing across the kitchen floor.

Nancy was relieved to be diverted. All the things Lindy had said she had also considered, of course, but she concluded that she and her friend had quite different philosophies when it came to men. Lindy wanted a lover round the corner, someone who wouldn't interfere with her life but would do as he was told, pitch up when required, push off when not. An arrangement that Nancy could never imagine for herself.

Now, as she leaned against the worktop, watching Lindy break spaghetti into boiling water for the children's tea, she was looking forward to getting home and finding Jim there, looking forward to sitting at the kitchen table having supper together, looking forward to sharing some wine and the sausages he'd bought, relating the wasp incident and listening to whatever he had to tell her about his day. In fact, she was longing for it.

CHAPTER THIRTY-THREE

'That's all I could find. I got rid of most of his old medication when I moved.' Joyce deposited a small cream Jo Malone bag on the table next to Frances.

They were in Joyce's house, a smart new slate-roofed, white-painted bungalow – one bedroom, one bathroom and a large, light sitting-room/kitchen area. Joyce's daughter-in-law, Fiona, had decorated the interior in muted Farrow & Ball colours: Cinder Rose, French Grey, Strong White. The furniture was all new, but elegant and comfortable – a bit *House and Garden* to Frances's mind. She couldn't understand why Joyce hadn't held out to keep her own stuff. But her friend felt on the back foot with Fiona, who had been kindness itself to her but was also over-conscious of appearances. And she had to admit, it did look very tasteful.

Frances peeped into the bag.

'The boxes give instructions about dose. Richard's doctor was a friend, so he was a bit naughty and gave him way more than he needed because Richard panicked so much about everything,' Joyce said. 'But you really shouldn't take anything without seeing the doctor, Fran. These are top-of-the-range painkillers – you can't muck about with them.'

Joyce was younger than Frances, not quite eighty, but she had suffered from rheumatoid arthritis for years – it came and went in severity – and was quite crippled with it sometimes. But her well-cut grey bob framed a plump, laughing, intelligent face. Joyce was not a complainer.

'Thank you,' Frances said. 'I'm so grateful, Joyce. It's just in case.'

Joyce lifted the arm of her spectacles, adjusting the frames more comfortably on her nose, peering intently at her friend as she did so. 'In case of what?'

Noting her expression, Frances smiled. 'Don't worry, I'm not going to use them to bump myself off. I just want to know that if the pain gets too bad I'll have something to hand.'

Joyce was clearly exasperated. 'That's what doctors are for, Fran. Why won't you go and get tested, find out precisely what's wrong? They can do so much, these days.'

Frances raised her eyebrows. 'Like they did for Richard?' She saw her friend wince, but she wasn't going to fall for the wonders-of-modern-medicine argument from Joyce, any more than she had from Nancy or that damn-fool child who called himself a doctor. 'I know it was what Richard wanted, but honestly, was it worth it? All that grisly surgery, those horrible lesions he got from the chemo, losing his hair, the mouth ulcers . . . He couldn't even hold a cup of tea with that neuropathy thing he had. And he was in so much pain towards the end.'

'You don't have to remind me,' Joyce said, her mouth tight.

'No, and I didn't intend to upset you, but I can't understand why you aren't on my side. I know I've got stomach cancer . . .'

'How do you know?'

'I went to the library and asked the girl to find the NHS site for me. I've got all the symptoms.'

Joyce sighed. 'When are you going to get your own computer, Fran? Then you could convince yourself you have cancer in the comfort of your own home.' She gave her a wry grin.

'Yes, yes, don't start that again.' It was a familiar bicker between them. Joyce was smugly internet savvy and never stopped reminding Frances of the fact, flaunting her sleek silver laptop, all its bells and whistles, with irritating frequency. 'Having a computer is not going to change the fact that I have cancer.'

'So you're basically going to ignore it till there's absolutely no chance anyone can help?'

'That's exactly what I'm going to do. You can call me a coward – I call myself one – but I cannot, I absolutely cannot, go through what poor Richard suffered. And he had you. You were an angel, Joyce. He was a very lucky man.' She stopped, seeing the tears forming in her friend's eyes.

'I do sometimes wonder . . .' Joyce lifted her glasses and wiped away the tears with a cotton hanky she drew from the sleeve of her navy cardigan. 'Yes, he lived a bit longer, but that bit was pretty horrible for both of us most of the time. It's just that, when faced with death or treatment, most people choose treatment.' She gazed out of the window. 'If he'd been cured, of course, we'd have made the right decision.'

'Richard was younger. Don't forget, I'm eighty-four. How much longer have I got anyway?'

The thought silenced the two women.

'What does Nancy say?' Joyce asked.

France shrugged. 'She wants me to have the endoscopy, of course. But she won't be pleased when I'm hauled in for major surgery, then chemo . . . the trips back and forth, the worry of having to look after me all the time. She hasn't thought it through, what hell it would be for the family.'

Both women were quiet again as they sat in the calm, neutral Farrow & Ball room, ensconced against the soft padding of expensively upholstered armchairs, a light summer breeze blowing through the open kitchen door, sending the petals of the overblown pink roses fluttering and falling onto the coffee table.

'So she's seeing the cowboy again, you say?'

Frances nodded, let out a long sigh. 'Not just seeing him, she's moved the bloody man in, according to Louise.'

'He's actually living at Applecroft?'

Frances nodded again. 'She insists it's only till he can get into his new flat, but I'm sure she's just saying that to keep Louise quiet.'

'Well, maybe he'll turn out nicer than you think, Fran. Nancy's never struck me as a fool. I'm sure she knows what she's doing.'

Joyce, Frances knew, had always been a big fan of her daughter. 'Normally, I'd agree. But this fellow has turned her head. She won't hear a word said against him. I've given up. I just pretend I know nothing and leave it at that.'

'Aah, bless her,' Joyce said, a faraway smile on her face. 'It must be wonderful to be in love again.'

Frances had been about to make some tart remark about the foolishness of love in general and love in old age in particular, but the words vanished as she was suddenly ambushed by a memory of the overwhelming thrill she'd felt when she was first with dear Kenny. The madness, the feeling that the actual cells of her body had been rearranged in a different order. So all she managed was a weak nod.

As Frances walked slowly back to her house, only three streets away from her friend's bungalow, she clutched the stylish bag with the black string handles that held the stash of Richard's old pain-killers. She would take some as soon as she got home. The pain in her stomach had been bad all day, but she hadn't wanted to alarm Joyce by swallowing one in her presence. The poor woman had enough pain of her own to deal with.

She felt exhausted. All she wanted to do was make up a hot-water bottle and crawl into bed, even though it was barely five in the afternoon. And she needed to get her strength up: Louise had asked her over for lunch tomorrow – Nancy was picking her up late morning. *The cowboy will be there, I suppose*, Frances thought, and suddenly felt an enjoyable shaft of anticipation at the potential of the day. Because however much she had played up her distress at having wine poured into her lap, there had also been a certain pleasure in the melodrama. And Jim was handsome, she had to give him that. Drunk and good for nothing, no doubt, but he did have a very charming smile.

CHAPTER THIRTY-FOUR

Things had changed for Jim. When he had arrived to stay at Nancy's while his flat was being sorted out, he had brought with him only his guitar and a small holdall. Three weeks wasn't long, he didn't need much. But today was different. He was moving in, not just 'staying', but *living* there. From now on this would be his home.

The reason was this. There had been a series of delays and farting around on the flat the week before he'd been due to sign the short-term tenancy agreement. Then early one morning the agent had rung, full of apology, to tell him the whole thing was off. The landlord, apparently, had discovered some major drama with the roof – it was a top-floor flat – when he was redecorating.

But when, panicking, he'd relayed the news to Nancy, she'd simply said, 'Stay here, then.'

'Until I find another place . . . Can I?'

'Yes . . . Or . . . seems silly, you paying a fortune for a separate flat when we're going to spend most of the time together. Aren't we?'

'What are you saying, Nancy?' he asked, watching the smile that was creeping tentatively across her face.

'I don't know. I think I'm saying . . . why don't we live together for a bit, try it out?' She waited for him to respond, but Jim wasn't sure what to say, so she added, 'You're here now . . .'

They discussed it back and forth for a couple of days, but in the end, Nancy prevailed. Something told him it wasn't a good idea, but he finally gave in to her enthusiasm. It wasn't that he didn't want to be with Nancy – and she was right: it was daft for him to pay a fortune on a flat he wasn't going to spend much time in – but still . . .

So today he was waiting anxiously for the removals men to pitch up with stuff from the storage unit. It was only seven-thirty. Nancy was upstairs having a shower, and Jim just wanted the day over with. He felt oddly reluctant to have his things in her house. He knew, almost before they'd been delivered, that they wouldn't really fit. So he'd kept the boxes to a minimum, just personal things, like clothes, papers and files, sheet music, a few books. All the furniture, like his beloved, battered leather chair and G Plan coffee table, would remain in store until he decided what to do with it.

He could definitely sense tension in the air in the days leading up to his things arriving. It wasn't just him: Nancy was nervous too. She had cleared out the spare room, pushed the bed to the side, emptied the cupboards of clothes. There was an armchair in the room, a small desk. It was to be his 'den', the place he could retreat to and play his guitar. But he couldn't imagine doing so, somehow, in this very feminine bedroom environment – not least because he banged his head on the sloping ceiling every time he stood up. *Early days*, he kept telling himself, as he checked the drive for the umpteenth time.

The two South African lads in the white van – broad-shouldered rugby obsessives whose rolling dialogue about a recent game picked up where it left off as they passed each other on the stairs up and down to the attic – had finished in less than an hour. He was just tipping them when Louise arrived back from dropping the girls at school. The van was blocking the drive, and he saw her face through the open car window tighten with irritation as she waited for the van to back out into the lane.

Nancy's daughter had been perfectly polite in the weeks he'd been staying, but she never made any effort to have a personal conversation with him. She just talked over him to her mother and seemed merely to tolerate him being there.

It was a shame because she was okay, was Louise. Jim found he liked her no-nonsense directness. But she was very uptight. Understandable, he thought. She had a lot on her plate, what with a failing gaff and a husband who never took his head out of a saucepan. But they hadn't exactly bonded and Jim still had the overriding impression that in Louise's eyes he didn't measure up. Which made him jumpy and not at his best around her.

'Finished already?' she asked, as she got out of her car.

'Yeah . . . didn't bring much.'

'Where's Mum?'

'Making coffee. Come in and have a cup.'

He saw her hesitate. 'Thanks, but I'd better get on.'

Jim sighed inwardly. 'Louise . . .' He glanced at Nancy's house, lowered his voice and moved towards her. 'I know you're not happy with me being here, but I promise you I have your mother's best interests at heart.'

Louise glanced up at him. Her small, neat features showed tiredness, despite the fading summer tan, her blue eyes pained. But as her gaze met his, her expression seemed to slide unwillingly from hostile to resigned. 'I know you have, Jim,' she said, and for the first time he heard some kindness in her words. Not approbation, definitely not that, but a softening from her usual response to him. Then she turned quickly away before he had a chance to reply.

Later that morning, Nancy stood in the doorway of the attic bedroom. 'Do you think you'll find room for everything?'

The small space was in chaos, boxes open, things strewn around, Jim kneeling in front of a pile of books, wondering which wall to prop them against. He wished he hadn't brought any of the damn stuff.

'I know it's not ideal,' Nancy went on, her expression anxious. 'But I want you to feel at home here.'

Which was what he wanted too. Not only for his sake, but for Nancy's too. He didn't have the heart to tell her that he thought it was unlikely, and the prospect depressed him. *Buck up*, he told himself, feeling suddenly very self-indulgent.

Jim filled the filter paper with ground coffee, clicked the funnel back into place and poured water into the back of the machine. He missed his cafetière, missed the strength of his old brew – four heaped tablespoons, only half filled with water. But Nancy didn't like coffee resembling treacle, and he'd had to comply. It was early, the misty September Saturday so beautiful it made his heart ache. He hadn't been able to sleep, so he'd finally given up trying, crept downstairs and sat outside on the wet wooden bench for a while, wrapped in his leather jacket, feeling the sun on his face. If he'd been at home, he'd have played his guitar now, but he didn't want to wake Nancy.

He let out a long sigh. Even though he'd been living there altogether for five weeks, he still felt awkward, unable to relax as he would have in his old house. He missed his room badly, missed his battered leather chair, the evenings sitting doing fuck-all with a glass of Jim Beam or three, missed the ease of being alone with his guitar . . . the odd sneaky fag. It had been a long time since he'd had to share his life because, despite what everyone thought about him and Chrissie, he had not had to consider anyone but himself for years now.

But this was Nancy's house, her enclave, in fact, what with the family across the gravel. And as he'd feared, he definitely did not feel he fitted in. Even sitting on the bench in the sunshine earlier, he'd been uncomfortably aware of Louise's house, the windows looking onto the garden, wondering if any of them were watching him, if Louise still disliked him being there. Paranoia, maybe, but still . . .

The upside, of course, was Nancy. It was incredible the way she made him feel. Just one loving look from those grey eyes of hers and he wanted to shout his good fortune from the rooftops.

He heard her on the stairs and reached into the cupboard for the large white coffee cups. She looked sleepy and gorgeous so he went over, put his arms around her and kissed the top of her head.

'Where did you go?' she asked, sitting at the table and accepting the coffee he offered, brushing her hair off her face, drawing her patterned, blue kimono-style dressing-gown round herself.

'Couldn't sleep. Sat outside in the sunshine for a bit – it's so beautiful out there. The mist was hovering in a layer above the fields at the back.' He leaned against the sink, sipping his black coffee, gazing at Nancy.

'Why couldn't you sleep? Were you worrying?'

'Umm, no, not really.' He hesitated, deciding not to tell her how he was feeling.

But she knew anyway. 'Jim,' she said. 'Listen, I feel we're treading around each other as if we're on eggshells at the moment.' She waited, and for a second their eyes met, then Jim looked away because he wasn't sure what to answer. 'It's not been easy for you, I know, losing your home.'

He took a deep breath. 'It's odd for us both, isn't it? Neither of us has lived with someone for a while now. Probably take some getting used to . . .'

She looked as if she might protest, her expression suddenly tight. Then she gave a short laugh and relaxed. 'Yeah, probably will. Lindy said I'll get fed up washing your underpants, having you under my feet.'

'Huh! Cheeky cow! When have I ever asked you to wash anything? In fact, I washed *your* knickers yesterday, and that sexy black bra that turns me on.'

Nancy gave him a flirtatious grin, which made him want to haul her back upstairs to bed that instant.

'Chrissie said you'd get fed up with me snoring,' he said instead, not giving up on the idea of a bit of morning sex, but wanting to clear up this snoring issue, in light of the discussion about their domestic habits. It had been bothering him ever since his wife mentioned it.

Nancy pulled a face. 'Umm, yes, you snore. Don't most men over forty?'

He groaned. 'Is it bad, though? Chrissie said I sound like a lawnmower, even from one floor down.'

She got up and came over to him, laying her hands flat on his chest, their warmth seeping through his threadbare white T-shirt, and gazed up into his face. 'I must be in love with you because I sort of like it. It's more like a diesel engine than a lawnmower, I'd say. A purr rather than a whirr.'

'Oh, God! I hate it whatever it sounds like. I'm so sorry.'

'Don't be ridiculous,' Nancy said, laughing as she dismissed the subject and reaching up to give him a firm kiss on the mouth.

But the kiss was interrupted by a hurried knocking, followed immediately by Louise poking her head round the front door. Jim and Nancy sprang apart, as if they were guilty colleagues caught in the stationery cupboard.

'Hi.' Louise, obviously clocking what they'd been doing, looked instantly awkward. 'Umm, sorry to barge in.' She wouldn't look Jim in the eye, just concentrated on her mother as if he weren't there. 'Mum, I'm going down to Granny's, but Hope's got a bit of a cold, so I wondered if you could keep an eye for a couple of hours. I don't want Granny to catch anything.'

There goes the sex, thought Jim, regretfully, busying himself with getting the loaf out of the bin and slicing some bread for toast. And the trip to the Lanes for a wander and the pub lunch they'd planned.

'Of course, bring them over,' Nancy said to her daughter.

'I'm taking her some of Ross's chicken broth,' Louise said, still hovering by the door. 'Do you want me to nag about the doctor again?'

Nancy sighed. 'You could try, but honestly, I think it's a lost cause.'

'We can't just leave her like this, Mum.' Louise's pinched face showed real concern as she shoved her hands into her jeans pockets, her stance stubborn and fierce. 'She's clearly ill. Can't we *make* her see someone?'

'Not unless she wants to, apparently.'

'But that's ridiculous.'

'I feel the same as you do, Lou, but, as Jim says, it's her life.'

Louise's mouth tightened. 'I know that,' she said, addressing him now, 'but just sitting here watching her die doesn't seem like an option.' She turned on her heel. 'I'll bring the girls over in about fifteen minutes, if that's okay, Mum.' And she was gone.

Jim pulled a face. 'That went well.'

'Sorry, shouldn't have dragged you into it.'

'It's true, though. It is Frances's life.'

Nancy's face fell. 'These last weeks, she's seemed a bit better . . . I suppose I've been kidding myself that whatever was wrong with her has gone away.'

CHAPTER THIRTY-FIVE

Nancy wasn't doubting her feelings for Jim, or his for her, but a certain awkwardness had seeped into their domestic exchanges. She wanted him to feel at home so badly, but she knew he didn't, so she spent much of her time watching him to find out if he was okay, and when she realized he wasn't, trying too hard to solve the problem. Like last night.

'Can I call Tommy on the landline?' Jim had asked.

'Of course you can. You don't need to ask,' she'd told him. 'Use it any time.'

But he didn't pick up the handset, just stood uncertainly beside it. 'We should talk about that, Nancy,' he said. 'You pay all the bills. If I'm living here, I want to contribute.'

Of course, with hindsight, she knew she should just have agreed. But instead she said, 'God, no. You don't need to do that,' aware that he didn't have a lot of money.

He said, 'I can afford to pay half. I want to pay half.' He obviously felt patronized, because his face shut down, his jaw tightened. 'This won't work if you treat me like a bloody guest.'

Which stung. She'd been bending over backwards not to do just that. 'Okay,' she replied, irritated, in turn, by his attitude. 'I'd be delighted if you'd pay half. I'll tot it all up and let you know.'

He had given her a stony nod, but the room was like a morgue for about two long minutes during which neither moved nor spoke. Then he had crossed the room and pulled her into his arms. 'Sorry, Nancy. Please, please, let's not argue about stupid things.' And, just as it always did, the closeness of their bodies, the mutual pleasure in being held and loved, had soothed their bad temper away . . . till the next time.

Today, though, Nancy felt out of sorts for reasons unconnected with Jim. It was Christopher's wedding day.

'I'm going across to see them off,' she told Jim, who was sitting at the kitchen table reading the newspaper.

He looked up. 'Are you okay?'

'Yes.' she muttered, although she wasn't. 'I'll be back in a minute.'

The house was in chaos. Louise, still in her dressing-gown, was arguing with Hope because the child wanted a French plait and Louise said she didn't have time. Jazzy was refusing to wear the lacy white tights Louise had put out for her to go with her pink flowered party dress because she said they were scratchy. Ross, the only one dressed and ready in a dark suit and blue shirt – both of which looked too small for him, the shirt straining at the waist – was bringing some croissants out of the oven, absorbed as usual in food, and making absolutely no effort to help.

'Go and get dressed, Lou. I'll do the girls,' Nancy said.

Her daughter shot her a grateful look and hurried upstairs.

'Croissant, Nancy?' Ross said, indicating the tray of warm, flaky pastries with an expansive sweep of his hand.

'Croisels!' Jazzy shrieked, and ran over to poke her nose over the side of the worktop and check out breakfast.

'Come here first. We've got to get you some more tights,' Nancy commanded, grabbing the child's hand. 'I'll do your hair when I come down,' she told Hope.

Having sorted the girls out and explained to Ross that he would die a very slow and lingering death if he let either of them get even one tiny speck of strawberry jam on their dresses, she went upstairs to see if Louise was ready.

But her daughter was sitting on the bed in her bra and pants beside the pale blue dress they'd bought back in the summer, crying.

'Oh, sweetheart . . .' Nancy sat down and put her arm round her shoulders.

'I hate the dress – I look like one of those Real Housewives of Beverly Hills or wherever. Blingy and cheap.' She sniffed loudly and wiped her hand angrily across her eyes.

'Don't be ridiculous! You'd never look cheap.'

'I might. But I haven't got anything else, anyway. They'll all be dressed like dogs' dinners and that woman will laugh at me and think I'm a sad try-hard.'

Nancy smiled. 'Nonsense. She's probably much more intimidated by you than you are by her.'

Louise didn't reply, just flopped back on the bed, on top of the dresses and jackets, and closed her eyes. 'Would he have told me about the baby, if you hadn't found out by mistake?' she asked.

Nancy sighed. 'He said he'd tried to.'

Louise's eyes shot open and she sat up. 'I'm not going, Mum. I don't see why I should.'

Nancy tried to work out if her daughter was serious or not. Part of her – the evil part – quite liked the idea of Christopher being upset that his daughter hadn't pitched up. But she did the right thing and pulled at Louise's hand until she had no choice but to stand up. 'Come on, put it on – show me.'

Her expression exactly like Hope's had been half an hour before over the French plait, Louise sulkily complied, pulling on the dress and standing there scowling at her mother, shoulders hunched. 'See?'

'Straighten up, put on your shoes, stop looking as if you're going to your own funeral,' Nancy instructed, unable to stop a smile at her daughter's melodramatic expression. 'And the necklace . . . There. Perfect.' She pushed Louise round to face the long mirror inside the wardrobe door.

Her daughter's face did not change as she hooked her freshly washed hair behind her ears. *At least she's taken it out of the ponytail today*, Nancy thought, smoothing the shiny dark tresses, which now reached to her daughter's shoulders and softened Louise's sharp features.

'It's nearly ten, Lou. If you don't leave now, you'll miss the whole bloody thing.'

Louise's face cleared. 'Will we?' she said, and they both began to laugh.

'God, I don't know what they'd do without me,' Nancy said, when she got back to the house, the family safely on the road to Suffolk, jam-free, Louise in her blue dress, Hope with her plait, Jazzy with some navy tights that didn't really match her dress but were the only option, Nancy had decided, if Lou didn't want to listen to the child whingeing all day.

Jim had made another pot of coffee and was sitting in a shaft of sunlight at the kitchen table. He looked so handsome, his strong features highlighted in his lean, tanned face, the sun playing on his silver hair. But Nancy couldn't enjoy him. She felt oddly left out of the family party. *I'd rather stick pins in my eyes than be at his ridiculous wedding*, she told herself. But the event seemed to drag her back into her past, with all the old feelings of betrayal, of not being heard, not valued. How easily Christopher had left her and started another family. How little she must have meant to him.

'I just spoke to brother Stevie,' Jim was saying. 'He says we should go down and visit him, now the main season's over. It'll still be sunny and warm, but not baking like in August.'

Jim's brother's gîte was in the South of France, near Apt.

'You mean for a weekend or something?' She tried to shake off her insecurity, concentrate on what she had now.

'Why not longer? We could go for a week. Stevie lets you alone, I can show you the countryside, we can sit in the sunshine, read, play music . . . We'll miss the lavender, though – that's July and August and completely breathtaking. Standing on his balcony it's just acres of deep purple – these long, domed rows of lavender bushes – as far as the eye can see.' She could tell he was transported by the memory. 'But it's gorgeous any time of year. I can't wait to show it to you.'

'A week?' Nancy felt a small shaft of panic. 'What about Mum? And my students . . .'

'Couldn't Louise keep an eye on Frances? You say she's not so bad at the moment. And your students won't mind, will they? I'm sure mine will survive a week without me.' Now Jim no longer had his house, he'd moved his lessons to Mal's shed because the students – mostly without cars – wouldn't come all the way out to Nancy's.

Reluctantly, Nancy nodded. 'I suppose a week's not that long. If Louise is okay about it . . .'

Jim looked deflated. 'Don't want to force you.'

'I *am* keen, just thinking it out.' She tried to weigh up how much more strain her absence would put on Louise, if Frances had a crisis, and the dilemma seemed so boringly familiar it made her already aching head ache more.

'I think I'll go anyway,' Jim was saying. 'Haven't been down there since the spring, and Stevie hasn't been well, he says. Bit worrying. The doctors have just told him he's borderline diabetic.'

'That's not good . . . Listen, I'd love to come with you,' Nancy said, annoyed with herself as she heard the doubt still lingering in her voice. 'It'd be great to meet your brother.'

'No pressure.'

Nancy shook her head. 'I can't always be hanging around waiting for the family to need me.'

Jim was silent and she saw him watching her, biting his lip as if he wanted to say something but had decided not to.

'You think I do too much for them, don't you?' She found she couldn't keep the sharpness out of her voice as images of Christopher and Tatjana swam before her eyes: smiling with happiness, kissing each other's lips, exchanging rings, declaring their undying love in front of all their – *her* – friends. More than thirty years she'd been married to him . . .

He took a long breath, fiddled with the newspaper in front of him, riffling the corner with his long fingers as if he were about to turn the page. She wanted to slap his hand to stop him.

'It's your family, Nancy,' he said finally.

'I don't think you understand. They've been an incredible support to me these last few years. I don't know what I would have done without them when Christopher walked out.' She pushed away thoughts of that day four years ago. 'And with Mum obviously not well, Lou struggling . . .'

'I do understand,' he said.

'You seem pissed off.'

'I'm not.'

'You are.'

'I'm not, honestly.'

Silence.

'It's just . . .' Jim sighed, raised his eyebrows a little as he looked at her. 'It's just I'm not sure how I fit in here.'

Nancy felt her stomach clench. 'Fit in?'

The expression in his blue eyes was very intense, as he said, 'Yeah. I mean this is your place, Nancy. I know you've bent over backwards to make me feel at home, and I really appreciate that, but there's the others across the drive and I know Louise doesn't approve of me . . . even though she hasn't said.' He stopped, but she saw he had more to say so she waited, her annoyance mounting. 'And when we plan something, like the movies or going into town for a drink or meeting up with Mal or Lindy, I just never know if something'll come up with your family and you'll just drop everything to accommodate them.'

The previous weekend exactly that had happened. Jim had been doing a lunchtime gig at a pub in Eastbourne with the band. Lindy was coming with some guy she wanted Nancy to meet, the whole thing had been arranged a week before. Then there was a crisis at the restaurant – Jason's mother had died – and Louise had had to take over his sous-chef tasks for the busy lunchtime service. So Nancy had agreed to look after the girls. She'd known at the time Jim was upset, but what could she do? Up until now he'd seemed not to mind when she cancelled stuff.

'What do you want me to do?' she snapped, in no mood to be having this discussion. 'Dump my sick mother? Leave my granddaughters hanging out in the office at the restaurant for hours because Lou can't find a babysitter?'

Jim shrugged.

'Well?' she demanded.

'Of course not. You have to do what you think best,' he said quietly. 'I was just saying that sometimes I feel you don't have room in your life for me . . . or anyone except the family.' His tone was cautious.

'Oh, for God's sake. I'm not giving you enough attention, is that what you're saying?' Her voice rose.

'You make me sound like a bratty child, Nancy. That's not fair.' He was sitting with his arms folded tight across his black T-shirt, while she stood, her arms similarly crossed, leaning against the worktop. Both of them seemed to be defending themselves against the other as they glared across the table.

Nancy felt tears gathering behind her eyes. 'It's not fair to make me choose,' she said.

'I'm not making you choose.'

'Yes, you are. You're saying I should ignore their cries for help so we can have some fun.'

Tension reverberated between them like a high-pitched whine. Nancy felt her heart pounding hard and fast in her chest. Jim got up and stood leaning on the back of the wooden chair he'd just vacated.

'How would Louise cope if you didn't live next door?'

'She'd find someone else, obviously. But I do live next door. I like living next door.'

He sighed. 'Yes, but . . . I'm not saying they take advantage of you—'

'You are.'

'Okay, maybe I am. But they don't do it deliberately. I just think . . .' He stopped.

'Think what?'

Jim shook his head. 'I don't know.' His eyes had softened and he looked at her beseechingly. 'Please. Let's not fight. I'm sorry, maybe I am being selfish and childish. But . . .'

Nancy realized she was holding her breath. 'What are you saying?' she asked, almost in a whisper.

He didn't answer, just came round the table and took her in his arms. 'Come here.' He delivered a kiss to the top of her head. 'I'm not saying anything except I think we deserve a life together. I see you worrying and dropping everything for the family – sometimes when it's not really an emergency at all – giving up things you were looking forward to, and it doesn't seem fair on you . . . or, selfishly, I'll admit, on me either.'

She pressed herself against his chest, hugging him close. 'I don't even think when they ask me, I suppose. I've got so used to just being there for them.' She noticed the strain in his eyes and knew hers contained similar tension. 'Before you appeared on my horizon, I thought that was my life from now on, the family my *raison d'être*. I felt lucky to have them so close and be able to watch the girls grow up.'

'And you are lucky. I wouldn't dream of taking that away from you. I couldn't even if I tried.'

'But?'

He didn't reply at first. Then he said, 'I suppose I'm wondering if we've hurried into something neither of us is ready for. Maybe I should find a flat, give you some space to do what you need to do.'

'Is that what you want?' Nancy, head buried in his chest, heard more than Jim actually said. She heard that he was over it, over her, that he wanted out. 'To leave?' The familiar, agonizing pain of being abandoned tore at her chest. *Not you too . . .*

But when she looked up she saw only bewilderment in his eyes.

'No, Nancy, don't be daft. Of course I don't want to leave you. That's an unacceptable thought. I'm just asking if it would be best to take it more slowly. I'm asking if that's really what *you* want, but you're too polite to say.'

Jim took her hand and drew her behind him to the sofa, pulling her down next to him. They sat side by side, clutching each other's hand as if they were both drowning, saying nothing for a long time. Nancy's brain was simmering. Did she trust him not to leave her? Because she couldn't see how she could have it all, Jim and the family too.

'Let's just take off to France, have a break,' Jim was suggesting. 'See how we feel when we get back.'

CHAPTER THIRTY-SIX

'Do you think your dad will help out?' Ross and Louise were lying in bed. It was a Saturday morning and the faint strains of cartoons wafted up from the television downstairs, where the two girls were ensconced in front of a decades-old *Tom and Jerry*.

Louise frowned at her husband. 'Help with what?'

Ross went on staring up at the ceiling. 'He seemed really interested when I talked to him at the wedding. Said he understood just how long it takes for a place like mine to click with the public.'

Dismayed, she asked, 'Are you seriously suggesting that Dad might invest in the Lime Kiln?' She sat up in bed, tugging her pillow behind her back until it was against the wooden headboard.

'Well—'

'You didn't ask him for money, did you?' she interrupted, her voice sharp. 'Please tell me you didn't, Ross.'

She saw him purse his lips, twist his mouth from side to side, the expression he always adopted when he was put on the spot. He, too, pulled himself into a sitting position, then gave her a quick sideways glance. 'I didn't, no, of course not. What do you take me for, Lou?'

It was on the tip of her tongue to tell him that she took him for a man who would sell his own children if it meant he'd save his restaurant, but she restrained herself.

The wedding – over a week ago now – still haunted her. Tatjana, swanning around like a goddess in her Grecian-style oyster silk dress, ostentatiously clinging to her rounded belly, a badge of honour, as if no one had ever been pregnant before. Her father, looking like an ageing fifties Teddy boy in his navy frock coat with purple velvet collar and trim to the pockets – clearly chosen by Tatjana, although Louise had to admit there had always been something of the dandy about him.

The guests were a mixture of people Louise had known from her childhood, all of whom greeted her with a cautious welcome, aware, perhaps, that she had sided with her mother and that they had not, and people she had never met. The flamboyant theatrical singers, younger women with big hair, dramatic décolletage and red lipstick, who were Tatjana's crowd, stayed apart from the small, shy knot of her Latvian family, who were separate again from the group of Downland singers and older musicians, lifelong friends of Christopher, dressed in understated but carefully tailored suiting with tidy flowers in their buttonholes.

Louise had stood among them feeling as if she'd wandered into someone else's life by mistake. None of it seemed to have anything to do with her and she kept having to remind herself that the old man getting married was actually her father. One moment, however, had surprised her. She, Ross, Hope and Jazzy were standing in the pub garden where the marquee had been set up, when Christopher approached. Louise made polite noises about the day as they stood in an awkward circle.

'So how is your mother?' her father had asked.

'She's good,' Louise had replied. And, without thinking, added, 'She's got a boyfriend.'

Her father looked curiously shocked. 'Nancy? A man?' he asked, unnecessarily. 'You mean she's going out with someone?'

'Living with him,' Ross corrected.

'Nancy's living with a man?'

Louise thought it was taking a mightily long time for her supposedly clever father to get the hang of this conversation. *Maybe he's drunk*, she thought.

'Jim's a singer,' Hope told her grandfather shyly, as she clung to her father's side. 'He plays the guitar and he's teaching me and Jazzy to sing harmonies.'

Her father shook his head in a bewildered fashion. 'How long has this been going on?' He sounded like a schoolmaster catching out some miscreant pupils . . . sounded as if it had something to do with him.

Louise, starting to enjoy herself, said, 'Ooh, about six months now. We all really like him.' She didn't dare look at Ross as she heard him spluttering into his champagne.

'Nancy never said a word.' Her father looked pained. He was clearly not enjoying the conversation. 'What sort of a singer?' he asked. And his jealousy was so blatant that Louise felt almost sorry for him.

'Country and western. He's brilliant.'

Her father was saved from her mischief by the advent of his annoying wife, all purring and silk-clad and nauseatingly smug. But Louise was surprised by how much he obviously still felt for her mother.

On the way back to the car at the end of the day, Ross had been roaring with laughter. 'So we "really like" Jim, do we, eh?'

She'd laughed too. It was a rare moment between them, these days. 'Well, you do, and the girls do. And when you compare him to the dreadful Tatjana . . .'

'Even though your dad curled his lip when you said "country and western",' Ross's face had creased with amusement, 'he still looked sick as a parrot. Maybe all is not well in Paradise.'

Now her husband was saying, 'He implied he'd be happy to have a chat about it after they get back from Latvia.' The Latvian wedding party would be part of the honeymoon, Tatjana had said.

'So you *did* ask him for money.'

'I didn't, I swear to God, Lou. I just said we were having some problems getting the attention we deserve. He totally got it.' He glanced at her. 'Wouldn't do any harm, would it?'

'There is no way in hell that I'd accept a penny from my father—' Louise did not have a chance to finish her sentence because her mobile went off.

'Granny?'

Her grandmother didn't reply at once, but Louise could hear her light, feathery breathing at the other end of the phone.

'Granny? Are you okay?'

'I'm fine, darling,' Frances eventually replied, but her voice was very weak. 'I've just had a bit of an accident . . .'

'An accident? What sort of an accident?'

'Oh, nothing dramatic. I'm afraid it's just rather embarrassing. I slipped getting out of bed and I . . . Well, I can't get up . . . My right leg doesn't appear to be working properly . . . and I . . . I was on my way to the bathroom when I fell . . .' She stopped and Louise heard only the breathing again.

'Are you still on the floor, Granny?'

'I'm afraid so. It's quite painful to move.'

'I'm on my way right this minute. I'll be as quick as I can. Keep yourself warm till I get there, pull the duvet off the bed or something. Can you reach it?'

'I think so.'

As Louise raced to get dressed, Ross said, 'Shouldn't you call an ambulance? If she can't get up, maybe she's broken something.'

She yanked on a sweater and pulled her hair back into a ponytail. 'I'll see how she is first. Granny would hate to be carted off to hospital for no reason.' She grabbed her mobile. 'Look after the girls. I might not be back for a bit if it's bad.'

Frances had wet herself.

'I'm so sorry, darling . . . I'm so sorry,' she kept repeating. Louise was shocked at how frail and insubstantial her body felt as she picked her up from the floor and eased her onto the bed.

'It's okay, Granny. Please, don't worry about it.'

She fetched the plastic bowl she found in the airing cupboard and filled it with warm water, gave the flannel to her grandmother and turned her back as the old lady washed and dried herself, then helped her put on a clean nightie she found in the drawer.

'Show me where your leg hurts,' she said, once Frances was dressed and propped up on the pillows.

Her grandmother gestured vaguely towards her ankle, her thin, spidery fingers fluttering, seeming to lack the control to be more specific. There was no sign of damage on her stick-thin leg, only the ravages of old age in the papery skin and prominent blue veins, bruises that looked historic, but Louise couldn't tell.

'You don't think you've broken something, do you?'

'Oh, no. Just bruised it, I expect. I'll probably be black and blue by tomorrow.' She managed a wan smile. 'I'm so sorry to drag you out, darling. I know you're so busy, but I didn't know what else to do, with Nancy away.'

'It's fine, Granny – please don't apologize.'

'Never get old, darling. It's all too embarrassing.'

Louise laughed. 'You don't need to be embarrassed with me.'

Frances gave a small shrug. 'You're very kind to say so.'

'I think you should stay in bed, don't you? I'll bring you up a cup of tea and some toast.'

'No, no, nothing to eat. And please don't feel you have to stay. I'll be right as rain after a little sleep, I'm sure.' She closed her eyes. 'I do feel quite tired.'

Louise went downstairs and called Ross.

'I'm phoning the doctor. Her leg looks all right, but how would I know? She might have some small break or something. Or she could have banged her head . . . I wish Mum was here. She'd know what to do.'

'What's going to happen with the girls? I need to leave for the restaurant in a minute.'

'Well, you'll have to take them with you, won't you?' she said, her voice tight with irritation.

'But if you're going to be there for a while . . .'

'They'll be fine.'

'They can't stay there all day, Lou. There's no TV, nothing for them to do.'

'For God's sake, Ross! Granny is ill. Can't you manage, just for once? There's a list of numbers by the phone in the kitchen . . . school mums. Try Patricia – she's always brilliant in an emergency.

And if she can't have them, they'll just have to amuse themselves. They can play outside or do stuff in the office. It won't kill them to entertain themselves for a few hours.'

She heard him sigh. 'Okay. But when will you be back, do you think?'

'*I don't bloody know*, do I? It depends on how poor Granny is. But I can't leave her alone, can I?'

'No . . . no, I suppose not.' Another sigh. 'Right. I'd better go and get them organized. Nightmare . . .'

Louise almost carried her grandmother to the car, then propped her up in the front seat with a blanket round her shoulders and another over her knees, although it was a warm day. The doctor had said very little except that nothing appeared to be broken and reiterating that Frances needed hospital tests for the mass he'd felt in her stomach, possibly an X-ray for her ankle, to which her grandmother had given him the usual short shrift – the poor man looked positively cowed by her fierceness. So Louise had made an executive decision, despite her grandmother's protests, that she would take her home, settle her in her room in Nancy's house and keep an eye on her till her mother got back.

'Shouldn't you tell your mum?' Ross had said, when she'd called to give him an update.

But Louise didn't want to ruin her mother's holiday if there was no need. She and Jim would be home in two days.

'You know Jim's living with Mum now, Granny?' Louise said, as she drove slowly through the streets, not wanting to jolt her fragile passenger. She found that what she'd said to her father wasn't so far from the truth. On closer inspection, Jim did seem quieter and more intelligent than she'd given him credit for after that first disastrous lunch. And the girls liked him a lot. Louise trusted their clear, unfettered judgement of people – look at their reaction to Tatjana. Jim had spent hours with them the day before he and Nancy had left for France, playing the guitar, singing songs with them, and they'd adored every minute. But, most of all, he seemed to make her mother happy. She wouldn't go so far as to say she trusted him yet, but it took effort to go on finding fault where none was apparent.

Frances nodded slowly. 'I'm saying nothing.'

'Do you think it's a mistake, though? I was pretty surprised when she told me he wasn't looking for a flat any more.'

Her grandmother raised her eyebrows. 'In my day, people married knowing considerably less about each other than your mother knows about Jim.'

Louise wasn't sure how to take this. 'So you approve?'

The old lady didn't reply, and Louise assumed she was drifting off.

'Your mother isn't very good at relationships, I'm afraid,' Frances said suddenly, after a long silence.

CHAPTER THIRTY-SEVEN

Nancy woke to the sun filtering through the pine trees outside the window, the wooden shutters thrown wide. Jim was leaning on the stone sill in his boxers, his eyes closed against the bright morning light, basking in the warmth. He must have heard her stir, because he swung round, a lazy smile on his lips, and let out a long, contented sigh. She had never seen him so relaxed.

'Isn't it heaven here?'

She lay back on the pillows and beamed back at him. 'Heaven.' And it was. Maison Lavande – Lavender House – was a seventeenth-century farmhouse in the hills above Apt. With a view from the terrace over the spectacular Luberon valley and the spreading lavender fields, olive groves, the mountains in the distance, Stevie's gîte was a sort of paradise. Jim's brother had bought it with his French partner, Pascal, in the eighties and slowly, lovingly, converted it to include four guest bedrooms and two bathrooms in one side of the house, their own quarters on the other – all downstairs – the large kitchen and living space across the whole upstairs, so that they could run it as a bed and breakfast. It had been very successful, Pascal loving to cook and bond with the visitors. Stevie, less sociable, could fix anything from a pump to a boiler to anything electrical.

Then two years ago last October, Pascal had died, cycling up the hill to the *mas*, baguettes and croissants for the guests tied to the back of the bike, just after eight on a similarly beautiful autumn day. A bin lorry speeding round the corner had clipped his front wheel, spinning him over the side. He had died in hospital later that morning from head injuries, a few days shy of his fiftieth birthday. Stevie, Jim said, had not recovered. He had continued to run the gîte, but without Pascal, the place had lost its spirit and the guests had started to fall off.

'Thought we'd take in Apt market this morning,' he was saying, as he padded across the terracotta tiles and sat down on the bed. 'It's huge and famous. You'll love it. We could do the meal tonight . . . There'll be stuff we can get that doesn't involve too much cooking.' He grinned.

Since Pascal's death, Stevie had hired a cook/housekeeper, Madame Laverne, during the season, but now that it was quiet she came in only a couple of days a week.

Nancy took Jim's hand. 'I don't know Stevie, but he seems quite withdrawn sometimes, like the light's on, then all of a sudden it flicks off and he's gone. Is he on pills for the depression?'

Jim sighed. 'He certainly was. But he's obviously not in a good state. I worry about the winter. He doesn't take guests from November to March and he's all alone here. He and Pascal used to love it when they had the place to themselves, but without him . . .'

'It's pretty isolated.'

'Yeah, there's Izzy in the house just down the hill, the one with the wooden dolphin sculpture outside. She's away at the moment, but Stevie says she may be coming back tomorrow, so you'll meet her. She's from New Zealand, a bit bonkers, I reckon, but a very good friend to Stevie since Pascal died.'

'Is that her sculpture?'

'No, her boyfriend's . . . ex-boyfriend now. Izzy does some kind of life-coach thing – she's got a studio in Avignon and I think she does online stuff too. But she must have money from somewhere, because she never seems short and I can't imagine she makes much from the work.'

'Life-coaches can charge a bomb.'

'Hmm, maybe, but when you meet her you'll see she's a bit of a hippie. But it's good to know someone's close at hand for Stevie.'

Stevie was not at all what Nancy had imagined. And, apart from his very blue eyes, he was not at all like his brother. At least four inches shorter than Jim and weighing considerably more, his kind smile and rather morose features peered from a sea of smooth flesh that bulked around his neck, giving the impression that his body started at his chin. He did not have Jim's long hair, and the sparse, greying, Caesar-style cut seemed to perch on his head like a wig. But the most marked difference between the brothers was their vitality. Whereas Jim demonstrated a contained energy, an elegance in the way he moved, Stevie dragged himself from place to place, heaving his bulk up from a chair with marked reluctance, breathing heavily at any exertion, slumping with a weary sigh that seemed to Nancy the biggest indication that he wasn't coping.

'You guys go, not sure I'm in the mood for a crazy market this morning.' Stevie was sitting in the sun on the first-floor balcony, which led from the kitchen and living area; his bedroom and bathroom were tucked into the hill on the ground floor.

'Nah, come with us,' Jim said. 'We can do a potter, show Nancy the stalls, then have a coffee. If we go now, it won't be too manic.'

Stevie didn't reply at once, just sipped from a French coffee bowl, his large hands cradling the fluted white pottery as he stared out over the plain. On the table in front of him was an Italian-style aluminium espresso machine, a plate of golden croissants, a jar of homemade apricot jam – Madame Laverne's speciality – and a small section of honeycomb on a blue saucer. Crockery and knives, two mustard-yellow cotton napkins, carefully ironed, had been laid out for Nancy and Jim.

'I suppose I could.' He turned his face up to Nancy. 'It's a pretty spectacular market, been going for nine hundred years, they say.'

Nancy gave him an encouraging smile. 'Come with us, then,' she said.

Sitting and gazing out at the extraordinary view, she took a deep breath. Such beauty seemed to require happiness, but perhaps for Jim's brother it served only to remind him of what he had lost. She had a sudden urge to hug him, pass on to him some of the strength, energy and love she felt right now. It was an unfair balance, his dull misery against her intense happiness. She looked up at Jim, who was leaning against the balcony rail also gazing out across the landscape. They had been so close on this holiday, both relaxing, having time just to enjoy each other without the awkwardness engendered by their domestic situation at home. Neither her house, nor his, the *mas* was a neutral place where Nancy felt no responsibility for Jim. Here, there was no pressure to make choices about how she spent her time. They would be going back on Monday, and Nancy felt the flutter of anxiety building in her gut at the thought.

Stevie had brought two traditional French shopping baskets – pale woven palm leaves with leather handles – and given one to

Jim. Every few minutes, someone would greet Stevie, drop the obligatory kiss, kiss, kiss on his cheeks, exchange a sentence or two in French, then move on. There were tourists among the crowd, but it seemed to be made up predominantly of locals.

Nancy's French was not bad, she had spent two summer holidays in Paris with a musician's family – all four children played different instruments, so they did nothing but practise, compose and perform with each other – at the impressionable age of fifteen and sixteen. But she lacked the courage, after so many years, to speak much. Jim, on the other hand, had no such reticence, although his grammar and vocabulary were patchy, claiming there was an acknowledged link between being a musician and a linguist. He seemed unafraid of trying out his skills on anyone who'd listen.

Nancy bought two small, brightly coloured Provençal-patterned bags for Hope and Jazzy, woven mats for Louise, a pot of mustard for Ross, and an embroidered organza lavender bag for her mother.

'Goat?' Jim asked, pointing to the tempting array of cheeses set out on straw mats on one of the stalls in the main square.

'The *banon*'s good,' Stevie pointed to a small round cheese, neatly wrapped in brown leaves, 'and I like the ashy one.'

They ended up with mountains of food: ripe, juicy tomatoes that smelt of the earth, *frisée* lettuces, salamis, cheeses, a warm rotisserie chicken, plump green beans, *rillettes*, celeriac *remoulade*, golden pears, fresh eggs and baguettes. Carrying their spoils they made their way to Stevie's favourite *tabac*, tucked back in a cool alleyway away from the throng, where they sat outside in the shade on hard aluminium chairs and sighed with relief. Nancy ordered a *cafe crème*, the two men, black coffee.

Jim, after a few minutes of inconsequential chat, fell silent, biting his lip.

'How's it going to be, over the winter?' he asked his brother.

Stevie, his round face pink and sweaty, his chest still heaving beneath his faded blue polo shirt, just shrugged. 'Okay, I guess. I survived last year.'

'Must get pretty lonely.'

Stevie blinked, and Nancy, wincing, saw the glint of tears. Addressing his remark to the house opposite, he said, 'Pretty lonely all the time. Winter's no different.'

Jim glanced at her, raised his eyebrows. 'Why not come home for Christmas, catch up with a few people . . . ?' He trailed off, as if even he were unconvinced by his own words.

'This is home,' Steve said softly, turning his blue eyes, now wet with tears, on his brother.

'I get that. But you seem so unhappy, Stevie. Do you think you should get another assessment, maybe take a different pill . . . or a different dose?'

'There isn't a pill on the planet that'll help how I feel.'

'But that's exactly what antidepressants do, isn't it?'

Stevie shrugged again, looked away.

'You are on them, aren't you?'

This time, when Jim's brother turned to them, his eyes were full of irritation. 'Leave it, Jim. I know you mean well, but just stay out of it . . . please.' He got up, wiping his sweaty forehead with a hanky and reached into the pocket of his beige cargo pants for his wallet. But as he drew it out, he suddenly staggered backwards, fell over the chair, crashed against the glass front of the cafe. Jim was on his feet in a flash, heaving his brother's bulk upright and guiding him onto a chair. A man passing by grabbed Stevie's other arm.

'*Merci, merci . . . je vais bien maintenant. La chaleur . . .*' Nancy heard Jim's brother mumble breathlessly to the Frenchman, obviously making a supreme effort to appear as fine as he said he was.

Jim hovered over him anxiously. 'What happened there, mate?'

Stevie pushed him away. 'Too much caffeine, I expect. Takes me like that sometimes. Stop fussing, will you?' He looked at Nancy. 'Sorry about all the drama.'

'Have you seen a doctor?' Jim was asking.

Ignoring his brother, Stevie tentatively got to his feet. 'Come on, let's get back.'

And that was an end to it, as far as Stevie was concerned. On the walk through the crowded streets to the car park, Jim kept glancing sideways at his brother and asking him how he was feeling, only to be brushed off.

Their last night loomed. Nancy and Jim sat on the balcony as the sun went down, both with a glass of cold white wine, silent as they took in the glorious panorama sweeping away in front of them. As the light dipped behind the far hills, the slopes of olive trees and fields of lavender – now reduced to green-brown rows after the harvest – took on a soft shadowy indigo hue, a small breeze lifting the heat from the day, Nancy felt a rare sense of peace steal over her. It was so beautiful, so still, so absolutely perfect. Jim caught her expression and reached over to take her hand.

'You like it here,' he said. It was not a question.

She nodded. 'I don't know it in the way you do, but I feel at home somehow.' She smiled at him. 'Maybe because you're here.'

'Don't know . . . It's just one of those places. I understand why Stevie doesn't want to leave.'

'Did you talk to him about the antidepressants?' Nancy lowered her voice, glancing back towards the house. There was no sign of Stevie in the darkening kitchen behind her.

Jim sighed. 'I tried, but he just keeps repeating that he's fine. I can't force him to open up to me.' He paused. 'He was always a brooder – used to drive Mum nuts when we were kids.'

They fell silent.

'Perhaps it's like my mother . . . We have to respect that it's his life.'

Jim gave her a wry smile. 'Yeah, easy advice to give when it's not your own relative.'

She laughed. 'I'm sure. Listen, we can come back . . . if Stevie's okay with it. Maybe visit over the winter. I'd love that.'

Jim squeezed her hand gratefully. 'Good idea.'

That night, Stevie was a different person. Freshly showered and dressed in pale chinos, with a pressed blue-and-white striped shirt, he was already getting the supper together when Nancy and Jim came upstairs. It was after nine and quite dark outside, the pin-prick lights from hundreds of homes glinting in clusters and trails across the plain, like gemstones in a necklace.

'Hey, there you are. Get yourselves a drink. White's in the fridge, red's on the side, or there's vodka in the freezer – Pascal's favourite.' The mention of his lover's name was accompanied by an unusually cheerful grin.

'Let me do that,' Jim said, wresting from his brother the knife with which Stevie had been slicing the tomatoes. 'We're supposed to be doing supper tonight.'

Stevie didn't protest. 'Great. I'll just sit back and get tanked then.' He took the bottle of red wine from the side and filled his glass, moving to the sofa where he plonked himself down, leaning back against the cushions with a sigh and a look of quiet pleasure. His blue eyes, normally so sorrowful, seemed suddenly full of life. '*Santé*, folks!'

'Are you so cheerful because you're getting rid of us?' Jim asked.

'Absolutely! Can't stand the sight of you.'

'Pity, because me and Nancy thought we might come back over the winter.'

Stevie's eyebrows raised. 'So you can check up on me, make sure I haven't slit my throat?'

'Something like that. Certainly not because we like you and want to hang out with you.'

Stevie chuckled. 'Wouldn't want to think anyone actually liked me.'

Nancy wondered at the transformation. Had he taken some sort of stimulant? Or was it just the see-saw nature of his depression?

The brothers' banter was interrupted by a call from downstairs. 'Hi there! Anyone home?' then the soft padding of feet on the wooden staircase, followed by the door opening and a woman appearing.

'Darling! I didn't think you'd be back till tomorrow.' Stevie hauled himself to his feet as she raced across the room, arms open to embrace him, apparently squeezing the life out of him until he begged for mercy and they both fell onto the sofa in a breathless heap. It was a moment before she seemed to notice there were other people in the room. Then she leaped to her feet.

'Jim! Oh, God, what a treat,' she said, giving Jim the same treatment, Jim's hand holding the knife waving dangerously behind her back as she hugged him.

'Very pleased to meet you, Nancy,' she said, when Jim introduced them, shaking Nancy's hand warmly. 'Didn't know you'd hooked up with someone new, Jim,' she said, smiling broadly. 'What have you done with Chrissie?'

'Shut up, Izzy,' Stevie said affectionately, going to the cupboard to find a glass for his guest.

'Have I said something wrong?'

'No, no, just your usual lack of filter.'

Nancy watched Izzy, fascinated. Tall and slim, dressed in a strappy white linen dress, short, mint-green cardigan and sandals, she had the sort of unselfconscious beauty that drew the eye. Her thick, corn-blonde hair waved halfway down her back, and her large light brown eyes were set in a face blessed with perfect tan-gold skin, free of any make-up, blonde eyebrows and lashes blending seamlessly into the whole. Nancy reckoned she must be in her forties, no older, and it was hard not to feel a small stab of envy at her beauty and comparative youth.

But Izzy brought a welcome boost to the party, recounting tales of her trip to Milan, where she'd been summoned to counsel a rich, high-powered client who was prone to panic attacks and needed on-the-spot help.

'The hotel staff must have thought I was a tart,' she said, as they sat round the oak table in candlelight, eating thick slices of *pissaladière*, the melting onions, black olives and salty anchovies delicious with the tomato salad, celeriac *remoulade* and chilled rosé that Jim had got together for supper. 'I was called to Didier's room at all hours of the day and night, whenever he felt a wobble coming on.'

'He was probably hoping you *would* have sex with him,' Stevie joked.

'You're not wrong. He kept asking me if I did massage, dirty beast.' She laughed. 'What we have to do to earn a crust, eh?'

Nancy found it hard not to like the woman. She thought Stevie was a bit in love with her, his eyes lingering fondly on her whenever she spoke. But as the evening wore on, he seemed to lose interest in the people around him. He sat back from the table, pouring down wine in alarming quantities, his previous animation evaporating, to be replaced by a morose drunkenness that seemed full of self-pity. She glanced at Jim, who was sitting next to Izzy on the other side of the table, but he was turned sideways, one long leg crossed over the other and seemed absorbed in an intense story Izzy was recounting in a low, intimate voice.

'You see,' Stevie grabbed hold of Nancy's arm, pressing his fingers into her flesh as if he were a drowning man, 'Pascal was a life force. He had this spirit . . . I wish you'd known him . . .' He drifted into silence, his grip loosening.

'You must miss him terribly,' she said softly. Stevie seldom talked about his lover, although his presence hovered over every word he uttered.

Stevie's eyes filled with tears. 'I can't seem to find a way to live without him,' he said. Which broke Nancy's heart. A few minutes later, he looked at her, a small smile on his lips. 'You love him?' He dropped his voice, inclining his head towards his brother.

She nodded.

'You seem good together,' he said, then closed his eyes, took a long, slow breath. When he opened them, he appeared to have found his spirit again. 'Stop flirting with my girlfriend,' he shouted across the table, making Izzy jump. Jim just grinned.

'Yeah, yeah. Your "girlfriend", as you put it, was telling me about this drummer she knows, lives in Avignon.'

'Bruno?' Stevie asked Izzy, who nodded. 'Yeah, he's good. Next time you come we'll introduce you.'

Stevie got up from the table and crossed the kitchen, pulling another bottle of red wine from the rack beside the fridge, searching for the corkscrew, peeling off the foil around the top and slinging it on the side. The others watched him as he twisted the metal coil into the cork, a tired silence in the room, the candles guttering in the breeze from the open doors onto the balcony. Nancy felt suddenly exhausted and had a desperate urge to be horizontal in bed. She looked at Jim, who raised his eyebrows a little in agreement. But neither of them moved.

'I ought to be getting home,' Izzy said, pushing her chair back as she stood, stretching her arms above her head with feline grace, a long yawn escaping her. 'Don't open that, Stevie, it'll go to waste.'

Jim nodded, got to his feet at the same time and they began to clear the table, Nancy gathering up the plates they'd used for cheese and the small golden plums Madame Laverne had left in a bowl on the side when they were out. Izzy took a handful of glasses between her fingers, and Jim blew out the candles, rolled the mustard-yellow napkins into the wooden rings, then laid them in a row at the end of the table.

No one noticed Stevie, who was breathing hard, leaning heavily against the worktop, the bottle with the cork sticking out of the top dangling uselessly in his right hand. But all of them heard the strangled cry he made as he teetered, then crashed to the tiled floor with a sickening thump, the bottle smashing as it hit the tiles, wine splashing up as the sea of red spread in a river along the bank of Stevie's inert body.

'Christ!' Jim was beside him at once, kneeling without care in the wine and broken glass as he shouted at his brother, 'Stevie!

Stevie!' He held the chubby face in both hands. But Stevie lay still, eyes wide, expression empty.

Nancy was rigid with shock. She didn't dare breathe as Jim looked up at her, frantic, feeling for a pulse among the folds of Stevie's neck.

'I can't tell if he has a pulse . . . I can't tell . . .' Then, turning back to his brother, 'Stevie! For Christ's sake, wake up – *wake up!*'

Nancy shook herself, then bent to pick up Stevie's wrist and feel for a pulse, but she didn't know how to do it and couldn't find the thump-thump that would signal life.

Izzy was on the phone: '*Allô . . . aidez-moi s'il vous plaît, aidez-moi. Une ambulance! J'ai besoin d'une ambulance . . . Vite, vite – il ne respire pas!*' She gave them the address of the *mas* in a breathless voice. '*Vite, vite! Dépêchez-vous!*'

Jim, silent now, had linked his hands and was pumping Stevie's chest frantically, his own breath rasping in grunts as he focused on his task, counting in a whisper, 'Five, six, seven, eight, nine, ten,' then starting again.

'Breathe into his mouth,' he said, not looking up, and Nancy took her place behind Stevie's head, extending his neck as she'd seen it done in various CPR instructions over the years, pressing her mouth to his, his lips cold and tasting of wine. Jim stopped pumping, she took a long breath and exhaled into his mouth. Jim, barely registering it, started pumping again. After another bout of compressions, he stopped and she repeated the task. But Stevie did not respond.

'How long will they take?' Nancy asked Izzy, who was standing beside her, clutching her phone, eyes fixed on the body on the floor. She knew it was an idiotic question to which there was no answer, but she felt she had to say something. In her peripheral vision, she could see Izzy's feet in their leather flip-flops, long, tanned, the toenails painted a deep carmine red, all ten toes clenched now, as if she were hanging from a cliff. *We are all hanging from a cliff*, she thought, as she bent to Stevie's mouth again.

'I don't know . . . I've no idea,' Izzy whispered. 'Here, let me do that for a bit.' She pushed Jim out of the way and knelt over Stevie, pumping his sternum as Jim had done. Jim staggered to his feet, knees dark with wine and doubled over as if he were about to throw up. Time had stopped, the three of them caught in a single, nightmarish moment that threatened to last for the rest of their lives. But Stevie never moved again.

CHAPTER THIRTY-EIGHT

Jim surfaced with a leaden lump in his chest as he remembered. He was alone and the house echoed with ghosts as he pulled on his jeans and T-shirt and made his way upstairs to put the kettle on the hob for his coffee. Everywhere he looked, he saw Stevie. In the three yellow plums, now rotten and surrounded by tiny fruit flies, that sat in the bowl in the centre of the table, the ones they'd eaten the last evening of Stevie's life; the bottles of Stevie's favourite Bordeaux poking out from the wine rack; the photograph of his brother and Pascal, arms round each other's shoulders in the sunshine of the balcony, grinning broadly, the Frenchman's slim, dark good looks in contrast to his brother's plump roundness; the book Stevie had been reading, a paperback Harlan Coben, pressed open in the corner of the leather sofa; the espresso machine that had never been far from Stevie's side.

Jim sighed, spooned too many grains into the glass beaker of the cafetière and poured boiling water on top. He stirred the sludge quickly, then slotted the filter on top. He didn't know what to do. It was ten days since Stevie had died, four since he had been buried, three since Nancy had gone home. And none of it seemed even remotely real. He pulled open the sliding door to the terrace and stepped outside. It was another stunning day, the autumn beginning to take hold, glowing spikes of yellow and red-gold warming the landscape in the misty October light. Unfairly beautiful.

He wished he had his guitar, wished he could sit there and numb himself with music, wished . . . what? That he had known his brother had an unstable heart condition, that he'd spent more time with him over recent years, that he'd taken him to the doctor when he nearly fainted that day in the market, that he'd noticed he wasn't well a few crucial moments sooner . . . On and on the regrets came, piling up until his brain shut down from overload and refused to think any more.

He saw Izzy's blonde head moving slowly up the path, but didn't call out. He pressed himself back in the faded wooden chair, stayed very still, hoping she was going for an early walk, rather than paying a visit – he wasn't in the mood to talk. She had been fantastic this last week, her superior language skills employed as they met the priest – Stevie had converted to Catholicism decades ago because of Pascal – and the funeral director, chose the coffin, informed his legion of friends.

But although she couldn't see him, she stopped and called up softly, 'Jim, are you there?' And he knew he had no choice but to reply.

Izzy was dressed in black jogging pants, a pink vest and trainers, blonde hair in a swinging ponytail. She was clutching a plastic water bottle and a ragged black cap with the All Blacks' white feather logo stitched above the brim.

'Coffee?' Jim offered, retrieving another cup from the dishwasher.

'Not for me, thanks. I won't stay, just wondered if you wanted me to come with you to see Fabrice this morning.'

Jim and Nancy had scoured the farmhouse to find his brother's will in the empty days before the funeral, but they couldn't get into his computer and there was nothing among the papers in his desk. It had been Izzy who suggested they contact Fabrice Royale, the lawyer Pascal had introduced her to when she'd needed help a few years back. 'He's a friend, he might know something,' she'd said. And she was right. Fabrice had a copy of the new will he'd drawn up for Stevie after Pascal's death.

'Thanks, I think I'll be okay. Fabrice speaks pretty good English.'

Izzy shrugged. 'If you're sure . . .'

He was sure. There was something slightly smothering about Stevie's neighbour, especially since Nancy had left. A sort of wide-eyed concern for him and an assumption that they were a team when it came to anything to do with his brother. He felt like a total bastard thinking that. He wasn't sure what he'd have done without Izzy's help with the funeral and stuff, but now he wished she'd back off a bit, stop dropping by without warning, staying too long, rubbing his back sympathetically as she went past his chair, constantly telling him he needed 'to talk' about his brother. It was annoying when all he wanted was to be alone for a couple of days, get his head straight.

'I'm going to Leclerc this morning. Do you want me to get anything? I could cook supper this evening, if you like. I haven't treated you to my legendary ratatouille yet.'

'Umm, thanks, Izzy, nice thought, but I think I'll go through Stevie's paperwork tonight, get things sorted a bit before I go back.' She was smiling kindly at him, didn't reply. 'I'll know more what's going on when I've seen Fabrice.' The thought of all the ends he would have to tie up made his head ache. He had no idea what he was doing and he didn't feel in a fit state to work it out. All he wanted was for his little brother to be alive. It still seemed impossible that he was not.

'No problem, but if you change your mind, text me. I don't want you sitting here all alone, brooding.'

He smiled. 'Promise not to brood.'

And she was gone.

Jim reached for his phone. He knew it was early still in England, but he needed to talk to Chrissie.

'Jim?' His wife sounded sleepy.

'Just wanted to touch base,' he said, but he couldn't go on: his throat had constricted and he realized he was crying.

'Oh, Jimmy, are you okay? I can't believe it about poor Stevie. It's just so shocking . . .'

'Sorry, sorry . . .' He tried to get himself under control, but the tears just refused to stop. It was like a tsunami welling up inside him, washing the unbearable pain through his body and making him want to bellow like a wounded animal. He felt as if he were being physically sick.

Chrissie repeated his name softly into the phone, and after a few minutes he managed to stop, breathe again, the rasping sobs gradually lessening as the minutes passed, leaving him weak, exhausted.

'Are you alone?' Chrissie asked.

Jim let out a long, shaky sigh and lowered himself onto one of the balcony chairs. 'Yeah . . . Nancy had to go home – her mother's ill.' He fell silent. 'But it's okay.'

'What are you going to do now?'

'I'm seeing the solicitor this morning – he's got the will – then take it from there. Honestly, I don't have a clue what I'm doing.'

'The solicitor will tell you, I expect.'

'Yeah.'

There was silence.

'Listen, thanks for being there, Chrissie. It's just you knew him better than anyone except me.'

'I loved him, you know that. You sure you don't want me to come out? I could take Friday off, pull a sickie . . . stay the weekend.'

Jim was touched by her offer. 'Thanks, kind thought, but I'm coming home tomorrow. I'll work out what needs doing and be back here in a few weeks. I can't cope right now.'

'Okay, but if you need any help, just let me know.'

Jim sat for a long time on the terrace after he and Chrissie had said goodbye, remembering the time his brother had come to stay with them in Brighton when Tommy was a baby and what a nightmare he'd been, lying around doing fuck-all, smoking too many spliffs, playing dumb video games that bleep-bleeped incessantly, forgetting to wash, until Chrissie had had one of her banshee moments and flown at him, screaming and ripping his Super Mario from his hands and throwing it in the sink, which was strategically full of soapy water at the time. Stevie had looked as if he might faint, but it had worked. Chrissie said it was as if the video game had been controlling him: without it he got himself sorted, found a job, stopped being such a bloody slob. And it was to Chrissie that he'd first come out, admitting he'd known he was gay since he was a child. Jim had been upset at the time, felt it should have been him Stevie told. But, hey, none of it mattered now, did it?

Jim was back on the balcony that evening, smoking a lung-rotting but exquisite Gitanes – he'd bought a packet on the way back from the air conditioned orderliness of Fabrice's Apt office. He had been so shocked by the news he'd received that he hadn't even considered resisting the temptation. It was getting dark now, the air chilly with autumn, but fresh with the scent of pine needles warmed by the day's sun. The silence was broken only by the phut-phut of a Mobylette slowly climbing the hill.

He leaned on the metal rail, cold to the touch, feeling quite different, as he surveyed the view, from how he'd felt that morning. Because it was his view now. Stevie had, unbelievably, left him Maison Lavande, its contents and the not-inconsiderable bulk of his bank account – Fabrice had said that much of the money had come from Pascal. Otherwise, there had been a small legacy for Madame Laverne, and a print of a Chagall painting – titled, *Paris through the Window*, according to the will – for Izzy.

There would be tax to pay, but Jim would still be left with money and the beautiful house. He couldn't get his head around it. *This is mine*, he kept telling himself. *Lavender House is really mine*. And the unfair thing was, he had nobody to thank. He would never be able to throw his arms round his brother and tell him how much he appreciated this extraordinary gift. Even so, now, as he gazed up into the darkening, star-strewn sky, he whispered, 'Thank you . . . Thank you, thank you, thank you, Stevie.' Then, as tears filled his eyes again, he added, 'I miss you, you silly bugger. Come back. I'd rather have you than this place any day of the week.'

He had left two messages for Nancy before she called him back.

'How's your mum?' he asked first, not wanted to blurt out his news if Frances were on her last legs.

'Not good. Looks like a skeleton, isn't eating, same old, same old.' Nancy dropped her voice. 'She's just too weak to look after herself properly.'

'I'm sorry . . . Are you coping?' His heart went out to her as he thought of the responsibility she was dealing with. He remembered his own mother's slow decline with dementia and how he'd had to steel himself before his weekly visit to the home, breathing a sigh of relief when it was over. 'I'll be there to help.'

'Missing you,' she said softly. 'How did it go with the lawyer?'

'It went well.' He swallowed. 'An extraordinary thing . . . Stevie's left me the house, everything.' He still couldn't believe it, even as he relayed the details to Nancy.

'But that's wonderful,' Nancy said, after a moment's stunned silence. 'I mean, not wonderful about poor Stevie, but wonderful for you. You love that place.'

Jim lay back, pulling up one of the blue-and-yellow cotton sofa cushions so he could rest his head on it. 'I know. But it's fucking odd, Nancy, being here without him, knowing he wrote that will wanting me to have it all. I mean, I'm eight years older than him . . . He must have been pretty sure he'd die first.'

'You said he was waiting to have some heart operation.'

'Replacing a dodgy valve, yes. But Stevie kept putting it off, Fabrice said.'

'He was depressed. Maybe the effort was too much.'

'The effort of living, more like.' Jim sighed.

'So sad. Wish I was with you.'

'I'll be home tomorrow. Flight gets in almost before it leaves with the time difference. Should be with you by about five, latest.'

There was silence for a minute.

'I'm afraid it won't be easy with Mum here, Jim. I've had to move your stuff out of the bedroom . . . I've put it in the piano room. Hope you don't mind.'

'No problem. You didn't have a choice.' He made sure his voice didn't give away his real feelings, but the thought of living with Nancy's mother hovering in that upstairs room, sick and disapproving of every breath he took, made his heart heavy. But an idea had taken root, had been floating around in his thoughts since he'd left the lawyer's office. *Why not?* he asked himself, brushing away the voice that told him it was a pipe dream, that it could never work in the real world. He closed his eyes and allowed himself to drift.

It was hard to take in, the whole thing. This morning he'd woken as a man pretty much without a pot to piss in, just some cash that had to last him for the rest of his life, apart from his measly state pension. This evening he had prospects. He almost called Nancy back that instant, but he held off. This really wasn't the time, when she was dealing with her dying mother. But it gave him hope for the future.

Izzy's voice on the stairs woke him from his doze. She appeared at the kitchen door bearing a basket, a baguette sticking out of the side, a question mark on her face.

'Change your mind about supper?'

Two bottles of Stevie's Bordeaux, one pan of very garlicky ratatouille, four Gitanes and half a baguette later, Jim was sitting opposite Izzy at the kitchen table, socked feet balanced on the rung of the chair beside him, supporting himself on his elbow, wrapped in a charcoal cable sweater of his brother's because he didn't want to shut the balcony doors. He was very drunk, he knew that. He had cried a couple of times in front of her, told endless stories about Stevie, including the one about the Super Mario meeting its end in the washing-up bowl. He had laughed almost hysterically at nothing, and there had been long, companionable silences. Now he didn't know which way was up.

'I should go to bed,' he mumbled, sucking the dregs from his long-empty glass. 'I'm wasted.' He closed his eyes, his head swimming.

'Yeah, I'll get off.' Izzy, also drunk, he reckoned, got up and rather half-heartedly began to clear the table.

'Thanks for supper. It was fun.'

She smiled. 'It was.'

Jim tried standing, to see if it would work, which it did up to a point, as long as he didn't stray too far from the support of a chair or table.

'Leave that. I'll do it in the morning,' he told her, wanting desperately to be in bed, but not to make the effort of getting there.

'When's your flight?'

'Taxi's coming at ten.'

'I'll see you soon, then,' Izzy came round the table and gave him one of her quiet smiles. 'Come on, give me a hug, cowboy,' she said. Taller than Nancy, she had only to reach up a little to lay her cheek against his, which she now did, pressing her cool skin, smelling faintly of lavender, against his hot face and passing her arms around his body, pulling him closer, then holding him there for what seemed like an inordinate length of time to Jim's befuddled mind. But he found himself devoid of the energy to break free as Izzy dropped a lingering kiss on his cheek, then gave a little sigh and finally let him go.

As she gathered up the basket and wrapped her rose-pink pashmina tighter round her neck, she stopped and looked at him intently. 'You'll sell the house?' she asked. 'Sorry, that was tactless . . . Way too early to say, I suppose.'

He blinked, tried to focus. 'Yeah, way too early.'

After she'd gone, Jim went outside, breathing in the cold night air with relief as he listened to her steps crunching down the hill on the dusty path to her house. Glancing up at the stars, he searched for Stevie. 'Where are you, you stupid bastard?' he muttered. 'Why didn't you tell me you were so fucking ill?'

He heard Izzy's question like a fuzzy echo in his head as he stood in the darkness, propped against the rail, reaching in his shirt pocket for his ciggies. Sell Maison Lavande? No, Jim was not about to do that. It wasn't too early to tell, even remotely. And not only would he keep the house, he would live in it. With the woman he loved.

CHAPTER THIRTY-NINE

Nancy's kitchen was full. Hope and Jazzy sat eating macaroni cheese and peas at the table, her mother leaned awkwardly against the work surface, holding a cup of tea and wearing a slightly spaced-out expression that puzzled Nancy, and Jim stood by the front door, recently home from teaching one of his students in Mal's garden shed. He had his guitar in his hand, which Jazzy immediately pointed to. 'Jim, can we do singing after supper?'

He grinned. 'Sure, finish up and we'll go through to the piano room.'

'Yay,' chorused the girls.

'Mum, sit down. You don't look comfortable there,' Nancy glanced anxiously between Jim and her mother, knowing the past two weeks, since Jim's return from France, had been full of tension. Frances had been charming to him, but in a very deliberate, purposeful manner. Jim, on his side, had been cautious, careful not to say much and engage in only uncontentious niceties. But there was no ease between them and Nancy felt like the referee at a boxing match. She was exhausted by her attempts to keep them both happy, but there seemed no solution except to wait and see if familiarity bred some degree of affection, rather than the fabled contempt.

'Tea?' she asked Jim. He looked effortlessly handsome, standing there in his black leather jacket, his face creased in a smile just for her. She wanted to hug him and kiss him immediately, but she didn't relish her mother's predictable disdain. A memory of the row she and Jim had had the previous night flashed through her head as she rummaged in the blue-and-white-striped china caddy for a teabag. They had drunk a bit too much, tense from a strained supper with her mother, where Frances had persisted in talking about Christopher and his bloody Downland singers until Nancy had been quite sharp with her, prompting Frances to retreat haughtily upstairs, leaving a sour note in her wake.

She and Jim had then sat in grim silence, knocked back another glass of wine each and gone to bed, but the desire they had felt for each other was stifled, half-hearted, the release they both craved eluding them as the bed creaked with each move they made, Nancy stiff and able to see only her mother's disapproving face in front of her, not Jim's.

'Her hearing's not *that* good,' Jim insisted, grabbing her and burrowing under the covers, making them sweaty and breathless.

'Old people can always hear what they want to,' she said.

'Surely she doesn't *want* to hear what we're up to.'

'Oh, but she does. So that she can be cross about it.'

'We can't let it get to us, Nancy,' he said, yanking the covers off irritably and sitting up. They hadn't made love properly since France. The only time they'd tried, Jim's erection had faltered just as it had on their first night together and he'd become agitated and upset.

'I know, but I can't help myself. I know she's listening.'

'For God's sake, Nancy. That's ridiculous. She's old and ill and deaf and probably fast asleep right now. Those pills she takes will make sure of that.'

'What pills?' Nancy snapped.

'Dunno what they are, but she seems quite dozy at times, doesn't concentrate when you talk to her, and her pupils are sometimes dilated.'

'She's not on any drugs, Jim.'

'Okay, maybe I got that wrong. She just reminds me of Jimmy P when he was taking all sorts.'

'Are you suggesting Mum's a drug user?'

He'd chuckled. 'I wouldn't put it quite like that. I just assumed the doctor had given her something for the pain.' He'd leaned close to her and kissed her nipple, but she'd batted him off.

'Well, he hasn't.'

'Sorry! I don't know what you're getting so upset about. Come here, let me kiss you.'

But she had been wound up, not least because she had noticed her mother being a bit strange and hadn't bothered to investigate. 'Stop it, Jim,' she'd said, pushing him away, and he'd taken umbrage. They'd moved to opposite sides of the bed and Nancy had lain there for hours, unable to sleep. She was angry with Jim for no reason, and worried about her mother.

It was the way things were, these days. Nancy felt she was continually monitoring her own speech, being careful not to let her mother overhear things, or discuss things in front of her that might offend, trying to include both Jim and Frances in conversations. She had no real time for Jim, having always one ear listening out for her mother, night and day.

Although Frances was adamant she hated being fussed over, she clearly required help, increasingly, in many areas, from bathing to eating to getting about. Nancy had summoned her own GP, Dr Khan, a couple of days ago when her mother had seemed particularly breathless, hoping she would be able to get through to Frances where the twelve-year-old hadn't – but her mum had given her short shrift too, basically told her in no uncertain terms to get lost.

'What happens when she gets really bad?' she'd asked Mariam Khan, in despair at her mother's intransigence.

'I spoke to Guy Henderson, and he says he thinks your mum might have a stomach tumour, but he can't be sure without tests. If she collapses, you must call an ambulance, of course. Perhaps if she's actually in hospital she'll go along with having a proper examination.'

'Eat your peas, Jazzy,' Nancy told her granddaughter now. 'Hurry up, or there won't be time to sing. It's getting late and your mum will be here soon.'

Louise was at the restaurant. Nancy had looked after the girls every day this last week after school because Jason was taking time off again, this time to look after his father – now in his seventies – who had suffered a collapse after the death of his wife.

The sounds from the music room made Nancy smile. Jim was singing a country song called 'Chicken Fried', which the children loved and which required frequent harmonies. Nancy listened as she heard Jim teaching them their part, then his deep, gravelly voice singing his own quietly while they thrashed around and ended up singing the main tune, which made him switch to the harmony. There was a lot of laughter, but in the end they got it and the cheers from the room were jubilant.

'Again from the top,' Jim said, as if he were speaking to Mal or Jimmy P. 'One, two, three . . . "A little . . ."'

'Wait, wait,' Hope said, clearing her throat.

'Okay? One, two, three . . .'

The sound of the guitar made Nancy's foot tap and on impulse she poked her head round the door. 'Need a piano player?' she asked. The girls were clustered round Jim, who was sitting on the piano stool, their faces flushed with pleasure.

'Always need a piano player.' Jim grinned, moving to the chair next to the baby grand. 'Know the song?'

'I'll pick it up,' Nancy said, and had no problem following Jim's lead.

'Nana, you sing too,' Hope said.

'Right . . . From the top.' And they were off, a mess of voices as Nancy found the right chords and joined in the harmonies with the girls, who, overexcited by her presence, were temporarily distracted and lost track of the notes they were supposed to be singing, collapsing in frequent giggles.

Nancy forgot all her problems in that half-hour, her joy in the music, her grandchildren, Jim, blotting out everything else.

They would have gone on for ever, but Louise poked her head round the door.

'Sounding good,' she said, grinning, as the girls rushed into her arms and began talking to her both at once.

Nancy and Jim were finally on their own, sitting together on the sofa, her mother safely stowed in bed with the television for company. Jim put his arm round Nancy's shoulders and began to speak. She felt he was about to say something important, something he had been storing up ever since he'd come back from France. On a few occasions he had started to tell her, his eyes intent on her face, his tone requiring her attention. But each time someone from her family had interrupted, either the girls wanting a biscuit or Louise on the phone or her mother calling from upstairs, and he had stopped, waved his hand, said it didn't matter, he'd tell her later. And she'd forgotten to ask. Now his voice was hesitant.

'Nancy, you know the house, Stevie's house . . .'

She nodded.

'Well, I've been thinking. I know it would make sense to sell it, use the money to buy something over here . . . but I don't want to do that.' He stopped.

'Okay . . .'

He drew his arm from around her shoulders and leaned forward, skewing his body so that he was facing her, his knees brushing against her thigh. He took her hand, looking solemnly into her eyes.

'You see, I think I want to live there . . . like properly live there.'

'Oh,' she said, her heart fluttering in her chest. But before she could say any more, he was talking again.

'And I want you to come and live with me. Make our life in France.' He was talking faster now and she realized he had thought this out in some detail. 'I've always loved it – as you said yourself, it's a magic place. Avignon is close, and there are loads of musicians and artists there, so we'd have a chance to explore our music . . . Then there's Lavender House itself if we wanted to do the whole gîte thing – which might be good for a few months a year – or not if we don't want to. And it's so beautiful, such a great lifestyle . . . the sun . . .' He stopped and held his hand up as she frowned and began to object. 'I know, you can't come now, what with your mum, but if . . . when things are resolved, would you consider it, Nancy? I know you wouldn't want to be there the whole time, but you could come back and forth . . . I really think we could be happy there.'

Nancy didn't know what to say. His proposition made her want to cry with the sheer impossibility of it all.

'What do you think?' His question was anxious as he watched her face.

'I can't,' she said simply. 'You can see, I can't.' A lump formed in her throat. Would he leave her, go and live in France without her?

He took her in his arms, laid his large hand over her head as she rested it on his chest. 'I know you can't now, and I wouldn't dream of asking you to. But say your mother . . . Well, you know what I'm saying and I don't want to upset you, jump the gun, but we both know this can't last. If it was just Louise and the girls you were leaving, could you do that? Make it your main home? Would you *want* to do that, do you think?'

She felt the tears on her cheeks, but didn't want to move from his embrace just yet. Could she leave the family, not see the girls every day, let her daughter cope with Ross and his problems on her own?

'I just feel it's such a fantastic chance,' Jim went on. 'It's our time, Nancy. We've put in the slog – or, at least, you have – and now you deserve to have some fun, do your own thing.'

She drew back from him reluctantly, wiped her eyes with her fingertips. 'Maybe this is my own thing,' she said quietly.

Jim sucked his bottom lip under his teeth. 'Is it?'

'Well, not all of it. Not . . .' she lowered her voice, 'not Mum, but the girls, seeing them grow up. And Louise, how would she cope if I suddenly upped sticks and moved to France?'

Jim smiled. 'You make it sound like Timbuktu! It's not even two hours to Marseille. They could come in the holidays and you could come back whenever you felt like it. They'd love it there.'

All of which was true, and Nancy knew it. But the thought felt too dangerous. She wasn't capable, right now, of projecting herself into the life she might have in the farmhouse: she wouldn't allow herself to. But the thought that Jim would leave her ran rings round her heart.

Jim let out a long sigh. 'Thing is, Nancy, it's never going to work, you and me in this house, is it? Not in the long term.' His voice was gentle, but he spoke a truth that neither of them had so far articulated properly.

She refused to answer, to validate his words, and felt a stab of annoyance in her gut. Moving away from him, shifting along the sofa cushions until their bodies were entirely separate, she said, 'You honestly think this is a choice? Me leaving the family and coming with you? You honestly think I could do that?'

Jim looked taken aback. 'Not now. I'm not saying now, Nancy. But some time in the future? Could you see it?'

'How, though? Tell me how, Jim.' Her voice had risen. 'How could I leave the girls when they spend so much of their time with me? Who do you think would look after them when Lou is at the restaurant? And how would my daughter cope, left in the lurch with all the shit she has to deal with?' Her eyes were flashing, she was sure, with anger, yes, but also with frustration at what she knew was a trap of her own making.

'I know what you're saying, obviously. I'm not a moron. All I'm asking is that you consider the possibility . . . No, all I'm asking is this. Family aside, is it something you'd *like* to do?'

Hot, angry tears began to pour down her face. 'It's never "family aside", though, is it?'

'Oh, Nancy.'

Jim pulled himself closer, but she held back. She didn't want to remind herself of how much she loved him. 'I can't come with you, Jim. End of. I have absolutely no idea what's going to happen with Mum, and even without that pressure, would I really want to abandon my family?'

His look was steady and determined as he asked again, 'But is it something you could imagine yourself doing . . . ever?'

And for a moment she did allow herself to imagine. The bewitching Maison Lavande, that incredible view, the soft light in the mornings, the warmth, the delicious French food, walks in the pine forest, *cafe crème* at that little *tabac* in town, the peace . . . and Jim. Her expression softened.

'I can definitely imagine it . . . yes,' she said.

'Ah,' he said, a soft smile on his lips. 'That's all I wanted to know.'

'It's no good, though, is it?' she added, hearing an almost petulant note in her voice. 'Thinking I might love it and there being no way I can go.'

'It's a start,' Jim said, and this time she allowed him to take her hand and plant a tender kiss on the palm.

CHAPTER FORTY

Frances knew she was dying. She could feel her body closing down, each day a little more. She supposed there was a point of no return, when the slide accelerated and she completely lost control, but that point had not yet been reached. Something still held her to her lifelong habit of 'keeping up standards' – her mother's phrase, drummed into her as she grew up in that grim house on the Welsh borders, no one in sight but an ever-changing mass of sheep.

Frances's father had been killed in the war when she was eleven, leaving her mother perennially depressed, but soldiering on. Which included regular church attendance in the nearest village, visits to the library, tea with neighbours, the Friday market, and once a month a dinner invitation from the local landowner and his wife, who liked to gather a large crowd so that they could all drink themselves under the table – not her mother, who barely managed a medium sherry with the vicar, but she went for the company.

And through it all – including the war years, which changed very little in their neck of the woods except for the reduction in young men on the farms – ran the constant litany of imperatives. Wear a hat and gloves to go out – even if it's only to the chemist. Keep your handshake firm. Never welsh on an invitation (unless you're actually dying, and perhaps not even then). Be unfailingly polite to everyone, including the servants. Never turn your fork over to eat your peas. The list went on. Frances had forgotten the finer details now, but the general message was ingrained in her DNA. Yes, she was snappish with her daughter at times, but she always made sure to apologize. And even when she was in pain, these days, and would have welcomed a quiet morning in bed, she would get dressed properly, put her face on, brush her hair.

Thank God for Richard's painkillers. She would not have managed without them these past weeks. But the stash, which she kept well hidden in her manicure bag, against Nancy's prying eyes, was dwindling alarmingly, not least because her need for them seemed to be increasing with every passing week. What should she do? she wondered, as she helped herself to a pill before going to bed. Give in and let the medics prod and fiddle and tell her what she knew already? At least they would give her drugs then. But she dismissed the thought, envisaging the tedious palaver that would ensue if she did. She wished she could just have a sensible discussion with Nancy and Louise, get them to accept that she was dying, without all these ridiculous protestations to the contrary. She was eighty-four, for heaven's sake! She'd lasted longer than most. It was only with Joyce and her older friends that she could talk about death in a straightforward, realistic way.

No, she would just have to tough it out: there were no more pills where these had come from. She could pace herself, perhaps, leave it longer between doses . . . and hope it wouldn't be for much longer. The thought made her feel suddenly very alone.

As she got into bed, the television still on low because she liked the company, she wondered what had been going on between Nancy and Jim earlier. She'd heard raised voices from the sitting room but, annoyingly, couldn't make out what was being said without opening her bedroom door. Nancy had sounded quite upset. Perhaps Jim was causing trouble again, although he seemed very polite most of the time.

There was something brewing between them, though, she was sure of that. Maybe now he'd inherited that house from his poor dead brother he'd disappear off and leave Nancy in the lurch. Because, despite his charming manners, Frances still didn't quite trust the man.

As she drifted off to sleep in codeine's soothing arms, she had a strange feeling that she'd already died and that she was watching the scene between her daughter and her lover from a convenient vantage point near the sofa.

CHAPTER FORTY-ONE

Louise frowned as she listened to her mother. 'You are kidding.'

'He's always loved it there, and he doesn't have his own place here any more. I understand.'

She and her mother were sitting in the car outside the girls' school, waiting for pick-up time. They had been into town to check on her grandmother's house, clean out the fridge, turn the heating down low, put out the rubbish, cancel the papers and pick up the post. It was the end of October and both women had come to the conclusion that it was highly unlikely Frances would ever go home now. Her mum was going to raise the delicate subject with Granny about sorting out power of attorney when she got home.

'But he's not going to live there without you, is he?' Louise asked, glancing sideways at her mother. She'd been looking quite stressed and pale, but Louise had put that down to coping with Frances.

'No,' Nancy replied, but she didn't sound too certain. 'No, he's . . . Well, it's early days, I don't know what he's going to do.' She took a deep breath. 'But he's asked me to go with him.'

Louise did a double-take, mouth open. 'What? You live in France? That's bonkers. You'd never do that, Mum.' She was suddenly uncertain. 'I mean, you don't want to, do you?'

'I can't, obviously, with Granny being so ill . . .'

Louise searched her mother's face. 'But if Granny . . . Are you saying you might if it wasn't for Granny?'

Nancy sighed, pulling the edges of her dark grey cardigan tight round herself. Louise waited, but her mum didn't speak.

'Sorry, Mum, I can't get my head around this. You'd honestly consider leaving the girls and me and going to France with Jim? That'd be a total and complete nightmare. We'd never see you.'

'Well, you would, but it's not going to happen, is it? I've got Mum to look after so I'm not going anywhere.'

'But Jim?'

'I don't know, Lou.' She sounded so bleak that Louise put her hand out and stroked her mother's arm.

There was silence in the car. Louise checked the time: the girls would be coming out soon. She reached to open the car door.

'Shall I come?' Nancy asked.

'No, stay here, I won't be long.'

Feeling a bit stunned as she walked away from the car, Louise simply couldn't believe that her mother was considering abandoning them. *The selfish bastard*, she thought. *As if Mum doesn't have enough on her plate looking after Granny, without being emotionally blackmailed by bloody Jim.*

But as she stood in the playground waiting for Hope and Jazzy, she began to calm down. Her grandmother might live for years, or Jim might just bugger off . . . or the horse might talk. Whatever, losing her mother to France and Jim Bowdry was not an option.

CHAPTER FORTY-TWO

That night Nancy rolled over in bed and put her arm across Jim's body. He was sleeping, but at her touch, he turned and pulled her into his embrace. 'Gorgeous woman,' he mumbled sleepily.

'Jim . . .' Nancy laid her face on his shoulder, brought her thigh to rest against his. She could hear his heartbeat beneath her ear, slow and steady, so unlike her own, which was racing double time. 'Jim, about France.'

She had his attention now, his body tense in the semi-darkness. 'What about it?'

'Are you really going to live there?' She felt his free hand stroking her arm gently. 'You keep saying it's not working for you here, so does that mean you're going to leave?'

He was silent. 'God, Nancy, I don't know what to do. I feel I'm in the way here. It's not a big house and you've got your mother to look after, the girls round all the time . . . You don't need me under your feet. But I won't leave you to cope alone if you want me here. I love you, you know that.'

Nancy heard that he loved her, and she believed him, but she also heard that he didn't want to be there, living in the cramped house with her sick mother, who was becoming more demanding, more crabby with each passing day, rarely having her to himself, when he could be enjoying the freedom of the beautiful French farmhouse. That he was staying because he felt he ought to.

Recently he had started making excuses to be out all day. Nancy knew they were excuses because he was running down his students – he didn't need the money now – and his gigs were mostly at weekends, in the evenings. She didn't blame him for his absences: there was nothing he could do to help, and his presence seemed to irritate her mother.

She experienced a leaden weight in her gut now, the weight of knowledge that their relationship was maybe too new to survive this tough test. What did Jim owe her? As Louise was always pointing out, they barely knew each other. And he was right: it was stressful in the house, all of them tense most of the time, no one happy.

Her body stiffened, as if to ward off the anticipated pain of loss. Without him, she knew she would just shrivel, give up. The family had been enough before, but knowing Jim had changed that. She'd finally found someone, miraculously in her seventh decade, who was her soulmate.

'Maybe you should go to France, Jim,' she heard herself saying. 'It'd be better all round. You're right, you can't help with Mum. That is what it is and there's nothing we can do except wait it out.'

At her words – their tone almost cold in her desperate desire not to care – Jim pulled away, reached over to turn the bedside lamp on.

'Nancy?' He sat up in bed, naked, his long legs bent under him, facing her as she lay against the pillows. His hair was loose, and he pulled it off his face as he stared at her. 'Are you saying you want me to leave you?'

She sighed, dragged herself into a sitting position against the bed-head. 'I don't see how it'll work otherwise.'

His expression was bewildered, shocked. 'You're actually chucking me out?'

'No, no, of course not. But maybe it would be better for you to go for a bit, while Mum's ill, see how things pan out for us both. You never know, you might not like France after all.' She gave him a wan smile, hardly believing what she was saying, but unable to pinpoint another option in the turmoil of her mind.

'Wait, Nancy. I don't want to live there without you, you know that.'

'I'd just hate us to fall out, start bickering, drive each other away because it's too difficult to be together here.'

He stared at her. 'So in case we drive each other away, you're driving me away first? Ha!' The sound was explosive. 'Doesn't make sense. I have no intention of living without you, Nancy.' His expression fell. 'Unless, of course, *you*'ve gone off *me*?'

Nancy felt cold and empty. 'Of course I haven't.' She blinked away the tears. 'But, Jim, we *will* drive each other mad. Look at that stupid row we had the other night . . . and sex is hopeless when Mum's upstairs. With one thing and another, we never have any time to be properly alone.' She paused. 'Just till Mum's . . . till things are resolved.'

Jim was silent for a moment. Then he said quietly, 'You've thought this out, haven't you? You do want me to go.'

She grabbed his hand. 'Don't be ridiculous. If you leave me, I shall die.' She let the tears fall this time, she was too tired to stop them as Jim lay down beside her again, pulling the covers up, cradling her in his arms.

'No need to go that far,' he teased, and very, very quietly they began to make love.

'Happy birthday,' Jim leaned over her as she woke and dropped a soft kiss on her mouth.

Nancy smiled sleepily. 'Thanks.'

She assumed the envelope he handed her was just a card, but when she opened it, two tickets fell out. Checking, she saw they were for a concert at the Dome that night: Brahms Symphony No. 3 and a Prokofiev violin concerto.

'Oh, Jim! That's fantastic!' Laughing delightedly, she was touched by the present: he knew how much she loved Brahms. 'How brilliant. Thanks, thanks so much.'

'I thought you'd put in too much time listening to me warbling away. Time for some proper stuff.'

Ross had made her a chocolate cake, which the girls decorated enthusiastically with a Smarties heart and lurid sugar sprinkles, stripy candles, chocolate buttons, pink sugar roses, their glee as they presented it to her at teatime making her want to cry. As she sat with them all in her kitchen – even her mother at the table for a short period before she got too tired – she thought how incredibly lucky she was.

That night, Nancy got dressed with care. It seemed an age since she'd paid attention to how she looked. She was desperate to get out, have a rare evening when she wouldn't have to listen for her mother. She looked at the clock: five-thirty. They were eating in town before the concert, Jim had booked the Italian they'd gone to all those months back, after the fracas in the bar.

'We ought to get going,' he called up.

Nancy finished her makeup and went upstairs to say goodnight to her mother. Louise was coming over to check on her once the girls were in bed, and had said she would pop in every hour or so. Frances had her mobile beside her if she needed help, and was in bed anyway, watching television – she wouldn't miss Nancy for a few hours.

But when Nancy went into her room, her mother was sitting on the edge of the bed, bent over, hugging herself and crying softly. She jumped when Nancy came in and shook her head, holding out her hand as if she wanted Nancy to leave.

'Mum?'

'It's nothing, darling. I'm fine,' she muttered, making an effort to sit upright. But she was clearly not fine.

'Is the pain very bad?' Nancy asked, sitting beside her on the bed, putting an arm round her shoulders, frail and bony beneath her nightdress. Her mother winced at her touch.

'Shouldn't you be getting off?' As she spoke, Frances gave a small gasp, her breath coming in short, feathery pants as if she dared not breathe more deeply. She turned to Nancy, her face white. 'I'm fine . . . Please . . . go . . .'

Nancy ignored her entreaty. Lifting her gently into bed, she pulled the covers up over her mother, tucking the duvet round her body, stroking her hair back from her forehead as she might for Hope or Jazzy. The skin was bone cold, clammy to the touch.

'Let me call the doctor, Mum,' she pleaded softly. But at the word 'doctor', her mother's eyes flew open.

'I don't need a doctor. It was just a spasm . . . It'll pass.' She laid her hand on Nancy's, pressed it briefly. 'You'll be late.'

Nancy heard Jim calling again as she stood looking down at her sick mother's face, tense and exhausted with pain.

Jim was waiting for her in the kitchen, texting on his mobile. He smiled as she came in. He looked gorgeous, smart in a navy shirt, black jeans and a charcoal wool jacket. Her stomach churned, as she said, 'Mum's not well.'

'What's wrong with her?' Jim frowned as he slipped his phone into his jacket pocket.

'I don't know. She seems in agony . . . She can't get her breath properly.'

Jim didn't say anything, then glanced at the clock. 'Shall I fetch Louise, then? We'll be late if we don't get a move on.'

A silence fell on the kitchen.

'I can't leave her, Jim. Lou has to put the girls to bed – she can't be here with Mum for a while yet . . . I thought she'd be okay on her own, but you should see her . . .' She knew she was gabbling, trying to make what was not all right, all right. 'I'd never forgive myself if I left her and something happened while I was away . . . when she was alone.' She prayed Jim would understand.

'Christ, Nancy, are you saying you're going to give up our whole evening, miss supper and the concert, when your daughter is perfectly capable of coming over and looking after Frances – is probably happy to, what's more? There isn't anything anyone can do if she won't see the bloody doctor, anyway.'

Nancy stared at him, shocked by his tone. 'I'm sorry, I can't,' was all she said, not wanting to repeat herself. She knew she could trust Louise, but it was more than that. Her mother was *her* responsibility. She wouldn't enjoy a note of the concert, thinking of her lying in bed in such a terrible state, even if there was nothing she could do for her. 'I'm going to make her a hot-water bottle,' she said, not looking at Jim as she went to fill the kettle.

'So that's it, then, is it?' Jim said, his voice low and angry. 'You're not even going to ask Louise to help, even though you rescue her every single bloody time she has a problem? It's your *birthday*, Nancy.'

Nancy glared at him. 'I'm sorry. I'm really sorry the evening's ruined,' she said, knowing she didn't sound at all sorry, even though she was. 'You went to a lot of trouble to get the tickets—'

'This isn't about the sodding tickets.' Jim interrupted her. 'This is about you sabotaging every damn thing that's fun in your life.'

'Yes, well, there isn't much fun in my life at the moment, with my mother dying upstairs, in case you hadn't noticed. Can't you see that I don't have a choice, Jim?'

Jim came over to her and clutched her arms, looking down into her face with an expression she wanted to pull away from, it was so intense, so full of frustration.

'You *do* have a choice. You do. You could go and get Louise right now, tell her what's happened, let her cope for a change. Frances is her grandmother, for God's sake.'

Nancy twisted away from his eyes. 'I can't,' she repeated. 'I'm sorry, I just can't.'

Jim's grip loosened and he turned away. Shaking, she poured the boiling water very carefully into the neck of the hot-water bottle, screwed the top down tight, shook the bottle upside down to get rid of any water drops and pulled the cover across the rubber.

'Right, well, I'm not going to waste the tickets even if you are. I'll see you later.' And in a moment he was gone, front door slamming, the cold blast of air left in his wake a chill reminder of his rage.

For a moment Nancy just stood there, clutching the warm, furry hotty to her chest. She knew Jim was right: she could have asked Louise. But she was right too, wasn't she?

Nancy didn't sleep. She heard Jim come in very late and imagined him at one of the numerous small bars he frequented – maybe his friend, Sammi's – drowning his sorrows in whiskey, disgruntled with her and her family in just the way her family had been with him. She wished she had played it differently from the start, but she didn't know what she could have done that would have made it better for them all.

Jim crept into the bedroom and slid quietly into bed, obviously thinking she was asleep. She listened to his breathing gradually slow as he lay beside her, smelt alcohol and the night air, wanted to turn to him, but she was still upset with him for walking out like that. In the end, her desire to resolve their fight now, rather than lie awake all night stewing, overrode her irritation and she rolled over to face him.

'You awake, Nancy?' he whispered, reaching a hand out to her, finding her arm, letting it rest there.

'I'm sorry, Jim.'

'I'm sorry too.'

'How was the concert?'

'I didn't go, just wandered around feeling sorry for myself. How's your mum?'

'She settled quite quickly and went to sleep. I could have come.'

In the ensuing silence, they both began to move over till Nancy lay against Jim's chest, his arm around her shoulders, the length of their bodies touching. His skin was still cool, but she felt an almost tangible relief to be back in his arms. A relief tinged with a dull sadness, however, which stemmed from the knowledge that this time he would not stay.

Two days later, during which time they had been carefully loving and polite to each other, Jim announced, 'I'm going to have to make a trip to France, check on the house.'

They were having coffee in the bright kitchen, the wet November morning still dark outside, even at eight o'clock. His tone was cautious, his eyes watching her face. 'I thought I'd go for a couple of weeks, get back before Christmas.'

When she didn't answer, he went on, 'I have to put all the bills in my own name, sort out a ton of stuff with Fabrice. Madame Laverne is keeping an eye on things, but I need to see for myself, make sure it's all watertight for winter.'

She nodded. 'You should do that.' She didn't look at him.

'Nancy?' Jim reached across the table and took her hand, but her own lay motionless beneath his. She hated herself for sulking, but she couldn't help it. 'It's only for a short time, then I'll be back.'

'No, no, I understand.' She finally looked up at him. 'I'll miss you.'

His face relaxed a little. 'God, I'll miss you too.'

'But you won't miss this grisly domestic drama, eh?' She inclined her head towards the stairs, giving him a wry smile.

'I wish I could take you with me,' he said, lowering his voice. 'I hate you being stuck here.'

Nancy shrugged impatiently. 'Nothing to be done about that.'

The following morning, she watched him get into the taxi, guitar and small duffel bag on the back seat, and a wave of misery engulfed her. It was the guitar that tore at her heartstrings. Jim always told her his Gibson was part of his psyche, his muse, his comfort blanket, and the fact that he was taking it now meant he wasn't just visiting – as they had before – he was intending to inhabit Maison Lavande, fill it with his music, make it his. She pictured the view of the distant hills, the warmth of the sun, which even now, in dark November, she imagined shining as if it were midsummer. She smelt the pine on the clear air, tasted on her tongue the astringent local wine, felt the cool tiles beneath her feet.

It was raining and bitter here. All she had to look forward to was the long-drawn-out process of getting her mother out of bed, listening to her pained gratitude, watching her play with some toast crumbs and cold tea, worry about Louise and Ross's marriage, their financial security, try to find some iota of pleasure in the endless day. Without Jim, there would not even be the evenings together, where they drank too much wine, listened to music, whispered their treasonous thoughts, crept about the cottage and indulged in the cuddles that had replaced their previously passionate lovemaking.

CHAPTER FORTY-THREE

Jim couldn't help himself: he breathed a sigh of relief as the taxi drew away from the house and the oppressive presence of her sick mother. Guilt for his lightness of heart quickly descended on him as the taxi made its way to the A23, and an overwhelming sympathy for Nancy, left behind to deal with her difficult family. But he knew, whatever she said, that he was not helping by being there.

Nancy was someone who felt responsible for making everyone happy, and he was sick of pretending that he was, sick of seeing her suffer because he wasn't, and she knew it. He felt suffocated in that house – both literally, because the heating was cranked up to intolerable levels for Frances, and mentally. He couldn't play his guitar when he wanted, couldn't blast the rooms with music. He felt big and too male, too . . . just too much somehow. He had tried and tried to make nice to Frances and Louise, but he felt constantly monitored, judged, in their company.

Jim found himself hoping Nancy's mother would die soon, even though he felt bad for thinking it. But Frances was clearly unhappy in every way, and in pain. And Nancy was miserable. Surely it would be better all round for Frances just to slip away. He began composing lyrics in his head about death and the stupid taboos about feeling as he did, tapping his fingers on his thighs as a melody presented itself to him. *We're all going to die*, he thought. *Why can't we say it how it is instead of disguising the subject, like ruffles on Victorian piano legs?*

Mal called him while he waited in the departure lounge for his easyJet flight to board.

'Hey,' Mal said. 'Where are you?'

Jim told him.

'Lucky bugger. Wish I was coming with you.'

'You can. Jump on a plane to Marseille and I'll pick you up. There's acres of space there, five bedrooms.'

He heard Mal sigh. 'Yeah, like Sonia would let me.'

'Bring her too,' Jim said, slightly regretting the invitation as soon as it was out of his mouth. He and Sonia, although they respected each other, did not really see eye to eye on many things. Sonia had always blamed Jim and Jimmy P for any bad behaviour she suspected Mal of indulging in, although Mal had never needed any help in that department.

'Ha! Fine chance.'

'Izzy, Stevie's next-door neighbour, knows a bunch of musicians in Avignon. She says there's a big music scene there. She might be able to get us some gigs. You'd have to come over then.'

'Just tell me when,' Mal said, chuckling with relish.

There was a pause.

'So you're really serious about living there, Jimmy?' There was a pause. 'What'll you do about Nancy?'

'I told you her mother's been ill? Well, she's worse.'

'You mean "worse" as in check-out lounge time?'

'Yeah, seems so. Looks like a ghost already, poor woman.'

'Right . . . So she'll come when her mum's popped her clogs?'

Jim couldn't help smiling at his friend's directness, but felt a shadow cross his heart at his question. 'I – I hope so, mate.'

'Don't sound too sure.'

'No, well, she's a bit under pressure at the moment, can't really make plans.'

'Fair enough.' Mal fell silent. 'But you're still into her, right?'

'God, yes.'

'Bloody hell. Who'd have thought it? You a man of property now, buggering off to France with Fancy Nancy, leaving your mates high and dry. Sonia thinks you're nuts.'

'Sonia always did.'

As he sat on the plane, gazing at the sunlit floor of billowing white cloud from the plane window, he wondered if Sonia was right and he was, indeed, nuts. He would miss Mal in particular, and Jimmy P occasionally – they weren't that close these days. But none of that would matter if Nancy were by his side. They would have people – family – to stay, they'd come home and visit. It could work, he was sure of it . . . if only Nancy were able to see that.

Izzy was at the airport, dressed in a multi-coloured knitted jacket, jeans and black boots. He'd forgotten how beautiful she was – he noticed the men around her, old and young, giving her surreptitious stares. When she saw him, she ran over, threw herself into his arms as if they were lovers – her habitual way of greeting, apparently. Jim, embarrassed, patted her shoulder and pulled away as quickly as was decent.

'So happy to see you,' she said, taking his arm as she guided him across the road to the car park. 'I've been really missing Stevie. We used to see each other all the time.' She clicked open the door to her Peugeot. 'I've asked some friends over for supper tonight . . . You remember the drummer guy I was telling you about? Bruno? Well, he's coming with his girlfriend, who's a singer, and another guy, Hervé, a sculptor who lives down the hill – used to be mates with my ex.'

'Uh, sounds fun.' He had absolutely no desire to spend the evening with Izzy's friends. He just wanted to hunker down, have a whiskey or two, play some chords, talk to Nancy. But if he was really thinking of living here, he would need friends. He hoped to God Izzy would be busy over the next two weeks, working or whatever she did, staying out of his hair. The last thing he wanted was for her to be constantly popping by, using him as a poor substitute for his brother.

Worried that the house would seem empty and creepy without Stevie, he was happy to find that it welcomed him, as it always had. Although it was colder now, the sun was out, filling the room with brightness. Madame Laverne had lit the pot-bellied stove in the corner, put some apples in a bowl, a small posy of pine leaves and cones in a jar on the table. Stevie's ghost still inhabited the place – everywhere Jim went reminded him of his brother – but he could already imagine a winter snugged up here in Stevie's broad yellow chenille armchair facing the balcony and the hills, the blue-gold rug under his feet, the ornate wrought-iron standard lamp with the globe shade shedding a warm glow. It was a friendly, relaxing room.

'Was your flight okay?'

Jim called Nancy before he went down to supper at Izzy's. It was an hour earlier in Sussex and he knew she would probably be getting tea for the girls. 'Fine. Izzy picked me up – which was kind of her.'

'Very kind.'

There was a silence. He could tell she wasn't really listening. 'Things okay with you?'

He heard Nancy walking across the floor and what sounded like the fridge door shutting, her voice low when she finally answered. 'No, I'm missing you.'

'I'm missing you too.'

'I wish you were here.'

Jim's heart contracted. 'I wish *you* were *here*. It's so beautiful.'

'Yes, I know, Jim. I know it's bloody beautiful. Don't wind me up.' Her voice was sharp suddenly. 'It's hardly fair to tell me about how gorgeous it is when I'm stuck here in the pouring rain, looking after my bloody mother.'

There was a tense silence between them.

'Sorry, I just . . .' There seemed nothing to say that wasn't contentious, and he stopped talking.

'Sorry,' she said after a minute, but he could tell she was still upset.

'I'll come back if you like,' he offered. 'Seriously, if you need me, I'll be on the next plane.'

'No, no, that's stupid . . . I'm just being stupid. We had Joyce over for lunch today. Those two are like a couple of schoolgirls – they kept giving each other conspiratorial looks, then getting into a huddle and going silent when I appeared. No idea what it was about.'

'Probably working out how to score some weed, now your mum's under house arrest.' Jim heard Nancy chuckle, and his heart lightened.

'Hilarious . . . Joyce, in her beige cardie, approaching some hoody on the corner and palming a bag of dope.'

As they laughed, he checked the kitchen clock and saw he was late for Izzy. 'Listen, better get on. I'll call you tomorrow,' he said.

'What are you going to get on with?'

'Umm . . . sorting stuff . . . Probably not a lot. . .' He'd made a decision earlier that Nancy didn't need to know about supper with Izzy. It was enough of a betrayal that he was out socializing, without driving home the point. And he didn't want Nancy to get the wrong idea about his neighbour.

'I love you,' he told her, and the knowledge brought tears to his eyes.

CHAPTER FORTY-FOUR

Frances knew that the time had come. Her body had finally reached tipping point and was sliding now – she no longer had the strength to resist. Standards had finally slipped. The knowledge, instead of frightening her, brought with it a profound sense of relief. She didn't need to do any more, she could just lie there and wait.

She had no real hope of meeting Kenny in heaven, not after all this time – twenty-four years: his soul had probably been shuffled off to merge with the Godhead or some such – although Joyce was sure her Richard would still be waiting. Frances hoped God would do his bit, though, find her a comfy spot somewhere after all those endless church services she'd sat through. It was easier to believe in him, because oblivion was the only other option, and who would willingly choose nothing? There wasn't a hell of a lot she could do about it either way, so she had resolved, long ago, not to worry. People had been dying since there were people to die, and so would she.

Now that Richard's painkillers had run out, however, things had become very tricky. She was tough, she knew how to endure, but goodness it had been hard not having that blissful cushion of respite every few hours. It had made her feel quite mad. She'd eked out the supply till the end of last week, but now she was reliant on paracetamol, and much bloody use that was, even taking twice as much as the packet advised.

It should be easier, she thought, as she lay in bed, waiting for Nancy to come up and help her wash. She was in constant dread that she would get too weak and her daughter would drag her off to hospital where they would insist on cranking up the whole ghastly medical machine. Every morning she was mildly disappointed that she had survived the night.

But Frances put on a brave smile when Nancy's face appeared in the doorway. The only wrench about knowing she was soon to die was leaving Nancy and the family, never seeing her dear granddaughter or those charming little girls again. The thought was astonishingly painful. Nancy had been a good daughter, despite being so much closer to Kenny than she'd ever been to herself. It used to make her jealous when Nancy was a child, witnessing the bond they shared and feeling so excluded, but none of it mattered now. One benefit of dying, she acknowledged, was that all the things that had bothered you in life were now spectacularly unimportant.

But although Nancy did her very best to hide her feelings, it was clear in her eyes the stress the bloody illness was causing. Frances would have liked to thank her from the bottom of her heart for being so kind; she would have liked to tell her she loved her before she died. But she wasn't good at saying those things and the words – so often on the tip of her tongue – just wouldn't come. She hoped Nancy knew.

'Good morning, darling,' she said, as if it were indeed good. But her whole body was just screaming to be left alone. She wanted to lie there and drift. She wanted it to be over.

CHAPTER FORTY-FIVE

Jim had been gone for more than a week. They talked every day, but Nancy was uncomfortably aware of the widening gulf between them, her only topic of conversation the claustrophobic nursing of a dying woman, while Jim was full of the new opportunities opening up for him in France.

'Bruno – Izzy's drummer friend – and I are getting together today to bash out some stuff . . . There's a club in Avignon he plays with his band – he says they'll be well up for some new blood.'

'Sounds great,' Nancy said, trying to be enthusiastic.

'How's your mum?' Jim asked, after a moment of silence.

'She's a bit calmer, not as jittery and anxious as she was earlier in the week – still don't know what that was about – although she hasn't got the energy even to get out of bed now. She sleeps most of the time. But I can't get her any pain relief without seeing the doctor, and you know where that suggestion leads . . . It's horrible, Jim.'

'God . . . poor woman. Poor you. Are you sure you don't want me to come back?'

'No, no, you can't help . . . It's better I'm on my own.'

'I'll be home Sunday.'

'Yes . . . good. Jim, I'm sorry I'm such a grump at the moment. All I do is moan – I never seem to have anything interesting to say.'

'For God's sake, Nancy, you're going through hell. I wish there was something I could do to help.'

There was silence for a moment.

'You would say if you wanted me there?'

'I would. Honestly, there's nothing anyone can do.'

They said goodbye and Nancy took a deep breath before climbing the stairs to find out how her mother was that morning.

She knocked on the bedroom door, but there was no response, so she pushed it open and went in.

'Hi, Mum.'

But Frances didn't respond. Nancy went over to the bed. Her mother looked as if she were asleep, but her breathing was laboured and slow, the sound painful, rasping, seeming to take over the whole of her frail body.

'Mum? Mum . . .' Nancy put a hand on her shoulder, shook it gently. 'Mum?'

Her mother gave no indication that she heard her.

Nancy, hands shaking, reached into her jeans pocket for her phone and dialled 999.

She stood with Louise in the hospital corridor, gazing into the room through the half-closed venetian blinds to where her mother lay, face covered with an oxygen mask, drip-cannula taped to a vein in her emaciated left forearm, a clip on her finger attached to a quietly beeping monitor beside the bed. She looked skeletal, clay-white, cheeks sunken, lips dry, eyelids fluttering, a light film of sweat on her brow. Barely alive.

'What did they say?' her daughter asked.

'They said what we suspected. She's riddled with cancer . . .' Nancy spoke without emotion. She didn't feel like crying. It was as if her life were suspended, as if she were holding a long, long breath.

'What are they going to do?'

'Nothing. There isn't anything they can do. Her organs are just giving out.'

Louise took her hand and squeezed it. 'Oh, Mum. Why didn't she have treatment when she first got ill, when it might have worked?'

Nancy shrugged. The question that had dogged her relentlessly for months was now redundant.

'So, what . . . ? Have they said how long they think she's got?'

'Hours . . . days at most,' Nancy said.

'*Hours?*' Louise bit her lip, her eyes filling with tears. 'Poor Granny.'

'I hope for her sake she goes quickly,' Nancy said. 'I hope she's already . . . not feeling any of this.'

The two women went inside the stifling room and sat either side of the high hospital bed. Nancy picked up her mother's cold hand and held it lightly in her own, squeezing it to let her know she was not alone. 'I love you, Mum,' she whispered.

But if her mother heard, she didn't acknowledge it. Frances died an hour later, never regaining consciousness.

Nancy lay in bed that night with a feeling of emptiness, of profound silence, of disbelief. But exhaustion took over and her thoughts stalled as she found herself sinking deeply – as if she were falling – into the softness of the mattress, her body gradually losing substance as she drifted into oblivion. When she woke the following morning, she realized she had slept solidly – not even surfacing to pee – for ten straight hours.

Her first thought was her mother. Her second thought was Jim. He was taking the earliest flight he could get and would be home by lunchtime.

Neither of them spoke. As Jim dumped his bag on the floor, she moved into his arms. They stood entwined, their bodies so tightly together that there was no distinguishing where she stopped and he began. It was such a relief to be held. She felt his lips in her hair, she inhaled the scent of his body, his clothes – stale from the plane and the pre-dawn start, but so comforting, so reassuring. She let out a long, shaky breath.

CHAPTER FORTY-SIX

Louise filled the kettle again, flicked the switch, emptied the big brown teapot of the four bags, which she squeezed over the sink and put in the bin. 'Take these round one more time, please, Hopey.' She handed her daughter the plate of smoked-salmon sandwiches. Hope, who had been on her way up to her bedroom to play with Jazzy, sighed, but did as her mother asked.

The voices wafting through from the sitting room were mostly female, her grandmother's coterie, not many in number but tough, independent women, who seemed to laugh loudly and a lot, despite the loss of their dear friend. *Maybe it's a case of you have to laugh or you'd cry*, Louise thought, *especially when you can't help wondering if you'll be next*.

As she waited for the water to boil, she heard Ross open the front of the wood-burning stove and bang another log inside, the squeak as the door was closed. She'd drunk too much wine and was aware of a dull ache behind her forehead, a stale taste of tea in her mouth. She wished they'd all bugger off. Ross had been whingeing all morning about having to shut the restaurant for lunch – as if it mattered any more – and they'd been arguing since dawn.

As she poured hot water over the fresh teabags, Jim wandered into the kitchen and came over to the sink, where he emptied the dregs of two glasses of red wine, then ran them under the tap, placing them carefully on the draining board.

'How's it going?' he asked, giving her a sympathetic smile.

'Okay, I suppose.' Louise hardly ever spoke to Jim alone and she felt awkward with him.

'Good turnout,' he was saying.

She nodded. 'How do you think Mum's coping with the whole thing?'

'Not sure. She hasn't said a lot, hasn't even cried much. I think she's exhausted.'

Louise nodded and they fell silent.

'Are you planning another French trip?' she asked. She worried he'd already been nagging her mother to go with him, now Granny was dead.

Jim shook his head slightly. 'Not sure what's going to happen.'

'Mum says you love it there.'

'I do. But I also love your mother.' His tone was resolute, but his expression suggested he wasn't sure how his remark would be received.

Louise fitted the lid back on the teapot, picked it up and gave it a gentle swirl to disperse the tea. 'She doesn't want to live in France, Jim. You must know that.'

Jim's face, which had gone very still at her words, told her he hadn't known that, and she wished she'd kept her mouth shut. 'I mean,' she hurried on, 'she'd never be happy so far away from us all.'

Jim gave a slow nod. 'Has she said as much?' he asked quietly, glancing towards the sitting room, where Nancy was standing in the doorway, talking to Granny's friend Joyce.

Louise hesitated. 'You should probably talk to her about it.'

'I will . . . I have. But it would help to know what she's told you.'

'She said, basically, that it would never happen.' Trying to think back to the last conversation she'd had with her mother about the French house, she thought she remembered her saying that, even without Granny being a factor, she wouldn't consider leaving them.

Jim cleared his throat. 'She said that, did she?'

Louise nodded. 'I'm sure you can see it from her point of view, Jim. You know how much she adores Hope and Jazzy. If she left, she'd miss their whole childhood.'

He didn't reply, just stood looking out towards the garden, arms folded, jaw solid, swaying backwards and forwards slightly in his boots.

'I shouldn't have said anything.' Louise felt sorry for him now. He looked devastated.

'No,' he said eventually, turning his blue eyes on her. 'Best I know.'

It *was* best, Louise was certain of that. The last thing her poor mother needed, after all she'd gone through with Granny, was to be shanghaied into living in some godforsaken house in the middle of France, where she had no friends, no family, with a man she barely knew. All right, he loved her, but that wasn't enough reason to tear her away from her beloved grandchildren. If he really had her best interests at heart, he'd sell the wretched house and buy something over here.

'Don't tell her I said anything,' Louise whispered, as she heard her mother saying goodbye to Joyce and saw her swing round to face them, making her way tiredly across the kitchen in her black dress.

'God, that was exhausting,' Nancy said, laying a hand on Jim's arm.

Louise watched him automatically put his own round her mother's shoulders and pull her into his side.

'I think they're beginning to go at last,' her mum added.

Jim didn't respond, his expression giving little away.

Louise couldn't look at him. Had he got the message? Would he back off, stop badgering her mother?

'Maybe I should hold the tea?' she asked Nancy.

'Yes, I don't want to encourage them. But *I* could do with another cup.' She looked up at Jim, let out a long sigh. 'Well, that's it, I suppose. Think it went as well as it could have.'

Jim smiled at her. 'Yeah, good job. Frances would have loved it.'

Louise saw her mother's eyes fill with tears. 'She would, wouldn't she? Mum adored a party. Can't believe she's not here enjoying it with us.'

Later, when she and Ross were lying back exhausted on the green sofa, Louise told her husband what she'd said to Jim because she was worried that she'd gone too far.

'You're such a bitch sometimes, Lou.' Ross's words were without heat and accompanied by a huge yawn. Perhaps he didn't even care enough to be angry, these days.

'Why?'

'Well, going behind your mum's back like that, interfering.'

'She needs to be protected. Jim's an okay guy, I don't dislike him, but it's not fair that he's pressuring Mum to go away with him. I'm glad I told him.'

'Your mum's quite capable of looking after herself, you know. You putting your oar in will only cause trouble.'

'He said he wouldn't tell her.' Louise realized that wasn't quite what had happened, but she didn't correct herself.

'Just leave her alone. Let her make her own decisions,' Ross was saying. 'If she wants your help, I'm sure she'll ask for it.'

Louise wasn't listening. Her father had just left her a message saying the baby, a boy – her half-brother, she thought, with a moment of shock – had been born last night. She knew she was too tired to reach the expected level of enthusiasm required if they spoke, so she texted him congratulations and pulled the 'Granny's funeral' card, saying she'd ring in the morning.

CHAPTER FORTY-SEVEN

Jim lay in bed, wide awake, beside Nancy. The digital display on the bedside clock read 04.11. It was nearly two weeks since Frances's funeral – Christmas Eve today – but Louise's words were still running around in his head, like some annoying mantra. He didn't know whether to believe her or not, and he hadn't plucked up the courage yet to ask Nancy if it were true. He told himself now was not the time, but in fact he was just shying away from knowing the truth.

So he said nothing, just looked after her, let her recover. Nancy played the piano a lot, they listened to music together – not just classical, but country, jazz, African music, his iPhone was packed with things she hadn't heard – they pottered round Brighton, sat in cafes, went to movies and did some Christmas shopping. And although Jim loved being with her, the time seemed like a sort of limbo, not their real life, as if they were waiting for the next act.

Rolling over now, he watched her as she slept, resting his palm very lightly against her shoulder. Without waking, she brought her hand up and laid it over his. He smiled in the darkness.

Louise had made him out to be so selfish. Was he? He just knew that their relationship would not survive such close proximity with Nancy's family – even now Frances was dead. He could never be happy in this small house, no breathing space, constantly playing second fiddle to Louise and the children. *Yes*, he thought, *that probably does sound pretty selfish*.

But it was more than what *he* wanted. It was to do with seizing an opportunity, having one last adventure in life, not just settling for what was. He didn't think it was entirely self-interest to believe that Nancy could be happy in Maison Lavande too, make a life for herself that didn't solely involve her duties as mother and grandmother. Maybe she could explore her music a bit more. She was so bloody talented it made him quite angry that she'd chosen to play second fiddle to that preening git of a husband. Now she was free of her main responsibility, didn't she deserve a break? Yes, it would be different, and he appreciated he didn't have grandchildren yet – maybe never would, Tommy so far not hooking up with any girl for more than a couple of months – so he couldn't know how it felt, but Nancy had a right to her own life too, if she wanted it.

But if she didn't . . . The thought was too complex for Jim to process right now and he rolled over onto his other side and decided to think about it in the morning.

Nancy and Jim stood beside each other facing the kitchen worktop. Jim had tapped his iPhone and sounds of the Everly Brothers' 'All I Have to Do is Dream', filled the room. He and Nancy were swaying side to side to the music, she taking Phil's harmony, Jim taking Don's, as they made the mince pies – the only part of Christmas cooking with which Ross had decided to trust Nancy. Jim spooned mincemeat into the pastry cases lying in the tins, Nancy wetted the edges of the pastry tops with her finger and covered each little pie, pinching the edges as she worked her way round. When the music finished they turned and smiled at each other.

'We should compose something together,' Jim said, putting the empty mincemeat jar on the counter, but still holding the teaspoon in his other hand.

'Like a country song?' Nancy laughed. 'Wouldn't know how to.' She took the spoon, exchanging it for a pastry brush and ramekin of milk, and he started brushing the pies she'd finished.

'Of course you would, sweetheart. You're a musician, for God's sake. I think you forget that sometimes.'

She flicked her fringe out of her eyes. Her thick hair was pinned back off her face today and Jim thought it made her look very young. 'Maybe,' she said.

There was silence as Jim watched Nancy cut a small slit in the lid of each pie, then slide the two trays into the hot oven.

'Seriously . . . Now you have more time, we should sit down and do it. It'd be fun.'

The oven door slammed shut and Nancy set the timer for fifteen minutes. Having done so, she looked up at him, her face suddenly serious. 'In France, you mean?'

Jim's expression froze. Yes, he did mean in France.

'You still think it's a good idea?' she was asking, her arms crossed over her blue-and-white butcher's apron.

'Do you?' he asked, hedging his bets.

She sighed, looked away.

'At least come for a week after Christmas, no pressure, just a break.'

'After Christmas?'

He nodded. 'Bruno has a gig on the twenty-eighth and he's asked me to join in for some of the set. I thought . . .' He held his breath, not knowing why. He was only asking her to come with him for a few days – no big deal – but her reply might be pivotal.

She was staring at him, but not seeing him, then her gaze focused. 'Twenty-eighth is a bit early. We're taking the girls to the pantomime on the twenty-seventh.'

'You don't have to be there for the gig. You could come out any time before the thirty-first. We'll have New Year together in France. What do you think?'

Nancy grinned. 'Why not?'

He wanted to shout for joy.

Jim drove home with Izzy after the gig. He had been a lot more nervous than he usually was – foreign country, different audience and all – and felt tired.

'You were amazing,' Izzy said, taking her eyes from the road to give him a smile. 'Your voice is beautiful, so sexy . . . they loved it.'

'Umm, thanks. Not sure . . .' He thought his performance had been a mess. Bruno had generously given him four slots for songs, but Bruno's band played modern country – stuff like Lady Antebellum – which was a much grander sound, heavier bass. He was used to Mal and Jimmy P's more laid-back rendition and he'd felt about a hundred and fifty, sitting there croaking out the likes of Kristofferson and Cash – although Izzy might be right: the audience had seemed appreciative.

'It was perfect,' she insisted, and he caught her smile in the glare of the oncoming headlights. 'Only the beginning.'

'Drop me at yours. I'll walk up,' Jim said, as the car climbed the hill.

'Don't be daft, I'll take you all the way – it's freezing out there.'

Jim, terrified she would ask herself in, was resolute. 'Nah. I want to walk – I love the cold air.'

As the car pulled up at her two-storey house, white-painted with bright blue shutters and a wavy terracotta-tiled roof, Jim got out and dragged his guitar from the back seat. 'Thanks for doing this, Izzy. Much appreciated.'

She stretched and yawned, breath like smoke in the beam of the security light that snapped on at their approach. 'Come in for a minute, will you? There's something I want to show you.'

He hesitated, not wanting to sound rude. 'Umm, show me tomorrow, eh? I'm bushed.'

Izzy laughed softly and came round the car. 'Okay. Ring me when you wake up.' She wrapped her arms round him, just as she had at the airport, and hugged him way too close. 'Really enjoyed myself tonight, Jim,' she said.

Nancy was arriving tomorrow, and Jim couldn't wait. He was really looking forward to a French New Year, buying the food in the little shops in town, going for walks in the frosty hills, sipping coffee in a cafe together, cosying up in front of the stove with a glass of champagne . . . making love. He'd already told Izzy, just in case she had other ideas, that he and Nancy would be having a quiet one. He had no desire to usher in the New Year with his neighbour and her friends, especially that grim sculptor fellow, who clearly thought he was some sort of fucking genius.

I need to make it clear, he thought, as he crunched his way up the hill in the darkness, guided by the torch on his mobile phone. *Me and Nancy are not negotiable*. He was pretty certain Izzy had a bit of a crush on him. Every time he'd looked her way in the club tonight, she'd been gazing at him with her large eyes in such a disconcerting way. And she was up at Stevie's house, uninvited, all hours of the day and night, with the flimsiest excuses, such as making sure he had enough wood for the stove, even though it was piled a mile high in the log store next to the house for all to see.

*

The following morning, his mobile woke him.

'Hi, Nancy, what's up?'

Her voice was hesitant. 'Jim, I know you're going to be furious, but something's come up.'

Jim pulled a face, let out a sigh, waited for the inevitable. It had to be Louise.

'The restaurant's doing this big New Year's Eve dinner thing, and the place is booked out, which is great, but . . .' he heard her sigh too, 'but Kyla has really bad flu and Ross and Jason can't manage with only Evie waitressing and no one doing front-of-house. It'd be a nightmare on a party night.'

'So you're going to babysit and Louise is going to help out.' Why had he thought it could be any different?

'I can't see how else they'll cope.'

'Couldn't they hire someone for the evening?'

'On New Year's Eve?'

'No, I suppose not.' He paused. 'God, Nancy, I'm gutted. I was so looking forward to you being here.'

'I was too. I'm gutted as well.' She sounded genuine, but he couldn't be sure. Perhaps she'd never really intended to come. 'I'm so sorry, Jim. Really, really sorry.'

He had heard that so many times before. And he was sure she was. But 'sorry' didn't mean a damn thing if you didn't address the reason for repeating it. 'Never mind. Next year, maybe,' he said.

There was silence.

'Do you want me to come back?' he asked, feeling a dull knot of resentment settling in his gut.

'Probably no point. I'll have to be with the girls most of the day, I imagine.'

'Right.'

'Missing you,' she said, which wound him up some more. Then she added, 'Jim, I'm so sorry about New Year's Eve. I know you think it's bloody predictable. I just didn't see what else I could do.'

He didn't want to start a row, so all he said was, 'No, well, don't beat yourself up about it.'

They said goodbye and Jim found himself on the verge of tears. This was more than just a missed New Year.

CHAPTER FORTY-EIGHT

Nancy sat alone in front of the television as Big Ben struck twelve and the crowd on the Thames went wild, fireworks exploding in the London sky, the presenter shrieking hysterically at the camera. Hope had begged to stay up, see the New Year in with her grandmother, and Nancy had had a moment of temptation, thinking how good the company would be, but she knew the girls would never last. Local fireworks, earlier on, had kept them from sleeping, but by ten she'd heard no more giggling and shuffling about, so she'd assumed they had finally dropped off.

She wondered what Jim was doing. He'd said he was staying in with a bottle of bourbon and his guitar, and she pictured him now, the wood stove burning, his boots off, the clear starry sky outside the balcony window, maybe some crisps or chocolate on the table, strumming quietly as he sipped his whiskey. She smiled to herself, her heart aching to be with him. They had agreed they would talk at her midnight, not his, which was an hour earlier, and she reached for her phone.

He didn't pick up, her call going to voicemail.

'Come on, Jim,' she muttered, dialling again, suddenly worried he was already asleep. This time it was picked up after two rings.

'Jim's phone?' a sleepy – or drunk – female voice muttered, before Nancy had a chance to speak.

She froze. On the verge of hanging up, she heard the voice say, 'Happy Noo Year!' in a bad American accent, then, 'Izzy here, who's this?'

'It's Nancy.'

'Hey, Nancy. Happy New Year,' Izzy repeated.

'Can I talk to Jim, please?'

'Umm . . .' There was a rustle of what sounded suspiciously like sheets to Nancy. 'Bit tricky. He's asleep, I'm afraid. We . . . he . . . There was a lot of alcohol involved and, well, he kinda passed out a while back.' Nancy heard her giggle drunkenly. 'We made a bit of a night of it, to be honest.'

Nancy held her breath.

'Are you at Stevie's house?'

'No, mine.' Izzy yawned.

Nancy didn't speak.

'Hey, don't get the wrong idea, Nancy. Jim wasn't in a fit state to get back up the hill, that's all. So I just put him to bed. Nothing odd going on, I assure you. Think he was just upset you didn't make it.'

Nancy wanted nothing more in that moment than to stab the beautiful Izzy through the heart. Instead, she forced herself to laugh, the sound harsh to her ears. 'Well, if you'd ask him to call me when he surfaces.'

'Course, will do. Hope you had a good one. We missed you.'

'It was great. Night, then.'

'Night, Nancy.'

She sat clutching the phone for a long time. She shivered, the house was getting cold. While her mother had been ill, she'd left the heating on all night – Frances was always freezing – but Nancy had barely been able to breathe in the stifling fug and now the system switched off at ten-thirty.

Nothing to worry about, she told herself firmly. *Jim doesn't find Izzy attractive – he's told me that enough times. Like the woman said, he was just upset I wasn't there and he got drunk. Serves me right.*

But telling herself wasn't working. She felt a piercing thrust of jealousy in her gut, so powerful that she almost retched as she imagined them lying together in bed, his hands all over Izzy's beautiful body, his— No! she shrieked silently, getting up off the sofa and pacing around the room, clutching her arms around her icy body, not knowing what to do with the intensity of her feelings, but instinctively aware that she must move about or be choked by them.

If the girls had not been asleep upstairs, she would have run from the house, jumped in the car, driven as fast as she could away from the fear that was consuming her. Instead she put on the kettle. Shaking, wrapping herself in the sea-green woollen throw that had been folded over the back of the sofa, she pulled a mug out of the cupboard, then found a chamomile teabag.

The liquid scalded her tongue and the roof of her mouth as she sipped it, standing rigid against the worktop, her socked feet numb on the chilly kitchen tiles, but she craved the heat. Without it, she was sure she would die.

She must have stood there for a long time, because the next thing she was aware of was the sound of Ross's car creeping slowly over the gravel. She wished she'd turned the lights out: the last thing she needed right now was a conversation with her daughter. But if they saw the lights, they didn't come over – it was after two in the morning. A minute later she heard the front door closing quietly.

Nancy didn't pick up when Jim called early the next day. He rang again half an hour later, and at regular intervals throughout the morning. Nancy still didn't pick up. She couldn't decide how to react. But it was too hard, not speaking to him, and by lunchtime she gave in.

'Nancy! Oh, thank God. I thought— Izzy said she'd spoken to you—' He broke off.

'Izzy said you were in her bed.'

'She said that? I wasn't. I slept in the spare room – passed out, more like. Listen, I know it doesn't sound good—'

'Why did she answer your phone, if she wasn't in the same room as you?' Nancy interrupted him, unable to keep the sharpness out of her voice.

'I have no idea.' He sounded bewildered. 'I told you, I was totally out of it.' He paused. 'For heaven's sake, Nancy, do you honestly think I'd do anything with Izzy? Do you honestly think that?'

'I don't know what to think. You said you were staying in, alone, having a glass of whiskey or two, and then I phone at what must have been one in the morning and that woman answers and I can hear . . . I can bloody hear, Jim, the sound of her moving about in the bed.'

She heard him let out a frustrated sigh.

'Don't treat me like I'm making a fuss about nothing. You obviously went down to her house when you said you didn't want to go anywhere, then got nice and cosy with her, partying away, and ended up in bed. What the hell am I supposed to think?'

'Please, listen, Nancy. I wasn't in her bed . . . or if she was in mine, then we weren't doing anything. I was fully clothed when I woke up this morning and Izzy was shut in her own bedroom. I swear, going over to hers was just a drunken impulse because you weren't here and I was missing you.'

'Don't blame me for your behaviour, Jim. We aren't children. I have responsibilities. Surely we can spend a few nights apart without you getting into another woman's bed.'

'I've told you, I *wasn't* in Izzy's bed.' He groaned. 'I mean she wasn't in bed with me, is what I'm trying to say.' Another sigh. 'God, my head hurts. I don't feel I'm making any sense, but please, please, believe me, Nancy. I got stupidly drunk, and that is absolutely the only bad thing I did last night.'

Nancy wanted to believe him. She did believe him. What made her sick with jealousy was the thought of him with Izzy at all, smiling and laughing with each other over the New Year candlelight in her cool little cottage, with her smooth, long-limbed, lightly tanned, *youthful* body, and – just as important – her brown-eyed, adoring gaze. Bloody cow.

'Nancy?'

'I'm still here.'

'Please, I'm so sorry about last night. But you know I don't fancy the woman. Okay, I should never have gone there, but I'd had a couple and I just thought . . .'

Leave a man alone for ten seconds, her mother used to say, *and they'll be up to no good.* With a jolt, Nancy remembered her mother was no longer around to deliver her bitter homilies. And although her conscious mind knew she had gone, the habit of concern for her – a constant backdrop to her day – was only just beginning to fade.

'It doesn't matter,' she said, not quite meaning it but feeling they were going round in circles with the argument.

Jim was silent.

'Let's talk later,' she added.

'Yeah, let's do that,' he replied, his voice tired and dull.

Lindy had been to Antigua for Christmas and was looking unreasonably gorgeous – more Goldie even than Goldie – when Nancy met up with her in the village pub two days later. Her blonde hair blonder, her skin glowing, she seemed to light up the dark, low-ceilinged pub like the Christmas tree they'd just dismantled. Nancy wanted desperately to talk to her friend about Jim, but she listened politely to Lindy's tales from the Caribbean, which inevitably involved a muscled diving instructor and a Chelsea-boy heir to a jewellery empire with a large yacht.

'Right.' Lindy eventually turned her attention to Nancy, a slight frown on her face. 'Spill the beans about our Jim. I know you've got something to tell me.'

Nancy didn't ask how she knew, she just launched into a breathless description of the events of New Year's Eve.

When she'd finished, her friend, raising her eyebrows, mouth pursed, took time to consider the situation. 'Sounds innocent enough.'

'You think?'

Lindy nodded. 'Yeah.' She laughed. 'He's a man, Nance. He's sitting there, all alone, having a glass or two, feeling a bit sorry for himself because you haven't pitched up . . . and there's this neighbour down the hill, whom he doesn't fancy . . .'

'So he says.'

'You don't believe him?'

Nancy sighed. 'Yes, I do. But she's very beautiful, Lindy.'

Lindy shrugged. 'Beautiful doesn't necessarily mean desirable, darling, and vice versa. You must know that by now . . . But that's not really the issue here, is it?'

'Isn't it?'

'No. Seems to me the issue is whether you love him enough to go to France. Or he loves you enough to give France up and come back to England.'

Nancy knew that. 'I can't leave Louise at the moment.'

Lindy looked sceptical. 'Well, there's your answer.'

'You think I'm wrong?'

'Not for me to judge. But if France means so much to Jim, you have to face the prospect of losing him.'

Nancy's heart seemed to contract down to a small, hard nub. 'Can't he live here?'

Lindy frowned. 'Sounds like he wants to make a break, try something new with you by his side. So romantic. But if you're dead set against it . . .'

'I'm not! I can easily imagine living there with him. I just can't imagine leaving the family. Especially as Lou's having a nightmare with Ross at the moment.'

'Fair enough. But, as I've said before, there's always some sort of drama with family. And if you're basically telling Jim you're putting them first . . . Well, that's a very strong message to a guy.'

Nancy nodded wearily.

'How much do you really love him, now the first flush of sex has worn off?' Lindy was peering at her intently.

'A lot,' she said softly, 'but I love my family too.'

Lindy laughed. 'Doesn't have to be either/or, you know, just a form of compromise that suits everyone. Thing is, hitching your star to your family and not having your own life can work for some people, especially if there isn't an alternative. But you've been offered a sodding brilliant alternative in Jim.' She shook her head, her glance almost pitying. 'You've done your bit, Nance. Couldn't you just throw caution to the wind for a change? Take a chance?'

CHAPTER FORTY-NINE

In the four days since the New Year, Jim had called Nancy a number of times, but she hadn't picked up, hadn't responded to his messages. He found himself increasingly reluctant to make the effort to get in touch, realizing he was still upset with her. Upset that she trusted him so little, believing he could be unfaithful on a mere whim. And with Izzy! Yes, he'd been drunk, but that wasn't a crime, as far as he knew. And, yes, he'd gone down to Izzy's when he'd said he'd stay indoors, but so what? It was New Year's Eve and Nancy had chosen not to be with him. Why shouldn't he socialize with anyone he chose?

Jim didn't know what to do. He still longed to see her, he missed her constantly – everything he did he wanted to share with her, even if it was just gazing out over the balcony at the winter landscape or sitting in front of the stove with a book and a glass of wine. But since New Year he had lost faith that she would ever be part of his life here, even for a visit. *What's the point in booking a trip for her, when I know fucking well that something will happen to stop her coming?*

He should go back, he knew that. Knew if he didn't it would be the end for him and Nancy. But he had another gig lined up, this time just him, in Bruno's club. He'd had offers of another couple with the band too, if he could persuade Mal and Jimmy P to get their arses in gear and come over. He was happy there, happier than he'd been for years. The place suited him somehow, and even though he missed Nancy, he didn't feel lonely in his brother's house. He'd started writing songs again too, which he hadn't done much of since the debacle with Chrissie – he reckoned that twerp Benji had stolen his spirit.

His phone rang. Izzy.

'Fancy a trip into town? We could do a beer and a croque-monsieur at Brazza . . . or go further afield. Bonnieux's cute.'

Jim had kept his distance from Izzy since the drunken episode, legging it up the hill before she'd woken on New Year's Day, then taking the car out for a long drive to avoid her. He'd texted an apology, she'd texted back, but this was the first time they'd spoken.

'Yeah, okay.'

'Such a bloody boring time of year,' she said. 'Nothing's going to happen till next week. Might as well enjoy ourselves.'

Might as well, thought Jim.

The cafe was crowded. Izzy and Jim squeezed into a table in the corner, glad to be out of the gale-force wind battering the hill town. She ordered for them both – the croques and two Kronenbourgs.

'Izzy, about the other night, I'm so sorry.'

She laughed. 'Hey, no big deal. We both got wasted, it was New Year, why the hell not?'

Jim nodded slowly. 'Yeah . . . but I . . . Nancy said you answered my phone?'

'Well, you weren't in any fit state.' Her eyes widened. 'I hope she didn't get the wrong idea.'

'Course not, but . . . were you in bed with me?'

Izzy glanced away, but Jim detected a slight blush on her perfect skin. When she turned back, her smile was distinctly shamefaced. 'Truth? Yeah, I was. But only because I sort of fell down with you and couldn't be bothered to get up.' She grinned impishly. 'I didn't, you know, take advantage of you, if that's what you're worried about.'

'Wouldn't have known if you had.'

They stopped talking while the waiter delivered their plates of food.

'But I wouldn't say no,' Izzy said.

'Wouldn't say no to what?' Jim asked, taking a sip of beer, not really listening to her and wishing Nancy was sitting opposite him, not his brother's rather annoying friend.

She began to laugh. 'God, Jimmy, either you're thick or just a total innocent.'

Now it was his turn to blush as he finally grasped what she was getting at. *Bloody shameless*, he thought, taken aback.

'Sorry, I've embarrassed you. Stevie used to say I have a "spectrum disorder" because I don't know how to filter stuff – but, hey, isn't honesty the best policy?'

He was baffled. She wasn't even flirting, just staking her claim with a confidence that took his breath away. Maybe she wasn't used to being refused. 'You might have got the wrong end of the stick, Izzy.'

She grinned. 'Now's the moment when you give me the speech about being in love with Nancy.' She spread her hands, cast a theatrical glance around the cafe. 'But, you know, where is Nancy?'

When he got home from lunch, he immediately rang Nancy. He wished he could wash Izzy's brown eyes from his thoughts as he would dirt from his body because he knew now that she was more of a threat than he'd first imagined. At lunch she'd begun to talk about sex without self-consciousness or constraint, rather as you might discuss travel or musical preferences. Jim had been like a fly on a pin, unable to move or speak. Her openness – delivered in a soft, low monologue to avoid offending the middle-aged Germans at the next table – was mesmerizing. He'd never experienced the like before. As she detailed the lovers she'd had – both men and women – the fantasies she indulged in and the explicit descriptions of how the sex games made her feel, it was like watching a porn movie. And, as with a porn movie, Jim had been horrified to discover he was aroused, right there in that stuffy cafe, surrounded by unsuspecting holidaying families. Worse, Izzy knew it, had obviously intended he should be. She seemed to be on a mission.

He had attempted to appear cool, making light of her revelations, as if this were the sort of chat he had every day. But Izzy had kept a firm hold of the reins. It was clearly not the first time she had seduced a man like that.

'Nancy?'

'Hi, Jim. How are you?'

He thought she sounded formal, not entirely pleased to be talking to him. 'Okay. . .' He found himself tongue-tied. 'Thought you were avoiding me, pissed off with me after the other night.'

'Nothing like that.' She sounded tired. 'There's just been another drama with Louise. The restaurant's gone bust.'

'God! When did that happen?'

'Yesterday, day before . . . I've lost track. They cut off the gas and electricity because Lou couldn't pay the bill. So they've had to close the place down, obviously.'

'Is it a lot, the bill?'

'Quite a lot, but that's not all. Louise says she can't pay the staff either. And to cap it all, bloody Ross has gone AWOL.'

'*AWOL?* What do you mean?'

He heard her sigh.

'Lou confronted him about the bills after service a couple of nights ago. Told him the utility companies were threatening to cut off the gas and electricity, told him they'd reached the end of the road. And he didn't take it well, as you can imagine. She's been warning him about this for months and months, but he just wasn't listening. Anyway, they talked – not even a row, Lou said – and then she went home. He said he'd follow in his car, but he never came back. Hasn't been home since. She's going out of her mind.'

'Christ, Nancy . . .You don't think he's done something stupid, do you?'

'I have no idea. She's rung all their friends, but they haven't seen him. Lou thinks he's just holed up, licking his wounds, but it's bloody selfish, not letting her know where he is for two nights now.'

'Shouldn't she call the police? He might be in a ditch somewhere.'

'I'm trying not to think that.'

They fell silent, both thinking what they didn't want to think.

'I'll come home,' Jim said.

Nancy didn't reply immediately. Then she said, 'Aren't you playing in the club on Saturday?'

'Yes, but this is way more important, Nancy.'

'Thing is, I've got the girls here a lot . . . It's all a bit chaotic. I'm trying to give them some stability, but obviously the poor things know something's up. Hope hears everything.'

'Are you saying you'd rather I didn't come back?' Suddenly he didn't feel like using the word 'home'. First her mother, then her daughter, now her grandchildren: there was always some sort of barrier between them, a reason to keep him at arm's length.

'I don't know . . . Perhaps you'd be better off there for the time being. It's such a small house.'

He heard her landline ring in the background.

'Better go. That might be Louise. Sorry, Jim.' She was gone.

Wait? Jim stared at the phone as it lay dead in his hand. He felt weak, as if someone had struck him, and he went over to the sofa, sat down hard and leaned back against the cushions. *Christ*, he thought.

But as he sat mulling over their conversation, it was himself he felt sorry for as much as Nancy. She was under a massive strain, he understood that, but in her hour of need she obviously didn't think he could help, didn't want him by her side. Didn't want him at all, maybe.

CHAPTER FIFTY

Christopher's voice woke Nancy just after six the following morning. She had cried herself to sleep that night, the unfairness of her situation with Jim making her feel trapped and hopeless. She'd hated their conversation, and she hadn't meant what she'd said, but she didn't feel she had anything to offer him at the moment. Having him there, knowing he was cooped up and unhappy, would ruin everything. It was all very well Lindy saying she should take a chance, but she'd never be able to enjoy herself with Jim if she felt she'd reneged on her family in its hour of need. Although, as Lindy also pointed out, one needy hour was endlessly replaced by another, and another, ad infinitum.

Louise had been round until late, the girls put to sleep upstairs in case their mum had to rush off at some urgent summons from the police or Ross. Her daughter was no longer distraught, just resigned and silent, worn out by it all. Nancy didn't know what to say to her because, despite all her cursing about Ross, Louise clearly loved the man – whether he deserved it or not.

'Nancy, I'm trying to get hold of Louise.' Her ex-husband's voice was plaintive.

'And good morning to you too, Christopher.'

'Uh, sorry, but I've called her repeatedly to tell her about Jasper, the baby, and she hasn't got back to me except for a couple of miserable texts. We were hoping she'd come over with the girls and meet him at Christmas.'

'No, well . . .' Nancy briefly filled him in.

'Hmm. I had a feeling that was on the cards, the restaurant going down. Poor Louise. Ross has his head in the clouds, it seems to me. Are they in the hole for very much?'

'You'd have to talk to Lou about that,' Nancy said, feeling the same way about her son-in-law, but thoroughly irritated to hear it from Christopher. She wanted to get off the phone before he started telling her how absolutely perfect Jasper was, what a musical genius, even at less than a month old. Which was obviously his intention, because when she said she had to go, he sounded decidedly put out.

She crept downstairs to make a cup of coffee before the girls surfaced. As she gazed sleepily out of the window, wondering what the day would bring, she noticed a dark heap of something on the brick apron outside her daughter's front door. Peering through the murky January morning, she leaned to the side to get a better view past her car. What was it?

Pulling her jacket over her pyjamas and crossing the wet grass to the other house, not wanting to wake the girls by crunching on the gravel – their window gave onto the drive – she approached the heap cautiously. But as the security light flashed on, it illuminated the sleeping figure of her son-in-law. He was lying on his side, his back to the door, curled up, his arms hugging his drawn-up knees. An incipient beard sprouting, he had no coat on and his clothes were crumpled, a strong stench of spirits floating up, like a miasma on his breath, as she leaned closer.

'Ross . . . Ross, wake up,' she whispered, terrified the girls would look out of the Velux window and see their father in a heap on the ground.

He opened his eyes, stared at her without seeing her and closed them again.

Nancy shook his shoulder firmly. 'Ross, please, wake up.'

He mumbled, groaned and opened his eyes again, blinking in the glare from the security light.

'What? What is it?'

'Get up, please . . . Come on.' She began to pull on his arm, but he was a heavy man and she made no headway. '*Ross*. The girls will see you if you don't get up right now! *Come on!*'

Maybe it was the mention of the girls, but Ross rolled over, slowly dragged himself onto all fours, then brought up one foot so he could push himself upright, Nancy clutching his arm for balance. Once standing, he swayed, then leaned his bulk back against the front door and closed his eyes.

'Key?' Nancy asked.

He shook his head. 'Left it in the car.'

'Where is the car?' It hadn't occurred to her that it wasn't in the drive.

'At the restaurant. Bloody thing wouldn't start . . . Had to walk home.'

'Sssh,' Nancy glanced up at the girls' window.

Ross shook his head. 'Where's Lou?'

Nancy pointed to the house. 'I'll go and get my key and you can clean up before you see them.'

His eyes were bloodshot and dazed as she left him propped up against the bricks by the door and ran back to the house. He had a lot of explaining to do.

Jim called. She stared at the screen for a couple of seconds, undecided whether to answer. Then she clicked the green button.

'Hi, Jim.'

'Hi. Any news?'

The sound of his deep voice, so full of concern, made her heart ache. She told him about Ross. 'He says he doesn't know what he's been doing.'

'On a binge, most likely. Must be a relief he's home.'

'You can say that again.' Nancy felt he was waiting for more, but she had no idea what to say without promising him things she might not be able to fulfil.

'Good to know he's all right,' he said.

'Thanks.'

'Ring me later. Bye, then.'

'Bye.'

Nancy swallowed hard to stop herself crying. She wanted to plead with Jim to come home. She wanted to lie in his arms and beg his forgiveness for being so cold, so rejecting. She wanted to watch the spark of amusement light up his eyes, to sing with him, to be free to love him again. But her gaze was drawn to the sofa, where the girls lounged in their pyjamas and sheepskin slippers, hair falling loose and tangled from sleep, eyes glazed in front of the television, empty cereal bowls on the coffee table in front of them.

CHAPTER FIFTY-ONE

Jim hadn't spoken to Nancy for nearly ten days now. Not for lack of trying, but his text messages went unanswered, voicemail ditto. He was beginning to feel like a miserable stalker, beginning to lose confidence in the love he had been so certain of only a few weeks before. Nancy's silence made him feel on edge all the time, his stomach seething with nerves, his heart pumping uncomfortably fast as he constantly checked his phone. He knew he was medicating his anxiety with too much whiskey – sometimes starting mid-morning – and smoking too many Gitanes, both in an attempt to dampen the loneliness he felt, looking at his future without her.

He refused to believe that it was over. Nancy loved him as much as he loved her. Would she throw that away without even a conversation? He wanted to get angry with her but understood she must be caught up in Louise's dramas and he knew she couldn't be happy. He decided he would leave it a few more days, let the dust settle, then try her again. Part of his reluctance to push for contact was the possibility that he might be forcing Nancy to articulate something final, something that would break his heart.

The weather was beautiful. Clean-cold, with bright blue sparkling-sunshine days that hurt the eye and would have gladdened the heart had not Jim's been so leaden with misery. Izzy had taken to collecting him as soon as the sun was up every morning, dragging him out of bed, making him thick, muddy coffee in Stevie's espresso machine that jump-started his system, whether he liked it or not, then handing him his coat and beanie, pushing him out of the house and up the hill without a word.

Every day he objected, buried his whiskey-soaked, fag-fugged head beneath the pillow, grunted at her to fuck off. But she didn't seem to mind his bad temper, just acted as if his curmudgeonly behaviour was the most natural in the whole world. And, of course, a brisk stomp up the hill among the pine trees, the sun beating down on them, the crisp air, like a blast of hope, entering his lungs did wonders. By the time she allowed him to walk back down, his mood, temporarily at least, was considerably improved.

This morning his neighbour seemed inclined to talk as they made their way, breath misting around their heads in the cold, up through the pines.

'You still haven't heard from her?'

'She's got stuff on.' Jim, who had been avoiding any intimate conversations with Izzy since that bizarre lunch in Bonnieux, had told her nothing. But she had walked in on him one night and he'd been crying – howling – Nancy's name, thinking he was alone.

'Too much stuff for one phone call? Three minutes, maybe five, max?'

Jim was silent.

'Just saying. Seems like she's punishing you for leaving.'

He frowned, looked sideways at his companion. 'How do you make that out? She told me not to come home. Said she had the girls there and it wasn't convenient.'

'Yes, but you're not supposed to believe her, Jimmy.'

He wished she wouldn't call him 'Jimmy'. Only Chrissie got to do that – and occasionally Mal – and that was because he'd got tired of arguing about it. 'Jimmy' made him feel like a big, dumb kid.

'Don't understand.'

'She's testing you. You're supposed to jump on a plane and go to her.'

'Even when she's asked me not to?'

Izzy nodded, the sun catching the highlights in her heavy, corn-blonde hair, which she was wearing that morning in a long French plait. She was much fitter than him, setting a pace he could barely keep up with, urging him on, arms pumping keenly, as they climbed the hill.

'Nancy doesn't play games, Izzy.'

Izzy raised her eyebrows. 'No?'

'No.'

There was silence between them for a moment.

'So you're just going to give up, drink and smoke yourself into a heart attack or a nice bit of cancer, are you? Die early, like your brother?'

Jim was shocked. 'No. Of course not.'

Another raised eyebrow.

'I'm just . . . I don't know what to do,' he said finally, his defences shot.

She took his arm. 'Loath as I am to see a good man go to waste on a woman who clearly doesn't appreciate him – especially when I'm offering what I consider a very viable alternative – you have to make more of an effort to win Nancy back. Or you really will lose her.'

'Doing what, though?'

'Jump on a plane and go home, Jimmy. Just do it.'

*

When he got back to the house, fired up by Izzy's goading, Jim went straight to his computer. Ignoring the doubts lining up to persuade him otherwise, not least the image of a cold-eyed Nancy turning him away at the front door, he booked a flight from Marseille for two days' time – there was a shedload of last-minute deals at this time of year – before he had time to change his mind. And ten minutes after he'd bought the ticket, as if he'd summoned her by his action, Nancy called.

'Hi, Jim.' Her voice was dull, without warmth, and Jim felt his gut clutch with anxiety.

'Nancy . . . at last.'

'I know. I'm so sorry I haven't called. It's just been so totally hectic since Ross got back. He's ill, seems to be having some kind of a breakdown, won't get out of bed. Louise is going crazy trying to sort out the problems with the restaurant and cope with him and the girls. I just haven't had time to think.'

'Sounds like a nightmare,' he said, prepared to let her off the hook. Despite her downbeat tone, he was so happy to hear her voice.

'Funny coincidence, you ringing now,' he said. 'I just booked a ticket back . . . flying on Thursday morning.' He waited, hoping, praying she would jump for joy, say how much she was dying to see him. But there was silence.

'Jim . . .'

He held his breath.

'Jim, listen . . .'

In the pause before she continued, he wanted to throw down the phone, block his ears, sing lalalalalalala very loudly so he didn't hear what was coming next.

'Jim, I don't see how it's going to work out, you and me.'

He didn't reply, his breath stuck in his throat like a stone, so she went on, sounding determined, as if she had to concentrate hard to get the right words out. 'I'm just totally swamped by the family, and I can't see how it's going to change. I know all the arguments, that I deserve my own life, I can have both you and them, but the truth is, I can't. And I don't want to live like a pig in the middle, feeling guilty if I'm with you, feeling guilty if I'm with them. Lou and the girls – Ross, even – need me right now, and if you come back, I'll be constantly feeling bad, trying to fit everyone into my life . . . I don't want to live like that.'

There was silence.

'Is this about France? Me wanting to live here? Because I can sell Lavender House, move back, buy somewhere in England. You mean that much to me . . .'

'It's not about France, Jim.'

And when she didn't go on, he pleaded, 'Don't do this – don't walk away, please . . . *please*, Nancy. I love you and I think you love me. Surely it's worth finding a compromise, a way of being with each other that makes it work for everyone else too.' He was keeping it together, just, although he could hear the quaver in his voice.

Another sigh, then she said, 'I do love you.'

'So let's find a way to be together. Let's not give up.' Now he heard her crying and his heart contracted. 'I'm not putting any pressure on you, believe me. I'm an independent guy, you've seen that. I won't be pulling on your coat tails, trying to stop you doing what you have to for your family. I never have, not deliberately.'

'I know you haven't,' she said, and he heard her sniffing, blowing her nose, but the soft sound of her sobs continued. 'You've been amazing, an extraordinary thing in my life, Jim. But right now I just don't have space . . . the energy for anything much. And I can't keep you hanging on, hoping things might change in the future, string you along with promises I might not be able to keep. It's not fair on you.'

Jim was shaking. 'Are you – are you really saying it's over? That you don't want me in your life any more?'

She had gone silent, stopped crying. 'I can't . . . It won't work.'

The words felt ice-cold, even though she spoke barely above a whisper.

'But I love you.' He, too, spoke softly, but the absolute devotion in his voice could not be misconstrued. He was sending his heart through the ether to rest with hers.

She didn't respond, and he sensed she had gone. Not actually, he could still hear her breathing, but she had said what she'd steeled herself to say and he knew her well enough to understand that she wouldn't change her mind, not now.

'It's not over,' he said. 'It can't be.'

'I'm sorry . . .'

The phone went dead. Cold and shaking, Jim didn't know what to do with himself. Dropping his mobile on the table, as if it were on fire, he paced the tiled floor, threw open the balcony doors to get more air, then picked up one of the wooden chairs and hurled it violently against the wall. The sound split the quiet morning, birds rising from the trees in alarm as Jim flung himself into another chair and buried his face in his hands. He felt a burning, out-of-control scream building in his chest and his body went rigid in an attempt to stifle it. Only a moan escaped his lips, but the scream sat there, waiting, his breath trapped by it, his heart sliding into a painfully uneven thump.

Getting up, he strode through the house, out of the door without a coat, up the hill he'd climbed an hour earlier. Adrenalin pushed a fast pace and he reached the top in double-quick time, barely aware of what he was doing. The view was spectacular, and he stared blindly at it, before bending over, clutching his head with both hands and opening his mouth to let loose his pent-up fury and despair, the agonized roar, renewed with each breath, reverberating around the valley below like a prowling, angry beast.

How long Jim howled, he didn't know, but eventually he lost even the ability to stand. Slithering to the cold rocky ground, knees bent under him, he wept.

CHAPTER FIFTY-TWO

Nancy told herself that breaking up with Jim was for the best. After the phone call – which was the full-stop she needed and had been pending for weeks – she made a singular effort to close down her feelings, force the man she loved into a box pushed to the back of the attic. And she didn't find it as difficult as she might have supposed, because she wasn't feeling anything much at the moment, except a dull numbness, which had gradually spread, like a spill of grey, across her consciousness, beginning shortly after her mother died.

It wasn't that she had no hope for the future: it was more that the future was a muted blank, a nothingness into which she was unable to project any feelings, any hopes, not even *herself*.

Even spending time with the girls did little to elevate her mood. She plodded through their care, smiled when she had to, hugged them when it was appropriate, listened to their chatter with one ear. And when she was alone, she cried. Long into the night sometimes, but without heat or hope of relief. It became a familiar process, which ended in exhaustion and sleep.

She hid her depression well. Louise was too busy to notice and Ross had his own problems. She avoided Lindy and cancelled her students, saying it was unlikely she would be able to teach them again in the near future.

'Where's Jim, Nana?' Jazzy took her thumb out of her mouth to ask as she lay in bed in Nancy's house one cold February night, sleepily clutching her battered giraffe, whose neck was hanging by a thread from years of cuddles. *I must mend that*, she thought.

'He's in France,' Nancy said quickly, as she sat on the edge of Hope's bed, preparing to read them another instalment of *George's Marvellous Medicine* – anything by Roald Dahl got the girls' vote.

'When's he coming back?' Hope was sitting up, clean hair – both girls had just had a long-overdue shampoo – falling round her shoulders, fiddling with two little Shopkins figures.

'I'm not sure . . .'

'But he promised he'd teach us the chicken song,' Jazzy complained.

Hope was looking at Nancy quizzically. 'He's still your boyfriend, isn't he, Nana?'

The unexpected question hit her in the pit of her stomach. It was almost a month since she'd talked to Jim and every day she made a point of carefully battening down the memories. They *were* memories now. Jim was a memory. But with Hope's brown eyes gazing at her so intently, she found her own filling with tears. 'I'm afraid he's not any more,' she said, swallowing hard and bending her head to the book so the girls wouldn't see her tears. Hope hesitated, then pushed the duvet back, crawling down the bed until she was close to her grandmother, snuggling into her side to give her a tight hug. A hug that was like a beacon in her bleak world: so loving, so understanding was the child's embrace that it broke through Nancy's haze of indifference and made her want to cry out in pain.

Jazzy glanced uncertainly at her sister, then at her grandmother, but didn't move.

'Don't worry, Nana,' Hope said, a very grown-up expression on her young face. 'I'm sure he'll come back soon.'

'Maybe.' Nancy managed a smile, clearing her throat as she tried to get herself under control. But her granddaughter's touching concern made it all the harder. Hope would be nine in a couple of days – she was growing up fast.

'He's going to teach us the chicken song,' Jazzy muttered again, with the innocent certainty of a six-year-old.

'Right, come on, it's getting late. We'd better get on with *George*.' She dropped a kiss on Hope's head, gave her a grateful squeeze, reluctant to let her go, then shooed her back under the duvet.

Ross jumped when Nancy appeared, although she'd knocked before letting herself in at the front door. It was early evening, already dark outside, and she was dropping back Hope's gym bag, which her granddaughter had left at her house the previous day. She knew Louise had gone to fetch the girls from Adventure Club and she hoped Ross was otherwise engaged – she wasn't in the mood to talk to anyone.

But her son-in-law was in the kitchen, a pile of chicken pieces on the island worktop, which he was chopping with a scary-looking cleaver. Nancy, despite her desire to avoid him, was pleased to see Ross back in his favourite place. Louise said he hadn't gone near the kitchen in the weeks since his breakdown.

'Hey, Nancy.' He stopped what he was doing and gave her a smile. She thought he'd lost weight, or maybe it wasn't actual bulk that he'd lost, rather the chutzpah that had made him seem so much larger than life. And his big dark eyes still looked weary, lacking their usual spark.

'How's it going, Ross?'

'Yeah, better, I guess.' He leaned against the worktop. 'You?'

She shrugged, put Hope's bag down on the kitchen table.

He gave her a knowing smile. 'You look like I feel.'

'Not good, then.'

He reached for the bottle of red wine, open on the side, waved it at her. She nodded. He went over to the sink and washed his hands, then found a glass in the cabinet beside the stove. 'Have a seat,' he said, picking up his own glass and coming round the island to sit opposite her at the table. 'Is it your mum?' he asked.

Nancy hesitated before replying. 'I suppose . . . partly.' She wasn't certain that was true: the different elements of her life seemed such a mish-mash, so indistinct yet intertwined, that she had lost the energy to unpick any one root cause. 'I never got on that well with Mum,' she found herself saying. 'I loved her, but we didn't have much in common . . . about life.'

'She kept people at arm's length, that's for sure.'

'I can't help wondering if I should have done more to persuade her to get treatment . . . If I'd loved her more, would I have insisted?' Nancy swallowed. The bloody tears, which sat waiting to ambush her minute to minute, would not win this time.

'You can't think like that. She'd made up her mind, Nancy, and she was a tough old bird. Nothing short of tying her up and carting her off would've worked.'

She smiled. 'I tell myself that.'

They sipped the fruity Cabernet, Nancy rolling the soothing, dark, blackcurranty liquid across her tongue.

'And Jim?' Ross asked, without the awkwardness her daughter

had brought to the question when she'd asked about him the previous week. Nancy had just said he was in France and Louise had accepted her answer without further probing.

Nancy swirled the wine gently, watching the light catch the surface. The cool, smooth roundness of the glass felt good against her palm and she cherished it as something simple and solid that she could understand in this baffling world. She finally looked up to meet Ross's eye. 'We've split up.'

'No! When?' He seemed shocked, which caught Nancy by surprise. To her, the knowledge was just part of the dull indifference that cloaked her life these days.

'Oh, about a month ago . . . maybe longer.'

'God, Nancy, why?'

And while she formulated her reply, he went on, 'Lou never said.'

'Lou doesn't know.'

Ross frowned. 'So what happened?'

'I – I couldn't . . . I don't know . . . It's been difficult, what with Mum . . .' She didn't add that it had also been difficult seeing her daughter and son-in-law fall apart, the restaurant go bust, her granddaughters bewildered. But Ross knew that.

'Was he putting pressure on you?'

'No, God, nothing like that. He wanted to help.'

'So . . .'

She shook her head. 'I can't do it all, Ross. I can't be with Jim and with the family. I can't make everyone happy. Go to France, not go to France, have him cramped in that house first with Mum, then with the girls. It just won't work.' Her voice crescendoed as she spoke, the words spilling out in a rush of frustration.

Ross, eyebrows raised, thought about this for a moment. 'No, I suppose I see. Sorry about that. I thought you two were in for the long haul . . . Feel a bit responsible for making such a fuck-up of things, causing so much trouble.'

'Not your fault,' she said, because finally it wasn't. It was *her* fault, her decision.

'It is. I've been such an arse,' he said, rubbing his hand across his face. 'I don't deserve your daughter. She's been so fucking good to me, even when I was . . .' He stopped, guilt flushing his cheeks. 'Even when I was so vile to her.'

Nancy didn't know what to say.

'You – you've been amazing too, Nancy. Just amazing. I can't thank you enough. I honestly don't know how we'd have got through this without you. And now Louise's dad . . .'

Which was one miracle that had come out of the last few weeks. One that Nancy still didn't quite believe. When Louise had finally called her father, Christopher – perhaps suffering from an excess of benevolence brought on by the warm glow of new fatherhood – had offered to bail them out, pay off the staff and suppliers, and give them a small amount to cover the mortgage on the house until they were back on their feet. A gift, he insisted, not a loan. Louise, despite saying she would never take a penny from her father, had been bowled over.

'Jim must be gutted,' Ross was saying. 'You must be, too.'

Nancy didn't want to think about that. In fact, she spent a lot of time forcing herself not to. She longed to change the subject but didn't know what else to talk about, her mind a weary blank. Luckily they heard car doors slamming, the front door opening, the girls piling into the house, filthy from head to foot with mud, hair straggling, huge grins on their pale, exhausted faces.

CHAPTER FIFTY-THREE

'Not long till you can marry Fancy Nancy, then,' Chrissie said, when Jim rang her from France to tell her he'd received the decree nisi in the post and had applied for a decree absolute.

'Didn't work out with her,' he said quickly.

'Oh . . . Sorry about that,' Chrissie said, not sounding sorry at all. 'So you're all on your lonesome in poor Stevie's house?'

'Yup. But it's good. I'm getting on with my music. Tommy's coming over at Easter for a few days. And I've got Izzy next door. You remember Izzy?'

'Yeah . . . Blonde piece of work.' She sniggered. 'Nice one, Jimmy.'

'Meaning?'

'Meaning Pascal used to say she'd fucked everyone with a pulse east of Marseille. What would that be in French now? *La bicyclette de la ville*?' Another disparaging cackle.

Jim remembered, yet again, why Chrissie irritated him so much. 'She's been a good friend,' he returned, against his better judgement, knowing he should just have shut the conversation down. Although what she'd said about Izzy was probably true – and Izzy would be the first to admit it – he felt suddenly protective towards his friend.

'I'm sure she has. Well, guard your virtue well, Jim-boy. If she's not had you yet, it's only a matter of time. Case of last man standing.' Which made his ex dissolve into yet more dirty laughter.

It was March, and Jim had spent the preceding months in a daze of disbelief. The whole structure of his life had tumbled about his ears. He felt completely crazy. He had written Nancy a heap of letters, which had ended up in the wood-burning stove. He had texted her a million messages, then deleted them. He'd composed emails, which were only saved as 'drafts'; he'd called her landline and hung up when the answer-machine kicked in. He was disgusted with himself. *You've just given up. You can't even manage to be a committed stalker*, he told himself, as he deleted yet another pleading text. And from Nancy there was just a deafening silence.

Izzy had been so wrong. Nancy wasn't playing games. She hadn't wanted him to jump on a plane and do a caveman act, dragging her by the hair back to his lair in France. She had wanted him to go away, leave her alone. He sat there in the darkening room, knowing he should put some wood in the stove but without the energy to get out of the armchair, feeling sorry for himself in the wake of Chrissie's phone call, realizing what a pig's breakfast he'd made of his relationships, feeling old and running on empty.

What have I got to lose? he asked himself a minute later, reading the text that had just come in from Izzy.

That night they got drunk together. Izzy had bought vodka at Duty Free on her flight back from Morocco, where she'd spent the previous week. Jim made supper – roast chicken and riced potatoes. He had taken to cooking for the first time in his life, testing myriad unfamiliar gadgets in his brother's kitchen, such as the potato ricer, a crêpe pan, a

Mouli, a tin egg poacher with holes in the bottom and a stalk to fix it to the edge of the pan, a rotating cheese grater – all of which were puzzling to his previous microwave existence and had to be explained to him by Madame Laverne, their purpose demonstrated. But it passed the time, shopping with his palm-leaf bag, trying out his French in the shops as he eyed the curious foodstuffs on display. And in the back of his mind, always, was the thought of sharing it all with Nancy.

'Okay,' Izzy said, getting up.

It was far into the night, the vodka long gone, the room a fug of Gitanes and wood-smoke, the lamps reflected in the glass balcony doors, giving the impression of an infinite space. Jim was restless, the emotionally charged voice of Souad Massi coming from the speaker, vibrating in his gut with an energy that seemed to speak directly to his misery, seemed to beg him to stop all this self-indulgent woe-is-me and *do* something for a change. He watched as Izzy came to stand in front of him as he lounged on the sofa, glass of wine balanced on the cushion, tilting dangerously to one side.

'Now is the time,' she said, swaying to the music, 'to treat you to the dance of the seven veils.'

Jim laughed drunkenly. 'Is that so? Not sure how a jumper and jeans is going to make that particularly possible.'

Ignoring him, Izzy raised her arms, twirling round slowly, her body undulating, head thrown back, hair floating around her face, eyes fixed on Jim at each turn.

'Pay attention. I'm Salome,' she whispered, as she drew the edges of her cream cable sweater sensuously up her body, revealing a pale pink vest-top beneath.

Jim, spellbound, just stared.

The sweater was thrown casually aside as Izzy continued to dance, the soft light from the lamp throwing shadows on her figure as she took hold of the hem of the vest, lifting it a few inches to reveal smooth, lightly tanned flesh, then dropping it again, pirouetting a couple of times before exposing a little more, until there was a fleeting glimpse of the curve of her small breasts. She was singing along with Souad Massi, her voice a light soprano, the words indistinguishable, the notes dissonant.

Drunk as he was, his senses were alert. He did nothing to stop Izzy, on her next pirouette, tossing aside the vest-top, laying bare her breasts – the soft-coral nipples bordered by a triangle of whiter skin against her otherwise tanned body. She was gyrating her stomach like a belly dancer now, her blue jeans unzipped, a line of black lacy knickers showing beneath her belly button. She held her hands behind her head, entangled in her thick blonde hair, her eyes never leaving Jim's face as she moved closer to him, pushing his knees apart with her own, dancing more slowly now . . . slower and slower.

Jim made no effort to resist her advances as he lay there, mesmerized. But he was suddenly aware of a warning light going on in his booze-addled brain. A light signalling a thought that grew to a clamouring insistence. *This is the line, Jim*, it said, *the definitive line. Step over it and you'll be separated from Nancy for ever.*

Another voice – visceral, thoughtless and emanating from his genitals – countered, *Fuck it, and why not? Nancy is lost to you anyway.* But his head-voice was urgent and imperious. *Cross the line just once and it's over. No going back. No second chance.*

CHAPTER FIFTY-FOUR

The April evening was like a long-forgotten pleasure, not least because dreariness, cloudy grey skies and rain had been persistent well into the spring, the countryside finally waking up to the delicate pink and white of the apple blossom, the pale cones of lilac and dense yellow broom. Even Nancy, whose torpid spirits had been in hibernation since her mother's death, felt a small waft of hope as she drove towards the pub on the South Downs to meet Lindy and Alison. The sun was low in the sky now, a deep-gold shaft of light layering the trees and hills with a dusty glory that made her hold her breath.

Lindy had insisted. It was her birthday again and she had badgered Nancy to join them for a drink and supper. Nancy had been on the verge of cancelling until the very moment she started the car. Even getting dressed up had been hard, each top she pulled out to go with her black jeans reminding her of some outing she and Jim had taken together – the first coffee, the first drink, the first gig. In the end she had opted for the black T-shirt with the faded butterfly – she felt comfortable in it. Her skin, worn from a cold winter and despair, looked lined and dry when she attempted to apply foundation, her grey hair so long and shapeless that she pulled it back into a loose ponytail, remembering with a painful jolt how much Jim had liked her hair off her face.

Lindy and Alison were already seated at a table near the door of the pub, a bottle of white wine in a cooler in front of them, alongside three glasses. Nancy, despite her earlier reticence, found she was glad to see her friends, grateful to be welcomed and hugged with such enthusiasm. Although she felt delicate, as if she were emerging from a long convalescence, she knew the despair was slowly lifting and tiny pinches of light were filtering into her dull mind.

They spent a while catching up before Lindy turned to her, as they were eating their fishcakes and salad, waving her fork in the air, and saying, 'You realize it's a year to the day since we met Jim.'

When Nancy didn't reply, her friend shook her head. 'Gorgeous guy. Still can't believe you let him slip away, Nancy. What were you thinking?'

Nancy still said nothing, her last mouthful stuck in her throat. All she could see was Jim's blue eyes, catching her gaze for the first time in that noisy pub, smiling his amused smile as if he'd known her for a lifetime. Something had stirred inside her that night, something that had changed her for ever.

'Don't tease her, Lindy,' Alison was saying. 'He obviously wasn't right for her. You can't *make* yourself love someone.' Her worried brown eyes were frowning reprovingly at Lindy.

'I'm not meaning to tease, Nance, but, God, I've been all over town looking for someone as cute and decent as Jim, and all I've found is paunchy bores with bad breath and limp willies – excluding the toy-boys, of course, who get equally tiresome after a few good bonks.'

The women laughed.

'A few good bonks wouldn't go amiss,' Alison said, with unusual brio.

Lindy looked shocked. 'Gracious, Ally, I've never heard you talk like that before. Are you on the lookout at last?'

Alison shook her head. 'No, no . . . God, no . . .' She sighed wistfully. 'But sometimes I remember . . . with Nick, you know . . .' Clearly embarrassed, she bent her head to her food.

A short silence was followed by Lindy pointing her fork at Nancy again, mouth full. 'You did love him a bit, though, didn't you, darling? Jim, I mean. Seemed like you were well into him for a while there.' She sighed. 'But we all know love isn't always enough, eh?'

'I did,' Nancy replied, then stopped, unable to offer the cogent explanation for which her friend was waiting.

After a minute, Lindy went on, 'I did warn you, though. Should have kept him round the corner, not moved him in. Wouldn't be over now if you had.'

'Is it really over?' Alison asked.

'God, yes.' Nancy breathed deeply, sat up straighter. The conversation was dragging her back to the dark place she'd inhabited since January. 'He lives in France now.' She knew she sounded frighteningly nonchalant.

Lindy harrumphed at her apparent sangfroid. 'So I hope your dear family is grateful for your sacrifice.'

'It wasn't a sacrifice,' Nancy said.

To which her friend just raised a sceptical eyebrow. 'How did Louise's restaurant debacle pan out, by the way?'

'Good. I think it's been the best thing for them both. Ross's pride has been hurt, but he'll get back on his feet – food is his life. Lou is very grateful to her father, which has helped their relationship no end. And Ross and Lou seemed to be slowly sorting their marriage out, now the bloody restaurant isn't driving them apart.

He's got a job interview tomorrow, in fact – a new place in Rottingdean.' She shrugged. 'So things have calmed down at last.'

'Told you,' Lindy said, always liking to be right.

'Told me what?'

'Told you they'd sort it out.'

'I didn't say they wouldn't.'

'Maybe not, but you thought you had to give up your own life to help them.'

'No,' Nancy said stiffly. 'I just couldn't seem to cope with things after Mum died, that's all.' She felt way too delicate to deal with Lindy's harangue.

The atmosphere suddenly became tense, and none of the women risked a glance at the others.

'Hey, girls, it's my birthday, let's not get maudlin,' Lindy said, raising her glass. 'Here's to love, freedom and a jolly good bonk.' She spoke so loudly that the people at the next table – four white-haired men who looked to be in their eighties – grinned over at them.

'If any of you ladies need help with that . . .' one piped up, in a high, thin voice, reducing the rest to wheezy guffaws.

'How very gallant of you, sir.' Lindy waved her glass airily in their direction. 'I'll certainly bear it in mind.'

It was after midnight when Nancy arrived home. She'd enjoyed the evening – talk of Jim notwithstanding. She'd laughed properly for the first time in a long while, not least at Lindy's description of some gruesome 'eight-point' face-lift she was seriously considering. She was pleased she'd made the effort.

But she felt restless. The past, brought back by Lindy's persistent digging, had unsettled her. She went through to the piano room and played softly for a while, but her hands unconsciously found the notes to the songs Jim used to sing and she couldn't risk that, not tonight.

Going through to the kitchen, she poured herself a glass of water, then checked her phone one last time before bed. The little red circle hovered above the mail icon. One email. She clicked, and her heart almost stopped. Jim. There was no subject line and her gut clenched with trepidation as to what he might be about to tell her.

But in the body of the email there was no text at all, just an underlined link in blue. Mouth dry, hands shaking, she tapped it, watching the download spin gradually round to completion. She sat down as she waited, staring at the small screen. Then he was there, Jim, just the same as if she'd seen him yesterday, sitting with his guitar, grey hair back in the usual ponytail, wearing the white shirt with the black piping, gazing at the camera, his eyes just as blue as she was remembering earlier. Nancy clicked the arrow to begin and watched as he smiled nervously.

'This is for you, Nancy, on the anniversary of the day we met,' he said, and began to sing, in his deep, gravelly voice.

'Old and alone with the memory of love,
My whiskey and songs kept me warm,
But you showed me your soul when your grey eyes met mine
In that instant I knew I was lost.
Be with me, Nancy, take one more chance,
I'll love you till the day I die.

Not free then to love, I lied in my fear,
Because losing you would lose me my mind,
But you let me come back, despite what they said,
And found me a place in your heart.

Be with me, Nancy, take one more chance,
I'll love you till the day I die.

That first time we kissed is burned on my heart,
It felt like the still point of time.
But I lost you to others, more worthy than me,
And without you I did lose my mind.
Be with me, Nancy, take one more chance,
I'll love you till the day I die.

Don't think of the future, don't make a plan,
Life's random, we can't know our fate,
But each precious moment I live in your love
Makes me braver to be who I am.
Be with me, Nancy, take one more chance,
I'll love you till the day I die.

Time has gone by but with each day that dawns
I live the enchantment we shared.
It was more than just lust, much more than a fling,
For me you're the link to my soul.
Be with me, Nancy, take one more chance,
I'll love you . . . I'll love you till the day that I die.'

At the end of the song he bowed his head slightly, his expression uncertain, then the image froze. Nancy closed down her phone and hurried to the laptop sitting at the other end of the table. In her eagerness to hear the song again, she fluffed her password twice and had to take a breath, get a grip of herself. But there he was again, the image bigger now, the sound clearer.

She watched, entranced, feeling that she could almost reach out and touch him as he played. Her heart was racing, her eyes misted with tears. *Take one more chance*, she sang softly. *For God's sake, Nancy*, she told herself, *do it, take the chance before it's too late*.

Nancy didn't have to think: it was almost as if the decision were already made, just sitting in the ether waiting for her to access it, Jim's song the trigger. She immediately booked a flight online to Marseille for the next day, arranged a taxi to pick her up at eight, packed a few things in a carry-on, crammed makeup and liquids into a clear plastic bag, had a shower. It was nearly two in the morning by the time she had finished, and she knew she should try to sleep. But her body was buzzing with anticipation, her mind running round in frenzied circles thinking about Jim. In the end she sat on the sofa and read, dozing for a while before the morning light woke her.

At a quarter to eight she put her case by the door and hurried across the gravel. The lights were on in the kitchen – the family was up, even though it was Saturday. She felt light-headed, her eyes scratchy from the hours of reading and lack of sleep as she let herself into Louise's house.

'Mum!' Louise looked up. Wrapped in her tartan dressing-gown, hair flopping around her face, she was sitting at the kitchen table, her hands round a mug of tea, a magazine open in front of her. The sound of the television filtered through from the sitting room, where Nancy knew her granddaughters would be ensconced under the purple fur throw, still half asleep.

Nancy pulled out a chair and sat down. 'Lou, I know this is a bit sudden, but I'm going to France to see Jim.'

'Jim? Really?' Louise was eyeing her up and down, taking in her jacket, her boots. Her expression was puzzled.

'Yes. I'm on the one o'clock to Marseille. I— He emailed me last night . . .'

Louise shook her head. 'Whoa. Out of the blue? I thought he was long gone.'

Nancy couldn't help smiling as she said, 'He sent me a song and I . . . It was a shock but, well, I want to see him again, Lou. I really want to see him. I've missed him so much . . .' She heard the broken, mumbled words and she thought she sounded a bit mad as she waited for her daughter's response, dreading the usual diatribe that accompanied any reference to Jim Bowdry.

But Louise was smiling, her eyebrows lifted in amusement. 'That's great, Mum.'

'Really?'

'Yup. I'm glad he's been in touch.'

'You are?'

Louise nodded. 'You think I haven't seen you pining?'

Nancy heard the beep of her phone. 'That'll be the taxi.' She got up and so did Louise.

'Have fun,' Louise said, giving her a loving hug that told Nancy more than any words could.

'Wish Ross good luck for the interview,' Nancy said, hovering, suddenly unable to leave. 'Say goodbye to the girls for me.'

'I will. *Go*, Mum.'

The doors from Customs to the arrivals hall opened and Nancy, dragging her wheelie, dazed from a deadening sleep on the plane and a consequent stiff neck, felt suddenly exposed, intensely self-conscious as the sea of curious faces stared at her, checking to make sure she wasn't the one for whom they were waiting. And as she stared back, glancing quickly from face to face, they all seemed to distort into a single, amorphous mass. She couldn't see Jim.

Then he was there, standing a little apart from the rest. Tall, handsome, tanned by the spring sun and, oh, so delightfully familiar. Her heart clenched as they moved towards each other. She was no longer aware of the hum of airport announcements, the shiny buff floor, the smell of coffee, the Mediterranean faces as she dropped the handle of her case and felt Jim's arms around her, inhaling deeply as she pressed her cheek to his, wanting to breathe him into the very centre of herself – the scent of his skin, of his leather jacket, the faint traces of his woody shaving cream intoxicating her.

She glanced up to catch a look of pure relief in his eyes and wondered if it were mirrored in her own.

'Hi,' he said, smiling down at her, still holding her close.

'Hello,' she replied, feeling a surge of happiness that threatened to overwhelm her.

As they drove towards Maison Lavande in Stevie's Citroën, they spoke little beyond the usual banalities: How was the flight? So glad to be here. It's raining at home. Did you eat on the plane? As if they were acquaintances meeting for a jaunt. There was no tension between them, though. Nancy found herself sitting very still in the front seat, hands in her lap, just luxuriating in being there beside him. When they stopped at lights in Cavaillon, he turned to her, raised his eyebrows in a tender smile.

'I loved your song,' she said.

Jim reached for his phone and scrolled down until he found what he was looking for. Suddenly his deep baritone filled the car as they drove through the town and out into the French country-side, the sunshine startling on the white cherry blossoms. Jim began singing with the track. Nancy joined in. And at the top of their voices they sang the chorus: '*Be with me, Nancy, take one more chance, I'll love you till the day that I die . . .*' pulling the last word out to its fullest extent.

As the music ended, breathless, they began to laugh, a joyous, uncontrollable burst of sheer delight that spilled around the interior of the Citroën, making Jim pull over, unable to drive, wiping the tears from his face as she did from hers. Then as silence fell, he leaned across and kissed her. It was a kiss like the first one, the still point in time, gentle, yet absolutely certain, burned for ever on both their hearts.

That night they did not make love. They ate an early supper – omelette and salad, goat's cheese, pears – drank a bottle of Bordeaux and went to bed. Naked together in the darkness, they held each other tenderly, as if they might break, like fragile glass, the painful months of separation still vivid between them. Sex seemed too raw, too soon, too exposing for them both, so they lay entwined, warm skin against warm skin, and slept.

Now, Nancy was propped on her side, facing Jim. It was early morning, the shutters pushed back, the glorious spring sun, already warm, pouring across the bed in dusty shafts. She placed her hand against his cheek. He held it there. They did not say a word as they began slowly to make love.

LAVENDER HOUSE READING GROUP QUESTIONS

1) Can you understand Nancy's reaction to Christopher's leaving her? Were you surprised at how little she protested?
2) Despite her repeated cheating, Jim takes Chrissie back – even after she leaves him for a year. Can you sympathise with his decision? What would it take for you to give up on your marriage for good?
3) Is Frances within her rights to feel entitled to so much of Nancy's attention? How about Louise and Ross, relying on her so heavily for babysitting? Does Frances or Louise have the stronger claim? How much do you think we owe to our parents and children as we (and they) get older?
4) What do you think of Lindy? Is her flirting 'humiliating', as Jim thinks, or is she just a woman who isn't afraid to go after what she wants?
5) 'Fathers aren't supposed to have sex' Louise says. Why do we struggle so much with seeing our parents as people beyond 'mum' and 'dad'? Does it matter?
6) 'Everyone's always telling us to exercise and eat lots of vegetables so we can live forever, but no one's found a way to make it fun'. Is it desirable for us to continue to prolong old age as

long as we can, given that we can't guarantee that any extra years we gain will be healthy ones? Conversely, can living longer be 'fun'?

7) What do you think of Nancy and her family's reaction to Jim's 'lie' about not being fully separated from Chrissie?
8) Why do you think Louise is so suspicious of Jim, even though she can see he makes her mother happy? Is it just snobbishness, or something deeper?
9) Do you think Jim has a point when he says Nancy is too willing to drop everything for her family, or is he simply out of touch with what being in a large family involves?
10) What do you think of Frances's determination to die on her own terms, even if it means lying to her family? Should she have just been frank with Nancy and Louise, or was she right to keep her illness a secret? Given the impact her ill health has on her family, could you call her decision selfish at all?
11) The closure of Ross's restaurant is devastating to him, but he clearly needed to listen to Louise's warnings earlier. At what point is it right to give up on your dreams?
12) What do you think is Izzy's role in the book?
13) Across the whole book, how far do you think Nancy and Jim create obstacles for themselves? Can you think of any times where a situation that could have been easily resolved is allowed to become a much bigger problem?
14) Who do you identify most with in the story? Whose actions can you empathise with the most?
15) Did you have any preconceptions about love affairs in later life before reading this book? If so, have they changed?